Death S

Kerry Watts was born and grew up in Perth where she still lives today. The daughter of a Rangers mad window cleaner and Daniel O'Donnell loving dinner lady. She began writing over twenty years ago after reading Isla Dewar's book *Giving up on Ordinary* and decided she wanted to do that. Becoming a best selling author is a dream come true.

Also by Kerry Watts

Detective Hazel Todd

Death Rite
Death Sentence

KERRY WATTS

death sentence

hera

First published in the United Kingdom in 2022 by

Hera Books
Unit 9 (Canelo), 5th Floor
Cargo Works, 1–2 Hatfields
London, SE1 9PG
United Kingdom

A CIP catalogue record for this book is available from the British Library.

Print ISBN 978 1 80436 021 7
Ebook ISBN 978 1 80436 919 7

Look for more great books at www.herabooks.com

Printed and bound in Great Britain by Clays Ltd, Elcograf S.p.A.

1

For a world that is battling an invisible enemy. This won't last forever. Better days are coming.

Whereof what's past is prologue, what to come
In yours and my discharge

William Shakespeare
The Tempest

Prologue

What was it you said? That's right – 'The past is the past,' you said. There was nothing anyone could do about what happened. Leave the past where it is and move on with your life. It was for the best. But I can't move on. Surely you must see that.

You were sorry but you didn't think there was anything left to say. Perhaps you had nothing to say. Perhaps you didn't care.

There was so much left I had to say. I had questions, so many questions and you knew that. I know you did. But still you walked away as if it didn't matter. It was an inconvenience. I was an inconvenience.

I watched you scurry away, checking the time on your watch as you hurried to meet your friends for coffee, clutching your phone to your ear, apologising for running late. You'd been held up, but it wasn't important. You'd be with them soon. You smiled as you flagged the bus down, thanked the driver for stopping for you. He smiled back. What did he say to you? What little joke did you share?

You didn't see me standing there, watching, listening, waiting in the pouring rain for you to turn back. But you never did.

You didn't see me that day and you haven't seen me since, but I see you. You can't hide from me. Despite your best efforts.

I haven't gone away. No matter how hard you tried to erase me.

I see everything.

I see what you're wearing. You've lost weight. You've had your hair done. A new colour. A new style. It doesn't suit you.

He'll tell you it does but he's lying. But he'll say anything, won't he, to make things right? You and I both know things will never be right. How can they ever be right?

You should have turned back. You should have talked to me. Listened to me. You owed me that at least.

That might not have been your first mistake, but it will be your last.

Chapter One

Saturday

The headache felt worse than it had before Hazel took the painkillers half an hour ago and that Godawful sickly, sour taste in her mouth made her want to throw up. Why had she finished the bottle last night? Even her back teeth throbbed, sending a shooting pain behind her eyes. The ringing in her ears was deafening and the thirst... she felt like she could drink the contents of the river Tay and still not quench it.

She should know by now how shit she'd feel in the morning because it was the same every time. But the memories didn't go until she drank herself to sleep. That was why. Images of his body felt tattooed to her eyes. Copious amounts of alcohol were the only thing capable of erasing it, allowing her to sleep, if only for a short time. Even though it was only temporary. The counsellors were great, but they didn't understand, not really. But they tried, and she appreciated that. The weirdest thing was, in the darkness of the wee small hours, when insomnia had robbed her of the rest she desperately needed, she still missed Rick, despite the way he'd betrayed her.

Hazel should know better than to try and numb her pain with alcohol. It hadn't worked for her mum. Why should it be any different for her?

She picked up the towel she kept on the floor next to her bed to wipe the sweat from her face and neck as the shrill ring from her phone sliced through her. Damn hot flushes. As if she didn't have enough to contend with. Hazel tossed the towel

3

back down and sucked air in through her teeth as she rubbed her temple, her eyes squeezed tight shut as if that could block it out. Two unread text messages came up on the screen. Both of them from Cara, she assumed. Hazel would deal with them later although she had a pretty good idea what they said already.

The same as they always did. Imploring Hazel to call her. She was worried about her. It was amazing how quickly her friend had got over the death of the man they both loved – but then, Hazel was the only one of them who had seen his body. Perhaps that was the difference between the two women.

'DCI Todd,' she answered the caller but had to cough to clear the dryness from her throat before feeling like she had to repeat herself. 'DCI Todd speaking.'

She licked what moisture she could with her bone-dry tongue to moisten her lips and listened to the incoming details from the station.

Christ almighty, it's Saturday morning, she wanted to scream. *I've got the hangover from hell, can't someone else go?*

Instead she said, 'Text me the address.'

She checked the time on the clock on her bedside table which read ten thirty.

'Bloody hell,' she exclaimed and struggled to sit up against the pounding headache.

She should shower first, get rid of the stench of stale sweat and wine, a stink she hated, but a splash of cold water on her face and a spray of dry shampoo was all she had time for. Fifty-five-year-old female. Victim of a hit and run right outside her home. Literally as she stepped onto her driveway, which was why Hazel had been called.

–

'Jesus Christ! Are you all right?' Detective Inspector Tom Newton asked, his big brown eyes narrowed in concern.

'Yes, yes,' Hazel batted away his question, hoping he'd leave it at that and nodded to DC Andrea Graham and DS Billy Flynn who she was pleased to see were already carrying out door-to-door enquiries nearby like she'd asked them to do 'Talk to me. Have we got a name? A motive?'

She tugged a pair of latex gloves from her cardigan pocket, glancing briefly at the paramedics securing the back of the ambulance which had sadly not been required this time then stepped inside the recently erected crime scene tent. She crouched down, the smell of faeces invading her nostrils uninvited. It took every ounce of willpower not to heave the half a cup of tea she'd managed to quickly throw down her gullet onto the neatly chipped gravel drive of the address in Meadowbank Gardens. The home of retired teacher Maggie Ramsay.

The recent heavy late March snow that had lain on the ground for days crunched underfoot. Samuel Ramsay, the victim's shattered husband, was being comforted inside the house by one of the uniforms who was also attempting to take a brief initial statement between the man's sobs.

'Involuntary opening of the bowels on the point of death.'

The softly spoken man's voice behind her made Hazel turn to see pathologist Jack Blair, dressed head to toe in white, wisps of his grey hair barely visible through the thin hood.

'Aye, you've told me that before,' Hazel greeted him as she stood. 'Given the witness statement, I'd say cause of death pretty straightforward. Impact trauma.'

The pair looked down at the crumpled, broken body at the same time. One leg was twisted and facing completely in the opposite direction to what nature intended, the foot hanging off the end, with the shin bone jutting out through a massive gash. A huge hole where the back of her head should be had bits of shattered brain matter sprayed outside of it; the remainder oozed out slowly, puddling on the ground beside her. The first uniformed officers on scene spoke to a neighbour who had witnessed the incident and who had described the victim's body as being like a ragdoll, tossed in the air, before the driver had reversed quickly and fled, at speed, from the scene. The witness had been quick-thinking enough to take down the reg number and they had already identified the vehicle as a Vauxhall Astra, reported stolen.

'Some of the brain matter will be on the windscreen so when you find the car, make sure forensics checks in the cracks of the wipers.' Jack Blair tightened his mask closer to his face and got down next to their victim. 'Her blood spatter will have been wiped away so the driver could see to make his getaway.'

'Or her,' Hazel suggested.

'What?' Jack replied.

'Or *her* getaway,' Hazel pointed out.

'Ah, yes indeed, or her, I suppose you're right.'

Hazel patted his shoulder. 'Cause of death seems pretty obvious. Let's hope the why makes the driver of the vehicle easy to find. Tom and I will go in and see if her husband can shed any light on that for us.' She nodded to the lifeless body of Maggie Ramsay.

'Indeed, yes,' Jack agreed. 'I'll be in touch about when the post-mortem will be carried out later on today. You'll want to be there I assume.'

'Thanks Jack. I appreciate that.'

Hazel smiled and started to walk out of the tent, until Jack called her back.

'Look, it's none of my business but you might want to get yourself some mints,' he whispered. 'And listen, I'm here if you want to talk about what happened to—'

'I'm fine,' she heard herself snap and recoiled. He was only trying to help. 'I'm fine, thank you.'

'OK but the offer still stands, and you know where to find me,' Jack repeated, turning his face to their victim's battered body before adding, 'Day or night,' without looking back up.

Hazel was mortified and rummaged in the bottom of her bag for the box of Tic Tacs she'd taken to carrying, her heart pounding when she had trouble locating them.

'Shit,' she mumbled under her breath when there was just one left, stuck to the bottom of the box which took several

6

attempts to dislodge. She was almost resorting to poking her pen inside the tub, just as Tom caught up with her.

'Maggie Ramsay, married to Samuel Ramsay, both retired teachers,' he began to read from his notebook. 'Fifty-five years old. Sentenced to six months, suspended for ten years, and a mandatory alcohol in-patient rehabilitation order, for a drink driving offence last year when the car she was driving hit and killed a ten-year-old boy. A horrible case from the brief outline I looked up before heading over here. There was a note added to the report that said one of the paramedics who attended the scene went on sick leave for a few weeks afterwards.' He took a breath, as if unnerved by the details he'd read 'She got out of rehab last month.'

Hazel's eyes stretched wide at that information, shocked by the judge's leniency, immediately suspicious of the reasons behind that decision. Did that have something to do with her murder? 'Wow, ten years suspended. Surely a custodial sentence was more appropriate?'

Tom turned over the page in his notebook.

'You would think so, especially given that ten-year-old Liam Wilson died instantly when the car she was driving hit him while she was twice over the legal limit as well as talking on her phone. Seems the poor lad stepped into the road outside the corner shop. Ramsay said at the time she didn't see him until it was too late. Family of the wee boy have been pretty vocal about their disgust at what they see as her getting away with murdering the lad. The older brother, in particular.' He scanned the page for the name he needed.

'David Wilson, eighteen years old, has been harassing the couple since and was given a warning for sending threatening letters. The family of the dead boy have got themselves a solicitor who is taking action on their behalf to appeal the sentence on the grounds that it was unduly lenient.'

Hazel listened quietly to Tom's information and couldn't blame the Wilsons. Then she thought about whether she'd have

7

passed a breathalyser test this morning and the idea of failing it horrified her. The drinking had to stop. She'd try and find time to call for a doctor's appointment to get something for her insomnia and night sweats. Anything had to be better than wine.

'Talking to David Wilson has to be our first priority once we're done here then – and is there an alert out for the Astra?'

Tom nodded. 'Yes, the details have already been passed onto Traffic.'

Hazel was relieved that so much had already been organised because she felt like shit.

'Thanks, Tom. Let's go and see what her husband can tell us, shall we?' Hazel replied, hoping the single mint would mask the stale alcohol on her own breath. 'Nice house,' she whispered to Tom as they entered the three-bedroom detached bungalow. Meadowbank Gardens was in a quiet, respectable neighbourhood which was unaccustomed to anything more than a little noise disturbance, let alone a deliberate hit and run – or in this case, more accurately, a murder – right on their doorstep.

Hazel rang the doorbell and the two detectives waited. Footsteps were heard coming quickly towards the door and they were let in by the uniformed officer who had been sitting with their victim's husband.

'How is he?' Hazel asked as she kicked snow from her boots, wiped them on the doormat and stepped inside. 'Has he said anything to you?'

'Not really,' the young, blonde officer replied. 'He seems absolutely devastated.'

'Thanks,' Hazel said. 'You can go now,' she told the young officer.

'Ma'am,' she nodded to both Hazel and Tom as she passed.

Hazel admired the large canvas on the wall in the hallway and recognised the scene immediately as the Piazza San Marco in Venice, a place she'd always wanted to visit, below which was an antique oak sideboard that must have been worth a bob or two, she thought. A bowl of keys sat between two large cactus plants and a thriving aloe plant which were surrounded by several cards. A quick glance pointed to them being anniversary cards for the couple. The smell of fresh furniture polish was a nice distraction. How they kept this almost-white wooden floor so immaculate she had no idea. Hazel's curiosity deepened on seeing the two small dogs sitting on Samuel Ramsay's lap when they entered the living room. Surely muddy prints left some kind of mess? The two detectives followed the sound of sobbing to where Ramsay sat in the living room where they could see yet more anniversary cards displayed on almost every surface.

'Mr Ramsay,' Hazel held out her identification for him to examine although she'd be surprised if he could see anything through those puffy red eyes. The young, uniformed officer's description of his apparent devastation was extremely accurate but that didn't affect Hazel's judgment. Until she'd spoken to him she wasn't ruling him out as a suspect. Everything was possible at this point. She held her ID closer to him. 'My name is Detective Chief Inspector Hazel Todd, and this is my colleague, Detective Inspector Tom Newton. Is it OK to ask you a few questions? I know this must be an awful time for you, such a terrible shock.'

'Sam, call me Sam, please,' the man answered, his voice hoarse from sobbing and barely audible, as the smaller and scruffier of the two terrier type dogs curled its lip and gave a low growl towards the two detectives.

'Do you mind if we sit down?' Hazel asked, concerned by the little dog's attitude.

'No, no, please sit. I'm sorry, don't mind Bella, she's not too keen on strangers, that's all.' His thin smile faded quickly as he stroked Bella's head.

Hazel offered him a sympathetic smile and sat down on the sofa opposite him. She glanced to the large bay window in the living room that looked out onto a large front garden covered by a carpet of thick snow. A new layer of fresh flakes from an overnight shower lay on top. A row of neatly pruned rose bushes, interplanted with lavender, held onto layers of snow alongside the immaculately clipped beech hedge; a thick mound rested on the foliage.

A sleeping black cat stirred briefly from the other end of the blue, flowery sofa. The cat took one look at Hazel, yawned, and closed its eyes again. How Hazel wished she were that cat right then. Curling up and falling asleep sounded bliss. The headache at least had reduced to become a dull ache stalking the top of her head. Hazel could cope with that; she would have to. She tried to ignore the first signs of a hot flush that she felt burn the back of her neck before landing on her cheeks, hoping that neither of the two men would notice it.

'Thank you,' Hazel said.

She could see Tom examining every corner of the room, allowing his eyes to scan everything from his seat on the high-backed grey armchair. Parker Knoll, if she wasn't mistaken. She spotted the book perched on the arm. The latest Jeffrey Archer novel with a red leather bookmark holding the reader's place. If it was their victim's book, it was destined to remain unfinished. A poignant thought.

'I can't believe this is happening, it's all so…' Samuel Ramsay burst into tears again and Tom grabbed a handful of tissues from the box on the low oak coffee table in between them and offered it to him. 'Thanks.'

'Take your time, I know this must be difficult for you.' Hazel assured him, while her stomach churned and growled for food. Not eating had seemed like a good idea an hour ago. She craved a bacon roll with a good dollop of tomato ketchup but thought perhaps it was best she didn't have that option – she was still feeling rough enough to fear anything she did eat might make a rapid return.

'It all happened so fast,' Samuel wiped the tears from his cheek. 'She waved, as she always does…' He stopped and looked as if he was swallowing back another wave of grief. 'Did, always did,' he murmured, as if reminding himself of what had happened. 'When she got off the bus before crossing the road.' He wiped his face again. 'Maggie isn't allowed to drive, you see, and…'

It was obvious to Hazel that he was struggling, embarrassed by having to tell her about his wife's conviction.

'We know about the accident.' She helped the man out, and her choice of words seemed to shift some of the burden he was feeling. Although calling it an 'accident' didn't feel right somehow. But she would let that go for now.

'It all happened so fast,' he repeated. 'So fast.'

'Did you manage to get a good look at the car or the driver?' She wondered if Samuel's account would match the eagle-eyed neighbour's.

Samuel shook his head, his face creasing into more floods of tears before one of the little dogs leapt up and began to lick away the salty liquid. Hazel could see he was in no fit state to give a proper statement yet. She would arrange for a FLO to come round before trying again. She opened her mouth to say they would come back later when Samuel's phone rang loudly behind him.

'Is it all right if I take that? It might be our daughter. She lives in Canada, and I left a message for her to call me.' He sobbed. 'What am I going to tell her?'

'Of course, go ahead, we'll see ourselves out.' Hazel stood and indicated towards the living room door for Tom to go ahead of her, as Samuel lifted the handset from the cradle. 'We'll come back later and have a chat. Is that OK?'

They had barely moved when she saw him frown then gasp, wide-eyed. 'Who is this?' he snapped down the line. 'Hello? Hello!' He pulled the phone away from his ear and looked at Hazel, his eyes wide and staring.

'What is it?' she urged, growing increasingly concerned by the expression on his face.

'I, I…' The man was in shock and talking seemed almost impossible.

'Mr Ramsay,' Hazel asked him again. 'Is everything OK?'

'I, I...' he stuttered again.

Hazel's eyes met Tom's, wide with concern.

'Samuel,' she tried again, watching in horror as the colour drained from the man's face, leaving a pale grey pallor behind.

'He said,' Samuel struggled for breath and let the phone fall from his grasp, landing on the cushions of the sofa before bouncing onto the floor at Tom's feet. 'He said...'

Tom picked up the handset and held it to his ear.

'Hello,' he said. 'Hello?' he repeated then shook his head at Hazel before resting the phone in the cradle on the living room unit. The shelves were adorned with various photos of a young girl, from very young to a graduation picture standing between her two proud parents. His eyes were drawn to a photo of a beaming Maggie Ramsay holding a new-born baby. A grandchild, he assumed.

'What did he say to you?' Hazel urged.

Samuel looked right at her. 'He said justice had finally been done.'

'Tom, dial 1471, see if there's a number,' Hazel pressed him but feared the caller wouldn't be that stupid. Leaving a number would be foolish in the extreme under the circumstances.

'Sure,' Tom replied and snatched the handset up again.

'Sit down, Samuel,' Hazel suggested. 'Did you recognise the voice? It was definitely a man, was it?'

Samuel lowered his wiry frame back down, wiping down his shock of unruly white hair.

'I, erm, I think so.' He dropped his head into his hands and shook it. 'God, I don't know now.' The man's breathing became faster, and a pink flush rose on his cheeks, a slight glisten of moisture on his brow. 'I, argh,' he grabbed his left arm. 'My spray, pass me my spray...'

'Your spray, where is it?' Hazel urged.

'Argh,' Samuel exclaimed louder. 'My GTN spray,' he gasped, his face growing redder, his breathing coming in desperate snatches 'For my angina.'

Tom rummaged amongst a pile of magazines on the table and found the container. 'Here,' he said and unscrewed the lid before handing it to Samuel, but the container slipped from his fingers before he could get hold of it.

'I'll get it, don't worry, just breathe,' Tom told him and shook the bottle before holding it close to Samuel's mouth, but it was no use, the man was clutching his chest more tightly now, squeezing his white shirt in his fingers. He had slipped down towards the floor before any of the medication could be sprayed.

'Samuel! Can you hear me?' Hazel asked, her headache returning with a bang as she and Tom watched in horror as Samuel Ramsay landed, hard, on the immaculate wooden floor.

'Is he breathing?' Hazel urged.

Tom leaned down and rested his ear just above Samuel's mouth.

'Shit,' Tom exclaimed and began CPR. 'Call an ambulance.'

Hazel did as he said, and the two detectives could only pray their witness survived to help them find out who had brutally murdered his wife.

It felt like a lifetime had passed until the sound of sirens wailed towards them. How Hazel wished the one sent to help Maggie was still there. She watched on in horror as Tom continued to try and keep Samuel Ramsay alive until help got there.

Chapter Two

'Hello, I'm Detective Constable Graham.' Andrea pressed the tips of her fingers against her auburn fringe to slide it out of her eyes as she held up her ID for the elderly lady to examine. The old, silver-haired woman who lived in the bungalow three doors down from the Ramsays' home peered over the top of a pair of black-framed glasses to see the card better.

'Is this about the accident earlier?' she said and had to tilt her head up to meet Andrea's eyes.

Andrea thought to herself, *that was no accident.* 'Yes,' she answered politely. 'I was wondering if I could ask you a few questions about it. Did you see what happened at all?'

The old woman glanced behind Andrea at the gathering crowd who were all chatting and pointing, sombre-faced, in the direction of the Ramsays' driveway.

'You'd better come in, dear,' she said, and held the newly painted white front door wide open and pointed further down the hallway. 'First door on the right, go right through,' she added.

Andrea caught the unmistakable whiff of fresh outdoor paint and spotted the neat lines of the paintbrush on the door frame as she tapped snow from her boots and wiped her feet on the coir doormat before stepping inside.

'Thank you,' she said and bent down to stroke the grey cat that came to greet her in the doorway.

The elderly woman, who looked like she was in her early seventies, carried a little more weight than she should for her diminutive height of what Andrea estimated to be no more than five feet.

'Have a seat dear,' the woman smiled and flopped down on a large mustard-coloured armchair next to a huge red brick fireplace that held a black stone log burner.

'Thanks,' Andrea spotted the knitting needles on the coffee table right away. The pink wool looked like it was about to become a cardigan – for a baby, perhaps.

'I'm not sure exactly how much help I'm going to be because I didn't see anything, but I certainly heard it.'

Andrea took her notebook from the pocket of her red duffle coat and unwound her long navy scarf. It was roasting in this house. Not that she wasn't grateful to get out of the bitter cold outside.

'I'm sorry, I forgot to ask your name,' Andrea began.

'Deirdre McNeil,' the old woman told her. 'Miss or Ms, as you young people might say today.' Her small smile lit up her pale blue eyes that looked out under her silver fringe.

'Miss McNeil—' Andrea started to say.

'Call me Deidre, please.'

Andrea smiled. 'Deirdre, you said you heard what happened; can you tell me exactly what you heard?'

Deirdre sighed and shook her head vigorously as she squeezed her eyes tightly shut on being asked to recall something so horrible.

'There was a scream.' The old woman seemed to shiver. 'It was a woman's scream. I remember that, all right. An almighty, deathly, blood-curdling scream…' She stopped to take a long slow breath. 'I've never heard anything like it, and I was in the Wrens for many, many years but…' She seemed to have to stop again. She shook her head. 'Then there was a loud bang then… then… nothing.'

Andrea frowned. 'Nothing?'

'Yes. When I heard the bang I ran to my bedroom window. I was putting laundry away at the time you see, and…' She took

15

a tissue from her sleeve and wiped her nose. 'That's when I saw a car skidding backwards out of the drive. It was green I think or was it blue?' She sighed and ran her fingers over her chin. 'It all happened so fast dear. I'm sorry I can't be more help.'

'That's OK,' Andrea tried to reassure her.

'It came out of the blue, you know. I don't suppose anybody can really prepare for something like that.' Deirdre shook her head before momentarily taking a wistful glance at her living room window.

'Did you manage to get a look at the driver or the licence plate?'

Ignoring Andrea's question, instead she fixed her eyes on her and said, 'It was Maggie, wasn't it?'

'Well it's—' Andrea started to say until Deirdre talked over her.

'She was such a lovely woman until...' Deirdre shuffled in her seat and fiddled with the sleeve of her blue woollen cardigan. 'Now, I'm not one to speak ill of the dead but,' she sighed. 'The accident,' she shrugged. 'She should really have been put in prison, shouldn't she?'

Andrea had been shocked to learn what their victim had been convicted of when Tom briefed her before they arrived at the scene. Leaving the little lad on the road warranted a custodial sentence she thought.

'So you knew her well, did you?'

Deirdre shook her head. 'Not really, but whenever we did meet in the street or up at Tesco, you know, she'd be nice enough.' She tutted as if remembering an uncomfortable thought. 'She gave me a lift home a few times before... well, before... everything.'

'When did you last speak to Mrs Ramsay?'

Deirdre looked like she was thinking, trying hard to search for the information Andrea wanted.

'Do you know what, lass, it's been at least a couple of weeks, maybe even three.'

'Is that unusual?' Andrea made a note in her pad.

'Probably not now that I think about it. She kept to herself a bit more after the accident. Like you'd expect I suppose.'

This information was useful, but Andrea needed to confirm the facts. 'So did you get a look at the driver of the car at all? Was it a man or a woman would you say?'

Deirdre shook her head. 'I'm sorry, no, I didn't. I'm afraid I can't help you with that kind of detail.'

'That's OK, you've been really helpful,' Andrea explained as she noted down what the woman had said. 'Can you tell me what time you heard this bang and the scream?'

'Yes,' the old woman nodded. 'The clock on the wall outside my bedroom door had just chimed ten o'clock so it must have been ten to ten.' She gave a small smile at the brief look of confusion on Andrea's face. 'It's been running ten minutes fast since my mother died two years ago. I haven't been able to change it since.' A look of sorrow briefly crossed her face and she avoided Andrea's eyes.

'I see.' Andrea wrote '9.50 a.m.' in her notebook.

'I know that's right too because the number fourteen bus had just pulled away from the stop over there. It usually gets here at that time.' She pointed to the bus shelter across the road through the narrow street. Andrea took a quick look to see the kind of bus stop that had a shelter and a seat for people queuing to hide from bad weather on a rainy day and which now had several people waiting.

'OK, that's great, thank you, Deirdre.' Andrea found herself gazing round the beautifully kept living room wondering how old Deirdre's mum was when she died. Her eyes fell on a photo of Deirdre standing behind a very elderly woman sitting in a wheelchair who looked as if she'd just had her hair done and who was dressed in a smart yellow dress.

'That was the last photo ever taken of Mum. We'd just been to a christening. She'd been so happy that day. Happy to see all of her family in one place.'

Andrea felt like she should apologise for snooping when she realised Deirdre had noticed.

'Oh,' she said instead. 'That's lovely. She looks happy.'

'Yes, Mum was a hundred and two when she died.'

Andrea's eyes widened. 'Wow, that's amazing.'

'She was a land girl in the war.' Deirdre's eyes lit up. 'Aye, she saw this country was fed when our boys were away fighting the Nazis.'

'My great-granny was a land girl too actually,' Andrea said. 'I don't know much about her. She died when I was very young.'

'I'm sure she'd have been very proud of you, dear,' Deirdre smiled. 'Becoming a detective.'

'I hope so,' Andrea replied.

Then the old woman looked serious again and pulled the topic of conversation back to the reason for Andrea's visit.

'It obviously wasn't an accident, was it?' she suggested. 'Otherwise they wouldn't have sent detectives round here to ask questions.'

'We just want to explore all avenues at this stage,' Andrea explained.

'Well, I hope you find out who did this quickly. For Samuel's sake. He must be going through hell.' Deirdre tutted and shook her head. 'Tell him if he needs anything, anything at all, he just has to knock on my door. Will you do that for me, lass?'

'I will,' Andrea reached into her duffle coat pocket on the chair behind her and produced one of the cards with her phone number on it. 'If you think of anything else, will you give me a call? My number is on this card.' She laid it on the coffee table and tapped it twice with her finger.

Deirdre reached for it immediately and held it up. 'I will, absolutely, lass.'

Andrea stood and slid her arms into the sleeves of her coat, not looking forward to leaving the cosy bungalow and returning to the freezing temperatures outside. She walked ahead of Deirdre as she made her way to the front door.

'Thank you for your time,' she said as she buttoned the toggles of her duffle coat up and tightened her scarf before stepping out into the cold air, her warm breath cutting streaks of condensation in front of her.

'You wrap up, now,' Deirdre insisted. 'You'll catch cold if you don't.'

Andrea smiled. 'Goodbye, Deirdre.'

—

'I don't think there's a lot more I can tell you,' Julian Grant told DS Billy Flynn. 'Like I said, when I spoke to your uniformed colleague earlier, I saw the back of the green Astra speeding away after...' he hesitated, the memory of seeing his neighbour's murder obviously still raw, '... You know, what happened, so I made a note of the number plate. I knew you lot would be needing it for sure,' he added, reaching for a cigarette packet on the coffee table between them. He offered the packet to Billy.

'No thanks.' Billy held up his hand.

'You don't mind if I do, do you?'

'Not at all,' Billy lied but could see the man's nerves were frayed by the incident.

'Cheers mate.' Julian Grant lit up and took a long, obviously soothing draw on it.

'Listen we are really grateful that you were able to take that number down,' Billy said wishing he was still cuddled up in his warm bed with Natasha and not doing door-to-door inquiries in the freezing conditions. The recent development in their on again, off again relationship was definitely welcome. As a result, he hoped it would be on forever, this time. He would have to tell Hazel soon.

'Is she going to be all right or—'

'Mrs Ramsay was killed, I'm afraid. I'm sorry,' Billy informed him.

Julian Grant quickly clasped a hand to his mouth. 'Jesus! I mean, I didn't really know them but,' he exhaled sharply. 'Jesus that's terrible,' he repeated.

'How well do you know the Ramsay's ?' Billy asked.

Julian shook his head. 'Not at all really, although…' He leaned his face a little closer to Billy and his words became whispers, 'I know about… what she did, to that wee lad. Everyone does.'

Billy nodded. 'Ah right, yes,' he said, giving nothing away. There was no doubt though that Liam's death was very much the motive at the front of his own mind.

'Terrible.' Julian shook his head and took a draw on his cigarette, blowing the smoke from the side of his mouth, away from Billy's face then seemed to correct himself. 'Not that I think she deserved what happened, don't get me wrong.'

'I wouldn't, no, not at all,' Billy said and wrote something in his notebook.

'Have you just made a note of what I just said?' Julian eyed Billy suspiciously.

'No,' Billy replied thinking what a strange question that was. 'Oh, OK.'

'So, is that all you know about the couple then? You've never spoken to either of them?'

'Not really, not like a real conversation, more just a "good morning" when I've been putting the bin out, that kind of thing.'

'Have you noticed anyone hanging around recently or has there been anybody in the street in the past wee while that you didn't recognise? Anybody at all?' Billy asked but was disappointed to see him shake his head.

Then Julian stopped as if remembering something. 'Actually, now you come to mention it, there's that young lad, you know, I think he must be the brother of the wee laddie she knocked down. He's been round a few times, shouting his mouth off about how she should be behind bars. Aye, you should talk to him,' he nodded and pointed his finger close to Billy. 'I bet he's done this.'

'Was it him in the green Astra, do you think?'

Julian shrugged. 'Sorry, I didn't get that close a look at the driver. My eyes were on the licence plate to be honest. Instinct I suppose.'

'Did you ever happen to see that young lad driving a green Astra?' Billy asked, making a note in his pad.

'No I didn't, sorry. I only ever saw the lad on the drive or the pavement outside their house.'

Billy thought for a minute. 'What kind of things did you hear him say?'

'Erm, do you know what? I can't say exactly the words he used, but his manner...' He sucked in air through his teeth sharply. 'He was angry – no, beyond angry, there was a rage in his demeanour, in his body language. Do you know what I mean? But can you blame him?'

Instead of getting involved in that conversation, Billy finished making his notes and thanked Julian for his help. He waved a hand to him when he saw him watching from the living room window and headed back to the Ramsay home to update DCI Todd.

Chapter Three

'Mum, you have to eat something,' David Wilson implored but the sight of his mum flat out snoring on the sofa made his pleas pointless.

He wondered if she'd moved at all since he left the house that morning as he looked at the clock on the mantel. Lunchtime. Memories of a cooked brunch on a Saturday hit him. Sausages, fried eggs, grilled tomatoes, heaps of streaky bacon and beans. Never mushrooms. His mum always remembered that. Sometimes though she teased him about his dislike of mushrooms. Those relaxed, joyful Saturdays were a thing of the past. The joy had gone, extinguished in the blink of an eye.

David had told her he had a college thing on that morning. She didn't know what day of the week it was at the best of times. David wasn't sure if she'd care, anyway. Carol Wilson hadn't cared about much, if anything, since that day. Especially not herself. David knew she would be with Liam if she could. He feared she would find a way to get to him and didn't like leaving his mum alone.

He tugged the tartan blanket from underneath her skinny bird-like frame, tensing at the feel of her bony hips on his fingertips, and draped it over the sleeping woman. At least when she slept she didn't think and if she didn't think, she couldn't remember. Memories weren't good. Not even the good ones – because enjoying the good was always followed by reminders of what had happened next. In such a short time his vibrant, smiling mum had withered to the point she was almost invisible. She'd been fading from the first moment.

That first knock on the door. That police officer's face, his eyes. David would never forget the man's eyes. The sorrow seared into them as he stood on the doorstep. The female officer, Hannah, had made a pot of tea for everyone. Her name was etched in his mind. She told them a woman had been arrested. They were so sorry for their loss. They could see Liam soon, they promised, just not yet.

Carol Wilson's eyes peeled open just as the empty glass rolled onto the floor.

'Mum,' David flopped down onto the sofa next to her, the foul smell drifting uninvited into his nostrils.

The thick sour stench of stale sweat and bad breath. He wasn't sure when she'd last showered, and her hair lay lank and greasy against the stained pillowcase. 'You haven't even touched your toast.'

'I know, son,' she replied, shivering.

She slowly pulled herself up into a sitting position then reached for the almost empty vodka bottle. Her face betrayed the disappointment she felt on seeing how little was left.

'I think I've got a bug or something. I just couldn't face it. I'll try something later when I feel a bit better maybe.' She spoke without looking at him. 'I promise.'

David didn't try to stop her. If saying she had a bug helped her, he wouldn't correct her. Once she'd had that first drink they'd talk. It was pointless until she'd taken the edge off. He grabbed the carrier bag and lifted out a big bottle of bubble bath. The cruel irony was that before all this, his mum had barely touched a drop. Not even at Christmas. It was only on Hogmanay she ever really drank and even then it was just a nip to see in the bells. 'A nip of a fine malt to herald in the coming year,' she always said.

She'd not even turned to alcohol to numb the pain when their dad died but losing Liam had utterly destroyed her.

'Your favourite was on a deal. It was half price, so I got you one,' he shrugged. 'Might be nice to have a soak in the bath, eh? I can run one for you if you like, I don't mind.'

David's words were ignored as Carol poured what was left in the bottle into her glass and gulped the contents in one.

'What are you on about?' she said and tipped the last dregs in. 'Listen, could you go to the shop for me?' Carol held up the vodka bottle. 'Get me some more.'

'Here look,' David held up the bottle of magnolia bath foam, trying to ignore her request. 'See? Your favourite.'

His mum's eyes didn't even register. 'Shift up, son,' she said instead and tried to lower herself back down. 'There's a twenty-pound note in my purse.' Then she frowned. 'Wait, I'm no sure, I canny mind, take my bank card if there's nae cash. Pass me the remote, will you?'

David lifted the two remotes and offered them into the hand that wasn't cradling the glass.

'I've got us some sausages that were reduced,' David persevered. 'I'm going to do some buttery mash and beans with it. What do you think? Loads of pepper and HP.'

'Bloody thing must be needing batteries.' Seemingly ignoring her son again, she tapped the remote on her palm and pointed it at the TV.

'Did you hear what I said?'

Carol blew against the end of the remote and tapped it again. 'Bloody thing.'

'Give it here, I'll see if we've got any batteries in the cupboard.' David gave up trying to talk to her. Again. It was becoming harder, but he had to stay calm. Shouting at her didn't help either of them.

Carol dropped the remote into his open hand then sought out the last drops from her glass. She held the bottle upside down, shaking it up and down, in a futile attempt to get more out of the empty bottle.

'Thanks son. Get yourself a sweetie at the shop as well.'

'Aye,' David sighed and snatched up the carrier bag and the other remote from the sofa. 'I might as well change them both.' *Get you and Liam a sweetie at the shop.* The memory slammed into him, almost knocking him off balance. He had to wipe a tear from the corner of his eye.

'What? Yes, good idea. Change them both. That's a good idea,' Carol Wilson repeated without looking at him.

'I'll go to the shop first, then.' He sounded defeated but what else could he do? He had to focus.

He'd seen his mum go through withdrawal before and he never wanted to experience that again as long as he lived. The shivering. The vomiting. The hallucinations. Watching her scratch her skin until it bled because she felt insects crawling all over her. No, not again, even if it meant he had to buy the booze himself. David took a long, slow sigh. He had to compose himself.

'I'll do you a wee plate then when I get back,' he persisted, trying to smile. 'It shouldn't be long. I'll do us a big pot of tea as well, and bread and butter.' He swept the plate of uneaten, cold toast and mug of equally cold tea into his free hand. 'What do you say? That sounds good, doesn't it?' Nobody could ever say David didn't try.

'Whatever, son, yes, if you're having one, I'll take one.' After glancing briefly at him – the tiniest of eye contact – Carol scratched her head and tucked her lank, greasy hair behind her ear. She pulled her blanket tighter against her body. 'Turn the heating up will you, it's freezing in here.'

'Aye, OK.' David nodded and stood up. 'I'll get these batteries for you first.' He squeezed his mum's knee and instantly regretted the bony feeling in his hand.

How could it be right that *she* could mow down a ten-year-old boy and escape a custodial sentence? What good was a ten year suspended sentence? What kind of justice was that for ending the life of a little boy? If she'd stopped and got help for Liam... His wee brother dying alone was hard to bear. David still had nightmares thinking about it where he heard Liam crying for him, for his mum, but there was nothing David could do to help him. In his dream he could never get to him in time.

No matter how fast he tried to run because his legs felt like he was wading through thick mud every time, squeezing them, holding him back. He was never able to fight his way out.

Mandatory inpatient rehabilitation was no prison sentence. Just because she couldn't go home didn't mean she wasn't still technically free. No, nothing about that was right.

A little boy who'd only popped to the shop to get milk for his mum's cup of tea. She left him lying in the road, his brains sprayed over the tarmac, sobbing alone for his mummy, as his life quickly slipped away. A suspended sentence was an insult to Liam's memory.

She did more than take Liam's life that day. She destroyed his mum's life, because Carol Wilson died that day too. The only difference was that her physical body still existed, her heart still beat, but she was just a shell. A husk was all that was left. David was struggling with his own grief as well as trying to get through college and look after her and the house.

If it weren't for Suzanne, David didn't know how he would cope. His phone chirped in his pocket. He pulled it out and read the text from Suzanne.

Can't wait to see you xx

Me too. I've missed you xx

You only saw me last night silly! Xx

I know but I love you and I hate not being with you. Xx

I feel the same. You know that. I'll see you soon
xx

X

David replied with a single kiss the way he always did. Going out to meet her would make him feel better, for a little while at least, but he wondered if she realised just how important she was to him. Essential, in fact. Meeting her that day had been like divine intervention. Kismet, she called it. Whatever that was. It wasn't a word he'd ever heard before and she'd smiled at his innocence.

He grabbed his baseball cap to keep his head dry from the falling snow. He took a last look in on his mum. Sighing, he closed his eyes for a moment, then set off, locking the door behind him. He'd get his mum's vodka and make her something to eat. It was probably a waste of time, but he had to do something. Then he'd go and meet Suzanne. She made everything better, somehow. Even on his darkest days, Suzanne could bring David back from the brink.

Chapter Four

Diva2008 – I can't believe how easy you are to talk to about this stuff.

KingPenguin – No bother. I'm glad I could help. Want to meet up and talk more?

Diva2008… is typing…

KingPenguin – It feels like I've known you all my life.

Diva2008… is typing…

KingPenguin – Shit man I'm not good at this stuff. Girls don't usually notice me.

Diva2008… is typing…

KingPenguin – What I'm trying to say is…

Diva2008 – I feel the same.

KingPenguin – Want to meet up?

Diva2008… is typing…

KingPenguin – You can come round tonight. My mum's got Zumba. We'd have the flat to ourselves.

Diva2008… is typing…

KingPenguin – I'd love to see you for real. I know we go to different schools but that doesn't matter does it.

Diva2008… is typing…

KingPenguin – What do you think?

Diva2008… is typing…

KingPenguin – You still there?

Diva2008… is typing…

KingPenguin – ???

Diva2008 – I'm still here.

KingPenguin – That's a relief. I thought I'd scared you off lol

Diva2008 – Nobody says lol these days. What are you fifty – lol?

KingPenguin… is typing…

Diva2008… is typing…

KingPenguin – You still there?

Diva2008… is typing…

KingPenguin – So want me to text you my address?

Diva2008 – Sure.

KingPenguin – I'll need your number first.

Diva2008 – 07698 245 657

KingPenguin – Just sent it.

Diva2008… Is typing…

KingPenguin – Did you get it yet?

Diva2008… is typing…

KingPenguin – Hey are you…

Diva2008 – Is that photo really you?

KingPenguin – Yes do you like it?

Diva2008… is typing…

KingPenguin – Maybe you could send me one of you.

Diva2008… is typing…

KingPenguin – I'd love to see what you look like properly.

Diva2008 – There did you get it?

KingPenguin – Not fair I sent you one with my top off.

Diva2008… is typing…

KingPenguin… is typing…

Diva2008 – There did you get it.

KingPenguin – yes wow you're cute.

Diva2008 – Nobody has ever called me cute before.

KingPenguin – Really?? You're actually hot.

Diva2008 – Wow thanks.

KingPenguin – If you weren't hot do you think your photo would do this…

Diva2008… is typing…

KingPenguin… is typing…

Diva2008 – Do you really like me that much??

KingPenguin – Hell yes. So you'll come over tonight.

Diva2008… is typing…

KingPenguin – ???

Diva2008… is typing…

KingPenguin – We could maybe get some beer if you like.

Diva2008… is typing…

KingPenguin – my brother's usually got some weed. He thinks I can't see him stashing it in the top drawer.

Diva2008 – I've never done that before.

KingPenguin – Never?? It's brilliant. I'll show you what to do. Is there anything else you want to try??

Diva2008… is typing…

KingPenguin – Have you ever been kissed?

Diva2008… is typing…

KingPenguin – Have you ever been touched…

Diva2008… is typing…

KingPenguin… is typing…

Diva2008 – No.

KingPenguin – Would you like to be kissed?

Diva2008 – Yes.

KingPenguin – Touched?

Diva2008… is typing…

KingPenguin… is typing…

Diva2008… is typing…

KingPenguin – I haven't scared you off have I?

Diva2008 – No.

KingPenguin – That's a relief…

Diva2008 – Does it hurt?

KingPenguin – Does what hurt?

Diva2008 – You know what I mean.

KingPenguin – It won't hurt. I promise.

Diva2008 – You promise??

KingPenguin – I promise I'd never do anything to hurt you.
I care about you too much.
Diva2008 – You do?
KingPenguin – Of course. Come about 7 and wear that
sexy top in the photo.
Diva2008 – Ok see you later.
KingPenguin – Can't wait x
Diva2008 – me too x
Diva2008 has left the chat.
KingPenguin has left the chat.

I can't wait. That's not a lie. I can't wait to see you tonight,
KingPenguin. Except this Diva2008 isn't exactly what you're
expecting. The judge believed all your pathetic, whimpering
excuses, gave you a suspended sentence for possession of thousands of images of underage girls being abused. Some as young
as eleven. You swore you'd never touch a little girl. You knew
it was wrong. You and I both know that's a lie, don't we?

I could go to the police with all this evidence but where's
the fun in that? No, KingPenguin and Diva2008 will have their
date tonight. Only it won't end the way you're hoping.

Chapter Five

Hazel gave her details to the paramedic before he closed the back door of the ambulance that had been urgently called for Samuel Ramsay. He was still alive, if only just. That had certainly wakened her up. All thoughts of her hangover were pushed firmly to the back of her mind, even if the headache did still linger stubbornly.

This heart attack, or whatever it was, had occurred at an incredibly inconvenient time. Not that Hazel dared say that to him. She had promised Samuel that she would ensure the house was locked up and he'd managed to tell her to call Maggie's friend Sandra to come and look after the dogs. She had a key, apparently. Hazel also promised she'd do that for him. And she would – but her key priority was finding out who had called Samuel, triggering his collapse.

Hazel dialled Superintendent Daly's number to update him about Samuel Ramsay's condition. She rubbed her cold fingers over her forehead against the headache and allowed a long, slow breath to exhale while she waited for him to answer. As she was about to hang up she heard his voice.

'Hello DCI Todd. What's happening?' he said.

'I'm afraid there's been an early setback, sir.'

Before Hazel could continue she heard her boss sigh down the line.

'Yes and that is?' he asked plainly.

'Our victim's husband was rushed to hospital before we had a chance to have a proper chat with him, sir.'

Hazel listened while he seemed to be quietly mulling over the information and she could picture the man she'd known for a number of years muttering inaudibly and shaking his head on hearing about the development. While she waited for his response she closed her eyes and took a long, soothing breath before opening them to see two uniformed officers moving on an inquisitive group of teenagers that were staring and pointing from across the road.

'Are there any other relatives there?'

'No, it was just Mr and Mrs Ramsay at the property.' She nibbled her lip before allowing her gaze to shift towards Tom through the living room window who was mouthing the word *what* at her. She waved her hand in his direction and returned her focus onto the call. 'Tom and I are going to take a look in the house to see if something in there can give us a clue to her murderer's identity sir.' Then she waited, knowing she was treading a fine line without a search warrant.

'That's fine. Go ahead DCI Todd,' Daly replied faster than Hazel anticipated. 'Did he manage to give you any indication of who might want to do that to his wife before he was taken ill?'

'The couple were being harassed by a man called David Wilson and he's on the top of my list. We're going to talk to him as a priority, sir.'

'I recognise that name. Remind me. Who is he?'

'He is the older brother of Liam Wilson. The young boy who...'

'Ah yes, that's right. The lad that was killed during Maggie Ramsay's drink-drive accident.'

'That's right, sir.' She was impressed by his knowledge. 'We also have the reg number of the stolen car that hit Mrs Ramsay and I've asked for CCTV to be pulled from the area to see if that can show us who was driving.'

'Good, then, good, good,' Daly said. 'Keep me in the loop DCI Todd.'

Hazel was about to thank him, but he'd rung off before she got the chance. She slid her phone into her jacket pocket and walked back inside the Ramsays' house to find Tom had already donned a pair of latex gloves and had opened one of the drawers in the sideboard under the living room window and was flipping through the contents.

'Have you found anything?'

'Not yet,' Tom told her. 'They look any other retired couple to me. It also looks like this last anniversary was a significant milestone one.' He nodded to the cards. 'Apart from Maggie's drink-driving conviction they could be any other insignificant couple.'

Hazel looked more closely along the line of cards displayed neatly on the mantel-piece above an electric fire. The kind that gives the appearance of a real fire, without the mess.

'Seemed they were a popular couple,' she suggested and pulled on a pair of gloves.

'Aye, it seems so.' Tom counted the cards, mouthing the words between his lips. 'I count sixteen in here and there must be at least ten on that unit in the hall.' He creased his brow, tilting his head gently. 'To be honest, I'm surprised they still have so many friends after the accident. Something like that tends to thin your network considerably.'

'Perhaps they've tried to erase it completely,' Hazel suggested.

She opened the drawer in the pine TV unit and found the usual take-away menus and a variety of old birthday and mother's day cards. A small pink folder caught her eye and she lifted it out. Flicking through the papers and old photos she could see that one of the couple had been doing some genealogical research with a rough draft of a family tree amongst the collection. As she laid it back down, a white A5 envelope attracted her attention. She picked it up and removed a letter from the envelope. Her eyes quickly widened as she read the content. The author of the note had not minced

34

their words. Hazel was surprised to find such an astonishing letter just sitting here with the other innocuous contents of the TV unit. Had it been thrown in there in a hurry? To hide it quickly, perhaps, she wondered.

'Tom, listen to this.' She read it aloud for him.

> *You're going to get what's coming to you. Do you really think you can carry on like nothing happened. Who the hell do you think you are. You think that because your fancy lawyers helped you get off with murder that it's all over. This isn't over. Not by a long shot.*

It was Tom's eyes that now stretched wide. 'That should definitely be taken as a threat to her life.' He held out his hand. 'It can't really be interpreted any other way can it, given the circumstances. ? Let's have a look.'

Hazel handed the paper over and returned to rummaging inside the drawer. She lifted out another two identical envelopes. She opened one and found the content to be almost identical to the first one. She leaned her hand in again and produced another one. Who had access to this drawer? Surely these letters should be more securely stored and why were they even there? Surely the police should have them. Hazel's mind buzzed with questions.

'What did we do about the threats David Wilson was making?' she turned and asked before handing Tom the other letters, fearing that Police Scotland, Tayside division in particular, had some serious questions to answer after what had just happened to Maggie Ramsay. 'God, if this is on us then the shit's going to hit the fan. Daly is going to be on the warpath. Not just him either. Top brass will be gunning for someone.' When she said the word 'we' Hazel was grateful that meant the universal 'we', as in the Police in general. Her team had never been alerted to Wilson's threats until today and she wondered who the reports were given to.

Tom took out his phone. 'I'll get Billy to do a more thorough background check on the case,' he said as he moved away.

'Aye thanks,' Hazel replied and dropped the letters into clear, plastic evidence bags, sealing the top securely. Reaching into the back of the drawer she found yet another envelope then looked up at Tom when she had a thought. 'Wait a minute, Billy is probably still on door-to-door. He'll have to do it when he gets back to the station.'

This time the envelope had something hard inside it and when she opened it she was shocked to find a bullet. 'Jesus,' Hazel muttered under her breath.

The sound of a vehicle pulling up made Hazel turn to see the private ambulance arrive to take Maggie's Ramsay's body to Dundee where their pathologist Jack Blair would carry out a full post-mortem examination. Even if her cause of death seemed obvious. The younger of the two men in the ambulance, who got out of the vehicle first, nodded to her when he saw that she was watching. Hazel acknowledged him with her own gentle nod to reciprocate.

'Is that a bullet?' Tom exclaimed, the pitch of his voice growing higher with the shock.

'Aye,' Hazel said and placed the bullet inside its own separate evidence bag. 'This is serious, Tom. He meant business didn't he? We really need to talk to this lad as soon as possible.'

'I can't disagree with you,' Tom said. 'But threats are one thing. Carrying them out is a whole other thing altogether. I mean we can all get angry, even say things but how many of us would actually carry it out. But don't get me wrong. I agree Wilson is our number one suspect for sure.' Hazel had to acknowledge his suggestion, but it seemed Maggie Ramsay had been able to get on with her life after what had happened when the Wilsons's lives had been shattered into irreparable pieces. She might have had ten years suspended sentence hanging over her but that wasn't enough. Hazel had to admit, it really didn't seem right. Wilson's anger meant that his threats could easily tip over into physical harm. Her thoughts were interrupted by a knock on the front door followed by the sound of it being opened and closed. Familiar voices drifted towards her. She looked over to the living room doorway to see Andrea Graham and Billy Flynn.

'How did you two get on?' she asked, hoping they had good news.

'Hey boss,' Billy replied. 'Julian Grant, the guy that wrote down the reg number, said he'd never seen the car before, but he had seen David Wilson on a number of occasions.'

'Did he say what David did when he was there?'

'Shouted and made a nuisance of himself, it seems,' Billy replied.

'Nothing more sinister, then?' Hazel pressed him. 'He didn't physically touch the couple did he?'

Billy shook his head. 'It doesn't appear so.' Then he frowned and pointed to the evidence bag in her hand. 'Is that what I think it is?'

'Aye, I found it in an envelope, stuffed in there.' Hazel pointed to the open drawer next to her.

'Is it real?' Billy asked and pulled on a pair of gloves.

Hazel handed the bag with the bullet in it to him and watched him narrow his eyes to examine it more closely.

'I dinnae think this is real.' He handed it back. 'It's a good fake, but it's definitely a fake.'

Hazel glanced at Tom. 'What do you think?'

'I think Billy's right.' Tom nodded towards their DS. 'That sounds more plausible, doesn't it? I mean, where would David get a real bullet from?'

'Has he got any connections to anyone in the armed forces?' Andrea chimed in. 'Or hunting and shooting perhaps.'

'Good suggestion.' Hazel pointed a finger towards her but could see Billy screwing up his face at that idea.

'Nah. I don't think so. I could show you how to tell if it was real but I cannae imagine you want me to bite it, do you?' he smiled.

'No thank you,' Hazel chirped and moved the evidence bag further away from him. 'We'll let forensics identify its authenticity thanks very much.'

'What are they?' Andrea asked, indicating the other evidence bag.

Hazel handed it to her so that she could read what was written on the top sheet of paper. 'Tell me what you make of that.'

'Wow,' Andrea said on reading the letter. 'He didn't hold back, did he?'

'Mm, but do you reckon he made good on those threats?' Hazel asked.

'He might have been all bark and no bite,' Billy suggested.

'We won't know until we find him, I suppose,' Hazel suggested. 'Andrea, could you stay behind and carry on helping uniforms with the door-to-door? I want more than just this street spoken to. That car passed through the whole area to get here. Hopefully, someone will be able to recognise the driver or at the very least give us a description. Speeding away from a crime scene is bound to attract attention.'

'Sure, boss,' Andrea agreed and handed the evidence back before she walked away.

'Billy, could you please get back and make a start on Maggie's phone? Dissect it, see if there's something on there that we don't know already. Find out the full details about the action that was taken on those threats as well.'

'Aye, sure,' Billy replied. 'I'll see you back at the station.'

'Aye, I'll see you in a bit.' Hazel patted his arm and watched him leave the bungalow.

She saw that Billy had stopped briefly to talk to one of the young female uniforms and shook her head gently. The way the pretty, blonde girl looked at him made it clear she was flirting. Hazel wasn't surprised. Billy was a good-looking man but she was glad to see that he didn't linger long. Hazel really liked his girlfriend, Natasha, despite the problems they'd had in their relationship.

'What do we know about the Wilsons?' Hazel turned to face Tom knowing he'd done some digging on Maggie's conviction and the family whose lives she'd devastated before Hazel had even arrived at the scene earlier. It was just as well he did, given the way Hazel had felt when she'd been wakened. She'd be lost without her DI if she were honest.

'Not much. Mum Carol had been raising the boys on her own after losing her husband to cancer five years ago,' Tom told her and started to flick through the pages of his notebook.

Hazel's heart broke for the woman on hearing that. 'God,' she sighed. 'That's awful.'

'Aye and then losing Liam has completely shattered them.'

'What about David, what does he do?'

'He's at Perth college,' Tom replied, on scrolling further through the notes in his book. 'Studying art.'

'Mm, I think we need to find out where David was a couple of hours ago,' Hazel said firmly. 'Come on, let's leave forensics to go over the rest of this place and go and find out, shall we?'

Chapter Six

Andrea Graham checked the time on her phone. The rumbling in her stomach had already alerted her to the fact it was lunchtime. She wondered how much longer this door knocking was going to take. It was all right for Billy; he was probably about to stuff his face in the station canteen before moving ahead on forensic examination of Maggie's phone. Andrea had noticed the easy way he'd chatted with that uniformed officer. Part of her wished she was as good with people as Billy was. Sure she could talk to anyone in the line of work but informally, that was different. If she was a bit more like him, then perhaps she wouldn't be single. At twenty-nine, she had hoped she'd have been a bit more settled by now. Sure, she was in no rush to have a baby but someone to come home to would be nice. Andrea had always been better with books and animals than with people which was probably why she'd joined the direct entry programme into the force rather than spending years on the beat. Andrea had wanted to be a detective since she'd watched old episodes of *The Bill* with her mum.

'Hello there.' She smiled at the little girl who answered the front door of number nine, a bungalow that was situated at the farthest end of the Ramsays' street. 'Is your mummy or daddy in?'

The little blonde girl shook her head. 'No, Mummy and Daddy are both working.'

Andrea crouched down to her level but before she could ask her anything else, the front door opened wider to reveal an almost completely bald, elderly man leaning heavily on a stick.

'Who is it—oh hello, can I help you?' he said and put his hand on the little girl's shoulder. 'Go back inside. Help your brother get some juice, will you, there's a good girl.'

Andrea smiled at the child as she turned and ran back along the hallway. The sound of a baby crying came and went when the kitchen door opened and closed behind her.

'Looks like you've got your hands full,' Andrea suggested.

'Yes, my daughter decided to go back to work full-time, so Grandpa has been left holding the baby, quite literally,' he chuckled.

Andrea held up her ID and saw the old man's eyes scan the details on it. 'I was wondering if you could spare me a few minutes. We're investigating an incident that occurred earlier this morning.'

The man frowned. 'I saw the police cars speeding past, but I didn't think too much of it. Please come in, come in.'

'Thank you.' Andrea wiped her feet and again enjoyed the contrast in temperatures between outside and inside this bungalow, just like in Deirdre McNeil's. She walked along the hallway where her presence seemed to attract the attention of the little girl again.

'You go and look after your brother,' the old man told her. 'I'm just going to help this lady for a minute.' He looked at Andrea. 'Please go through.' He pointed to the white door to her right.

Andrea walked into a clean but untidy room that was littered with newspapers, one lying open and draped over the arm of a chair, with colouring books, tubs of Lego and jigsaws covering the carpet.

'Excuse the mess.' The man smiled and lifted one of the newspapers from the red armchair closest to the door. 'The kids make a bit of a mess, I'm afraid.'

'Don't worry,' Andrea smiled.

'Please take a seat.'

'Thanks.' Andrea sat on the cream leather sofa that sat in front of a huge cherry-wood dresser. Judging from the photos that covered the shelves, she figured this man must have lots of grandchildren. 'Is it just yourself that lives here or...'

'Yes, it is now. My wife passed away last year.'

'Oh I am sorry.'

'Thank you.'

Tears looked close to falling from his eyes and Andrea felt guilty.

'Can I take a note of your name?' Andrea pushed on.

'Yes of course. I'm Jacob Sheldon.'

Andrea wrote his name in her notebook. 'OK Mr Sheldon, could you tell me if you heard or saw anything unusual around ten o'clock this morning?'

'Erm,' he frowned. 'Now you mention it, I did hear what I thought was one of those boy racers tearing up the street. You know the kind I mean. Tyres screeching.'

Andrea nodded. 'And this was around ten, you say. Did you happen to see the car at all?' She noted that detail down, thinking to herself that was probably an accurate description of a car fleeing a crime scene.

Jacob nodded. 'Just the back of it. It was green but I couldn't tell you what make or model, I'm afraid.'

'Did you recognise the driver?'

'I'm sorry, I didn't get a good look at them,' Jacob said. 'What's this about? What's happened? It must be something serious if detectives are asking questions.'

Before Andrea could answer, the living room door opened, and the little girl walked in. She smiled at Andrea, then lifted a colouring book from the table before Jacob helped her take a tub of crayons.

'Good girl,' he said gently as she headed back towards the kitchen.

'She's a sweet little thing,' Andrea mentioned.

'Aye, she is that.' Jacob's face lit up and he chuckled a little when he spoke. 'Hard work, though. Her and her brother.'

'I bet,' Andrea said.

'So what's happened, then?' Jacob repeated.

'A woman was knocked down and killed this morning.'

Jacob gasped. He clasped a hand to his mouth. 'That's terrible. Oh how sad. Did it happen in this street?'

Andrea nodded. 'I'm afraid so, yes.'

'Who was it?' he asked, the anxiety in his voice palpable.

'Her name is Maggie Ramsay.'

'Maggie!'

'Did you know her?' This piqued Andrea's attention. His reaction suggested they were close.

'Yes, yes, I know Maggie very well. She and my wife were very good friends.'

This was good, Andrea thought. Very good. Before she could continue, Jacob started to throw a barrage of questions in her direction.

'What happened? You said she was hit by a car, is that right? How, I mean...' he rambled. He took a navy cotton handkerchief from his trouser pocket and rubbed his eyes. 'I'm sorry, this is just such a shock.' His eyes widened. 'Samuel! Is Samuel all right?'

'He's OK.' Andrea didn't think it was a good idea to tell him about Samuel's heart scare.

'I must call him,' Jacob reached for his phone handset that was behind him on a telephone table, the wood matching that of the unit.

'Erm, he's a bit busy just now,' Andrea said quickly. 'Maybe later.'

'What? Yes, of course,' Jacob sighed and rested the phone in its holder again. 'Of course, of course.'

'It sounds like you were close to Maggie,' Andrea pointed out.

Jacob sat back in the chair and took a long, slow breath. 'It was my Sadie that was friendly with her.' He sighed. 'I occasionally went for a pint at the club with Sam but...' He stopped.

43

Andrea frowned. 'But…' she repeated, wondering if he was holding something back.

'Och, Sam's nice enough,' he shrugged. 'He's just not exactly the chatty type.'

'What do you mean?'

'He always seemed so serious,' Jacob told her. 'Maggie was so different. She was always so bubbly and laughing. Mind you,' he shrugged. 'After the accident she changed, of course.'

'I can imagine.'

'They argued, too.'

'Did you witness them arguing?' Andrea pushed.

Jacob nodded. 'Samuel was…' He stopped to find the right word.

'Do you think he was abusive to her?'

'No, no, that's not what I mean,' he tutted. 'I can't quite put my finger on it. He didn't seem to like that she was so friendly. I think he was jealous, that's all.'

'Did your wife ever tell you anything that she'd witnessed?'

'Not really. I think Maggie enjoyed the relief she found when she went out with Sadie.' He smiled. 'Those two often went out to the theatre and, oh yes, the Edinburgh Festival!' His eyes lit up. 'They always went there on the train at least three times every August.' Then those eyes saddened quickly. 'Aye, well, neither of them will get there this summer now, will they?' His voice broke under the strain.

'I'm sorry if I've upset you,' Andrea said gently.

A warm smile grew slowly on Jacob's face. 'It's not your fault, dear. It's actually nice to talk about Sadie.' Then his eyes stretched wide as if a memory had suddenly returned. 'That man!' He held his hand up. 'I saw Maggie getting out of a car. An Audi, I think. A red Audi, yes, that's it and when she realised I'd seen her, her face went beetroot-red.'

'Oh, is that right. When was this?' Andrea made a note of that. 'Did you get a look at the driver?'

'Aye, I did. It was erm, let me see, it was…' He wiped his nose with the handkerchief. 'Two weeks ago. Yes, it was a

44

couple of weeks ago and I made sure to have a good look given the beamer she had. Her face was beetroot when she'd seen that I'd clocked them.' He tutted and took a small breath. 'The driver was younger than Maggie and they looked suspicious to me. I mean don't get me wrong it wasn't my business or anything.'

'In what way? What does 'suspicious' mean exactly?'

'Well, he was dropping her off two blocks away from her house.' He pursed his lips tightly. 'Now, why would she ask him to do that? Why didn't she want him to drop her outside her front door?'

Chapter Seven

David Wilson jogged across the cobbled road which was covered in a carpet of snowy slush after the gritters had been round, lifting his hand up to apologise to the driver of the white van he'd stepped out in front of without noticing. When he reached the door he stamped his trainers on the step to shake off the loose snow he'd picked up. He did feel guilty for leaving his mum again but sometimes he had to think of himself. She would soon be in a drunken stupor again anyway after he'd given her the vodka bottle she'd sent him out for.

David was getting used to this new Saturday routine and he liked it. If he couldn't have the brunch that he'd loved, this was a good replacement. The sound of the bell on St John's Kirk chimed behind him as David opened the door to Willow's coffee shop. He waved to Suzanne when he saw her sitting waiting for him inside. Their place. At their table. The one in the corner by the window which they always seemed to be able to get, no matter what time they went in. Luck, he thought. Fate, Suzanne always suggested. He blew hot air into his cold hands then unzipped his jacket as he walked, the warm air in the café hitting him a stark contrast to the bitter chill outside. He nodded a brief greeting to the young waitress he recognised, a girl he remembered from school but whose name he couldn't recall. He was sure she'd been in the year above him.

Suzanne smiled at him as he came towards her, kissing her cheek gently before sitting opposite her.

'Hey,' he said softly.

'I've ordered you an Americano,' Suzanne said and shuffled a little uncomfortably in the seat. 'Bloody leg,' she muttered and seemed to be manually moving it into position.

'Is it bad today?' David asked, a look of concern on his face.

'The numbness is being a right prick today – well, no, not numbness exactly, more a combination of irritating pins and needles and numbness.' She sighed briefly then corrected herself before smiling. Suzanne didn't want the focus to always be on her symptoms. The sudden onset had taken her doctors by surprise, but the truth was, she'd been hiding the symptoms for a long time. Until she couldn't any longer, that was.

She reached across the table to take hold of his outstretched hand. 'Never mind that. How are you?' Then she rubbed his hand in hers. 'Gosh, your hands are freezing.'

'Aye, I left my gloves on the kitchen table.' He shrugged, then smiled at the waitress who laid their coffees in front of them. 'I'm all right,' he replied to Suzanne's question. 'It's good to see you. I missed you.'

'You only saw me last night,' Suzanne teased but didn't admit how much she loved it when he said that.

Suzanne's smile became hidden beneath her hair that had fallen when she dipped her head on hearing his compliment. He always made her feel like she was a shy teenager again.

David coming into her life six months ago had been like a bolt from the blue, parachuting in just when she needed someone. Just when he had reached rock bottom too, it transpired. The circumstances of their meeting could have been better but the way he made her feel, especially after the MS diagnosis, was wonderful. Sure people frowned at their age difference but, like David said, she still looked like she was in her early twenties. Not mid-thirties. The one thing she appreciated about her genes. But something about him made Suzanne feel comfortable. He'd never put any kind of pressure on her to do anything that other couples might take for granted. He just seemed to want to be with her. Even their silence was comfortable.

'How's your mum?' Suzanne asked.

David shook his head gently and avoided her eyes moment-arily. 'Same as ever.'

Suzanne squeezed his arm in her fingers. 'I'm sorry,' she whispered.

'You look nice,' David complimented her, clearly trying to steer the topic of conversation in another direction. 'That colour really suits you,' he said, pointing out the pale blue T-shirt she was wearing. He narrowed his eyes as he glanced at her neck. 'Is that new?' He reached over and touched the silver locket he'd not seen before.

'What?' she replied. 'Erm, no.' She reached her own hand down and brushed her fingers over the chain, then tucked it out of sight. 'Are you sure you've never seen it?' she smiled.

'Maybe I have.' David shrugged and sat back in his chair, lifting his cup to take a sip of coffee. 'It looks good on you.' He kept his eyes on her the whole time.

Suzanne looked up, catching his huge green eyes and couldn't stop the smile that grew on her lips. Not that she'd want to. Being around David had that effect on her.

'Thank you.' She felt herself blush at his compliment and knew that a good-looking lad like David could be with almost any woman he wanted but he'd chosen her. Why he'd done that she couldn't fathom but she was grateful that he had. More than he realised.

'What do you fancy doing this afternoon?' David took a sip then licked traces of coffee from his lips. 'We could go to the cinema if you like. I think the new Marvel one is out.'

Suzanne appreciated that he knew how much she loved those movies but screwed up her face then had to stifle the yawn. 'I'm a bit tired, to be honest. I'm not sure I could face it.'

'We could just go back to yours, if you like, then.'

'That sounds perfect,' Suzanne agreed. 'I'll cook.'

'Or we could get a takeaway,' he grinned.

'Hey, my cooking isn't that bad,' Suzanne laughed just as the ringtone from her phone burst into life. On seeing the caller ID she picked it up. 'I'm sorry, just give me two ticks. Hello.'

Suzanne listened to the caller carefully as David mouthed 'Is everything OK?' across the table at her. She rolled her eyes at him and nodded gently. The way he smiled back at her made her stomach flip. This gorgeous young man saw her, the real her. Not the woman whose life was slowly disappearing after being diagnosed with a degenerative disease.

'Listen, I'm going to have to call you back,' Suzanne said into the phone. 'I'm busy just now but I'll come over later, I promise.' She stopped to listen, squeezing her eyes tightly shut as she took a slow, deliberate breath. 'Yes, I said I promise, didn't I?' She paused. 'OK, I have to go. I'll see you later and stop worrying. Everything is going to be fine. I promise.'

'Who was that?' David asked once she'd hung up.

'Och, it was just my wee cousin.' Her eyes flicked sideways to where a small boy sat nibbling a piece of sandwich at the table next to them. 'She was panicking as usual over nothing. She has anxiety problems, bless her. Remember? I think I told you.'

'Aye, I think you've mentioned it before, yeah.' He sipped from his cup then wiped his top lip with his fingers. 'It's nice she's got you, though,' David pointed out.

'I suppose,' she said. 'But she doesn't half go on.' She smirked and shook her head.

'It must be nice though, to have someone in your family that can…' David's expression darkened, and he looked away.

Suzanne hated it when he did this. He seemed to disappear inside himself, into his grief. A grief that she would do anything to make better.

'But you have got someone, David.' She spoke softly and laid her hand over his. 'You've got me.'

David looked back at her. 'Do you promise?'

'I promise,' she whispered.

Chapter Eight

After persuading Tom that they should grab a burger from the drive-through on the way to talk to David Wilson, Hazel pulled up in the parking space closest to the Wilson home. She'd been starving and was grateful that the queue at McDonald's was pretty much clear of both snow and cars. The only obstacle had been hungry gulls who appeared to have a death wish, stubbornly parking themselves on the road while they picked at the crumbs and rubbish. She had avoided eating anything earlier when her stomach had been churning but now she was famished. The drinking had to stop. It wouldn't end well if she didn't; she knew that more than most.

The two detectives knocked on the front door and waited, listening for movement inside the Wilsons' council-owned end-of-terrace home in the neighbourhood Hazel knew very well. Flakes of white paint stuck to Hazel's knuckles while others floated down onto the front step. She wiped her hand on her trouser leg then pressed her finger on the doorbell, holding it there for several seconds, lifting and pressing repeatedly. Surely nobody could ignore that din.

Hazel leaned her head closer to the glass pane in the front door. She looked at Tom.

'There's nobody in. What do you want to do?' Tom asked.

When they still got no response, Hazel held her finger on the doorbell and let it scream out through the property. If someone was inside, there was no way they'd tolerate that noise for long. Tom moved to the living room window and peered in through the dusty film covering it. He pursed his lips and shook his head as he rubbed his hands together to shed the dust.

'Nothing.' He glanced back in Hazel's direction then knocked on the glass and waited for a response. When he got nothing, he started to walk towards the gate. 'I'll check round the back.'

Tom tried the handle, shaking it several times, but it seemed jammed rather than locked. He'd climbed over the six foot gate with ease before Hazel could say anything. The fact that there was a gaping hole halfway up the ramshackle structure meant his foot could easily use it as a foothold to spring from. From the state of the fence and the front door, it seemed the whole property was in need of maintenance.

Hazel rung the bell again then heard Tom talking to a woman, their voices coming from the back of the house.

'Tom!' Footsteps came towards where she was standing, attempting to also get in the gate.

Tom eventually, after several attempts to shift the warped wood, yanked the gate wide open for her to join him in the garden. 'The next door neighbour says she's not seen either of them for a couple of days.'

Hazel held her ID up so the neighbour could see it as she approached.

'Hello, Detective, what's happened?' the elderly woman asked, while a small long-haired black cat curled its body round her legs, leaving fine black hairs on her beige tights.

'You've told my colleague that you haven't seen either of the Wilsons for a couple of days?'

'Yes, that's right,' the woman agreed. 'Mind you, Carol could be passed out and he…' she tutted. 'Well, let's just say David keeps strange hours these days. Comes and goes at all hours of the day and night, he does.' She folded her arms and puckered her lips disapprovingly.

'Is that right?' Hazel asked.

'Yes, but, mind you,' her attitude softened, 'he's got a lot on his plate after… you know what happened, don't you, about

51

losing little Liam the way they did, I mean?' Her voice lowered so much she was barely audible.

'We do,' Hazel confirmed.

'I've told him that if he needs anything, anything at all, I'm more than happy to help,' the neighbour continued. 'It can't be easy taking care of his mum when she's like that.'

'When she's like what exactly?' Hazel asked.

The elderly neighbour shook her head and tutted. 'You know, the drink.'

'Has he ever asked you for help?' Tom chimed in.

The old woman shook her head with her lips pursed so tightly it looked like she was sucking a boiled sweet.

'No, and he seems to do everything for her these days. I mean, I've not seen Carol go any further than the back garden for months.' She tutted and shook her head again. 'It was terrible what happened to wee Liam.' She looked away and dabbed the outside edge of one of her eyes before composing herself. 'He was such a little sweetheart.' Her voice dipped with emotion.

'So he's his mum's carer, is he?' Hazel hadn't realised that. She glanced at Tom who was shrugging back at her. *Interesting – another consequence of the accident impacting on David personally.*

'Not exactly. Just since the drink got hold of her, you know. He does the shopping and the washing. I think he even cooks and cleans the place for her.' She tutted again and shook her head. 'Damn shame he should be doing that. The boy should be out making his way in the world, not taking care of his heartbroken mum. I mean, hasn't he got his own grief to think of too?' She kept talking until Hazel made to turn away.

'Thank you, you've been incredibly helpful,' she said.

'You'll know where to find me if you need anything else,' the old, grey-haired woman called out then turned to walk back inside her own back door with the black cat running ahead of her.

'What do you want to do?' Tom asked.

'We'll come back. Carol might be in there, but it sounds like, if she is, she'll be in no fit state to be interviewed. It's David we want, anyway.' Hazel remembered vividly her own mother's drunken stupors as another light flutter of snow started to come down. 'But what do you make of that? David has got more than enough motive to want Maggie Ramsay dead.'

'Aye, she's ruined their lives,' Tom pointed out. 'Not only that; she seemed to have been getting on with hers like nothing happened. That's bound to make them angry.'

'Angry enough to kill her?' Hazel suggested.

Chapter Nine

Hazel had told her team to head home. They'd trawled through as much CCTV as they could get hold of and found nothing. It seemed that there were no cameras pointing in exactly the direction they needed. Hazel had updated Daly in a brief catch up that they'd managed to have in his office before he'd been called away to a meeting after a phone call that had left him flustered. She had opened her mouth to ask if everything was OK, but she'd been ushered out of the office before she'd had the chance. Hazel had also tried to get hold of the Ramsays' daughter, Louise, in Toronto but hadn't been successful. Unwilling to leave a message, she decided to try again later although Daly had said he'd do it. Hazel feared he'd not remember given the fluster he'd hurried away in. They'd move forward with the investigation first thing tomorrow morning. For tonight she'd arranged for the night shift to keep a close eye out for David Wilson.

She logged into the police database to find out more about Maggie Ramsay's conviction for killing Liam Wilson. It seemed she'd had one of the best solicitors defending her against the charges. Causing death by dangerous driving. 'Dangerous driving' didn't seem accurate. It was far worse than that, in Hazel's opinion. Clearly, it paid to have the means to pay for a good solicitor.

Wilson had been spoken to already several weeks ago about the letters. He'd been issued with a warning by a couple of uniforms that had been sent to tell him to stop harassing the couple informing him that further, more serious action, would be taken if he didn't stop.

As for the whereabouts of his mother Carol, the elderly neighbour, that she and Tom had spoken to earlier, had been more than happy to update the uniforms Hazel had sent who'd visited later. She told them that she'd seen Carol on one of her rare trips to the wheelie bin that was kept by the back gate. She had apparently been staggering but managing to stay upright so Hazel decided she'd drop by and see if Carol would be fit to talk to her now. Her phone read just after eight. Given Hazel's experience with her own mother, she wasn't optimistic that she'd get much out of her but wanted to try regardless. She was going home to an empty flat anyway. A flat with housework well overdue that she'd like to avoid for a little longer.

At the Wilsons' home, Hazel pushed the doorbell and held it down, allowing the noise to reverberate around the property. She lifted her finger and leaned in to listen. This time she could hear the sound of music coming from inside. One of Heart's most famous songs, if she wasn't mistaken although she couldn't recall the name of it. Hazel bent down and lifted the letterbox to peek inside.

'Mrs Wilson,' Hazel shouted. 'Carol, could you come to the door.' She dropped the letterbox and straightened back up, wincing from the stiffness in her back. When no footsteps appeared to be coming towards the door, Hazel rapped the letterbox, hard, several times then leaned down and shouted again.

'Carol!' This time she got a response. The music was switched off and Hazel could see Carol staggering towards the front door.

Hazel held her ID up as the front door swept open, Carol's hand slipping drunkenly from the handle before she tried to right herself. The stale smell immediately hit her. Stale vodka was a smell she recognised right away. Her own mum's tipple of choice.

'Who're you?' Carol slurred and swayed as she screwed up her eyes to focus on Hazel.

'Can I come in, Carol? There are a few things I think you could help me with.' Straight to the point. Hazel knew from experience that was the only way.

Carol glanced slowly between the ID card and Hazel's face several times, narrowing, and widening bloodshot slits before stepping back, almost losing her balance as the front door squealed open.

Hazel closed her eyes tight against the sound of the front door banging shut as it slipped out of Carol's grip. She watched the obviously inebriated woman fall briefly against the wall then steady herself.

'What things...?' Carol slurred and followed Hazel into the living room.

Hazel could see that the room was tidy to a degree. David had done his best, it seemed, but thick layers of dust caught the back of Hazel's throat and she had to cough, wiping her nose that had started to run. She watched Carol fall onto the sofa and struggle with a thin blanket that she'd stumbled on top of.

Hazel lifted a pile of laundry from the brown patterned armchair in the opposite corner of the small, almost exactly square living room that had a long window stretching the entire length of the front wall, a grimy layer of dirt on the outside. The dust on the surface of the fireplace in front of the chair made it look almost grey where it should be a dark, cherry-wood colour. Photo frames covered the mantelpiece, filled with the smiling face of a little boy. Liam. An unexpected lump caught in Hazel's throat. She had to look away. The sound of laughter distracted her. Looking up, under the streetlight right outside the house, she could see a group of teenage girls walking past, all crowding around a phone, giggling at whatever was on the screen. She saw a brief flicker of interest in the commotion in Carol's face before her eyes fell away to the floor again.

Carol sighed and lifted the glass from the sticky coffee table and sank the contents.

'What did you say your name was again?' she asked without looking at Hazel.

'My name is DCI Hazel Todd and...'

Carol's eyes stretched on hearing that. 'What else do you lot want fae us?' she snapped. 'Fat lot of gid you were when...' She gulped from the glass and immediately refilled it, holding back the rest of her comment.

Hazel knew she would have to handle this carefully. She also knew exactly what Carol meant with her barbed comment. Hazel could have cried for her, but she was there to do a job.

'I was wondering if you could tell me where David was this morning and where he is now actually.'

Carol frowned. 'What?'

'Where's David?' Hazel persevered.

'Why do you want tae speak to David?' This time Carol's full attention was fixed on Hazel. Her mood had darkened. She gulped down the contents of the glass and refilled it again. The more she sank, the more brittle her mood became.

Hazel was undeterred. 'Have you got any idea when he'll be home?'

'What business is it of yours where ma boy is?' Carol snapped and made to stand before toppling backwards.

Hazel could see where this conversation was going. In the direction that many of her own mother's had when she was growing up. She knew what an ugly-drunk woman was capable of, so she stood and headed for the door.

Hazel's heart raced as she closed the front door to the sound of Carol crying. It had been a long time since that had happened, but she'd seen so much of her own mum in Carol it had scared her. The realisation that she might be doing the same thing hit her and it didn't feel good. Not good at all.

Chapter Ten

Hazel was too unsettled after that unnerving visit with Carol Wilson to go straight home to her flat. She would have loved to go to the house she still considered home – the house that was, as it happened, only a five-minute walk from the Wilson home and have a hot chocolate with her dad, but those days were over. Her wonderful dad's dementia meant that he had moved from the home she'd grown up in and into a care home after his needs became too much for Hazel to handle alone.

Long gone, too, were the days of landing on Cara's doorstep to talk through what was bothering her. The weird thing was that, even though Cara had betrayed her, there were still parts of the friendship that Hazel missed. But running off with someone's husband tends to put distance between even the closest of friends. Following her ex-husband's sudden death, the two women had been civil to each other. That was all Hazel was prepared to commit to although she knew Cara wanted them to go back to the way things had been.

The thought that she might end up getting a cat for company horrified Hazel but she could see how it might happen. Heaven forbid she might not stop at one.

Hazel popped into the hospital on her way home instead, in hopes that another chat with Samuel Ramsay could help. She was to be disappointed.

'I'm sorry, detective, but Mr Ramsay isn't fit to be spoken to yet. His heart is too weak for the kind of pressure your conversation might cause.'

The flustered, skinny doctor's words were short and to the point before his pager sounded in his pocket and he rushed away, so Hazel had little choice but to call it a night after all. Her efforts of persuasion had fallen on deaf ears. There was a time she'd have been able to sweet talk that young man into getting her way but not tonight, it seemed.

She yawned and stared in through the glass panel of the side room door at the man, his face covered by an oxygen mask with loud beeps coming from a variety of equipment around his bed. She was sure he could tell her something useful, if only she was allowed to talk to him.

'It's getting late.' A young nurse startled Hazel when she came up behind her. 'I think it would be better if you came back tomorrow morning.'

'Yes, of course.' Hazel smiled briefly then yawned again and took a final look at Samuel Ramsay. 'Thank you, goodnight,' she said to the group of nurses gathered round a desk as she made her way out of the ward.

Hazel was exhausted and although she knew she shouldn't, she bought a bottle of white wine from the garage when she'd filled her Fiesta with fuel. Her chronic insomnia meant she needed a little help to get to sleep. She resolved to use this bottle to prove to herself that she could just have one glass – which would be the one she needed to help her get to sleep – and hopefully this regime would get her sleep pattern back to something resembling normal. She'd cut that whole glass to half a glass in a few days. That sounded like a reasonable plan. Didn't it?

She opened the fridge to put away the few bits of shopping she'd bought and found a lasagne ready meal that had yesterday's date on it. She was sure one day wouldn't matter and sniffed the contents of the thin cardboard container. Yes, hell, it was fine. Hazel had eaten worse. She switched on the oven and poured a glass of wine. She saw that the answering machine's orange light was flashing boldly and hit the play button while she tried to sip without guzzling. The mechanical voice burst into life.

Message one

Hello this is a message from your internet provider.

Hazel rolled her eyes and sipped again before pressing the button.

Message deleted. Message two.

Hi Hazel, it's me. I've had a letter from Rick's solicitor. He wants to talk to both of us. Can we meet so I can talk to you about it? Call me.

What the hell could that be about? Why did the solicitor want to talk to them after all this time? Her ex-husband Rick had been dead for a year. There couldn't be anything left to sort out now, surely. Unless it was tax. That had to be it. Rick must owe the government tax. Her mobile rang before she had a chance to ponder over it more.

'Cara, I thought it might be you,' she answered. 'What's this about a solicitor?'

The red light on the cooker blinked off and Hazel put the call on speakerphone so she could have her hands free to open the oven door where the smell of burnt cheese hit her. She put the food in the oven and quickly opened the kitchen window to dissolve the smoke that had wafted out. Hazel was so hungry that even this out-of-date ready meal looked and smelled delicious.

'I spoke to the solicitor on the phone last night.' Cara's voice sounded tinny through the speakers of Hazel's iPhone 6. She really should upgrade. Hadn't she been inundated with online offers recently? 'He wants to meet to discuss Rick's share of the inheritance.' There was a silence before Cara added: 'You had heard that his mum just died, hadn't you?'

No Hazel had not heard that bit of news. But why would she? She wasn't married to him when he died but neither was Cara. She'd always found Rick's mum to be a cold woman and hadn't been surprised when she'd not kept in touch despite the decades they'd been together. That was what the solicitor needed to speak to them about. It had clearly stated in Rick's will that his entire estate was to be split equally between the two women. The new inheritance would be likewise.

'No, I didn't know that,' Hazel replied. 'When did this happen?' She asked because despite not liking the woman all that much, she felt she should attend the funeral.

'Over three months ago, Hazel. His brother didn't bother to tell us.'

That didn't surprise Hazel. Perhaps he had hoped the entire estate would fall to him. But by the tone of her voice it had clearly upset Cara.

'When is the appointment? I'll try and make it if I can,' Hazel told her. 'But I can't promise anything.'

'I know you can't, the solicitor is away at a conference but wants to arrange something when he gets back,' Cara acknowledged. 'I realise you're busy with work.' Then she paused before asking, 'So how have you been?'

There it was. The start of the small talk. Hazel yawned. She was too tired for this.

'Fine, yes, I'm good,' Hazel replied. 'And you?'

'How's your dad?' Cara continued, her voice breaking a little as the signal flickered.

'Dad's OK, thanks. Listen I have to go, there's another call waiting,' Hazel lied.

She clicked the 'end call' button before Cara had a chance to protest, although knowing Hazel as well as Cara did after all these years, she must have known that had been a lie. Hazel's stomach was rumbling too loudly for her to give a shit. She took a sip from her glass, but the chilled wine was just too moreish. She sank half the contents and filled her glass to the top. A little more wouldn't hurt. It had been a stressful day, after all. She'd start cutting down tomorrow.

The figure across the road in the car park snapped another photo of Hazel standing next to the kitchen window. They were annoyed that she'd got home before they'd got there. Five minutes, that's all it would take. At least to sow the seeds in her mind. Surely she'd want to control the narrative and this would have been the perfect opportunity to get to her before anyone else. She was about to become very busy, too, with a murder case to tackle. A brutal one, it seemed, if early reports on the local newspaper's social media accounts were anything to go by. They'd been quick off the mark. The woman had only been dead for twelve hours.

If Hazel would take the time to listen, she would surely see this was an offer she couldn't refuse.

Chapter Eleven

Sunday

Detective Constable Andrea Graham slunk in hoping not to be noticed, tidying her auburn ponytail as she sneaked towards the team meeting, beads of moisture glistening off her forehead. She glared at the smirk on Billy Flynn's face as he stood in the small office kitchen doorway with a mug in each hand.

'Nice of you to join us, DC Graham,' Hazel said, her thin smile an attempt to put her at ease.

'Sorry, boss,' DC Graham replied, flicking her hand in Hazel's direction gently. 'Traffic was bad. Those roadworks on the Crieff road are a nightmare to get through. If you miss the green light then you're waiting ages until it changes again.'

'On a Sunday?' Tom asked.

'Every bloody day.' Andrea announced, peeling off her duffle coat and slinging her scarf across the back of the chair. Still flustered, she pulled the green scrunchie back out of her hair and re-did it, again. 'I hope this new road is worth all this hassle.'

'Right, guys, sorry about the early hour on a Sunday but...' Hazel flashed Billy a warm smile as he laid her mug on the desk. 'Did the phone guys manage to get anything for us on the call that Samuel Ramsay received?'

Hazel looked in Tom's direction before stealing a brief glance back at the smiling face of Maggie Ramsay pinned to the board behind her, then allowing her eyes to drift onto a picture of her broken body laid out on her driveway.

'Nothing,' Tom replied. 'The call was too short and from an unknown number, probably a disposable pay-as-you-go phone.

I've asked for a deeper forensic exam, but they weren't optimistic when I asked them.'

Hazel was disappointed to hear that.

'Billy, what about Maggie's mobile phone?' Hazel pressed on, quizzing her 'digital detective', as she called him. An invaluable member of her team. 'Actually, hang on,' she raised a finger in the air. 'Did any of you manage to get hold of witness statements from passers-by? There were people in the street weren't there? Tell me there were.'

'Uniform spoke to a couple of women who had been on the bus with Maggie, but once they got off they'd walked away in the opposite direction. They heard a car screeching away. That's all,' Billy told her.

Another dead end. 'What about the driver of the bus? Has anyone spoken to Stagecoach yet?'

She was disappointed to see them shaking their heads and looked at each of them.

'Billy, you chase that up, will you?'

'Aye, nae worries.'

'He must have passed the car that hit her,' Hazel suggested. 'So Billy, what about Maggie's phone, what have you got for me?'

'I'm afraid it was too damaged for me to get anything. The tech boys will have better luck I think.'

'Where are we on the stolen car?' Hazel looked at her team, hoping one of them would say something that would drive this case closer to its conclusion. 'ANPR got a hit, boss,' Tom said. 'It was clocked half an hour away. It's only now been reported stolen from an address in Letham. The owner says it was probably taken some time on Friday night.'

'But it's Sunday. They waited two days to report it,' Tom suggested. 'That's a bit strange.'

'It seems so but the owner was working a weekend on call – a sleepover shift in the kids supported accommodation in Auchterarder. She car-shares with a colleague and didn't notice until this morning that the car was gone.'

'Ah, I see.'

'The cameras did snap a picture of the driver, though.'

Hazel loved the sound of that but wondered why Tom didn't look as happy. 'Really, that's brilliant.'

'It's not a very clear image I'm afraid.' Tom scrolled through his phone and showed the picture to her.

Hazel had to narrow her eyes to see the fuzzy photo but the only thing she could tell for sure was that the driver was wearing a baseball cap, the peak pulled low over the top of their head, obscuring their face. 'Is that a man or a woman driving the vehicle?'

'I don't know but I've sent it down to the forensic tech guys. They'll hopefully be able to scrub it up a bit.'

Tom tucked his phone away.

'Right. I did manage to speak to Carol Wilson last night. Well, when I say I spoke to her...' Hazel continued, informing them of the futile attempt she'd made. 'Let's just say I didn't get anywhere. When I asked where David was she got defensive and aggressive, so I beat a retreat. I know not to bite off more than I can chew. We'll get back over there this morning.'

She chose not to add the way the brief meeting had left her feeling. The waves of emotion stirred up by the memories it had triggered. She was grateful that Tom moved the topic away from Carol Wilson.

'Are we talking to Ramsay again this morning, boss?' Tom asked while he fiddled with his watch strap.

'Aye, that's the plan.' She frowned and nodded at his wrist. 'Is that a new watch?'

'Aye, John got me it.'

'John is a very generous man,' Hazel pointed out, recognising the watch as a Rolex and knowing Tom's partner was the son of a wealthy, well-known Perth garage owner.

Tom rolled his eyes. 'Yes, well, I wish he'd asked me first.' He held his arm out closer to her. 'It's huge, look at it!'

'It looks heavy,' Hazel commented.

'He said he didn't think we could do the whole engagement ring thing, so we agreed to buy each other something else instead.'

'What did you get him?' Billy asked.

'I got him a tie from—'

'A tie!' Andrea chirped. 'He got you a Rolex and you got him a *tie*?'

'If you'll let me finish,' Tom interrupted. 'I got him a tie from Turnbull & Asser.'

'It's the thought that counts,' DC Graham piped up, shooting a smile towards Hazel.

Hazel could see Tom open his mouth to speak and wanted to cut him off.

'I think it was a lovely thing to do for your engagement,' Hazel remarked, genuinely pleased that Tom had found happiness. 'He's a good man.'

'Tell that to the angry, itchy red skin I've got, then.' He pulled the watch face back to reveal an angry-looking patch of red skin.

'You must have an allergy to the nickel,' Andrea told him. 'It's quite common.'

'Shit, is that what it is?' Tom unfastened the watch and put it away in his drawer. 'There we go then, problem solved.'

'You're going to have to tell him,' Andrea said.

'I know,' Tom sighed. 'But—'

'When you two are finished swapping jewellery tips…' Hazel interrupted.

'Sorry, boss,' Tom said as he rubbed his wrist. 'How is Ramsay, anyway?'

Memories of their victim's husband lying motionless on his living room floor came flooding back to Hazel. The man had stopped breathing for at least five minutes before paramedics arrived. It was only immediate CPR that had stood between him and certain death. It was not a situation Hazel wanted to repeat in a hurry.

'I did attempt to talk to him again in hospital last night, but I had no luck. The doctor said he was too poorly.'

'You should have said you were planning to talk to Carol and Ramsay again,' Tom pointed out. 'I'd have gone with you.'

Hazel knew he meant it, but he had a life outside of work. She wanted him to enjoy it.

'It's fine. Turns out it was pointless anyway. At least it didn't waste both our times.'

'The shock must have triggered Ramsay's angina attack,' Tom suggested.

'I'm no' surprised,' Billy remarked. 'She was a mess lying on that driveway like that.' He screwed up his face. 'It was bad enough for us so it must have been a horrific sight for someone who loved her.'

'What came up on the door-to-door?' Hazel looked at Andrea then across to Billy and back. 'Andrea.'

Andrea opened her notebook and flicked through the first couple of pages. 'I spoke to Deirdre McNeil who lives a few doors down who said she heard a scream – "blood-curdling" she called it – and looked out of her window to see a green car speeding away. She says it happened at ten to ten.'

'She's absolutely sure on her timing?' Hazel questioned.

Andrea nodded. 'She is, bless her. She told me a story about the clock and about her mum dying and her not wanting to change the time on it so that's how she's so sure.'

'Did she see who was driving?'

Andrea shook her head. 'Sadly, no, she didn't.'

'Never mind, what else have you got for me?'

Andrea flipped over to the next page. 'OK, now I spoke to a man called Jacob Sheldon who said he heard tyres at exactly the same time. He said he thought it sounded like boy racers. He saw the back of a green car, but he didn't see the driver either and couldn't tell me the make.'

Hazel sighed. 'So many sightings of this damn car but no positive ID on the driver.'

'Maybe not but he did tell me something that I think you'll find interesting,' Andrea said.

'Tell me more,' Hazel smiled.

'Sheldon knows the couple well. His wife, who passed away recently, was a friend of Maggie's.'

'Oh that's interesting,' Tom interjected.

'Isn't it,' Andrea remarked.

'What's his take on them?' Hazel asked.

'He said that his wife and Maggie were good friends. The two of them went out socially together. Said that Maggie was a happy, gregarious woman but all that changed after the accident.'

'I can imagine it did,' Hazel commented. 'Did he suggest it caused a strain on the couple's marriage?'

Andrea nodded. 'Yes, he said there had been arguments.'

'Did any of them get physical?' Tom suggested.

'I've not seen any domestic abuse complaints from the house come up,' Billy told them.

'No, Sheldon didn't think so, but he said that Samuel Ramsay was the polar opposite to Maggie. His exact words were he wasn't "the chatty type". But that's not the most intriguing part.'

Hazel swallowed what was left of her cold tea. 'Oh yes, what else did he say?'

Before Andrea could say any more the phone on Hazel's desk rang. 'Hang on a sec,' she said and jogged to answer it. She listened as she was told a call had come in from someone at Stagecoach buses. 'And he's sure?' After a moment or two she continued. 'Great, thank you.'

Brilliant! She mumbled under her breath.

'Right, it turns out the bus driver did see something. Apparently, he read something about the incident on social media, one of the local groups, and came forward to report a green car speeding on that road. The driver was wearing a baseball cap he said, but that's about all he can say.'

'Don't buses all have dashcams now, boss?' Andrea suggested.

Hazel looked at Billy. 'Aye, I'll check.'

'Right, Andrea, what were you saying?' Hazel moved the conversation on. She was keen to hear what else this Sheldon had said.

'Yes, so he said, a couple of weeks ago, he saw Maggie getting out of a car he didn't recognise driven by a much younger man. When she saw that he'd spotted her she turned beetroot with embarrassment.'

'Mm, that's interesting.' Hazel turned and looked at Maggie's photo again.

'Not just that,' Andrea beamed. 'He said she got dropped off two blocks from their street.'

Hazel looked at Tom, eyes wide. He stared right back. 'Are you thinking what I'm thinking?' she asked him.

'Possibly,' Tom suggested and took a long, slow breath before blowing it out through puffed cheeks. He stared up at Maggie's photo. 'Why would you want to be dropped off where your neighbours can't see you?'

'My thoughts exactly,' Hazel said.

Chapter Twelve

Sean Jacobs' eyes peeled slowly open. Sunday morning. His mouth felt like a badger had shit in it when he'd been sleeping. He coughed to clear the dryness stalking his throat. His head pounded and goosebumps had already starting popping up on his arms. Sitting up slowly, he tried to rub warmth into them, but it was futile. It always was. The heating was on in the shelter. He wasn't cold because the room was cold. One good thing about the place was that they didn't skimp on the heating. His teeth started to chatter for another reason altogether.

'Fuck's sake,' Sean muttered under his breath and dropped his head into his hands against the growing pain tearing at his brain that felt like it was being shaken against his skull. A loud knock hit his room door. A room he usually shared with two other residents.

'Sean,' a woman's voice slammed into him. 'Sean, are you up?' she said from behind the door.

Sean looked up and sighed. Coughing again, he struggled to answer her. The door handle dipped and one of the support workers in the men's homeless unit popped her head round the door.

'You'd better get a move on, or they'll no' be any toast left on the table.'

Sean swallowed hard. 'I'm no hungry,' he mumbled, desperately trying to stop the shivering.

'All right then,' she replied, tucking her long, blonde hair behind her ear as she pushed her glasses higher on her nose. 'If you want anything washed, the washing machine is free for the next half an hour.'

The sound of her voice, tinny and grating, cut right through him. God, she was irritating, standing there all chirpy and perky. Could she not see how much he was suffering?

'Aye, thanks.' He lifted a hand to acknowledge her.

'Come on then,' she repeated and left him to it, pulling the door gently behind her.

'Fuck!' Sean threw his pillow angrily at the door. 'Argh,' he gripped his head in his hands.

He hoped Benny would still be in the dining room. Sean rummaged in his jeans pocket, turning the material inside out.

'Shit,' he exclaimed. He was sure he had a fiver in there. Some arsehole had dipped his pocket. When he found them he'd give them a slap, all right.

Sean spotted that one of his roommates had left their denim jacket on the floor next to their bed. He flipped through the pockets, struggling to control the trembling in his arms, until he found a ten pound note and some shrapnel. Leaving the coins, he pocketed the tenner and slammed the door behind him.

Benny was still there. Thank fuck.

'All right, B?' Sean sniffed and glanced around to make sure none of the staff were within earshot.

'All right,' Benny nodded. 'How's it gaw'n, man?'

Sean looked nervously over his shoulder and leaned closer. He sniffed and scratched at the itch that was growing on his skin. It felt like spiders were crawling all over him.

'Am fucking rattling, man,' Sean murmured and pulled the money out of his jeans pocket, squeezing it tight in his fingers. 'Geez a swedger, man.' He took another quick glance behind him. 'Or have you got a bit a green ah could hae?'

Benny gazed over Sean's shoulder and smiled as a support worker passed the open door on the other side of the room. Sean sniffed then nibbled on his thumbnail. His body was aching. Every muscle burned and he felt sick.

'Come on man,' he urged.

'Here's a couple of jellies. It's aw I've got until I meet my chemist.' Benny grinned and pressed a tiny plastic bag into Sean's outstretched hand.

Sean had thrown the money at him before he could say anything else. He ripped the bag open and devoured the contents. It might get him through the next hour or two but wouldn't be enough to get him through the rest of the day so he headed to where he knew he could find something for that.

Chapter Thirteen

'How was Samuel Ramsay when you saw him last night?' Tom asked as the team briefing pressed on.

'I won't lie. He looked grim. He actually looked quite grey.' Hazel shuddered at the image of Samuel Ramsay in her head. 'Listen Could you and Andrea get over to the Wilsons' place? See if you can track David down. Hopefully, you'll have better luck this morning. If not then his absence is making him look guilty. He'd surely be home now if he had nothing to hide. I'm going back to the hospital to talk to Ramsay.'

'Sure,' Tom nodded to Andrea as he grabbed his jacket.

Andrea tucked her navy scarf round her neck and grabbed her duffle coat then followed Tom out.

Hazel picked her mug up from her desk, her eyes giving the photo of her ex-husband Rick the briefest of glances, a habit she wished she could break. She wasn't quite ready to take the photo off her desk but looking at it was still hard. 'Being stuck between a rock and a hard place' was how Tom described it and he was right.

'I'm making another,' Hazel held her mug up. 'Do you fancy one?' she asked Billy.

Billy looked up from concentrating on something on his laptop. 'Nah, I'm all right, thanks.' He smiled then returned his focus to his work.

The sound of the office door banging shut after Tom and Andrea left preceded the silence until it too was broken by the whirr from the boiling kettle. A text landed as she dropped a teabag into her mug. Thinking it was probably Cara, again, Hazel grabbed the phone from her pocket and sighed. She really wasn't in the mood to see what Cara wanted this time. She was surprised to see that it wasn't from her at all, but from someone Hazel had not spoken to in a while but who had never been too far from her mind. She would never be able to forget Rachel. The two women were forever joined by tragedy. Hazel clicked to read the message.

> I remembered it was a year ago today and I just wanted to let you know I was thinking about you. About Rick. About what happened. I'm probably not your first choice but I'm here if you ever want to talk about what happened. We have so much in common after all X

Hazel ignored the unexpected tear that leaked from her right eye, until it trickled down over her cheek before dripping off the edge of her jaw, onto the collar of her black shirt. She wiped her face with the back of her hand. The anniversary. A whole year had passed since that day. Part of her was glad that none of the team had mentioned it. Another part of her was angry that they'd forgotten. Life carried on. Many more people had died since then. Overdoses. Suicides. Road traffic accidents. Hazel had seen them all, but nothing came close to the pain caused by the death of her ex-husband, Rick. The text from Rachel Fox felt good whether Hazel wanted to admit it or not. And Rachel was right. They did have a lot in common. Something so unique.

> Thank you. I appreciate that.

She stopped short of ending with a kiss and stuffed her phone back down into the pocket of her black jeans then pushed the mug away and switched the kettle off. She'd grab a cup of coffee from Costa on the way to the hospital instead. She was in the mood for a hot, sweet latte now with at least four sachets of brown sugar. Perhaps she'd add a blueberry muffin to her order.

—

'He's still very weak but he's keen to talk to you.'

Hazel had to look up to meet the eyes of the wiry, flame-haired doctor outside Samuel Ramsay's hospital room.

'I won't keep him for long,' she promised. 'But it's really important we talk to him.'

'I heard what happened to his wife,' the young doctor mentioned. 'Tragic.'

'Yes, tragic,' Hazel acknowledged and reached for the door handle before he could go on.

The continuous high-pitched beeping from the heart monitor was actually quite soothing, Hazel thought, as she pulled one of the black plastic chairs closer to Samuel Ramsay's bed. He looked like he was sleeping until his eyes peeped briefly open then, on realising Hazel was there, he tried to remove the oxygen mask.

'Detective,' he gasped. 'Have you found them? The person who did that to...' His words disappeared into tears.

Hazel laid a hand on his arm. 'Not yet, Mr Ramsay, but we're doing everything we can, I promise.'

'Have you spoken to the Wilson boy yet?' Ramsay's breathing slowed and the tears subsided. 'I'm sorry, I...'

'You've no need to apologise and no, not yet, but two of my team are on their way there now,' Hazel assured him. 'Now, if you're up to it, just take your time and tell me what happened yesterday. I know it's hard but if you can give me as much detail as you can remember.' She gave his arm a gentle squeeze then released her grip on him and took a notebook from her jacket pocket.

'I'm sorry, could you fill my cup for me? The oxygen makes me so thirsty.' He pointed to an empty plastic cup on the unit next to his bed.

'What? Oh, of course.' Hazel poured water from the jug and offered it to his shaky hand.

'Thank you,' Ramsay replied, and Hazel was surprised to see him down the contents without spilling a drop. He handed the cup back to her and rested his head on the pillow. Taking a long slow breath, he closed his eyes just momentarily.

'No problem.' She placed the cup back down next to the jug and wiped her damp hand on her jeans before flicking open a page in her notebook.

'I still can't believe this is happening.' Ramsay shook his head. 'Any of this.' He pointed to the cannula in his hand and the heart monitor next to the bed. 'I got up yesterday morning and I was looking forward to seeing the Agatha Christie play at the theatre last night. The girl from *Emmerdale* is in it, I can't remember her name. Maggie and I were going to have dinner at The Bothy before the show and—'

'I know this is hard,' Hazel interrupted him before he had a chance to add what they were planning to order for dessert. 'Do you remember anything out of the ordinary before Maggie left the house yesterday morning? Did she seem different in any way?'

He shook his head. 'Nope, she had an early hair appointment at Liza's. It was at eight thirty, I think. She liked to be Liza's first customer. That's why she'd arranged to have coffee so early with Sandra. They both like a breakfast roll and pot of tea in Willows which is very close to the hairdressers. Do you know it?' His eyes filled with tears again and he struggled to make much sense. 'I'm sorry...'

'Yes, I know Willows,' Hazel replied and wrote the words *Willows* and *Liza's* in her notebook. 'It's OK, take your time.'

'I'm sorry,' Samuel repeated.

'Sandra?' Hazel tried to press on.

'Erm yes, Sandra Bell, they've been friends since teaching college.' He wiped his eyes with the back of his hand then pulled a tissue from the box and rubbed it over his nose.

'I'm going to need Sandra's details, if you don't mind.'

'Of course yes, her address is 116 Birch Place.' He reached for his phone and began to scroll through his contacts. 'She's the woman I asked you to contact to arrange to take care of my dogs.'

'Oh yes, that's right. Thank you. Of course. I do already have her number thank you. Do you know if she met with Sandra as planned yesterday?'

'Yes she did. Sandra called last night after she heard what happened. I only managed to talk to her for a minute. Everything was so chaotic last night.'

'Did she say if Maggie said anything to her?' Hazel asked.

Samuel frowned. 'Said anything?'

'Yes,' Hazel explained. 'Was she worried about anything? Did she think there was someone following her, perhaps?'

Samuel looked shocked by her question. 'Do you think he was following her? That David Wilson?'

'Right now we don't know but everything is a potential line of inquiry,' Hazel explained. 'So did Maggie tell her friend anything?'

'No,' Samuel's voice began to tremble again. 'No; they talked about having a weekend away in the autumn, like they always do. The Lake District this time, I think Sandra said. I wasn't at my best when she called my mobile.' Tears fell easily again. 'Something else she won't get to do now.'

For a brief second, an image of the unfinished Jeffrey Archer novel sitting on the arm of the chair flashed into Hazel's head. Samuel wiped his face with his palm and took a deep breath.

'I'm sorry, me crying isn't going to be much help to you, is it?'

'I do understand,' she said. 'It can't be easy having a stranger ask you questions about the worst thing that's ever happened to you. Especially when you're lying in a hospital bed.'

'It helps when they're as lovely as you.' His thin smile, which disappeared as quickly as it had appeared, suggested this was meant as a compliment.

Hazel's phone buzzed in her pocket before she could respond.

'Andrea,' she answered then listened in disbelief. 'Is he OK, is he hurt?'

This was all Hazel needed. Shuddering, her mind flashed back to a time her DI had been seriously hurt in the line of duty once before. 'Stay with him. I'm on my way.'

Chapter Fourteen

Hazel could see Tom sitting holding a white handkerchief against his head in the passenger seat of his car when she pulled up outside the Wilson home. It had a little blood on it which was alarming. Tom and Andrea had knocked and waited but were shocked to hear raised voices coming from inside. An experienced detective, Tom didn't hesitate to go and check on Carol, who he feared might be in danger. A huge mistake, as it turned out.

Hazel nodded a greeting to Andrea then crouched down next to where Tom was sitting.

'What happened?' She indicated towards the Wilsons' front door.

'We heard shouting, like an argument. A man and a woman,' Andrea explained. 'We thought it was David fighting with his mum.'

'It sounded heated, whoever it was,' Tom added.

'But you don't know if it was David and his mum?' Hazel said – as more of a question than a statement.

'Honestly, no I don't, but a man in a black hoodie came surging towards us and slammed Tom hard before fleeing like a bat out of hell. I was worried about the way Tom fell, so I didn't go after him. Sorry.'

Hazel frowned. 'Neither of you got a good look at his face, I assume. Could it have been David?'

Tom shook his head, his awkwardness obvious. 'No, sorry, boss. He whacked me then scarpered. I don't know who it was.'

'He had a black hoodie on, Andrea said, is that right?' Hazel asked.

'Aye, navy or black, I'm not sure exactly.' Tom admitted.

'Height?' Hazel scrolled through the photos on her phone to find a picture of David that Billy had found and emailed to her.

'About six feet, maybe.'

'Was it him?' she showed her phone to them.

Seeing both her detectives shake their heads was disappointing.

'I don't think it was,' Tom said, pulling the handkerchief away.

'OK, don't worry about it, you concentrate on yourself for now,' she said. 'I'm going to get Andrea to take you to A and E, just as a precaution.'

'It looks worse than it is, I'm fine,' Tom protested. 'It's just a scratch.'

Hazel's eyes widened, her lips puckering in a way that said he'd be doing as he was told. Tom nodded gently in resignation.

'DC Graham, take him to get checked out, will you?'

'Sure, no problem,' she replied as Tom tossed his keys towards her.

'Call me when you've been seen,' Hazel added then closed the passenger door on a forlorn-looking Tom. She looked at Andrea. 'What's Carol's mood like?'

'Honestly, she's a pretty sad individual,' Andrea informed her. 'I didn't get much sense out of her when I asked about the fight.'

'That's not much help is it,' Hazel tutted and momentarily thought of her own mother again.

'Aye I don't think you'll get much out of her either but you can try. I'll see you later,' Andrea said then got into the driver's seat of Tom's car.

Hazel was surprised to hear that, given that Carol had appeared to be arguing loudly with someone not that long ago. She watched Tom's car retreat from the rundown street the

Wilsons lived in. A variety of abandoned pieces of furniture sat piled up between two of the properties, the windows of which had paint peeling from the frames. Black bags that had been ripped open by cats or possibly crows, lay scattered across the small front gardens of at least four of the houses in the row of council terraced houses. A rusting bike sat outside the Wilsons' front door. Liam's, perhaps. It looked about the right size.

Hazel knocked and listened for movement inside. When only silence returned she tried the handle and the door opened. A glance up at the snow-laden sky told her another shower was imminent. It was unseasonably cold, even for Scotland in late March. The bitter wind made it feel more like early January and she rubbed her arms to get some warmth into them.

'Mrs Wilson, it's Detective Chief Inspector Todd,' she called out as she wiped her snowy boots on the doormat and closed the front door after herself.

The house smelled bad. A mixture of stale food, dirt and sweat hit her nostrils. She couldn't remember it smelling this bad last night. The property was dirtier than she'd noticed, too. Even in this cold weather, opening a few windows would work wonders. The hint of male body spray caught her nose, barely there, but still a pleasant addition. David's, she thought, as the scent wafted down from upstairs. He'd been here recently then.

Piles of unopened post lay on a small table at the bottom of the stairs. The table itself was thick with dust. A stain on the hall carpet caught her eye, something brown and sticky, so she stepped over it, just to be sure. Country music played from inside the living room, the door ajar. Hazel pressed a finger on it and pushed it open slowly.

'Carol,' she said gently and stepped inside to find the thin woman sprawled over the heavily stained sofa, her hair lank and greasy, her clothes covered in a wide variety of stains. A smell drifted towards Hazel. Sweat and stale vodka, a hint of urine too. Andrea Graham wasn't wrong. She looked so sad lying there, pathetic, even.

Carol Wilson had an empty glass cradled in her grasp, the bottle of vodka half full on the floor next to her. A newspaper lay open on the television pages on the sticky coffee table. An untouched cheese sandwich sat on top with a KitKat next to it on the plate. The woman didn't look like she was in any fit state to have made that food. David, perhaps. Was it him she'd been arguing with? Tom didn't think so. So who was it? What was their argument about? Hazel doubted she would get much out of Carol but had to try. At least her mood was less brittle this time, but experience taught her that could change in a heartbeat.

'Carol,' Hazel tried again. 'It's DCI Todd, we met last night. Is it OK to have a chat?'

Carol Wilson's eyes opened then closed again before she sighed loudly then tutted. She said something in response, but Hazel wasn't sure what exactly.

'Carol,' she repeated. 'I'm...'

'I heard you the first time,' Carol snapped and pulled herself up slowly, almost dropping the glass she was cradling. She was white as a sheet as she met Hazel's eyes. 'What do you want?'

'Do you mind if I sit?' Hazel pointed to an empty armchair, one that looked reasonably stain-free.

'Fucking knock yersel out.' Carol sniffed and lifted the half empty bottle of vodka up to pour a large measure into the glass.

Hazel watched her sink the entire contents without flinching before refilling it.

'Thanks,' Hazel sat, casting her eye briefly over a blue foolscap folder with David's name on it surrounded by ornate, detailed drawings, on the shelf under the glass-topped coffee table. The pink roses, in particular, were very impressive. She took her notebook out of her pocket and cleared her throat against the thick dust in the room. 'My colleagues told me they heard you arguing with someone earlier. They were worried about you.'

'What are you talking about?' Carol's words were brittle and defensive.

'Who were you fighting with?' Hazel tried the direct approach. 'Was it David?'

'What?' Carol snapped. 'He's not here, he's…' She looked at her watch. 'He's at college, isn't he?'

'Is that right?' Hazel answered just as an older Volkswagen Polo pulled up outside. She saw a young man fitting David's description getting out, smiling at the driver then heading up the path. He wasn't wearing a hoodie, but a camouflage-patterned T-shirt with a pair of black jeans. He had a jacket slung across his arm, but he was wearing a baseball cap. He couldn't possibly have been at college though. It was Sunday.

The front door opened and shut before a man's voice echoed through the house.

'Mum,' he called out. 'Class finished early so I…' He stopped when he saw Hazel. 'Who are you?'

As polite as your mother, clearly.

Hazel lifted up her ID so that David could see it. 'I'm DCI Hazel Todd. I'm…' She paused as David snatched her warrant card out of her hand to examine it, narrowing his eyes at it, then at her, before handing it back.

He sniffed as he scratched at the stubble on his chin, then ran his hand up and over his closely cropped brown hair.

'Yes, so, what do you want from us?' he asked then stared at the uneaten food on the plate, which seemed to irritate him. Ignoring Hazel he said, 'Mum, I've told you, you've got to eat.'

Hazel observed the dynamic between the pair. The son was clearly now taking the role of parent while having to watch his mum disappear into her grief. *Motive for murder of the person who caused this pain.*

'I know, son,' Carol replied quietly to him. 'I just couldn't manage it. I'm sorry. My stomach is still a bit iffy.'

The way they spoke to each other struck Hazel. It was like they were the only people in the room. Hazel was the interloper, the intruder. She coughed to remind them of her presence before two pairs of matching green eyes burned into her like she was an irritation.

'What do you want, then?' David said as he sat next to his mum, draping an arm round her shoulder. 'You can see Mum's not feeling too good.'

For a moment Hazel felt she was the one being questioned. The way their eyes bored into her from the other side of the small room…

'I'm investigating the murder of Maggie Ramsay and—'

'Woah, woah, what the fuck did you just say?' David interrupted, snatching his arm back from his mum's shoulder and dropping it onto his legs. 'What do you mean, murder?'

'Mrs Ramsay was hit by a stolen car yesterday morning.'

'What did she say, David?' Carol seemed confused. 'She… she…'

David beamed the widest of smiles at his mum and took her hand in his, giving it a hint of a squeeze.

'She's dead,' he announced. 'The bitch is dead.'

He turned his attention back to Hazel. 'That is the best news we've heard in a long, long time.' David grabbed his phone from his pocket and scrolled through his contacts for the number he needed.

'Hang on a minute,' Hazel held up her hand, appalled by their reaction. 'I have a couple of questions to ask you.'

'Yes, yes, give me five minutes,' David stood up, his phone clasped to his ear, and walked out of the room.

Hazel could hear the absolute joy oozing from the words she overheard him say to whoever it was he had rushed to call. She frowned. Carol's facial expression remained the same. Dazed and confused. Her response to the news was muted. From the alcohol, Hazel supposed. Hazel put the question to her that she had to ask.

'Where were you yesterday morning?'

Carol stared blankly at her. 'I have no fucking idea,' she retorted. 'Here, I expect, like I am every day.' Her words were filled with bitterness.

Of course you don't.

'Have you any idea where David was?' Hazel persisted.

'At college.'

'Oh yes, what time did he leave the house?'

Her question would remain unanswered as David re-joined them.

'You have no idea how happy you've made me,' David informed her, his wide beaming smile seemingly even bigger than before. He flopped down next to his mum and took her hand in his. 'Did you hear what she said? That fucking bitch is dead.'

'I'm not sure that's an entirely appropriate response, do you?'

'What?' David looked confused by Hazel's statement, angry even. 'Of course her death is going to make me happy. Are you mad?' Then his eyes narrowed, almost to the point that his thick eyebrows met in the middle. 'Wait a minute, why are you here?'

From where she sat, Hazel took in his appearance. He couldn't be the man that whacked Tom over the head. David wasn't quite six foot and neither did he have a hoodie on. He could have ditched it, of course, but still, her gut said it wasn't him.

'Where were you yesterday morning? It couldn't have been college because it was Saturday.'

'There are Saturday classes,' he answered defiantly, without looking her in the eye.

'Yes but not on a Sunday.'

'What?'

'You told your mum that your class ended early when you came in.'

David frowned, then his face said he realised he'd been caught out on a lie. He sighed.

'It's just easier that way,' he admitted, keeping his voice low. The pair looked at Carol who was oblivious to their conversation. 'Mum's not been the same since…' He stopped.

'I know about your little brother,' Hazel told him. 'I'm sorry.'

'You guys weren't sorry enough to put that bitch away, though,' he scoffed and snatched up the plate of uneaten food and headed for the living room door. 'She was a teacher, and we were...' His anger seemed to be increasing as he moved away. 'We were just council scum.'

Hazel took a last glance at Carol, sitting, staring into space then followed him, finding him in the kitchen tossing the sandwich into the bin.

'Look, I can't help you,' David said, his mood darkening.

'You can make a start by telling me where you were yesterday morning because we both know you weren't at college so don't insult my intelligence by continuing with that line.'

David scratched his head angrily, dropping the plate into the sink. 'I was with my girlfriend, all right?' He looked right at her, directing the words into Hazel's eyes. 'OK?'

'I'm going to need your girlfriend's det—'

'What the fuck?' David snapped back. 'Do you seriously think I had something to do with it?'

His reaction had an undercurrent of a temper Hazel didn't fancy being on the receiving end of.

'I know about the threats you made against Maggie Ramsay.'

David's expression fell into a grimace, his hatred for the woman was crystal clear. Then he shrugged. 'What do you expect me to say?'

'Did you mean the things you wrote in the letters?'

'I was angry, all right?' His words came out in a deep growl. 'Can you blame me? She killed my wee brother. Hit him and left him to die alone in the road.'

'What about the bullet?'

'What about it?' David's dark mood deepened further, and he held Hazel's eyes seemingly without blinking.

'That's a very serious thing to do,' Hazel said. 'I think we can both agree there was no doubt you were threatening to kill her.'

'So what if I was? Doesn't mean I would go through with it. Maybe it just made me feel better. Anyway, the bullet wasn't even real.'

'Did it make you feel better?'

'No,' he huffed. 'Nothing could make me feel better about what she did.'

'You were given a warning by the police, I believe.'

David nodded. 'Aye, that's right.'

Hazel glanced around at the state of the kitchen. Dishes were piled high on the draining board and a greasy frying pan had been left on one of the back rings of the cooker. But it wasn't in as bad a state as it might have been. David clearly had been trying to hold things together.

'I have to rule out all of the wrong possibilities until I get to the truth. You know that,' Hazel informed him. 'And you threatening her the way you did makes me want to look very closely at you.'

David shook his head. 'The worst bit is the good Samaritan that killed her will get punished more than she did for killing my wee brother!' He angrily grabbed the kettle and held it under the fast-flowing cold tap, shaking his head all the while, spits of water spraying on him. 'Please go before I say something I regret.'

Hazel saw the tears he was fighting back. 'I'm sorry, David, but I need your girlfriend's name. Your alibi for the time of the murder is very important. I'm going to have to talk to her.'

'Suzanne Gerrard,' he snapped, 'but go easy on her OK, she's not been well.' He slammed the kettle down and grabbed his phone from the worktop. Once he'd scrolled through his contacts he pushed her entry close to Hazel's face. 'Are you happy now?'

'Thank you,' Hazel said. 'Just one more thing before I go.'

'Jesus,' David muttered under his breath. 'What now?'

'Who was the man your mum was heard arguing with?'

The defiant look on David's face changed in an instant. 'What do you mean? What man?'

'My two colleagues overheard a heated argument before one of them was assaulted by a man in a black hooded top, maybe six feet in height. Do you know who that is?'

She was alarmed to see David's eyes darting in several different directions. 'Erm… no, I don't know. Did he hurt Mum?'

'Who was he?' Hazel pushed him for an answer.

'I, erm…' he stuttered, avoiding her gaze.

'Because I want to speak to him about his attack on my detective, amongst other things,' she informed him.

'Look, I don't know anyone that looks like that.' David was edging closer to the kitchen door, avoiding her gaze. 'Listen I forgot,' he changed the subject. 'I have somewhere I need to be so…'

Hazel took her card from her pocket and tried to hand it to him, but David seemed uninterested, so she laid it on the counter instead.

'If you think of who that man might be then please call me. My mobile is on there too so, anytime, OK?'

'Yes, yes, all right,' he said then fled out of the kitchen, peeking briefly in the living room door at his mum.

Hazel watched him from the kitchen doorway that led into the hall. She saw David drop his eyes down to the floor and shake his head before he took a brief last glance back at her. Then he headed out, the loud slamming of the front door making Hazel jump.

Hazel hadn't had the chance to ask him anything else. He'd been in such a rush to get away. It was clear he knew exactly who the man was. His behaviour made it obvious he recognised his description immediately. It would have been helpful if he'd taken a moment to fill Hazel in, too. She checked in on Carol and saw her laid back on the sofa, the blanket half covering her thin body. Such a sorry sight. Hazel closed the living room door quietly and followed David out of the front door.

'I see you finally found him, then.'

Hazel turned to see the Wilsons' neighbour standing outside her own front door.

'Erm yes, thanks.' Hazel pulled the Wilsons' front door shut and headed back towards her car. Then she stopped and turned before striding across the snow which lay heavily on the patch of front grass between the two houses. Given that the snow almost came right to the top of her ankle boots, Hazel quickly regretted taking that route. 'Actually, maybe there is something you can help me with.'

'If I can help in any way, I will.' The old woman smiled, her cheeks pink from the biting cold wind. 'Would you like to come in?'

'If you can spare me five minutes,' Hazel smiled back. 'I would be really grateful.'

If David wasn't willing to help identify the man, Hazel would have to ask someone else who might be able to. Especially when it looked like nothing much got past this old woman.

'I was about to put the kettle on, actually,' she beamed. 'Would you like one?'

Hazel declined the offer. As kind as it was, she didn't have time for tea. She gave her the description of the young man who had attacked Tom.

'Yes, that tall, thin, lad goes next door all the time. I couldn't tell you his name,' the Wilsons' neighbour said, tutting loudly. 'I'm not one to judge, you understand.' She picked fluff from her blue skirt then took a tissue from the sleeve of her blouse and wiped her nose. 'But David doesn't keep the best of company these days.'

'Oh.' Hazel's eyes widened. 'Did you see anyone going in next door today?'

The old woman nodded and pursed her lips tightly. 'Like I said I don't know his name, I'm sorry, but it was the young lad that's always got that dirty baseball cap on.' She looked like she was shuddering at the thought.

Hazel's interest was piqued by that. Another baseball cap. Was this the driver of the car? Not David? 'Can you describe this baseball cap?' she asked hopefully.

Chapter Fifteen

Hazel's phone had buzzed just as she was getting ready to drive away after her interesting chat with the Wilsons' neighbour. She had wondered if the old woman was ever going to stop talking, eventually realising that she might be lonely.

'Hi Billy, what's up?' she said, answering the call while she stared at her reflection in the rear view mirror.

Her heart sank at the news. There had been another murder. One even more gruesome than Maggie Ramsay's. This time in an area that couldn't be more different to the Ramsays'. Instead of asking Billy to meet her at the scene, she asked him to keep going through the evidence they already had on the Ramsay murder. She had more than enough uniforms for the door-to-door on this new murder which had been carried out in the same council scheme that the Wilsons' lived in. The significance of that fact meant Hazel couldn't rule out a connection, coming so soon after Maggie's death, and David Wilson was her key suspect.

The victim's niece who had called the police was talking to one of the uniformed officers outside the run-down block of eight council flats, a dripping overflow pipe causing a dirty brown stain down the exterior wall of the property. Hazel offered the clearly shocked young woman a gentle smile before slipping on some latex gloves and making her way inside the block where she was met with a flurry of activity, including the presence of pathologist Jack Blair who was bent close to the victim's shattered body, as well as DC Graham.

Hazel had grown up on this estate in the seventies and eighties when her family had been offered one of the brand new North Muirton houses, and always told people she was proud of her scheemy heritage. Even when residents from the estate were looked down on over the years. The deterioration in the area was striking, particularly in the last twenty years. This block in particular looked worn and tired, in need of a great deal of maintenance. She was shocked to see that the crime scene was less than five minutes' walk from the kids' park and the primary school – and five minutes from the home she had spent her childhood in. Most of it, happy. Until it wasn't. Hazel shuddered at the thought of its close proximity to the school given the details she'd been told about their victim.

'What can you tell me?' Hazel asked and gave a quick nod in Andrea Graham's direction. 'Have you got a time of death for me?'

Jack Blair pulled down his mask and stood up from kneeling next to their victim.

'Initial examination tells me death occurred between fifteen and eighteen hours ago, give or take,' Jack replied. 'Cause of death is probably fairly obvious at this stage but I won't be able to give you a definitive answer until I've examined him properly.'

Hazel stared at the lifeless, dishevelled, dirty-looking man sitting on the navy-blue sofa surrounded by piles of empty beer bottles and a pizza box containing a half-eaten large cheese-and-tomato. A large knife stuck out of his chest as if suspended in mid-air, a pool of thick dried blood soaked into his green, tattered T-shirt. His face had been severely beaten, his nose broken, and lips split in several places. Hazel spotted a bloody tooth resting on his collar bone – not whole, but half a tooth. Blood had leaked from his ears and a single trail of dried red crusts led towards his collar. One of his cheeks appeared lower than the other, the bone broken and hanging out of place as if it too was suspended in the air.

It must have taken a great deal of rage to beat his face into this state and the amount of blood indicated it had happened when he was very much alive. This looked personal. Her gut said this man knew his attacker. A pool of blood further down his body caught Hazel's eye. She looked at one of the forensic officers standing by the living room door.

'Was there any sign of forced entry?'

Her theory that their victim had known their attacker and let them into the property looked correct when the officer shook his head. She turned her attention to Jack.

'Is that what I think it is?' Hazel asked.

'I'm afraid so,' Jack acknowledged her suggestion. 'Penis removed, possibly with the same knife that we can see sticking out of this unfortunate soul's chest.'

Again, the volume of pooled blood indicated when the castration had taken place, but Hazel asked, for confirmation.

'Before death?'

Jack nodded and cast a brief glance at the discomfort on Andrea Graham's face. 'Again, I'm afraid so, yes. The amount of blood loss suggests it was all carried out before death.'

Hazel blew a large breath from puffed cheeks. 'Thanks, Jack, I'll hear from you.'

'I'll be doing the Ramsay post-mortem tomorrow morning,' Blair told her. 'You're more than welcome to join me.'

'I think I will, yes,' Hazel confirmed. 'I'll see you in the morning. I might even bring coffee.'

Blair smiled. 'Excellent,' he replied and tugged the mask back over his face before kneeling back down in front of their victim.

Hazel and Andrea headed for the dead man's kitchen. They walked through the short hallway, past bulging black bags.

They'd be filled with rubbish, Hazel thought, but just to be sure, she called back to where the forensics officers were busy searching and pointed to the bags. 'Could you go through these as well please?'

Hazel smiled back at the officer who had nodded that he would undertake that unpleasant task. She followed Andrea into the kitchen.

'What do we know so far?' Hazel asked as she scanned the room for anything out of the ordinary, but the state of the place made it difficult to know. She couldn't see a surface that wasn't covered by something. From laundry – both clean *and* dirty by the looks of it – to dishes, again in various stages of filth. She spotted the calendar hanging above his kitchen. The letter 'D', written in capitals had been circled with deep, thick red lines on yesterday's date. She removed the calendar and placed it in an evidence bag.

'Peter King, fifty-five, convicted sex offender,' Andrea began. 'Suspended sentence for possession of ten thousand indecent images of children.'

Hazel sucked in air through her teeth. 'Bloody hell, that's a lot! And he only got a suspended sentence?'

'Judge ordered background reports.' Andrea referred to her notebook for more details. 'Psychiatric reports etc. You know the drill.'

'Aye, I do that,' Hazel agreed. Her eyes fell on the neglect in the room.

Plates were piled high next to the sink, various stages of mould living its best life on the surface of many of them. Mugs, thick with brown tea stains, littered the worktop. Two on the kitchen table caught her eye.

'Bag these two for DNA. See who popped round for coffee with him last.' Her eyes moved around the room, stopping at a beige plastic laundry basket, unsure whether the clothes were on their way in or out of the machine. 'Oh and I almost forgot. Have you heard from Tom?'

'Yes, he texted to say Doctor told him to rest tonight, he should be fine tomorrow.'

'Good, that's good,' Hazel replied but wondered why he hadn't contacted her first.

'How did it go with the Wilsons?' Andrea asked.

Hazel rolled her eyes. 'You were right. Trying to talk to Carol Wilson was a waste of time.'

'Damn shame,' Andrea suggested. 'What happened to them, losing that boy like that.'

'Aye, his brother, though, is highly delighted to hear that she's dead,' Hazel pointed out. 'He's given his girlfriend as his alibi for the time of the murder. Could you go and talk to her for me?'

'Sure. Text me the address.'

'Great, thanks, but could you do the door-to-door on the immediate neighbours here for me first? The uniforms can do the rest.'

'Aye, no problem. That's fine.'

'He said she's not been well,' Hazel added as she typed Suzanne's details onto the text for Andrea. 'So take it easy.'

'Will do. Did he say what was up with her?'

Hazel shook her head, then a shopping list next to the kettle caught her eye.

> Coke
> Monster
> Sweets
> Bread
> Milk
> Ham
> Cheese

Hazel put the small piece of paper into an evidence bag.

'Monster, is that one of those energy drinks that teenagers buy?' Hazel was curious. 'Why would he have that, I wonder? Was he expecting teenage visitors perhaps?'

'Could be but that's one hell of a risk and yes, it's disgusting as well. Stinks like sweet fruity piss.'

'Sounds like you're speaking from experience, DC Graham,' Hazel teased.

'My flatmate at university used to drink it to keep him awake for all-night cramming study sessions.' Andrea's face contorted in disgust. 'The flat used to stink of it because he'd leave his half empty cans around the place. Foul stuff.' She shivered. 'Even when they did make it to the recycling basket they hadn't been rinsed so the smell still lingered.'

'Go and check the bedroom, will you?' Hazel instructed Andrea, guiding the conversation back to where it should be. 'See if there's a laptop or an iPad or a phone, even.'

'Sure,' Andrea replied and walked back into the hall towards another room that led off it.

Hazel tugged open the drawer next to the fridge, pulling it roughly several times before dislodging a phone charger that had been trapped. The contents were no real help. Just a variety of takeaway menus, old keys, a screwdriver, a penknife, a pile of old shoelaces as well as a brand new pair, a pile of receipts and a couple of bills. Mainly utilities and mobile phone. She took the phone bills out and saw they were the most recent statements so bagged them as well. Her stomach lurched on seeing a copy of a teen girls' magazine, for younger teens at that, and she fought the urge to be sick.

Hazel flipped open the cupboard underneath and rummaged amongst the pots and pans, disgusted by the pungent smell of what she thought must be stale vegetable oil. The sight of the fryer made her gag, drips of grease clinging to the cold silver pan. She was about to close the door when she spotted a small grey mini laptop, the type that can be used as a tablet or laptop, pressed against the back of the cupboard. It was the same colour as the back panel; she'd almost missed it. As she pulled it out, Andrea came back into the kitchen.

'Boss, I've got a laptop,' she said.

Hazel stood and held up hers. 'Now why did he need two laptops?'

'One in the open and one hidden away,' Andrea added.

'Mm,' Hazel said. 'Get both of these to Billy. See what he can tell us, shall we?'

Andrea took the smaller laptop out of Hazel's hand and placed them both into an evidence bag, sealing them tightly and trying to find a surface to lay them on.

The ringtone from a mobile phone sang from behind them. The two detectives turned and opened drawers and cupboards but couldn't find the source of the sound. Then it stopped.

'Shit,' Hazel exclaimed, narrowing her eyes, and tilting her head a little as if that would help.

'It was definitely coming from nearer you,' Andrea suggested and pointed behind her.

'That's what I thought too but…' Another ringtone. Hazel's, this time. 'You keep looking, I'd better take this,' she said, patting Andrea's arm as she passed her. 'Check on top of the fridge, in the fruit bowl, maybe. Hello?' She said into the handset as she moved away.

Hazel listened to the officer, while she stared out at the gathering crowd outside the block: an elderly couple, the tall, wiry man standing next to his dumpy, plump wife with a lead in his hand that led down to an equally elderly Yorkshire terrier; two young mums with toddlers in buggies, chatting and gesticulating wildly at the events unfolding in front of them; a group of hooded teenagers of various shapes and sizes, huddled together, one of them drinking from what looked like a can of that Monster drink. A boy and a girl on bikes stood a little way back from the older kids. A man in a grey suit spoke loudly on his phone, so loud that Hazel could hear him. Something about the murder. *The police are everywhere. He reckoned it was that perv that had been done in.*

Vultures, she thought, or maybe they were just glad King was dead. The way David Wilson was glad Maggie Ramsay had been killed.

The officer on the phone told her that a woman called Sandra, who said she was Maggie's friend, was asking to speak to her at the station. Very keen, it appeared. 'I'll be back in fifteen minutes, tell her. Put her in room one and make her some tea, will you?'

Hazel instructed Andrea to talk to Peter King's niece first, before talking to King's immediate neighbours then to head over to David Wilson's girlfriend's place to confirm his alibi one way or another. Hazel's first priority had to be to speak with Sandra Bell, Maggie's best friend who had told the desk sergeant that she needed to tell the detective in charge about something that Maggie hadn't wanted Samuel to know.

Chapter Sixteen

'Hello, I'm DC Andrea Graham, I wondered if I could have a few minutes.' She held up her ID for the young woman, being consoled by a uniformed officer, to see. 'I was hoping you could answer a few questions.'

'Of course yes,' Rona King looked up, tidied her long hair out of her eyes and nodded, rubbing her fingers over her face and sniffing back tears to compose herself. She blew out a long slow breath, glancing once over Andrea's shoulder at the gathered crowd.

'Miss King, you were the one that found your uncle, is that correct?' Andrea continued, aware of the growing crowd behind them. She held a hand in front of her to usher Rona away from them. 'Come on, we can talk better over here where it's a bit quieter.'

A heckle from the crowd hit Andrea's ears before the rest of the group erupted into jeers.

'They're happy Uncle Peter is dead,' Rona said.

Andrea indicated towards an empty patrol car. 'Come on, we'll have a seat in there shall we?'

Closing the door of the vehicle didn't obscure the chatter completely but it helped take some of the sting out of the barbed jibes while a group of uniforms began to disperse the increasingly unruly crowd. Andrea looked over to see the teenage boys giving a mouthful of cheek to the officers before moving away. An elderly couple walked, arm in arm, away towards the shopping arcade nearby. A man in a suit was pointing his finger close to the officer's chest then at the block of flats before seemingly reluctantly moving off.

'You know about his convictions, I assume,' Rona began. 'It's been like that round here since then.'

'That can't have been easy for you. Did you live with—'

'God no!' Rona interrupted her, seemingly keen to shut down that suggestion quickly. 'Of course not. He's my dad's brother and he's literally got nobody else. Not any more. My dad died last year and nobody else in the family will talk to him after...' She shrugged. 'You know.'

'That's a lot to take on for someone so young, if you don't mind me saying,' Andrea suggested.

The teenager gave another gentle shrug.

'If you don't keep tabs on men like my uncle then you don't know what they're up to, do you?' She picked at the corner of her green nail polish. 'Someone had to, didn't they? And I'm afraid I didn't trust you lot to do it properly, no offence.'

'None taken,' Andrea said plainly. The girl had a point. 'Have you any idea why he would have two laptops – one being hidden in the back of a cupboard?'

Rona looked shocked but her expression quickly evolved into resignation. 'I don't think it takes a genius to figure that out, does it? One nice, clean one, available for inspection by his probation officer any time and the other...' She hesitated to continue, screwing up her face in disgust. 'A suspended sentence!' she exclaimed, her frustration growing. She shook her head and rummaged in her bag then took out a packet of cigarettes. 'Do you mind if I smoke?'

Andrea rolled down the window. 'No, it's fine, go ahead.'

'Thanks, my nerves are shredded,' Rona explained as she lit her cigarette and took a long draw before blowing out in the direction of the open window. She took a moment. 'A suspended sentence, I mean, what kind of punishment is that? That's no kind of deterrent, is it?'

Andrea remembered the shopping list. 'I know this might sound like a strange question, but do you drink Monster?'

Rona narrowed her eyes at her. 'Why would you ask that? No, I can't stand the stuff. Stinks and tastes like sweet liquid speed.'

That comment momentarily stumped Andrea. She'd never heard that expression before but just as she was beginning to suspect, King had been catering for a teenager. Just not this one.

'Did your uncle drink it?'

'Not that I'm aware off,' Rona replied. 'Why do you ask?'

Andrea was unsure how much to say but went on her gut. 'A shopping list we found in the flat suggests he planned to buy some.'

'Oh,' Rona answered, her body language tightening right before she began to nibble her nail.

'Oh,' Andrea repeated. 'Does that mean you know something? The person he was buying it for, perhaps?'

Rona shook her head. 'No, no it's not that,' she sighed. 'It just looks bad, doesn't it? But I can't imagine any young girl in her right mind would be hanging around with him, not after what he did. I mean, everyone is talking about him so there's no way that anybody couldn't know.'

'It's certainly an unusual purchase for a man in his fifties,' Andrea admitted. 'When did you last speak to your uncle?'

'End of last week. I called to ask if he wanted anything from Asda because he doesn't go in there anymore. He feels...' She stopped to correct herself as she sighed. '*Felt* uncomfortable. People staring and pointing, muttering behind his back, that kind of thing. Some not even muttering. Some people have been openly hostile.'

Andrea wanted to say – *can you blame them?* But resisted. She may have been a strong advocate for rehabilitation as well as punishment but there were some crimes that even pushed her limits. 'I understand,' she said instead. 'Can't have been easy for him.'

Rona scoffed: 'Jail would have been easier. How ironic is that?'

'How did he seem when you last spoke? Did he suggest anything was wrong, out of the ordinary at all?'

A sadness crept over Rona's face. 'The usual suspects had been banging on the door again.'

Andrea flicked over to a new page in her notebook. 'Oh yes, and who are the usual suspects?'

'Two lads I went to school with, mostly. They hang around the block, shouting stuff, knocking on his door. Sticking dog shit through his letterbox. The usual. He had an argument with them when he'd had enough.'

Andrea needed more than that. 'What kind of argument? When was this?' she asked — but she was thinking that the state King's body had been left in had been caused by a vicious attack and not a heated argument gone too far. 'Did the argument become violent?'

'He just told them to fuck off, that he'd call the police if they didn't leave him alone.'

'And they did, did they?' Andrea probed.

Rona shrugged. 'They seemed to. But not before one of them kicked his door.'

That explained the deep gouge in the paintwork that she'd noticed earlier, Andrea thought. 'Do these friends of yours from school have names?'

Rona's eyes widened and she scoffed: 'They're no friends of mine, I can assure you.' She fiddled with the leather bracelet on her wrist and took another long draw on her cigarette. 'The one you want to speak to is Sean Jacobs, junkie waste of space asshole and he's got a temper on him. I remember that much from school.'

'Do you have an address for him?'

Andrea scribbled down the address she gave her. It was the shelter for homeless single men in town. Interesting, she thought.

'You might want to talk to his pal David, too. He was always with Sean as well.'

'David?'

'Yes. David Wilson.'

Chapter Seventeen

Andrea texted Hazel a quick message to let her know that David
Wilson's name had come up again before ringing the doorbell
of the flat above Peter King's. She held up her ID as she heard a
key being turned in one lock, then a second. The spyhole grew
darker followed by a chain being slid across.

Andrea offered the harassed-looking young woman a warm
smile. 'Hello, my name is DC Andrea Graham. Could I possibly
ask you a few questions about—'

'Come in, come in,' the woman said before Andrea could
finish and left the door wide open for her to come inside.

'Thank you.' Andrea wiped her feet on the doormat and
closed the front door behind her.

The contrast between the two properties was enormous.
The occupant of this one clearly looked after her home, and
herself, better. She took pride, Andrea thought, that was the
word she was searching her mind for. The smell that wafted
into Andrea's nostrils was beautiful. She couldn't think of what
it was exactly, but it was ten times better than King's place. She
followed the young woman into the living room where a little
boy was playing on the floor with a box of bricks next to a small
coffee table that had a colourful jigsaw of farm animals on it.

'Come through. We can talk in here.'

Andrea sat down on one of the kitchen chairs opposite the
woman, who introduced herself as Mary.

'What's this about? Is it about him downstairs?' Mary
pointed down towards the floor.

'How well did you know Peter King?' Andrea asked as she opened her notebook, placing it gently on the table in front of her.

Mary frowned. 'Did?' she repeated. 'How well *did* I know him?' Then she gasped, covering her mouth with her hand. 'Is he...' she whispered the word: 'dead?'

Andrea nodded. 'He is.'

'What happened?' Mary asked. 'Was it suicide?'

'Why do you ask that?'

Mary shrugged. 'Och, I don't know. I'm just guessing after the recent court case. You know about that I expect.'

'No, it wasn't suicide and yes we do.'

Mary gasped again. 'So he was murdered!' she exclaimed.

'Why do you assume he was murdered?' Andrea asked.

'Because you wouldn't be here if he'd had a heart attack would you?'

'Mummy, I need a drink.' The little boy who had been playing in the living room wandered in and tapped Mary's arm.

'Mummy's talking,' Mary tried to say, but he tapped harder. 'OK.' Frazzled, she got up and handed him a carton of apple juice from the fridge. 'Take it in there and be careful with it.'

Andrea smiled as the little boy swept past her and back into the other room.

'Sorry about that,' Mary said.

'It's fine,' Andrea assured her. 'So have you seen anyone hanging around lately? Anyone coming or going from the block that you didn't recognise?'

Mary shook her head. 'No, I can't say I have.' She stood up again and lifted the kettle to check how much water was in it before switching it on. 'I need a cup of coffee. Would you like one?'

'No thank you,' Andrea replied. 'Did you happen to hear any kind of disturbance coming from Mr King's flat recently? His niece has told me that he was being harassed by a couple of young lads.'

Mary rolled her eyes. 'Yes, they come round sometimes, banging, and shouting at him but they couldn't have done it,' she frowned again. 'Nah, they're all bark and no bite.'

'Do you know them, then?' Andrea was curious.

Mary hesitated and nibbled her lip then nodded. 'One of them is my wee cousin.'

'Oh yes and what's your cousin's name?' Andrea was poised to write the name in her notebook.

'His name is Sean,' Mary said and sat back down at the table. 'But you can't possibly think he's had anything to do with that. He's got his faults.' She shook her head. 'My God he's got his faults but...'

Andrea immediately thought about the two names Rona King had given her. That can't be a coincidence. Two people telling the same story. About the same two people.

'My cousin Sean,' Mary continued before Andrea could say anything. 'He's got himself into drugs and my auntie had to put him oot. He'd been nicking money oot of her purse. He hangs aboot with a guy he went to school with. David something. I can't remember his last name. I think it's that lad whose wee brother got killed. The two of them harassed him downstairs. I told Sean to behave himself but,' she shrugged, 'but he ignored me.'

'How well did you know Peter King?'

'I didn't but I knew what he did.' Mary's expression was filled with disgust. 'Sick perv.'

'Did Sean ever mention him to you?' Andrea pushed her.

'No, why would he?' Mary was becoming defensive suddenly.

'So he didn't tell you he wanted to—' Andrea didn't have time to finish when Mary's expression changed.

'Wait a minute,' Mary blasted. 'My wee cousin is a lot of things – a junkie scumbag maybe – but a murderer is not one of them.'

'I wasn't trying to—'

'I think you should leave,' Mary insisted.

Mary's little boy wandered back into the kitchen as the two women stared at each other. Andrea had enough for now. Mary had repeated the names that Rona King had said so she flashed a smile at the toddler and got up to leave.

'I'll see myself out,' she said, holding Mary's gaze while she took a card from her duffle coat pocket. 'If you think of anything that can help us, please give me a call.'

When Mary didn't take the card from Andrea's outstretched hand, she laid it on the worktop behind her.

The state of King's body and the fact there was no forced entry suggested that this murder was personal. That he knew his attacker. According to Mary, King knew Sean Jacobs and David Wilson. The saying – *the lady doth protest too much* – kept spinning in Andrea's mind. Was Mary's defence of her cousin normal or had she overreacted? Was she covering something up? Not only that, could King's death have anything to do with Maggie Ramsay's? It seemed David Wilson was the connection. She dialled Hazel's number to let her know what she'd learned as she walked down the flight of stairs to see that King's body was being removed from his flat. She stopped on the bottom step and watched them carry it carefully and respectfully away while waiting for her call to be answered. Their two victims were connected by harassment. David Wilson was disgusted by the outcome of both their victims' cases. Andrea certainly didn't think David should be ruled out as a suspect. Had the death of his little brother turned him into some kind of vigilante? And if so, how many more people was he prepared to kill?

Chapter Eighteen

Andrea's text had been illuminating, Hazel thought. According to Rona King, David Wilson was also connected to Peter King. Her DC's follow-up phone call after talking to the neighbour was also very interesting. Couldn't be a coincidence, could it? Andrea's use of the word 'vigilante' was a bit much but perhaps she wasn't too far from the truth. On learning that Sean Jacobs was staying at the Skinnergate homeless shelter, she asked Andrea to go over and have a word once she'd finished with Suzanne Gerrard. Rona King had warned Andrea that the lad had a temper, so she needed to be careful. Andrea said she could handle it. With his young body ravaged by drug addiction did Jacobs sound capable of what had been inflicted on King? His cousin certainly didn't think so.

Hazel intended to ask Sandra if the name Peter King meant anything to her or if Maggie might have mentioned him. The fact that both murder victims had been given suspended sentences was a flimsy connection but the niggling fact that David Wilson had verbally abused both victims recently couldn't be ignored. His alibi bothered her. Did Sean ever go with him when he went to harass the Ramsays? The eyewitness, Julian Grant, didn't mention a second person. God, she could do with Tom this afternoon and hoped he'd be cleared fit for work tomorrow.

'Sandra Bell, I'm DCI Todd, come on through.' Hazel held out her hand to the small, plump woman, whose short grey hair had a hint of auburn still clinging to it. She smelled of pears, Hazel thought.

'Thank you so much for seeing me.' Sandra took the outstretched hand and shook it gently.

'Can I get you anything, tea or coffee?' Hazel pointed to the chair on the other side of the desk. 'Please have a seat.'

Sandra shook her head as she sat. 'No thank you, I'm fine. Your officer already asked me that.'

'Good, then what can I do for you?'

The look on the woman's face said she had something important to say. Hazel waited while Sandra gathered her composure, her eyes glistening with tears ready to burst out. She had a feeling something significant was coming.

'Maggie was my best friend,' Sandra began, a thin smile briefly etched on her lips before quickly disappearing. 'We met at school fifty years ago this year. We met on our very first day and were put in the same class.' She smiled. 'Our seats were next to each other. I mean, we lost touch for a while, but we got close again a few years ago.'

'Wow,' Hazel said. 'That's a long time.'

She thought of herself and Cara in that moment. Their own friendship stretched back almost that far. Except they'd had a major betrayal come between them during that time. But it had taken the brutal murder of the man they both loved to bring them back together – sort of. It could never be the same.

'So you see, when she told me her secret, I knew I had to keep it.'

Hazel frowned. 'What secret was that?'

Sandra leaned forward in her chair and Hazel realised the smell of pears was coming from her breath.

'Maggie had met someone else.' Sandra's face flushed pink as she spoke.

The man in the red Audi. It had to be. The obvious question sprang to mind immediately.

'Did Samuel know?'

Sandra shook her head. 'Maggie didn't think so. I told her to be careful. She knew what Sam was like.'

Hazel frowned at that comment. 'And what exactly was Sam like?'

Sandra fiddled with the cuff of her navy cardigan and Hazel spotted the start of fraying around the edge. A habit she'd had for a time, perhaps.

'I told her, I warned her...' She stopped fidgeting and laid her hands on the table between them. 'He was always a little overbearing, right from when they first got together but the past few years, he's been so controlling. Always wanting to know where she's been, what she's been doing and especially who she's been speaking to.'

Interesting.

'Did this control ever end in physical violence that you're aware of?' Hazel asked but knew from years in the job that a man didn't have to lift a hand to his wife to hurt and abuse her.

'I don't think so; nothing that I ever saw, and Maggie certainly never told me it had,' she shrugged then dropped her eyes to the floor. 'But she wouldn't, would she? Not if she were scared.'

'And was she scared, do you think?' Hazel suggested. 'After knowing her for so many years, would you say you knew her well enough to spot the signs?'

Sandra sighed again, tears glistening in her eyes. 'I don't know.' Her voice trembled.

'What was your relationship with Sam like?'

Sandra sniffed and reached into her pocket for a tissue to dab her face. 'Erm, it was OK I suppose. It's just...' the short pause told Hazel something else was coming. 'Recently he'd been...' It seemed she was searching for the right words, so Hazel waited, unwilling to put words into this potentially crucial witness's mouth.

'My gut.' Sandra patted her stomach. 'My gut said something wasn't right. Do you know what I mean?' She stopped and blew her nose. 'I'm sorry, I'm not making much sense, am I? I wondered if he'd found out about the other man.'

'You're doing great,' Hazel encouraged her, wanting to move the conversation onto this new man in Maggie's life. 'So, this new relationship, tell me about that. Did you ever meet him?'

Sandra's eyes widened in time with a short breath. 'Gosh, no, I never met him. He was someone she met at AA. You know, after the accident,' she said quietly. 'She said he was really helpful and supportive to her when she first started going to meetings and things just evolved from there. They started meeting for coffee outside meetings which became lunch dates. I know she'd told Sam a few times recently that she'd been with me when she'd been meeting with him.'

'So you covered for your friend.'

Hazel's suggestion made Sandra's eyes fill up again and she nodded.

'I knew it was wrong, but Maggie was my best friend and she needed whatever it was she had with this man. It, I mean he… he really seemed to help her after what happened. She said she was in love with him.'

Hazel knew intense relationships often sprang from mutual addiction issues, whether that was from a support or enabling perspective. Whether it was love she had her doubts.

'So do you think this relationship was serious, then?'

'Oh yes,' Sandra nodded emphatically. 'Maggie was planning on leaving Sam.'

Hazel knew that the most dangerous time for a victim of domestic abuse is when they've decided to leave. It can trigger a violent outburst from the abuser in response, but Maggie's death didn't fit that profile. Sam was at home and Maggie's killer was behind the wheel of a stolen vehicle. He had the perfect alibi. He was an incredibly intelligent man after all.

'Do you think he knew about her plans?'

'Honestly, I don't know any more.' She seemed flustered again. 'I don't know if I've helped or hindered your investigation, but I thought you should know.' The volume of her voice lowered to almost a whisper. 'I owe it to Maggie.'

'Maggie was very lucky to have a friend like you and I'm always grateful for any information. I promise I'm going to do everything I can to find out what happened to your friend.'

Sandra's thin smile quickly dissolved. 'Thank you.'

'One more thing,' Hazel continued. 'Do you know the name of the man she was seeing? Or better still do you know how we can contact him?'

To see Sandra shaking her head was disappointing.

On a hunch, Hazel asked. 'Have you got any idea what kind of car he drives? Could it have been a red Audi?'

'No, I'm sorry but I do know he was listed in her phone as "Brenda" if that helps.'

Yes! A lead.

'That's incredibly helpful,' Hazel acknowledged. 'Listen, does the name Peter King mean anything to you? Did you ever hear Maggie mention someone by that name?'

When Sandra shook her head at that question too, Hazel was disappointed but, if she was honest, not surprised. The chance of the two victims being connected in life seemed slim. Perhaps David Wilson's involvement was just coincidence. She had to hope now that the tech boys could retrieve this mystery man's details from what was left of Maggie's phone.

Chapter Nineteen

Andrea rang the doorbell of the small council bungalow not far from Peter King's block of flats. Her stomach rumbled when she realised she'd not eaten for hours. Thankfully, she'd had a Snickers bar, which she had devoured and half a bottle of water in her car.

Talking to the neighbours in the rest of King's block had proved fruitless. Most residents were not home – or not answering – and Andrea had pushed her card through their letterboxes, and the one neighbour she did manage to catch spoke very little English, so she had arranged for an officer who could speak Romanian to go round instead.

She stamped her feet on the step of Suzanne Gerrard's front door and blew warm air into her freezing cold hands, wishing she'd not left her gloves on the passenger seat of her car. Despite wearing her boots with the fluffy inner lining, her feet were freezing too. She cursed that she hadn't worn the thick wool socks her mum had bought her for Christmas. She rapped the letterbox loudly a couple of times before a woman's voice sounded inside.

'Hang on, I'm coming, I'm coming.' Footsteps moved slowly closer until the front door squeaked open.

'Yes,' Suzanne Gerrard said without emotion, her eyes moving briefly to the block of flats to their left.

Andrea held up her identification. 'Hello, are you Suzanne Gerrard?'

Suzanne took Andrea's ID out of her hand and read it carefully. She looked from the card and back to Andrea's face a few times then handed it back to her.

'Yes that's me, what can I do for you?' Suzanne replied finally.

Andrea was immediately struck by how thin she was. Her collar bones protruded, and her cheekbones were prominent. Andrea corrected herself, hoping that Suzanne hadn't noticed the shock on her face.

'Would it be all right to come in for a few minutes? I have a few questions I'd like to ask you.'

'Questions about what?' Suzanne asked, leaning heavily on a stick.

A woman pushing a screaming toddler in a buggy walked past behind them.

'It won't take long,' Andrea pressed, without answering Suzanne's question directly.

Suzanne sighed. 'You'd better come in then, I suppose.' She moved slowly away from the door.

Andrea followed her inside and closed the front door behind them.

'Come through,' Suzanne said as she made her way into a room to the right. 'Excuse the mess.'

'Thanks.'

Suzanne sat down in an armchair by the living room window. Next to the chair was a large birdcage with a red and blue parrot in it. The bird started to squawk as soon as Suzanne sat down.

'I'm sorry, do you mind if I let him out? He'll keep making this racket until I do.'

Andrea wasn't exactly happy about it, but she agreed. 'Sure, no problem,' she said anxiously.

'He'll not harm you. He's just a big softy, really.'

Andrea was reluctant to agree with that as she watched the huge bird sitting on Suzanne's shoulders, pecking her hair with his sharp beak.

'What did you want to ask me?' Suzanne continued and held her hand out for the bird to rest on before lifting her hand in the direction of his cage. 'There, that's better,' she said as he flapped his wings and landed on the top of the bars. 'He just wanted to come out to see that I was OK.'

'That's nice.' Andrea heard the anxiety in her own voice and felt a little silly. She steered the topic of conversation back to the reason for her visit. 'Do you know a man called David Wilson?'

A look of alarm crossed Suzanne's face. 'Yes, yes, I do, David is my boyfriend. Is he OK?'

'Yes, don't worry,' Andrea reassured her. 'David is fine.'

'Oh thank God,' Suzanne lifted a hand and pressed it against her chest. 'For a minute there I thought something had happened to him.' She frowned. 'Why are you asking about David?'

Andrea watched carefully for how Suzanne reacted to her next words.

'David has said he was with you yesterday morning. Can you confirm that for me?'

'Why on earth…' Suzanne seemed flustered. 'Why are you asking me that? Do you think he's done something?'

'Was he with you?' Andrea persevered, thinking that was a strange thing to ask.

'Are you asking me that because he needs an alibi for something? What the hell does David need an alibi for?' Suzanne insisted.

'Was he with you or not?'

It seemed to take Suzanne a minute to think before answering.

'Erm, yes he was. We met at about nine thirty, had coffee and then we spent the rest of the day together. Why do you want to know?'

'And where did you have coffee?' Andrea wanted to double-check that the couple were in fact where she'd said they were. It would help if others could corroborate it too.

'What?' Suzanne asked. 'Why on earth does that matter?'

Andrea waited, watched, taking a breath, allowing Suzanne the chance to think, to decide that she should tell Andrea what she wanted to know. Her strategy worked quickly.

'Willows,' Suzanne told her. 'We met at Willows.'

Andrea made a note of that information.

'Does the name Maggie Ramsay mean anything to you?'

'Of course it does,' Suzanne sneered. 'She killed David's little brother. What's she got to do with this?'

'Maggie Ramsay was killed in a hit and run accident yesterday morning outside her house.'

Suzanne's eyes stretched so wide, her thin, wispy eyebrows disappeared into her blonde fringe as she gasped. 'What, are you serious?'

Andrea nodded, then saw the look of comprehension on Suzanne's face.

'Oh my God.' Suzanne clasped a hand firmly on her mouth then quickly pulled it away. 'You think David killed her!'

'I'm here to clarify the alibi that David gave us for his where-abouts at the time of her death,' Andrea said firmly, alarmed to see Suzanne get up awkwardly from the armchair.

'Get out,' Suzanne shouted and pointed to the living room door. 'David was with me and even if he wasn't, he wouldn't do something as awful as that.' Tears filled her eyes. 'He is the kindest, sweetest man I've ever met and if that woman was murdered, then, then…' Her words were spewing out with angry tears. 'She deserved it.'

Suzanne limped slowly towards the front door and snatched it open. 'Get out of my house and don't ever come back here spreading lies about him.'

'Can you confirm for me that the firm you work for has been—' Andrea made a futile attempt to keep going.

'Yes, my firm has been putting together a civil case, if that's what you were about to say. What has that got to do with anything?' Suzanne's words were hostile.

'Is that how you and David met?' Andrea persevered.

'How David and I met is none of your business,' Suzanne sneered, her hostility growing. 'Now, if you don't mind, I've answered your question. Please leave.'

Andrea had barely stepped outside when the front door was slammed in her face. Twice in one day she'd been unceremoniously removed from a house. That couldn't be a coincidence. She pressed Hazel's number as she walked back to her car. 'Yes, it's me, Suzanne Gerrard confirms Wilson was with her – if somewhat reluctantly and angrily.' She listened to Hazel's response. 'Sure, yes, I'm on my way now.'

Suzanne stared at the back of the retreating detective, barely able to disguise the sneer curling her face. How dare she? She picked up her phone and scrolled the contacts. Hitting the option next to the name she needed, she waited anxiously for the call to be answered.

'Come on, come on, pick up.' Suzanne rolled her eyes and huffed on hearing the call go to voicemail. 'Call me back as soon as you get this. It's urgent. You're not going to believe what's just happened.'

Chapter Twenty

David Wilson paced back and forth, waiting for Sean Jacobs to come outside and meet him. That detective had told him all he needed to know. If Sean thought coming round and bullying his mum was all right, he was very much mistaken. That was too much. Even for him. Their friendship only went so far. Did he think because he'd helped David, he could take advantage like that? Like his good deed was an open-ended invitation to take advantage.

'Awright, man.' Sean slurred his words and swayed a little off balance because of the Temazepam he'd taken. He was immediately stunned by the speed of the attack.

David had him by the throat and was pinning him to the wall outside the men's homeless shelter. The elderly couple taking a shortcut through the vennel were appalled and sped up to avoid the altercation, muttering something under their breath that David neither heard nor cared about.

'What the fuck, man?' Sean fought back, but his efforts to push his friend off were futile against David's fury, even though he was the taller by two inches. His intoxication meant his coordination was all but gone, along with the strength in his limbs that felt like jelly against the onslaught.

'If I ever hear you've been harassing my mum again, I'll do more than threaten you, you piece of shit. I'll rip your fucking throat out, ya got that!' David oozed venom as drops of spittle flew into Sean's face. 'No more, Sean. I said we were even, and I meant it,' he growled, low and breathy, into his face.

'Oy, what the hell's going on?' The manager of the shelter had opened her office window after hearing raised voices. 'Quit it now. I'm calling the police,' she warned them and could be heard giving details to the operator.

David was undeterred and squeezed his fingers tighter round Sean's throat, pinning him closer to the brickwork. He pressed his face right up to Sean's. So close he could smell coffee on Sean's breath.

'My mum's had enough to deal with. She doesny need scumbags like you hassling her for money,' he hissed low next to his ear. 'Coz that's what you were there fur, wasn't it? You thought you'd be able to rob her while she was passed oot on the couch. Or were you planning to try and sweet talk her into giving you it? Was that it? You hink she's some kind of soft touch don't you because she's ay pished.'

Sean, subdued by Temazepam, struggled to defend himself, frantically patting David's hands on his neck until David's body was swept backwards by two of the shelter's care workers. Sean fell to the pavement on his knees, gasping and clutching his throat. He coughed and spat onto the ground. Nausea burned into his throat as his coffee threatened to return.

'What the fuck, man?' he protested hoarsely and coughed again before falling onto his side, clutching his fingers to his throat.

'Gerroff me!' David snapped and fought until he'd managed to wriggle free, sending one of the workers flying with an elbow to the stomach.

He surged for Sean again, flattening the prostrate teenager on his back and raining blows down on his face, until blood sprayed from his wounds onto the pavement and wall.

'The police are on their way,' David heard the woman in the window saying but her voice sounded like it was inside a cotton wool cloud as he continued to pound Sean's face despite the best efforts of the care workers to get him to stop. He snatched a handful of Sean's hair in his hand and started slamming his head onto the concrete as the sound of sirens got louder.

Chapter Twenty-One

Hazel poured the dregs of her cup of tea down the sink and rinsed her mug under the hot tap then left it to drain just as a text hit her phone in her trouser pocket. She dried her hands on the tea towel then sniffed it, turning away at the smell before tossing it onto a pile they put aside for the cleaners. She grabbed her phone, relieved to see it was a message from Tom.

> They're letting me home. I'll be in early tomorrow
> to catch up.

'All right, boss.' Andrea's voice from behind her made her turn round before she had a chance to answer his text.

'Hello, Andrea, I hear David Wilson got to Jacobs before you did.' Hazel typed Tom a quick reply then tucked her phone away again.

> Great. I'll see you then. Take care.

'Aye, he did that. Sean Jacobs has been taken to A and E. He's in a right state. The lad's face is pretty messed up,' Andrea informed her.

'Have we any idea what the fight was about?' Hazel asked as she headed out of the small kitchen and into the incident room.

'Not yet. Do you want me to talk to him?' Andrea suggested.

'No, we'll do it together,' Hazel told her. 'Let's just go over what we've got so far – oh, and I've just had a message from Tom. They're not keeping him in. Thank God.'

'Yes, he texted me too. Doc wanted him to have tomorrow off but he's persuaded them to sign him fit, apparently.'

Billy's concerned expression caught Hazel's attention.

'What's up?' she asked.

'Can I have a quick word?' Billy said, his usual smiling face nowhere to be seen. He flashed a brief glance at Andrea then back to Hazel.

'Sure, come on through,' Hazel pointed towards her office.

'Thanks,' Billy replied and followed quickly behind, closing the door after them.

'What's up?' Hazel repeated.

'Look, I know we're short-handed with Tom not being here, but can I go home?'

'Is everything OK?' Hazel asked.

Billy sighed. 'I'd rather not go into details,' he informed her.

This wasn't like Billy so Hazel didn't hesitate to let him go. He thanked her and assured her he would be in first thing. She headed back to where Andrea was sitting at her desk. Andrea was about to speak when Superintendent Daly's face at the door caught her attention.

Great, that's all I bloody need.

Hazel smiled at him as he approached the evidence board with Maggie Ramsay and Peter King's photos on it.

'A word, DCI Todd,' Daly said without acknowledging that Andrea was also there, his expression impossible to read as he walked ahead of her into her office.

Andrea shot her a concerned glance and Hazel tried to shrug without being seen before following her boss. She closed the door quietly behind her, irritated that he'd taken the seat behind her desk. Her seat. Leaving her standing.

'Is everything OK, sir?'

'You tell me, DCI Todd.'

It took Hazel a moment to process what he meant. 'Sir?'

'Two brutal murders in less than two days,' he said. 'And one of your detectives is sick.'

Hazel didn't like the insinuation that was coming here.

'DI Newton will be back on duty tomorrow, sir. He sustained—'

Daly's hand waved away the rest of her comment. 'One of your victims was Peter King,' he said, more abruptly than Hazel was happy with.

'That's correct, sir, we found his body this afternoon.'

'The newspapers are going to have field day with that,' he grumbled. 'That's all we need.'

'I'm sorry, sir, I'm not sure what you mean.'

'It has occurred to you that we have a vigilante on our hands.' He pointed out, with more than a hint of sarcasm in his tone. 'That the public are going to support what this lunatic is doing if we don't stop them quickly.'

'It's too soon to speculate, sir,' Hazel replied, hoping to cut him off. 'There are several lines of inquiry I want to follow. Maggie Ramsay, for example, was planning to leave her controlling husband.'

Daly's face changed. 'Sam was nothing of the sort. Who told you that?'

The real reason for his visit became clear.

'How well did you know the victim's husband, sir?'

'That's irrelevant. What is relevant right now is…' Daly's phone ringing in his shirt pocket stole his attention.

On seeing the identity of the caller he got up and left without even saying goodbye, leaving Hazel bamboozled by his visit. He'd seemed genuinely rattled by thoughts of a vigilante and what it meant for them. He was right, though; they didn't want the public getting wind and hailing this guy a hero. The sooner this was quashed the better. She saw that Andrea had opened her mouth to say hello to him, but he'd walked past again as if she wasn't there. The sad truth was that even in the twenty-first century, female officers had to work twice as hard or shout twice as loud to be seen and heard. Hazel certainly felt that. The years as a DI seemed to go on forever until she'd won this job. Using the word 'win' wasn't an exaggeration because it had felt like a competition all the way. Being passed over twice had stung.

'Rude,' Hazel whispered and walked back out of the door he'd left open.

'What was that all about?' Andrea asked.

'Doesn't matter, it'll keep,' she replied, keen to put his outburst out of her mind for now.

She lifted the handset on her desk and dialled the front desk. 'Hi, it's DCI Todd. Has David Wilson's solicitor arrived yet?' She glanced down at her watch as she spoke. Her shoulders dropped on hearing that the answer was no. 'OK, thanks. Call my mobile when they do, will you?' she said and hung up. Hazel checked her watch again. 'Grab yer coat. Let's nip across to Hortons for something to eat while we're waiting. I don't know about you but I'm starving.'

She'd not had to ask Andrea twice and the two detectives walked the short distance to Tim Hortons. They'd have time for a quick bite, it seemed, before interviewing David Wilson who was safely tucked up awaiting his solicitor.

'Happy anniversary, by the way,' Hazel said, before tucking into a potato wedge. She smiled at the confusion on Andrea's face and unzipped her jacket in the warmth of the restaurant.

'Anniversary?'

'You've been on my team for two years now,' Hazel reminded her.

Andrea's eyes widened. 'Wow, has it really been two years already?' she replied and slurped from a large cup of Coke.

Hazel nodded. She couldn't agree more. Where the hell had the time gone? She swallowed the rest of the potato wedge and wiped the grease from her lips with a napkin. She picked up a chicken strip but before taking a bite, she asked curiously, 'Had you always wanted to be a detective?'

Andrea swallowed her bite of food and took another long sip of her drink. 'Kind of. It was when I was at university doing my psychology degree that I really started thinking about it. I saw the direct entry course and thought, why not?' She shrugged.

'Why not, indeed.' Hazel smiled. Although initially she'd not been too sure about adding a direct entry detective to her team, Andrea Graham had proved herself to be an efficient and effective member straight away. Her insights into human behaviour were incredibly useful in this job. Hadn't she been good with the girls who'd fallen into prostitution too, in their last harrowing case, the one that Hazel could never forget, the one with Andrea seeming to know how to understand and communicate with the girls caught up in that case.

She knew, though, that Andrea's route into the job was still frowned on by other officers who still believed only years of beat experience made a great detective. Once upon a time, Hazel had thought likewise.

'What's up with Billy?' Andrea asked as if trying to steer the conversation away from herself.

'He's all right,' Hazel replied. 'Something came up at home that he needed to sort out. That's all.'

A text told Hazel that they had to eat up quickly. Wilson's solicitor had finally arrived.

Chapter Twenty-Two

'No comment,' Wilson replied to another of Hazel's questions about his assault on Sean Jacobs.

'So you'd like us to believe you decided, on a whim, to beat the living shit out of Sean Jacobs, a man who, by all accounts, is an old school friend of yours,' Hazel persisted, fearing that everyone in the room could see the hot flush that was burning through her. What she wouldn't give for a nice blast of the Arctic air outside to sweep through there!

'No comment,' Wilson repeated while throwing a look of contempt her way.

Hazel thought that his mood was considerably darker. A worrying sign that he had a volatile personality, prone to mood swings. Maybe she could use that to her advantage now, persuade his tongue to loosen.

'What happened, David? You seemed happy earlier, especially when I told you about Maggie Ramsay's death.'

She watched his jaw tighten and relax briefly at her remark, his breath exiting in almost a growl, as the solicitor whispered something in his ear.

'No comment.'

'Some people might not blame you, of course,' she persisted. 'I mean, who wouldn't be happy to see her dead after what she did to your family? In fact, some might suggest you killed her.'

David's solicitor intervened. 'I have to insist you stop that line of questioning, Detective. Mr Wilson is here to discuss the alleged assault on Mr Jacobs. Nothing else.'

Hazel's eyes met David's and she was sure she saw the hint of a smirk appear then fade quickly.

'No comment,' he repeated as a loud knock landed on the interview room door.

'A stolen car, David, what a genius idea. Was it just a random vehicle or did you plan that bit as well?' Hazel pressed on, undeterred. This was her chance. 'I mean you did a great job of pretending not to know she was dead. I'll give you that.'

David frowned at her and nibbled on his thumbnail. He looked at his solicitor.

'I really must insist this stops right now,' the solicitor repeated.

Hazel took a breath. 'I get it,' she said gently. 'If Liam was my baby brother—'

David slammed his palm against the table and leaned across until his face was so close to Hazel's she could feel the heat of his breath.

'You don't get to say my brother's name,' he snapped. 'None of you gave a shit about him before.'

The knock landed on the interview room door again, this time louder.

'Come in,' Hazel called out, irritated by the interruption.

A female uniformed officer came in and handed her a folded piece of paper before exiting but not before David's eyes devoured her slim frame. Hazel opened the note, its contents not exactly a surprise. Sean Jacobs had said he didn't want to press charges. David probably knew already and had been stalling until confirmation came through. She held the note out for Andrea to read then leaned over to switch off the tape. Hazel didn't have enough evidence yet to charge him with Maggie Ramsay's or Peter King's murder. There were no eyewitnesses putting him there at those exact times. No DNA. She had no choice for now.

'Interview terminated at 17.44.'

'You get off home,' Hazel said to Andrea while she stared out of the office window to see a smiling David Wilson get into the passenger seat of a Volkswagen Polo driven by Suzanne Gerrard. 'There's not much more we can do tonight.'

The woman was exactly as Andrea had described. She was so thin and pale.

'Thanks, boss,' Andrea replied and grabbed her duffle coat from the back of her chair.

'Thanks for all your good work today. I know I gave you a lot to do.' Hazel knew the importance of showing her appreciation.

'You're welcome. See you in the morning,' Andrea smiled.

A text landed on Hazel's phone. It was from Rachel Fox. Hazel looked up to ensure she was alone before reading it. An involuntary response. She still didn't want people to know the two women had become friends, of sorts. Their strange connection was something that most people couldn't understand when their friendship had been born out of such horror a year ago. A tragedy that had pulled the two together.

> Just checking in. Hope you're well x

That made Hazel smile and she was about to reply when another text chirped. She rolled her eyes at the sender of this one and pressed *open message*. Cara. Her heart sank.

> I'm coming over. Put the kettle on xx

Hazel pressed Cara's number whilst trying desperately to come up with a believable excuse to put her off. Why did she still feel the need to save this woman's feelings? Hazel's numerous late night conversations with Tom couldn't come up with an answer. One suggestion he made was that Hazel was just by far the better person which had made them both laugh and pour more wine.

When her call to Cara went straight to voicemail twice, Hazel resigned herself to her unwanted visitor. After such a damn long day all she wanted to do was put her feet up and chill.

Chapter Twenty-Three

'Cara, you'd better come in,' Hazel said reluctantly, her smile not as genuine as it looked.

The last thing she felt like doing was having a forced heart-to-heart with her. It had been a trying day and wasting time on the farce that was David Wilson's interview had left her exhausted. That and her damn thyroid – which reminded her; she really should make an appointment to have her bloods done soon. She felt there was a possibility that she needed the dose increased. Between the tiredness and her skin drying out further she figured it was time for a check-up. What with that and the menopause insomnia, caused mainly by nocturnal pissing and hot flushes, her energy levels weren't exactly top notch. A bath, a glass or two of pinot and an early night was what she wanted. She would only have two glasses, she'd promised herself. She could stop at that. She had to.

Cara leaned in and hugged her. 'I hope you don't mind me turning up unannounced,' she said and stepped deeper inside Hazel's flat.

Unannounced? Didn't your text announce your arrival?

'No problem,' Hazel lied and closed the front door, stopping to lean her forehead on the frame briefly. She exhaled a long, slow breath before locking the door. She followed Cara to the kitchen where she'd poured herself a glass of wine and was taking her cream woollen coat off and slinging it across the back of the chair next to her.

'What have you been up to?' Hazel began, realising the effort had to be made if she was going to get rid of her soon. 'Any joy on the job front yet?'

Cara screwed up her face. 'No, nobody is taking on women over fifty, are they, these days?'

'I'm sorry,' Hazel said, and perhaps she meant it. It couldn't be easy to be fifty-plus and unemployed.

Rick's life insurance had come to both of them, which was as much of a surprise to Hazel as it was to Cara. Hazel had tried to say she didn't want it, but Cara had insisted even if it did leave her a little short after losing her job during the pandemic. Hazel hadn't touched a penny of her share and assured Cara it was there if she needed it. Seventy-five grand wasn't an amount to be sniffed at. Something about spending it made Hazel shudder. They weren't married when he was killed. Did he feel guilty? Was that why she was still named in his will? It would have made sense if they'd had kids, but they didn't. But now there was this new inheritance. This could change things.

'Something will come up,' Hazel continued. 'I know it will.' She patted Cara's shoulder as she passed, pouring herself a glass of wine before flopping down opposite. 'Any more word from the solicitor?'

'You look like shit,' Cara said, seemingly ignoring her comments.

'Thanks for that,' Hazel replied drily. 'You always say the nicest things.'

'Are you still not sleeping?'

Hazel scrunched up her face before gulping a large swig of the chilled white wine. God, that was good. If Cara hadn't been watching she'd have guzzled the entire glass in two before refilling. That first glass always helped, followed by the second, then the third…

'When I sleep, I sleep. It's staying asleep that's the issue,' Hazel explained. Her night-time waking to pee probably wasn't helped by the excessive drinking but without it Hazel feared she'd not get to sleep in the first place. It seemed she was trapped in a vicious circle.

'Have you been back to the doctor?' Cara suggested.

'When have I got time for doctors?' Hazel scoffed and waved away her suggestion.

'You've got to make time.'

Cara's suggestion made Hazel's skin crawl. How did this woman still think she had a right to give her advice? She was lucky that Hazel still spoke to her at all. Anyway, that was all well and good for Cara to say. She had bags of time. She didn't have murderers to catch. Hazel sank the second half of her wine and refilled the glass before handing her a sarcastic retort.

'I'll just tell killers to take a few days off then shall I?'

'I hardly think that's appropriate do you?' Cara bit back.

'Have you eaten?' Hazel asked, ignoring Cara's reprimand, and scrolled through her phone to the takeaway app. 'I am starving.' Which wasn't a lie despite the quick bite she'd had with Andrea although that felt like hours ago. Hazel's appetite was an enigma these days. Either she was famished or just not hungry at all. Just another one of mother menopause's delights, she thought.

'What are you ordering?' Cara sipped from her glass then reached for her bag.

'It's on me, put your money away. I could really go for Chinese, what about you?' Hazel drank another large gulp then looked up to see the disapproving look growing on Cara's face. 'What?'

'Do you think you should maybe slow down a bit, mate?'

'Who are you, my mother?' Hazel snapped but instantly regretted it. She hated to think Cara had seen her lose her cool. She put down her glass and focussed on the food order. 'I'm sorry.' She quietly conceded.

The short awkward silence that always descended when Cara mentioned the booze was quickly swept away.

'I'll take a sweet and sour,' Cara said. 'Get me it with fried rice, would you?' She sipped from her glass.

'Sure, no problem,' Hazel spoke more softly, staring at the glass, wishing she could grab hold of it and neck the contents.

The text that landed should have been a distraction, but it wasn't, and Cara's questioning didn't help.

'Who's that?'

Hazel couldn't tell her the truth. 'It's, erm, Tom.'

'Doesn't he know you're off duty?'

'Yes, it's just, he's erm, he got hurt on a job today and…' She felt a hot flush threaten to burn through her with the lie.

'God, is he all right?' Cara asked.

Why did Cara always make her feel so guilty?

'Yes, yes, he's fine now, don't worry. Just a bump on the head,' Hazel smiled. 'Docs are just being cautious, that's all.'

'Oh no what a shame, poor guy.' Cara took a sip. 'I like Tom.'

'Yes, me too, he's a good lad.' But Tom was way more than that to Hazel. He was her best friend.

Hazel's mind drifted away from Cara's words. She read the text from Rachel again while Cara continued to witter on, about what Hazel didn't know because she'd zoned her out.

> I meant what I said. I'm available if you need to talk. It doesn't have to be about what happened. I'm a good listener. We could maybe meet for a quick coffee before you start work tomorrow. I can be at the Costa in the retail park if you fancy it. I know that's where you sometimes grab a coffee before work. Just text me in the morning. Look, I've seen the news. It might be good to talk
>
> x

DI Tom Newton paid the taxi driver and walked along the path towards the house he shared with his partner John. He'd been disappointed that John hadn't been able to collect him but the fifteen-quid taxi fare wasn't the problem. It wasn't just the taxi. Coming home to an empty house didn't fill Tom with joy, either. He stared at the lights in the houses on either side of theirs. One of their neighbours, a lovely young nurse, hadn't shut her curtains yet and waved when she saw Tom. Tom smiled at her then took another look at the darkness in his own window and turned, grateful to see that the taxi driver hadn't left yet. He jogged quickly back to the vehicle and opened the passenger door, startling the driver.

'Change of plan,' Tom said.

Chapter Twenty-Four

The sound of the security buzzer rang out minutes after Hazel had managed to persuade Cara that she had a headache and told her that she wanted to go to bed. It had been surprisingly easier than she'd anticipated. She laid down the two wine glasses and rubbed her temples.

'Hello.' Hazel answered the buzzer and smiled on hearing the voice on the end of the line. 'Oh hey, come on up.'

Hazel unlocked the front door for her unexpected visitor.

'I'm not interrupting anything, am I?' Tom asked and closed the door behind him.

'No, not at all. How are you feeling?'

Hazel was pleased to see Tom looked better than the last time she'd seen him.

'Och, it was just a bump,' he skimmed his fingers over his brow. 'I'm fine. How did you get on today? Are we any further forward?'

Hazel smiled and held up the wine bottle to offer him a glass. 'You know we're off duty, don't you?' She checked the time on her watch. 10pm. It had been a long day.

Tom frowned. 'What? Erm, yes, I'm sorry, I know,' he said then shook his head. 'No wine for me. They've given me painkillers for my head.'

Hazel looked at the wine bottle in her hand, realising that her heart rate had increased. She chose to put the bottle back in the fridge instead of having another glass. She'd already had enough although she knew that the truth was, if Tom hadn't turned up, she'd have necked the rest of it.

'I bet John was pleased to see you were all right. My ears should have been burning,' she smiled. 'He must have been fuming. Me sending you out and getting you hurt again. He'll be having my guts for garters when he sees me again.'

Memories of the time Tom had been seriously hurt last year made her shudder. The case that had changed Hazel and Rachel Fox's lives forever and had thrust the two women together. Hazel quickly spotted that Tom wasn't smiling back.

'John wasn't in when I got home so…' Tom shrugged.

'Oh,' Hazel replied and flopped down on another of her kitchen chairs. 'Do you want to talk about it?' Hadn't he been there for her when Rick left her, and some? That was an understatement.

Tom sighed. 'No, I don't.' He shook his head. 'Get me up to speed on the case instead.'

'Cases, plural,' she told him.

Tom's eyes widened. 'What?'

'Have you heard of a guy called Peter King?' Hazel asked.

Tom nodded. 'The name sounds familiar. Who is he?'

'Our second victim,' Hazel announced. 'That's who.'

'Is he connected to Maggie Ramsay?' Tom asked.

'Not exactly but David Wilson is connected to both of them. David and his friend Sean Jacobs have a history of harassing and abusing Peter King.'

'What do you mean by abusing? Who is this guy?' Tom pressed her, rubbing his brow as he spoke.

'Are you OK?' Hazel was concerned. 'Do you need me to get you anything? Do you want a glass of water?' She stood up and grabbed a glass from the cupboard. 'I'll get you a glass of water,' she repeated in a fluster.

'I'm fine. Doctor said I might have a headache. Scans were clear. I'm all right, honestly.'

'You look tired, Tom,' Hazel pointed out then realised she was stifling a yawn herself.

'You don't look exactly bright-eyed and bushy-tailed yourself,' Tom smiled then yawned, too.

Hazel couldn't disagree. The bags under her eyes had bags. She knew that.

'Are you still having trouble sleeping?' Tom's question took her by surprise.

'Is it that obvious?'

Tom's smile was meant to reassure. 'Maybe you need a holiday,' he suggested.

'Aye, maybe you're right.' Spending time with her dad would be good. Or renting a cottage in the middle of nowhere with no Wi-Fi or phone signal. Hazel would enjoy that too. 'When all this is over, maybe.'

'Do you think David Wilson is good for both murders?' Tom asked, his expression more serious. 'He's just a young lad. How did King die? How is he connected to Maggie Ramsay?'

'Peter King was killed in a very different way to Maggie Ramsay,' Hazel began. 'He was stabbed multiple times. I think his attacker was in a fit of blind rage, given the state his body was found in. It felt more personal.'

Tom's eyes widened. 'Peter King, I know who he is now.' He screwed up his face in disgust. 'He was the guy that got a suspended sentence for possession of thousands of indecent images of young teenage girls.'

Hazel nodded. 'That's him.'

'Is that the connection? The suspended sentences?' Tom suggested. 'Jesus, a suspended sentence for that! What were they thinking?'

'I know, you're so right and yes it could be,' Hazel agreed.

'Have we considered it might be the same judge that handed the sentences down?'

'I have considered that.' Hazel replied which wasn't a lie. She just hadn't shared that with the team yet.

'They could be in danger, too?' Tom suggested. 'If these killings are connected by a vigilante. I'll check the details on the judge or judges in the morning.'

'Thanks, Tom.'

Hazel knew he was right, and she hoped the two murders were connected but knew things were not always that easy. The nagging feeling that Samuel might have known about Maggie's mystery man cast some doubt in her mind. Until he'd been conclusively ruled out then Samuel's name was still on her list.

Black Eyes, It was collected the night the party ended
were eaten in a blur from the room where she might have been. The
young couple than drunken might have been tidy room knows
dresses, that contains drunk in the room. Until the drunk
to harshly tidied into drunk, under attack, and I don't know us

Chapter Twenty-Five

The hand poked through the small gap in the open window.
Not very security conscious, are they? He pushed hard against
the window frame, nicking his skin slightly, until he'd got his
hand inside. He jimmied the window lock until it became free
and opened it with ease.

'Bingo,' he muttered under his breath and licked the tiny
trickle of blood from the back of his hand before wiping it dry
on his jeans. A small price to pay.

He was inside the Ramsays' kitchen. Taking a long breath, he
eyed the room with its modern fittings; a cooker hood above
a huge double oven and six hob rings beneath. Clearly a top
of the range cooker. He noted the immaculate decor and the
fridge freezer with one of those fancy water dispensers with an
ice tray next to it. Their lives were more than comfortable; they
lived extremely well. Wanted for nothing. The anger fizzled
from the soles of his feet, and he felt it burning his skin. With
clenched fists, he punched the wall, making barely a dent until
he punched again, this time jarring his wrist.

'Argh.' He pulled his hand back and cradled it in the other
momentarily.

The pain did nothing but fuel his rage. He screamed into
the silence and ripped the fridge from its place and watched it
crash to the floor at his feet, knocking off a glass bowl filled with
fruit, some of which he had only ever seen in supermarkets. It
crashed to the ground sending tiny splinters of glass across the
dark wood floor. He allowed his eyes to drift around the room,
coming to rest on the huge dining table set immaculately with a

long, red cotton runner draped across the centre. A clear crystal vase of daffodils took centre stage.

With one swift move, the vase was swept into his hand and hurled against the wall, splintering into chunks, spraying water everywhere. He pressed his foot onto the flowers, crushing them into the floor. Pressing so hard, his toes ached.

He ripped open all the drawers in the kitchen and tossed the contents to every corner of the room, staring at the carnage he'd created, breathing heavily, savouring every piece of chaos he'd wreaked. He snatched a large knife from the block on the counter and made his way out of the kitchen. He'd only just begun.

Expecting to be greeted by the two yapping terriers, he crept into the living room to find their beds empty. Even those dogs lived well, with large beds filled with soft cushions and lots of toys. He grabbed a foam rubber pig that grunted when it moved and slashed it over and over with the knife then tossed it back inside the bed. The dog's cosy blanket was ripped in two then thrown into a bin next to the coffee table. He upturned both dog beds and smashed his foot into the bases, breaking the hardened plastic down the middle before throwing them across the room, the snapping sound sending a thrill through his body.

His heart racing, he turned, focussing on the luxury sofa behind him. He squeezed the knife tight in his grip, beads of sweat glistening above his eye, threatening to sting his eyes as it trickled down past his eyebrow. He quickly wiped it away then raised the knife before slashing and tearing at the fabric of the sofa. Over and over, he pierced and shredded until his arm ached. The burning in his muscles was a small price to pay.

Exhausted, he fell to his knees, fighting to catch his breath. It was the sound of the front door opening and closing that snapped him back to the present. Barking and yapping echoed through the hall.

The woman's scream burst into his ears as the intruder barrelled past her and fled out of the front door towards the waiting car.

Chapter Twenty-Six

Monday

'Shit,' Hazel murmured when she spotted Rachel Fox outside Costa. She'd forgotten about her text last night. She hadn't made any arrangement with her, though. Had she? Hazel genuinely couldn't remember. Brain fog. She'd slept well when she'd slept. Hazel had been so tired after such a long, exhausting day but knew the next few days would be like that until this case was solved.

Hazel had offered the bed in her spare room to Tom as it got later last night but he'd declined. Hazel could tell he had something else on his mind other than the job, but she'd not wanted to push it. He knew she was there whenever he wanted to confide in someone.

'Hello, Hazel.' Rachel walked towards her, her new short, bobbed hair looking like it had been freshly cut. It really suited the silver colour.

'It's good to see you, Rachel,' Hazel smiled gently, trying to ignore the throbbing headache that was crushing her temples.

'Are you feeling OK?' Rachel frowned. 'You look pale.'

Nausea was churning Hazel's guts, but she wasn't about to admit that.

'I'm just a bit tired,' she said instead. 'How are you doing?'

'Fine, yes. I know we didn't make an arrangement, but I thought I'd catch you grabbing a coffee before work.'

Good, I haven't forgotten a coffee date.

Hazel noticed the serious look on Rachel's face as she spoke.

'Is everything all right?'

'I'm fine, it's you I'm worried about,' Rachel admitted.

'That's very kind of you but honestly, please, don't worry about me.' Hazel wasn't in the mood for this. 'If you don't mind, I'm in a bit of a rush this morning so...'

'I've seen the news,' Rachel blurted out.

Hazel quickly swept her aside, so the gathering queue didn't hear.

'I'd rather you didn't talk about that outside,' Hazel said plainly. 'It's an ongoing investigation.'

'Were his offences a factor in his murder?' Rachel asked. 'I know what he did. I read about it in the papers.'

Hazel had a question for her.

'Did Peter King ever come to the community kitchen?' she asked. 'Have you ever seen him on the days you've worked. I know, from what I've learned about him, that his wife kicked him out after his conviction. I know he spent a little while in the hostel before the council gave him that flat.'

Skinnergate hostel – of course. Sean Jacobs. David Wilson.

Rachel nodded. 'He did, about six months ago and as you can imagine, he wasn't popular with the other people who use the kitchen. He sometimes came for foodbank parcels too.'

'I can't imagine him being popular with many people,' Hazel suggested.

'Exactly, yes. I have to say I wasn't all that comfortable in his company, either.'

Hazel found this comment interesting. 'What was he like?'

'There was something about the way he looked at me...' She shuddered.

Hazel's mind ticked over fast. Was Sean Jacobs living in the hostel at the same time King was there? He would know all about King and his conviction. Hazel grabbed her phone and scrolled through the images to one of Sean, although his facial injuries didn't exactly match an image Rachel might have of him.

'What happened to him?' Rachel exclaimed.

'An old school friend gave him a hiding. Do you know him?'

'Some friend,' she scoffed. 'No, I can't say I do but his face is so bashed, it's hard to say.'

'Sean Jacobs. Does that name ring any bells?'

Rachel's eyes widened. 'Yes,' she gasped and looked again at the screen. 'Tell me that's not Sean! Gosh, I only saw him on Friday. He came in for a meal at lunchtime. He looked bad but not as bad as that.'

'I'm afraid so.'

'Who did that to him?' Rachel asked without taking her eyes off the gruesome image.

'David Wilson. Does that name mean anything to you at all?'

Rachel shaking her head was disappointing, but Hazel didn't think David had ever been homeless so it wasn't surprising that Rachel hadn't come across him in the context of her voluntary work. His home life might not be great, but it had never got that bad.

'No, was it him that did that?' Rachel pointed at the screen. 'I hope you've locked him up for it.'

Rachel was actually quite naïve. Given the history of her own devastating crimes that she'd committed a long time ago, before she'd put her life back together.

'Sean doesn't want to press charges,' Hazel informed her.

'What?'

'Seems Sean was pestering David's mum for drug money and David found out. He wasn't too pleased to hear about it.'

'My God!' Rachel looked genuinely shocked.

'Did Sean ever talk to Peter King?'

'I really don't remember, I'm sorry,' Rachel said.

'OK, it was just a hunch, never mind.'

Hazel looked at Rachel. She'd come so far from the woman she once was. A murderer who hadn't just killed once or even twice. If someone like Rachel could change, it just showed it was possible. It seemed that Maggie had been trying to change

her life, before that chance had been ripped away from her so
brutally. It seemed unlikely that King was trying to change,
Hazel figured.

'Do you think Sean might have something to do with Peter's
death?' Rachel asked.

Rachel's question was interrupted by a text.

'Excuse me a minute,' Hazel told her.

PM 10 a.m. sharp.

Jack Blair's reminder wasn't required. Maggie Ramsay's post-
mortem examination had been on her mind since she woke up
this morning. The pressure was mounting. It had been two days
since she'd been killed, and they didn't have enough evidence
yet to charge anyone. She hoped the rush hour traffic on the
A90 to Dundee would be gone by the time she hit the road.

'Listen, I'm sorry,' she glanced at her watch, which read eight
forty-five. 'I need to grab the coffees and get going but it was
nice to see you. I really appreciate you checking on me.'

'OK,' Rachel smiled and reached for Hazel's hand. 'You
know where I am if you need me.'

Hazel nodded, an unexpected lump appearing in her throat.
She wasn't about to cry in front of Rachel so coughed it away
quickly and gently pulled her hand out of Rachel's grasp.

'Thank you, I appreciate that. I'm sorry but I really must get
going.'

'OK then, I won't keep you. Take care of yourself, Hazel.'
Rachel smiled and turned towards the Morrisons supermarket
across the road.

'Yes and you.'

There was something about Rachel's concern for her that
she liked. Not that she could tell anyone that. Especially not
Cara. Hazel's friendship with Rachel wouldn't sit well with her.
She would have a fit if she found out that Rachel had kept in

touch with Hazel. Her deep grief meant that Cara wouldn't understand, probably not ever.

Lady Margaret Campbell switched off the engine in her Jaguar and sat back in the driver's seat. What a fabulous weekend. She wouldn't forget that for a long time. Catching up with old friends was something she loved to do. The fifteen-minute drive home from Pitlochry had taken longer in the snowy conditions but she'd declined the offer of a lift.

'I know it's taken longer than usual, you silly pup,' she said over her shoulder at the white West Highland terrier on the back seat who was barking excitedly.

Lady Campbell smiled and slowly got out of the car, rubbing her hip before heading towards the front door of her bungalow. As she got closer to the door, she was horrified to see that it was ajar. She unclipped the catch on her bag to find her phone, knowing she shouldn't go inside. Whoever had broken in might still be there. Lady Campbell looked behind her to see that her dog was barking furiously and jumping up at the car window.

A noise from behind her made Lady Campbell turn before a young girl barrelled past her, dropping something from her pocket as she fled.

Twenty years as an experienced High Court judge couldn't prepare her for the shock of this. Should she call out? What if the girl turned back and hurt her? A tightness spread across the sixty-year-old's chest, and it became hard to catch her breath. Her dog barked frantically to attract his owner's attention. Lady Campbell wiped the tear that had escaped down her cheek.

'Hello,' she stuttered into her phone. 'Police please,' she urged and waited while the operator connected her, fearing that her housekeeper might be lying injured, or worse, inside.

In the field behind her property she could see a small, thin figure move further and further away, cutting a path through the freshly fallen snow, scattering the flock of sheep that had been nibbling the turnip tops before she'd crashed through their home. Lady Campbell spotted the cigarette packet that the girl had dropped and hoped that would be enough to find out who she was. What the girl might have wanted would have to wait.

two reckless, one the other. ... shield enable ... You won't rush Name? Any complaint secured the recourse. ... her though ... but a hope that would be cool to read for who — With me and his you wouldn't would have to wait

Chapter Twenty-Seven

The clock above the mortuary door said it was quarter to ten. Hazel hadn't exactly broken the speed limit to get to Dundee after stopping to chat to Rachel Fox then having to wait to queue for the coffees. Her old fiesta may have been close to the limit but not quite. Despite that, she was glad to get there on time. She held up Jack Blair's coffee before laying it on the counter and taking the lid off the disposable cup to let it cool. Or more accurately, to go cold. Just the way he liked it. Hazel had never met anyone before who ordered a hot coffee then allowed it to go cold before drinking it. Her suggestion that he order a chilled coffee or a Frappuccino instead was swiftly and emphatically pooh-poohed.

She pulled the paper mask over her mouth and joined the enigmatic pathologist by the cold, steel table that had Maggie Ramsay's body laid out, naked, on it, a discreet sheet covering her genitals to maintain her dignity. Something that was important to Jack. Hazel had always admired that about him.

Just because they can't see us, we can see them.

'Good morning, DCI Todd.'

'Hi, how are you doing Jack?' Hazel caught her breath after rushing to meet him. Navigating the warren of corridors always seemed to take longer when she was in a hurry. Parking in Ninewells hospital was such a nightmare too. Not that she was late. Thanks to the relatively traffic-free road.

'Can't complain DCI Todd. How are you? How was the road this morning?'

'Och it was fine.'

His smile of greeting was obvious under his mask. It was the creases at the edge of eyes that gave it away. 'Good, good.'

'So what can you tell me?' she asked, noting as usual just how tidy the room was. Hazel wondered how he kept the place so perfect given the nature of what he did there. The darkness of his job had never got to him. Or perhaps it would get to him if he didn't control his environment like that. It would certainly haunt Hazel if she had to dissect dead bodies all day. At least the ones she found could be handed over.

'Cause of death was catastrophic head trauma as we expected, and time of death matches witness statements.'

Hazel looked down at the body on the cold, steel table, Maggie's head supported by the solid pillow under her neck. She found it hard to take her eyes off Maggie's face. From the front, she looked almost uninjured which was unnerving given that most of her brain had been expelled at speed and sent pouring onto the driveway.

'Any luck on finding the stolen car yet?' Jack Blair asked.

'Not yet.'

'Her husband is Samuel Ramsay, isn't he?'

'Yes, that's right, do you know him?'

'I didn't realise when we attended the scene who they were.'

'How do you know them?'

'Samuel Ramsay is a past master of number seventy-four.'

He was a mason – and not just any ordinary brother. A past master. Daly and Jack both knew him through their masonic connections. It didn't mean they knew the real Samuel, though. People had secrets.

'Is that the same lodge as you...' she hesitated briefly, unsure if she could continue, 'and Superintendent Daly?'

'You know if I told you that, I'd have to kill you,' Jack responded, with his characteristic deadpan humour, without looking up from Maggie's body.

'Oh ha-ha,' Hazel chirped. 'What's Samuel Ramsay like? Had you ever met Maggie before?'

She watched his eyebrows narrow. 'No, I've never met her before. What are you getting at?'

'What was their relationship like?' Hazel pushed. 'Were they happy?'

'As far as I can tell, yes,' he answered without hesitation. 'I certainly haven't heard anything to the contrary.'

Perhaps now wasn't the time to mention the other man labelled in Maggie's contacts as *Brenda*. As much as she liked and trusted Jack, his friendship with Sam risked that information getting back to him before Hazel was ready. It was best if it was kept on a *need to know* basis. She knew that the 'old boys club' could ruin her case.

'Fair enough,' she said instead then wondered if Maggie was successful in kicking the booze. 'Toxicology check came back clean, did it?'

'Clean as a whistle,' Jack confirmed.

'I thought it might. She'd been attending AA regularly, I believe,' Hazel commented. 'Anything else stand out to you?'

'No; she was a remarkably fit woman for her age. Heart and lungs all in good nick. Obviously never been a smoker. Liver, kidneys, pancreas – all good. Surprising, given the history of alcohol abuse. I'd have expected to see some scarring on the liver but there was none. A little shrinkage in the ovaries and uterus but nothing remarkable. Oh, I almost forgot.' He reached behind him and grabbed hold of a clear evidence bag and handed it to Hazel. 'This was in her jacket pocket.'

'What's this?'

'Tut tut, DCI Todd, you of all people should know I wouldn't open it.'

Hazel stared at the heavily bloodstained handwritten envelope.

'Thanks for that,' she replied, ignoring his gently barbed comment. She pointed to another body, still wrapped in a black body bag containing the remains of Peter King, on the table across the other side of the room. 'Have you had a chance to look at him yet?'

'He'll be next after I've enjoyed the coffee that you so graciously treated me to.'

Hazel smiled. 'Let me know as soon as you've examined him, will you?'

Hazel's phone rang as she ripped off her mask in the ante room.

'DCI Todd,' she answered and stopped dead in her tracks to listen. She frowned. 'Are you sure?'

She listened to Andrea Graham filling her in on a development that helped push the case in one direction. David Wilson's fingerprints. That had to be good.

When she got back to her car, she looked at the envelope Jack had given her. Curiosity got the better of her and she grabbed a pair of latex gloves from the glove box.

Hazel peeled the bag open and took out the bloodied envelope. She turned it over and examined each side and wondered if Samuel would recognise the handwriting. Inside was a single sheet of A5 paper with a short, unsigned note on it. It looked like an invitation or confirmation of an arrangement but had no time or date on it. Friday being the only definitive detail. What was meant to happen on Friday? Hazel wished the author had been clearer; presumably, the writer had expected Maggie to know what they meant. Sadly, Maggie wasn't in a position to clarify. Hopefully, Samuel could fill in the blanks.

Chapter Twenty-Eight

Hazel yawned as she made her way to her office and was pleased to see her whole team assembled, waiting for her. Especially Billy, who looked less worried than he had when she'd let him go home yesterday. Hopefully, whatever had been troubling him had been sorted now. They had so much to get through and the note she'd been given by the desk sergeant just added to her growing list of things to get through. The Right Honourable Lady Campbell had called the police in a panic to say someone had broken into her home. A young girl had fled the scene but not before leaving behind potential forensic evidence. A cigarette packet, dropped on the ground. This was important to Hazel's team, as it turned out. Tom had texted her late the previous night to say that he'd found out that Lady Campbell was the judge who oversaw both Maggie Ramsay's and Peter King's criminal cases. It sounded like Tom was having trouble sleeping too.

'Right, now we're all here…' Hazel laid the evidence bag containing the letter on her desk and couldn't wait to remove her jacket. She was embarrassed to think that her team could see the line of sweat gathering around her hairline. *Would it be too awkward to switch off the heating until she'd got on top of the hot flushes? Probably.* 'Before we start—' she started to say until Tom interrupted.

'What's that?' He nodded to the evidence bag.

'What?' Hazel frowned, briefly distracted. 'I'll get to that in a minute.' She tapped the letter with her finger. 'Now, I don't know if the rest of you have already heard but Lady Campbell's home has been broken into and as you may or may not know she was the judge who handed down the suspended sentences in the Ramsay and King cases. So I think there is a strong possibility that the break-in is connected to our cases.' She turned and pointed to the photos of Ramsay and King.

'How do you fancy a drive up to Pitlochry, Billy? See what Lady Campbell can tell us about the girl she saw running away. Her initial statement to the local uniforms was a bit vague but maybe, with a bit of persuasion, you can help her remember. Forensics have the cigarette packet that the girl dropped as we speak.'

'No problem,' Billy replied.

'Thanks,' Hazel smiled, remembering Andrea's call. 'Now let's recap what else we've got. Andrea, it's definitely David Wilson's prints on the table in King's hall, is it?'

'Yes. Forensics are testing for samples of DNA now to be sure.'

'Excellent,' Hazel exclaimed.

'But what about the alibi his girlfriend gave him for the time of Maggie Ramsay's death? Can she confirm he was with her when King was killed?' Tom butted in. 'What do we know about her?'

'She works part time as a paralegal at the firm who are helping the Wilsons push for an appeal against Maggie Ramsay's sentence.' Billy flicked to the next page in his notebook. 'Suzanne Gerrard, thirty-five.'

'Thirty-five! How old is David Wilson?' Tom asked.

'Almost nineteen,' Andrea told him.

Hazel's eyes met Tom's.

'What are you thinking?' she pushed him.

'It's a bit of an age gap.' He shrugged.

'He's maybe looking for a mother figure,' Andrea suggested then stopped on seeing the look on Hazel's face. 'What? It happens. A big sister, at the very least. She was incredibly hostile to me when I spoke to her. A bit overprotective, I thought,' she scoffed. 'She chucked me out just like Sean Jacobs' cousin did.'

Hazel glanced at Maggie Ramsay's smiling face, then allowed her eyes to drift to the picture of her lying dead on her drive. David Wilson's prints might be in King's flat but was the nineteen-year-old capable of stealing a car, lying in wait then mowing down a woman in cold blood? His motivation was obvious, there was no denying that, and his dislike of Peter King was also understandable. There weren't many people with a good word to say about him after his conviction. David Wilson had also shown that he was more than capable of violence after beating someone who was supposed to be a friend.

'Are we any closer to finding the identity of Maggie's mystery man?' Hazel pressed on, directing her question to her digital whizz, DS Billy Flynn.

Before he could answer, Billy's phone rang on his desk. He lifted a finger. 'Hang on a minute. Hello, DS Flynn?'

Hazel let him take the call but before she'd even opened her mouth to speak, Billy had hung up.

'That was burglary; they had a report of a break-in last night that they thought we should know about. Fingerprints match someone we're looking at. Their name was flagged as a person of interest in our case, so they've passed it along. The place was left in a considerable state by the sounds of things, too.'

'Another one?' Hazel frowned. 'Who, the same person that broke into Lady Campbell's perhaps?' she suggested.

'The Ramsays' home was broken into last night. The friend, Sandra Bell, walked in just before a man fitting Wilson's description fled the scene. Fingerprints found there match his. Some spots of blood on the windowsill will probably match his DNA too. Looks like he cut himself when he broke in.'

'Very interesting, clearly not the same person, then.' Hazel pursed her lips and looked at Tom. 'What do you think?'

'I have a suggestion,' Andrea said.

'Go on,' Hazel replied.

'Maybe it was an impulsive act of destruction. He's a teen-ager, still emotionally immature,' she suggested. 'All the grief that we've stirred up by interviewing him… maybe it's triggered a rage response. I mean, look at what he did to Sean Jacobs.'

Hazel was impressed by Andrea's knowledge as well as her instinctive way of reading people and was inclined to agree. Her DC's psychology and criminology degree came in very handy, and she knew she was damn lucky to have her. 'That is a bloody good point. It also adds weight to the possibility he is capable of the kind of violence inflicted on Peter King.'

'Exactly,' Andrea nodded. 'King's injuries were inflicted by someone with some serious anger.'

'But what's his motivation for killing King?'

'Perhaps he has developed a vigilante complex,' Andrea suggested.

Hazel hesitated for a moment, allowing her comment time to whirl through her mind. She wouldn't deny the possibility, for now.

'You go with Tom and bring him in. I think it would be safer if two of you go.' Hazel stole a quick glance at her evidence board and wrote the words *burglary* and *Wilson*. Then she looked at Billy. 'What about Maggie's phone, then? What's happening with that?'

'Digital forensics are still working on it,' Billy told her. 'They've had a right job on their hands but they've retrieved the contacts and are cleaning up what they can for us. They said they'd give me a buzz as soon as—' Right on cue, Billy's phone buzzed. 'Ah, it's them now. Hello.' He scribbled down a phone number then ended the call after being assured they would send the full contact list over as soon as they could. 'They've found a number for the mystery man labelled as "Brenda".'

'Excellent, let's have it.' Hazel reached for the piece of paper. 'What about the laptop?'

'Nothing significant on it. King's is still waiting to be processed.'

Hazel looked at Andrea. 'Did we ever locate the ringing phone at King's place?'

'I'll check with forensics.'

'And it's just Wilson's fingerprints we've got,' Hazel said. 'What about Sean Jacobs?'

Andrea shook her head. 'Only Wilson's name was mentioned.'

It felt like a lot of little pieces of a large puzzle. She would go and talk to Maggie's mystery man. See if he had a missing piece. Did he know of a connection Maggie had to King? She turned to Tom. 'Are you and Andrea good to go back and bring in David Wilson for questioning? It really would be better if you both went. We know how volatile he is.'

'Sure, yes,' Tom agreed. 'You were going to tell us what that is.' He pointed to the bloodied letter that Hazel had been given by Jack Blair.

Embarrassed that her brain fog had almost let it slip out of her mind, Hazel picked up the evidence bag.

'This was found in Maggie Ramsay's pocket.' She held it up. 'It suggests that Maggie was invited to meet someone. Or had an arrangement with someone.'

Tom grabbed a pair of gloves from a box on the unit that ran along the edge of the room.

'Let me see,' he said.

He removed the paper from the bloodied envelope and read the note. 'It's not very clear, is it?'

'Sadly not,' Hazel agreed. 'What do you make of it?'

'*Friday*,' Tom read aloud. 'Not much to go on, is it?'

'I'm sending it to forensics to see if they can get anything off it,' Hazel told them as Tom slipped the note back into the evidence bag. 'You two get off and bring David in and be careful,' she urged.

She was pleased to see her two detectives nod eagerly then head off. She liked the way her team worked so well together.

Billy checked the time on his watch and grabbed his blazer from the back of his chair. 'I'll get going, I'm no' sure what the road to Pitlochry's like so I'll maybe need to take my time.' He sighed. 'Bloody snow! I hate the stuff.'

'Thanks, Billy,' Hazel said. 'Actually, hang on a minute.'

Billy stopped. 'Aye sure what's up?'

'Aye, that's what I wanted to ask you.'

'Yes, everything's fine,' Billy replied. 'And listen, thanks for letting me go early like that.' He smiled without holding her gaze. 'I really appreciate it.'

'OK,' Hazel said. 'If you're sure everything's all right.' She was disappointed he'd not expanded on what his trouble had been, but perhaps it wasn't her business.

Hazel watched the back of Billy disappear through the double doors as she typed in the number on the paper Billy had given her that had the mysterious 'Brenda's' number on it and listened to it ring four times then go right to voicemail. The man's voice on the other end was deep – husky, even – as it growled that she should leave a message and he'd get back to her as soon as possible. She detected a hint of an accent too. Australian perhaps, maybe even South African. She wasn't sure.

'Hello, this is Detective Chief Inspector Hazel Todd,' she began leaving a message. 'I'd appreciate it if you could call me back as soon as possible. Thank you.'

Hazel laid her phone down. If he didn't call back in the next ten minutes, she would get a trace on the number. Without the reg number of his car that was all they had. She logged into her laptop with the intention of looking up the law firm that was working for the Wilsons but before she could even finish typing in her password, her phone rang with an unknown number.

'DCI Todd.' Hazel answered the call and listened to 'Brenda' tell her he was returning her call and asking her what had happened, his voice full of concern. He asked if it was his dad, back at home in Cape Town. Had something happened?

So your accent is South African.

Hazel assured him that she wasn't calling about his father and asked him about his relationship with Maggie Ramsay. Given that he spoke of her in the present tense she decided not to mention about her death over the phone. She made arrangements to meet Casper Vermeer in person to give him the awful news.

—

'Do you reckon he's at college?' Andrea suggested as the two detectives waited for the door to be answered.

Tom knocked again and leaned in to listen more closely for movement inside the end-of-terrace house while Andrea stepped aside to peer in the living room window.

'Could be, but the boss seemed to think he'd be here.'

'Tom!' she exclaimed. 'It's Carol Wilson. She's lying flat out on the floor, we need to get in there!'

'Shit, let me have a look.' Tom could see her laying on her face between the sofa and the coffee table, not moving, with the television blaring in the background. 'Hang on, she might just be passed out drunk.' He hammered on the window to see if he could rouse her then turned to Andrea. 'Press the doorbell again and keep your finger on it.'

Andrea did as she was told, rapping the letterbox at the same time. Tom scrolled the details in his notebook.

'Have you got a number for her or the landline? Shit, I don't.' Tom said as he scrolled through his phone, his concern for the woman's welfare deepening.

'Wait a minute.' Andrea flicked over the first couple of pages of her own notebook then typed a number into her iPhone. The mobile phone on the coffee table started ringing and vibrating across the surface, almost toppling off the edge.

Carol Wilson didn't move, not even when they rang the number again. This time, the vibration caused her handset to tip off the edge of the table onto her back. There was still no response. They had no choice; they had to enter the property now. Tom tried the handle.

'Shit, it's locked.'

Andrea scanned the ground then grabbed hold of a large boulder that was lying in the dishevelled flowerbed under the living room window and smashed the glass panel in the front door. A heavily tattooed man who was holding tight to the lead of a large American bulldog called out to them.

'Oi, what ya doing?' The dog barked and lunged in their direction.

Tom quickly grabbed his ID from his pocket and held it up. 'It's fine, sir, we're police officers.'

'The key's in the lock,' Andrea said and reached in to unlock it. 'Mind the glass,' she added.

Tom stared at the man and his dog until they started to walk away then went inside the house ahead of Andrea.

'What on earth is going on?' The old woman next door poked her head out on hearing the commotion.

'Go back inside, please,' Andrea held up her ID.

'Well, I'm not sure...' the Wilsons' neighbour tried to protest.

'Go back inside,' Andrea repeated, this time more loudly. 'This is a police matter.'

Andrea stared the old woman down until she had retreated back inside her house then followed Tom inside.

'Carol, it's DC Graham,' she called out to her, crouching next to where she lay motionless on the sticky carpet, her face pressed onto the floor. She reached her hand down to search for a pulse but the cool temperature she felt on contact with Carol's skin told its own story. She wasn't cold but there was no warmth there either, despite the heat in the room. Her lips had a blue tinge to them.

'Fuck, she's dead.'

'You're joking!' Tom exclaimed. 'Shit!'

'I'll call it in,' Andrea told him and moved into the hallway to make the call.

Tom pulled a pair of gloves from his pocket and checked for a pulse. 'Shit,' he mumbled. He leaned his hand against the mug on the table to find the contents cold. Next to the mug was a plate of cold food.

'The boss says forensics are on their way,' Andrea said. 'She said don't touch anything else. A couple of detectives from Dundee are heading over here to go over the scene for us.'

'Looking at the place, does it look like there's been a struggle or a fight to you?' Tom asked, grateful to see a couple of uniformed officers walking up the path when he looked out of the living room window. He was less happy to see a couple of older women standing nearby, staring, and chatting about what was happening inside the Wilsons' home.

'Honestly, it's hard to say. I don't think housework has been Carol Wilson's priority lately.'

'That's what I thought,' Tom agreed. 'Heart attack maybe or a stroke. I mean, her health wasn't great, was it and I can't see any blood or obvious injury.'

'We'll need to see what the post-mortem shows up. Weird timing, though,' Andrea suggested. 'Her son is prime suspect in a double murder and now she's—'

'Mum!' David Wilson's cries hit their ears and they had to fight hard to stop him from grabbing hold of his mum and cradling her in his arms. He fought back hard. 'What the fuck have you done?' His words burst out with panic and it took both detectives several tries to get him into a pair of handcuffs. They helped the distraught teenager into an armchair in the far corner of the room.

'David, I'm so sorry,' a woman's voice echoed from the doorway, and she walked towards him, leaning on a stick. She held him close to her as he sobbed. It was Suzanne Gerrard.

'Mum! Mum, I'm sorry I wasn't here,' he sobbed. 'I should have been here.'

'David, honey, I'm so sorry.' Suzanne kissed the top of his head and ran her hand up and down the length of his back. She threw a barbed stare at Andrea. 'His mother has just died, for God's sake! Can you take these things off him, at least?' She indicated his hands cuffed behind his back. 'He's got rights as you well know.'

Andrea shot a concerned glance at Tom. Neither of them were looking forward to the next part but Hazel had sent them to bring him in, so bring him in they would. Dead mother or no dead mother. Forensics were on their way. For all they knew, he could be responsible for her death too.

'Mr Wilson,' Tom began. 'You're going to have to come with us…'

'What?' Suzanne yelled. 'What the hell do you mean? Why does he have to come with you? Are you two fucking blind? His mother has just died!'

'I'm going to have to ask you to step back,' Andrea announced and moved closer.

Suzanne kissed David's cheek and threw the two detectives another scowl. 'Hang on, I'll go and make a couple of calls. I'll get the solicitor to meet us there. Don't take him anywhere until I come back.' She snapped at them as she walked away, a little faster but still leaning heavily on the stick.

Tom looked at Andrea then down at David's grief-stricken face.

'Mr Wilson.' He leaned down to take David's arm. 'Come on.'

David looked at Tom then to where Suzanne was walking away.

'What about Mum? What's going to happen to her?'

'Don't worry. We'll take care of her.' Tom sighed. This was horrible. 'But listen, you have to come with us now.'

Tom was relieved that David seemed to understand. It was Suzanne Gerrard who was proving more difficult.

'Step back,' Andrea repeated when Suzanne returned and tried to get close to David as they took him outside.

'David,' Suzanne called after them. 'Don't say anything. Don't let them put words in your mouth. I'll be right behind you.'

Sean Jacobs walked up to the Wilsons' front door, if a little awkwardly given the beating he'd had from David, just as David was being loaded into the back of Tom's car.

'Mind your head,' Tom said, and his eyes met Sean's. He closed the car door. 'Hang on a sec, Andrea, I'll not be a minute.'

Tom walked towards Sean who had stopped dead in his tracks. He was surprised to see Sean up and about so quickly after the beating.

'Where are you taking David?' Sean asked.

'What are you doing here, Sean? I would have thought David was the last person you'd want to see after he did that to you.'

Tom indicated the bruises on Sean's face and glanced back to where David was watching them from the back seat. He spotted the two men staring at each other and he was sure he saw David nod, just a touch, then look away.

'It's fine, I'll catch up with him later. It's not important.'

Before Tom could respond, Sean had turned and was heading in the direction of the bus stop. Tom glanced back at David who was watching Sean intently, his expression unreadable. He caught Tom watching and immediately turned his face in the opposite direction.

'Is everything OK?' Andrea asked as Tom got behind the wheel.

Tom stared at David in the rearview mirror, narrowing his eyes at him. 'Fine, yes,' he said and started the engine. 'It'll keep.'

Chapter Twenty-Nine

Billy wasn't surprised to find that Lady Campbell's home wasn't in the town itself. Her sixteenth-century cottage was situated a mile further north in the quiet village of Moulin. Close enough to the town but far enough away when peace and quiet were what you wanted, and he supposed that was exactly what she wanted, given her job as a High Court judge.

Out of season, Pitlochry was quiet with tourists mainly coming during that time to stay in one of the luxury hotels and take in a show at the famous Pitlochry Festival Theatre. Summertime though filled the small Highland Perthshire town with a whole host of other tourists from walkers to wildlife-watchers. Anglers also came for the area's world famous salmon and trout seasons. Billy knew some famous names often came to the area for the fishing.

The fact that Lady Campbell lived in Moulin, though, meant the final part of Billy's drive was a little hairier than the rest with the council gritter's attention being paid to the main roads rather than the outlying villages. He passed a field of Highland cattle and envied their dense red coats that must keep them incredibly cosy in these wintry conditions.

Billy indicated right automatically despite the fact there hadn't been a vehicle behind him for the past fifteen minutes. Lady Campbell was outside her front door when he pulled up in her extensive driveway. A statue to his left caught his eye, and he realised it was a water feature as he got closer. He wondered if it was marble, but it was hard to tell under all the snow.

Billy locked his car and instinctively checked his tie to ensure it was straight, the way he always did when he was about to enter a courtroom to give evidence. He recalled standing before the judge once many years ago but didn't think she'd remember him.

'Lady Campbell.' Billy held out his hand to shake hers. Her eyes looked red as if she'd been crying. 'My name is DS Billy Flynn.' He pulled his ID out to show her.

'I remember you, Detective Sergeant.' Her thin smile faded quickly. 'Come in, please. Some of your forensic colleagues have just left.' She stepped inside and pointed to a room at the end of the hall.

Billy bent his head as he crossed the ancient cottage's threshold. He could see immediately that Lady Campbell had restored the place sympathetically. The beams all stood out, catching his eye as he made his way into a large kitchen. His attention was instinctively attracted to the huge fireplace at the opposite end. An original, he imagined. Where once a roaring fire might have burned, Lady Campbell had put piles of logs, strategically placed for maximum effect. A couple of tall white candles either side.

'Please take a seat,' she told him and sat down at the long pine table, picking her West Highland terrier up as he barked at her knee. She took a tissue from the sleeve of her blouse and wiped her nose. 'Forgive me, I'm still a little shaken by what's happened.'

'Don't worry,' Billy tried to reassure her but couldn't help feeling nervous in her company. He adjusted his green tie again. A nervous tic. He coughed to compose himself and took his notebook and pen from his blazer pocket. 'OK,' he began, 'I realise you've already spoken to one of the local officers but if you wouldn't mind going through what happened again, for me...'

'Of course, of course.' Lady Campbell took a breath.

Billy could see that her hands were shaking. 'Can I get you a glass of water?' he asked.

'Could you pour me a brandy instead?'

'Yes, yes, I erm...' Billy stood.

'There's a decanter on the counter over there.'

Billy followed where her finger was pointing and found it. He poured her half a glass and handed it to her.

'A generous measure.' She smiled thinly and sank half of the contents in one gulp.

Billy sat back down and opened his notebook to a new page. He waited until she'd taken another large drink. He watched her sigh.

'That's better,' she smiled and slid the glass away. 'I'm sorry about that. My nerves are frayed.'

'It's OK, you've had a terrible shock.'

'She doesn't seem to have taken anything, at least,' Lady Campbell said. 'Perhaps I arrived home in time. My housekeeper was out too, thank goodness.'

Before he could open his mouth to say anything else, she continued. 'Do you think this has anything to do with those ghastly murders?'

Billy didn't realise she knew about the murders of Ramsay and King.

'We're not sure at the moment,' he told her honestly.

'But you can't definitely say it's not,' she pressed him.

'I can't, no. I'm sorry but I'd like to ask you some questions.'

'Of course, go ahead,' Lady Campbell said. 'Oh, do you have a match for the fingerprints on the cigarette packet yet?'

'Not yet but we're still trying.' He found himself reaching for his tie again. 'You told my colleagues it was a girl that fled the scene.'

'That's right,' Lady Campbell agreed. 'She couldn't have been more than twenty, if that, but it all happened so fast.'

'I know,' Billy said. 'But do you think you could describe her for me? Did she have any distinguishing features like piercings or tattoos?'

He was disappointed to see her shaking her head until she spoke again.

'I'm not sure if this helps but she was wearing a baseball cap… erm, a blue one, I think.' She stopped. 'Or was it brown? I'm sorry, my mind has gone blank. It all happened so fast I can't really remember much I'm afraid.' She lifted the glass to her lips. 'We ask people to recall information accurately in court don't we. We ask them to be sure of what they've seen but now I know how hard that is for some people.'

'That's OK you're doing great. She was definitely wearing a baseball cap though. You're sure of that much.' Billy repeated and wrote that in his notebook.

'Yes.' Lady Campbell nodded.

'Have you received any letters threatening you in any way or strange phone calls recently?' Billy asked.

Lady Campbell frowned. 'No, I haven't. Why do you ask that?'

'Before Maggie Ramsay was murdered she had been receiving threatening letters.'

Lady Campbell's eyes widened and she brought the glass to her lips again.

'Are you saying I'm in danger, Detective? Do you know who this young woman is? Is she involved in Maggie Ramsay's murder?'

Billy wished he did know who she was but he wondered if this might be the driver of their stolen car. It couldn't be a coincidence, could it? What did this girl have planned now that she'd scoped out Lady Campbell's home? The danger might not yet be over. He had to ask the Honourable Lady a question now without scaring her.

As if she could feel his anxiety, Lady Campbell asked, 'What is it, Detective?'

Billy could feel his heart rate increase and he coughed to clear his throat. 'Erm, do you have a friend you can stay with for a few days?'

Chapter Thirty

Hazel hung up the phone to Tom, reminding him to get Wilson's clothes for forensics, then corrected herself. Of course Tom would do that. A flashback from her own childhood smashed into her, uninvited. Finding her own mum lying dead, face down on the floor, would live with her forever. Sudden death in alcohol syndrome. That's what her death certificate read. She'd been minded many times to ask Jack Blair to explain that one to her fully, but she'd never had the nerve or the time, if she were honest. The cruel irony that Hazel really fancied a tall, chilled glass of white right now wasn't lost on her.

Tom had told her that David had walked to the back of the waiting car quietly and without resistance which was a nice surprise. The girlfriend, Suzanne Gerrard, was arranging legal representation for him this time so they couldn't talk to him until then. When asked what he thought of her, Tom had told Hazel that Suzanne was a small, thin woman. Skinny, even, with wrists that looked like they'd snap easily. She might best be described as 'fragile'. Her cheekbones were prominent like she'd recently been ill, and she was pale with white-blonde hair, which was thin and wispy, hanging loose by her shoulders. She walked with a stick, leaning somewhat heavily on it at times.

He'd suggested he thought her eyes looked haunted and sad. Sunken. Not the sort of woman he saw a young, attractive lad like David Wilson with. Holding him in her arms, she looked more like a concerned aunt than a girlfriend. What she lacked in physical power though she certainly made up for in strength of character. She'd been quite the bulldog, it seemed. He mentioned Sean Jacobs' arrival too and said there was something off about it but couldn't explain exactly what. Hazel knew that gut feeling well.

She was pleased that Billy had helped Lady Campbell to organise a few days with a friend. He'd said that she took his suggestion with less fuss than he'd thought she might. The relief in his voice had been obvious. He'd suggested how odd it was that nothing seemed to have been taken so what this girl had planned to do was still a mystery. The possibility that she might return was still there.

Right now, Hazel was standing outside Superintendent Daly's office, waiting to ask him for permission for a surveillance operation outside Lady Campbell's home. Exactly where they would hide was still to be arranged because her cottage was so isolated.

'Come in,' Daly said from inside his office.

Hazel took a breath and reached for the handle just as she felt a hot flush hit her face.

'Bloody great,' she mumbled.

'DCI Todd, come in,' Daly welcomed her. 'Take a seat.' Then he frowned. 'Are you OK?'

Hazel quickly realised he'd seen her flushed face. 'What? Yes, yes, I'm just a little hot, that's all.'

She managed to bluff it but this couldn't go on.

'How is the investigation going?' Daly asked, seemingly satisfied with her answer.

'That's why I'm here,' Hazel responded. 'The judge who was involved in both of our victim's cases has had her home broken into and—'

'What?' Daly gasped and it was clear to Hazel that he deemed the judge's upset more important than the two dead victims. That irked Hazel. Goosebumps spread across her skin at the thought.

'I'm afraid so, we—' she began again until he interrupted her.

'Who was the judge?'

'Lady Margaret Campbell.'

'Lady Campbell,' he said in surprise. 'Is she all right?'

'Yes, yes, she disturbed her intruder who ran off but—'

'Good, good, that's a relief,' he said, cutting Hazel off again. She had to bite her tongue, given his rank and seniority.

'That's why I'm here,' she pressed on. 'I'd like to send a surveillance team up there to keep an eye on the place. Lady Campbell has gone to stay with a friend for a few days. It may have just been a coincidence – I mean, perhaps the motive was just burglary although nothing appears to have been taken. Lady Campbell's home is isolated. An opportunistic robbery isn't out of the question.'

This time Daly stared, listening. He perched his elbows on the edge of his desk, clasping his fingers together and leaning on them before nodding.

'Yes, absolutely, let me know what you need, and I'll make sure it happens.' His answer was exactly what Hazel needed. 'You don't think the motive was robbery though, do you?' he suggested.

'No I don't,' Hazel said firmly. 'Sadly I don't, sir.'

—

Hazel texted Billy with the good news and said he should get back to the station as soon as he'd ensured Lady Campbell was out of harm's way. She wanted Billy to brief the surveillance team on the case and said she'd be back once she'd spoken to Casper Vermeer, who after a quick internet search she'd discovered was the owner of a very successful bespoke furniture business selling handmade furniture which he made himself. According to his fancy website it was a business he'd built from scratch, firstly out of his garage then from his brand spanking new premises in Bankfoot, a village nine miles north of the city centre. Thankfully the heavy snow on the A9 had been recently cleared by the council.

'Detective, please come in.'

Casper had opened his front door as Hazel was getting out of her car on his extensive chipped gravel driveway, lined with flowering cherry trees that she imagined would look spectacular in full blossom soon. The soft virgin snow beneath them glowed white under the low sun. A robin sitting in one of the trees caught her attention. It was as if it was staring right at her, watching her.

Parked on the drive was a car she'd had a hunch she would find. A red Audi with a personal number plate. She locked up her own vehicle and followed him inside.

'Please take a seat.' Casper pulled an exquisite black leather chair out from the long, dark wood kitchen table then sat opposite.

Hazel had to admit that if she had to choose between this tanned, muscular man with a deep gravelly voice and a thin, wiry Samuel Ramsay, she knew which she would choose. Casper Vermeer obviously looked after himself. His face was bronzed, and his jaw was chiselled. The hint of one day's growth of stubble suited his dark features. The specks of silver peppered through his short brown hair looked good on him.

'Thank you,' Hazel said and laid her keys and phone onto the table, wincing at the sound they made when they hit the heavy wood. Clearly a bespoke table, probably made by Casper himself.

'You said on the phone you wanted to talk to me about Maggie.' His face was filled with concern and Hazel felt bad about what she had to do now.

'That's right, Mr Vermeer.'

'Call me Casper, Mr Vermeer is my dad.' The thin smile was meant to hide his anxiety but faded quickly. 'Would you like a cup of coffee?' he asked, cracking the knuckles on his left hand as he spoke. He must have noticed Hazel wince at the sound because he added, 'Sorry, it's a bad habit, I know.'

'It's fine, don't worry,' Hazel said plainly, trying to keep herself focussed. 'Listen, I have some bad news.'

Casper gasped, his eyes widening. 'What? Is it Maggie? Has something happened to her?'

'I'm afraid so. Maggie died on Saturday morning. I'm so sorry.'

The tall, well-built man in front of Hazel crumbled. He let out a flurry of sobs, struggling to find the words he was obviously searching for.

'I, erm… what…' He coughed to clear the emotion from his throat.

'Maggie was hit by a car in front of her home. She died instantly.'

'So it was an accident.'

Hazel's hesitation made him clasp a hand to his face.

'If it wasn't an accident then was she—' He stopped and stood up from the table to pour himself a glass of water, sinking half the contents immediately.

'I'm really sorry for your loss.' His whimpers were awful, and Hazel wished she could make him feel better. 'Is there anyone who can come and sit with you?'

'My wife will be home soon.'

His wife. Both of them were married.

'Lara doesn't know about Maggie,' he pleaded. 'I would prefer it if you didn't say anything.'

The sound of the front door opening and closing hit them.

'Please,' he begged. 'I'll tell her.' He spoke with tears dripping down his face and had to rub them away quickly before his wife saw them.

A wife. A potentially scorned wife. Hazel couldn't ignore that fact.

'Darling could you get the bag from… oh hello,' a tall, pretty woman said to Hazel as she shifted a cream and blue patterned woollen shawl from her shoulders and draped it over the back of a chair. 'I didn't realise you had a customer, I'm sorry.'

Hazel smiled at her, admiring her flawless skin and immaculately manicured and painted purple nails. Something she would like to have but didn't have the time nor the inclination to put in the effort. Not these days. Underactive thyroid and menopause did that to you. Hard work and sleepless nights were also a factor. This woman looked at least ten – perhaps fifteen – years younger than Casper and if Hazel could be frank, she was considerably prettier than Maggie. Lara was hot, with breasts that defied gravity and legs that accounted for most of her amazing height. The woman could easily have been a model. She could see Lara with Casper more than she could picture him with plain old Maggie Ramsay. Was it their shared addiction that had brought the two together?

'I won't be long, darling,' Casper said.

'Sure, I need to shower anyway,' Lara told him, smiling at Hazel briefly before leaving them. If she thought Hazel hadn't noticed her derisory gaze over Hazel's slightly overweight figure and greying short haircut she was mistaken. Lara's beauty was clearly only skin-deep.

Casper closed the kitchen door. 'Thanks for not saying anything.'

'I can't promise I won't in future, you must know that. This is a murder investigation.'

'I know,' he acknowledged as he dropped down onto a chair.

He flopped his head into his hands, and it was then that Hazel spotted the spider web tattoo on the back of Casper's neck. Not the expensive kind, either. It seemed Casper's life hadn't always been this good and she'd asked for a background check on his life in South Africa.

From the preliminary checks, his life in the UK had been relatively straightforward after a short stay in Sunnyside hospital many years ago for alcohol rehabilitation. Sunnyside. What a waste of time that place had been for her own mother. When visitors brought in oranges laced with vodka, how did they expect their patients to get sober?

'Are you sure Lara didn't know about your relationship with Maggie Ramsay?'

'Yes I'm sure,' he snapped and squeezed his hands roughly over the back of his neck. 'I know my wife. She would not be able to hide a discovery like that, I can assure you.'

'How long have you and Lara been married?'

'Why is that important?'

Casper's mood was becoming brittle, but Hazel wouldn't be deterred.

'I can ask Lara if you'd prefer.' Stony-faced, she tested him. Hazel didn't have time for his bullshit. He should have kept his dick in his boxers if he didn't want to answer her questions.

'Five years,' he relented quietly with a long, slow sigh. His mobile phone buzzed on the counter behind him, and he reached for it before rejecting the call and dropping it back down.

Hazel watched him rest his elbows on the kitchen table, covering his face with his palms before shaking his head gently. Sniffing back tears, he looked at Hazel while he rubbed his wet face with his fingers.

'What the hell happened to her?' he asked and wiped his nose with the back of his hand.

Unless Casper was a great actor, this display of emotion appeared genuine to Hazel. She almost felt sorry for the guy. His vehement denial that Lara could know about the affair intrigued her. Maybe the younger woman wouldn't care. Casper was a wealthy man. Would she want to give all this up for his indiscretion? Was she faithful to him? Hazel imagined Lara had men falling at her feet every day.

'A car mounted the pavement and struck Maggie outside her home. It was a deliberate move by the driver of what we now know to be a stolen car.'

'Are you sure?' he asked.

'I'm afraid so,' Hazel nodded. 'I'm sorry.'

'God, that's…' He seemed to be searching for the right words but inhaled a long deep breath instead before blowing it back out through puffed cheeks, shaking his head. 'I can't believe this.'

'When did you last speak to her?'

'Last Thursday. After the meeting.'

'Is that the AA meeting, you mean?' Hazel wanted him to confirm. 'How did she seem to you?'

Casper sighed. 'She was fine. We went to my flat in Perth and...' he paused. 'Well, we spent some time together there talking and, you know.'

'Is that where the two of you usually went to be together? Have you ever been to Maggie's home?'

'Never.'

'Where were you on Saturday morning?'

'You can't seriously think I had anything to do with this!'

'You understand I have to ask.'

Casper sighed. 'I was here. With a customer.'

Hazel didn't think Vermeer was responsible but she had to ask.

'I'll take a note of that customer's details if you don't mind.'

She took the number from him and tucked it away for now.

'Lara doesn't know about the flat,' Vermeer admitted.

It seemed there was a great deal Mrs Vermeer didn't know. What a strange relationship, Hazel thought. She chose to brush over his last remark.

'So would you say she was her usual self when you last saw her?' Hazel suggested.

Casper hesitated. He stood abruptly and poured himself another glass of water, sipping this time before pouring the rest of the contents away. Hazel spotted the trembling in his hands. He leaned on the edge of the sink and stared out at the view of open countryside as far as the eyes could see, broken only by a few trees on the horizon. Their nearest neighbour must be at least half a mile away.

'Do you know what, no she wasn't.' Casper turned quickly. 'She told me she was going to tell Sam about us.'

Hazel was intrigued. Samuel didn't mention any of this. Had she changed her mind about telling him?

'Did she ever talk to you about her relationship with her husband?' Hazel was curious to see how much of Sandra Bell's account would match his. 'They'd been married for a very long time, hadn't they?'

'Only that she wasn't happy with him any longer and wanted to leave.'

'Is that all she said?'

Casper nodded. 'Yes.' Then he frowned. 'Why, what else was there? Was he abusing her?'

'We don't know. Her friend has suggested that Samuel was controlling rather than abusive. Did she ever suggest that to you?' she asked.

'No, God, he couldn't.' He stared blankly at her. 'He couldn't have, could he? Sam wouldn't have done it, would he? To get back at her, I mean. A crime of passion.'

'Do you know if she told him about the pair of you?' Casper's idea had crossed Hazel's mind, if somewhat fleetingly.

Casper shrugged and stared outside, smiling thinly, and waving to the horse and rider that walked past. Hazel narrowed her eyes at the back of him while she waited for his response. He turned back to face her.

'I don't know,' he answered plainly. 'We weren't going to see each other until tomorrow so I didn't know anything had happened to her until you called me.' His eyes swam with tears again. 'We usually don't speak between meetings you see and...'

He turned back and refilled his glass with cold water. 'I'm sorry, m–my sponsor,' he stuttered, 'this is something he does when he gets the craving. He guzzles water. He says it works in two ways. Your hand and mouth are occupied and then your stomach gets too full for anything else.'

'Ah, I see.' That made sense to Hazel. As did the collection of empty water bottles in the recycling bin by the kitchen door. 'Is it a strategy that works for you?'

'It used to,' he replied sarcastically and swallowed down a large swig. 'Until today.'

'How long have you been sober?' Hazel was genuinely interested to know the answer to that. The man had clearly built a very successful carpentry business. From scratch, it seemed. That couldn't have been easy while he battled an alcohol addiction.

'I'll be fifteen years sober next week.'

Hazel was impressed. 'That's great, quite an achievement, in fact.' An image of her mum's face filled her mind and Hazel had to shove it aside. It often saddened her that her mum hadn't managed to beat the demon booze that had such a grip on her.

Casper scoffed. 'My sobriety has been tested lots of times over the years but not like this.'

'I'm sorry.' Hazel felt like a broken record. 'I really am.'

'Do you have any idea who would do that to her? Was it that Wilson boy?'

Casper's eyes blinked hard when he said David's name and his jaw clenched.

'What do you know about David Wilson?' Hazel asked.

'I know he threatened her many times. Have you arrested him yet?' Casper urged, his South African accent becoming thicker with the stress of the conversation. 'It has to be him. Maggie was so upset about what happened to that little boy. She said if she could go back and change it, she would. Of course she would. Anybody would.' A look of recognition crossed his face. 'She'd argued with Sam that morning. Did you know that?'

'She told you that, did she?'

This was news to Hazel. From the reports she'd seen, there had been no suggestion about any argument with her husband. Maggie had been to lunch with her friend Sandra where she'd had a couple of glasses of wine, as testified by the waiter who'd served her, before getting behind the wheel. The suggestion she was on the phone when it happened made Hazel now question whether she'd been fighting with Sam at the time.

'What was the argument about, do you know?'

Casper shook his head. 'No, I've got no idea, sorry. So have you arrested Wilson or not?'

'David Wilson is a person of interest in our investigation, I can assure you.'

While it was looking more and more like Wilson was in the frame for both murders, Hazel had to keep an open mind. She'd be looking more closely into Casper's background as well as his wife Lara's. It may be that Maggie and Peter King's deaths were not connected at all. Just a horrific coincidence. But then, why had Lady Campbell's place been targeted? Again, a coincidence? Hazel didn't think so.

Hazel left her details with Casper and asked him to call if he thought of anything else that could help in her investigation. She suggested he should have a long talk with his wife, code for *if you don't tell Lara, it might be embarrassing when she finds out later* which he appeared to understand. Hazel hoped so.

An elderly man walking his chunky black Labrador waved a greeting to her as Hazel unlocked her car. Perthshire villages had always been friendly, even to incomers these days. Growing up in a council housing scheme, Hazel wasn't sure she'd cope with the silence, though. Not a single vehicle had been heard the whole time she'd been there. Only the clip-clop of horses hooves on the road past the Vermeer house. A lovely sound.

'Hello there,' the old man shouted over. 'Are you buying one of Casper's masterpieces, then?'

This man appeared to know Casper Vermeer. A five-minute chat couldn't hurt. She closed her car door, her eye catching a figure in the upstairs window. Lara. Hazel looked away before she did.

'I'm considering it,' Hazel said which wasn't strictly a lie because she had admired the gorgeous table and chairs.

'We've just bought a table and chairs for the conservatory,' he continued. 'Cost us a pretty penny, mind you,' he winked.

'How well do you know Mr and Mrs Vermeer?' she smiled.

'Not that well, really.' The old man took a cotton handkerchief from his pocket and wiped his nose. 'Such a shame what happened to his workshop.'

Hazel's interest was piqued. 'What happened to it?'

'The fire! You don't know about the fire?' The man sucked air in loudly through his teeth. 'Damage could run into hundreds of thousands, folk say.'

'Is that right?' Hazel glanced up to see Lara wasn't in the upstairs window now.

'Yes, he's got a workshop on the other side of the village. Someone set fire to it a couple of nights ago. Terrible business. So close to the stables, too. Thankfully, nobody got hurt.'

Raised voices carried from the open kitchen window and she saw the couple were arguing.

'She's got some temper on her, that Lara.'

Hazel flicked round on seeing him indicating towards the house. 'I wouldn't want to be on the receiving end of that. It's not the first time I've heard shouting coming from that house.'

'Is that right?' she asked without looking at him. 'Listen, do you know what time the fire happened on Saturday night?'

'Oh well, me and the Mrs had been in Perth, at a family wedding and by the time we got home at just gone eleven the fire brigade had put the flames out. Neighbours said they heard the sirens coming at ten o'clock. Awful business.'

'Ah, I see, yes, terrible business.'

His dog whined, distracting the elderly man. 'Anyway, I'd better be going. Buster looks like he's fed up waiting.' He chuckled then looked at the sky, tutting loudly. 'Looks like another snow shower's on the way. I hope you find something you like.'

Hazel thanked him. So why had Casper neglected to mention the fire? And exactly how bad was Lara's temper?

Chapter Thirty-One

Before heading straight back to the station, Hazel found herself standing outside of what was left of Casper Vermeer's workshop. Whoever had started this fire had caused major damage, leaving barely a frame in place. Flimsy tape fluttered in the late March wind as Hazel pulled on a pair of blue overshoes and gloves. The drifts of snowdrops poking proudly through the white carpet under the oak tree didn't fit with the scene of devastation. She rang Tom and asked him to look into the details of the arson investigation for her. She wondered why this hadn't come up when she'd looked Vermeer up herself. Perhaps she'd been in too much of a hurry to speak to him. Or worse, had brain fog got in the way. Within two minutes, Tom had called her back.

'Hey Tom, that was quick, what did you find out?' Hazel's eyes widened on hearing who the senior investigating officer was. It was a man she'd known very well a long time ago but had no idea he was back in Perth. 'Thanks,' she said and ended the call.

The sound of car tyres came from behind her. 'Ah shit,' she muttered under her breath while she smiled at the driver.

As if he'd heard her thinking about him, DI Gerry Smith waved at her, his stupid grin plastered over his face.

'Well, Hazel Todd, this is a lovely surprise,' he beamed at her as he locked up his car.

Gerry hadn't changed in the thirty years since they'd met at Tulliallan police training college where, much to Rick's amusement, Gerry had had a serious crush on Hazel. Hearing he'd managed to get a job in Inverness after graduating had delighted her, especially as she'd managed to stay in Tayside. Many miles away from her admirer. He'd been harmless but irritating.

'Gerry, it's great to see you,' Hazel smiled until she was bustled into his arms for a hug.

'God, how long has it been?' he asked once he'd released her. 'We should have arranged a thirty-year graduation do, shouldn't we?'

Hazel couldn't think of many social events more cringey than meeting up with middle-aged peers like herself.

'Mm maybe, yes,' she agreed reluctantly. 'How long have you been back in Perth?'

Gerry rolled his eyes. 'Since the divorce. I put in for a transfer as soon as I could when I heard a position had become available back here.' Then his expression softened. 'I heard what happened to Rick. I'm sorry.'

'Aye, it was grim, all right,' Hazel agreed but immediately made to change the subject. She pointed to the remains of Vermeer's workshop. 'What's gone on here, then? Have you got any leads?'

'Nah, CCTV is useless and the cameras in the other warehouses were switched off,' he frowned at her. 'What's your interest in Casper Vermeer? Anything I should know about?' Gerry tucked the stray strands of his ginger hair behind his ear before rubbing his fingers across the equally vibrant ginger beard, not a fleck of grey to be seen. The man looked barely ten years older than the last time she'd seen him and that was thirty years ago. How different her life was then! Suddenly Hazel felt old.

'I'm not sure yet,' Hazel admitted. 'He was having a relationship with one of our murder victims.'

Gerry looked surprised. 'Was he? Who was that?' he asked and pulled out his notebook. 'Naughty, he didn't tell us about that. Makes me wonder what other secrets Mr Vermeer is keeping.'

'Her name was Maggie Ramsay.'

'Maggie Ramsay?' Gerry's eyes revealed his surprise.

'Yes, do you know her?'

'Yes, she was the woman who knocked the lad down, wasn't she? That teacher.'

Hazel nodded. 'Aye, that's right.' Then she watched him stare quietly from the burnt-out warehouse to Hazel. 'What are you thinking?' she asked because Gerry might be an irritating man, but he was a really good police officer. She was confused when he walked away without answering her.

'Are you coming in or what?' he shouted without looking back.

—

'They completely destroyed the place,' Hazel said, staring around inside the frame. She could smell charred wood and metal, a stench that clung to the air. Making it hard to breathe.

'This is the source.' Gerry showed her to a pile of burned rags in the corner next to the remains of what might have once been a sofa. 'They used an accelerant on a sofa he'd taken in to restore for a client.'

'He was a restorer as well,' Hazel suggested.

'Yes, Vermeer is an incredibly talented man.'

'Have you spoken to the client who asked him to restore it?' Hazel asked.

'Not yet but he's on my list,' Gerry replied. 'It was Samuel Ramsay. A surprise for his wife, apparently. It was an inherited piece he wanted him to restore.'

Hazel couldn't believe what she was hearing. Both men might not have lied directly to her but what they had omitted to say spoke volumes.

Chapter Thirty-Two

Bumping into Gerry Smith had been more helpful to Hazel than she'd imagined on seeing his silver BMW pulling up outside Vermeer's burnt-out property. The two murders had looked so closely connected by David Wilson but thinking about the Ramsays and Vermeer was giving her a headache.

'Here you go.' Billy Flynn smiled and laid a hot cup of tea in front of her. 'How did it go with "Brenda"?' He added the quotation mark gesture when he said it.

Hazel sipped. The tea was perfect and exactly what she needed. Her mouth was so dry.

'Have you ever heard of Casper Vermeer?' she asked.

Billy shook his head. 'Nah, who is he?'

'He's a furniture designer and he's our "Brenda".' She mimicked his quotation marks with her own fingers. 'He had also accepted a recent commission from Samuel Ramsay, it seems.'

'Did Samuel Ramsay know about Vermeer and Maggie, do you think?' Billy suggested.

'Sandra, the friend, doesn't think so but Vermeer says that Maggie told him she was planning on telling her husband last Thursday night.'

'Interesting,' Billy said as he opened the drawer in his desk. He laid a KitKat in front of her.

'Yes, very.' Hazel swallowed down the tea. 'Aw, thanks, buddy, I'm starving.' She snapped the chocolate sticks and bit down. 'Remind me. The laptops? Oh, and the surveillance team are up to speed, are they?'

Billy nodded and flipped open his notebook. 'Yes, there's a couple of shifts going up there. They think they've got a good spot and one of them is sitting inside the house.'

'Good idea,' Hazel admitted. 'The laptops?' she repeated.

'Maggie Ramsay's laptop had nothing. Facebook didn't give me anything of note. She didn't even talk to the guy, what was his name, Vermeer, on there. She had about fifty or so friends and nobody stuck out. She was mainly in groups for Auld Perth and some teacher education ones.'

'What about—' Hazel started to say as Andrea chipped in.

'The stolen car has been found!' she announced.

'Get it to forensics. I want it stripped for fingerprints and DNA.'

'That might be a bit difficult,' Andrea said. 'It's been pretty badly burnt.'

'What? Please tell me you're kidding?'

Andrea shook her head. 'If they'd thought to remove the reg number we might not have known it was the car we were looking for.'

'Shit!' Hazel sighed. 'Thanks, Andrea. It might still have something useful to us,' she tutted, trying to convince herself as well as her team.

Hazel turned back to Billy.

'Tell me you've got something on King's laptops.'

Billy looked at her in surprise.

'I'm afraid his had already been taken before I got a chance to look at it,' he said.

'What do you mean "taken"?' Hazel was confused.

'Daly came in and took them both.'

'What the hell?'

Billy shrugged. 'He came in about an hour ago and asked for the two laptops to be handed over.'

'Why didn't you tell me this before?'

'I assumed you knew. That you had arranged for a deeper forensic examination.'

'No, Billy, I hadn't done anything of the sort,' Hazel answered, fuming that Daly had done this. She walked into her office and immediately dialled Daly's office number hoping for answers.

Tom arrived before she managed to get an answer, so she hung up.

'Tom.' Hazel raised her hand to greet him. 'How's David Wilson?'

'Subdued but then his mum has just died, hasn't she?'

'Has the solicitor arrived yet?' Hazel checked her watch. She had been dismayed to learn the solicitor was finishing up a case in Edinburgh before coming through to attend his interview.

'Aye, she's waiting for you.'

Still reeling from Billy's revelation about Daly and the laptops, Hazel had to focus. 'Good, good. Come on, let's see what he has to say about the prints.'

Chapter Thirty-Three

To say David Wilson looked broken would be an understatement. Part of Hazel knew how he felt because her mum had died suddenly too. She knew that pain. That shock. She'd been a good bit younger than him, but David was still just a kid and had already been through so much. First losing his dad to cancer. Then losing Liam in such a violent and horrific way followed by the lack of justice. That would break even the strongest person and now the last member of his family was gone. Hazel felt sorry for him. But two people had been murdered. This interview couldn't wait. David was the only person that connected both of them.

The lad was barely audible when asked to confirm his name, but Hazel was undeterred. She was about to begin asking him a question when David spoke first.

'Where's my mum?' he asked without looking up; instead, his head remained down while he picked at his nails.

'Your mum has been taken to Dundee for—'

'Dundee!' David exclaimed, lifting his gaze finally. 'Why has she been taken through there? Why isn't she at the funeral home?'

Hazel realised he didn't know the procedure. Why should he? He shouldn't be dealing with this at his age. 'Your mum has passed away unexpectedly at home so a post-mortem will be carried out to determine a cause of death.'

Hazel had a vague recollection of this same conversation happening around her when her mum died. Not to her, but around her.

'Can't they do that here? Mum doesn't like Dundee.'

A strange thing to say under the circumstances. But these weren't normal circumstances.

'She'll be brought back as soon as they've finished.' Hazel spoke slowly knowing he needed time to take it all in. 'We just want to establish why your mum passed away so suddenly.'

David stared blankly, narrowing his green eyes as if trying to process what was going on around him. Eventually, he nodded. 'OK. What will happen to her then?'

'Well,' Hazel began, quickly realising he would be out of his depth with arranging her funeral. 'We'll find out how your mum died first then take it from there. Do you have someone who can help you make the arrangements?'

David frowned and shook his head, then he looked at Hazel. 'Maybe Suzanne? Oh, I don't know.'

'We'll put you in touch with people who can help,' Tom interjected. 'Don't worry about all that for now.'

Hazel was grateful for Tom's intervention but knew that David wouldn't have to worry about any of that if he was found guilty.

'OK,' David agreed and rested his arms on the edge of the table. He stared down at his feet. Then he looked up. 'Why am I even here? I've already told you I had nothing to do with that Ramsay woman's death. I was with Suzanne. Hasn't she told you that?'

'She has,' Hazel confirmed. 'But your fingerprints have been found at two more crime scenes since then.'

'What?'

'Does the name Peter King mean anything to you?'

David screwed up his face in disgust. 'Fucking pervert.'

'You admit to knowing Mr King, then.'

'Unfortunately,' David scowled. 'I don't know what the council were thinking putting him in that block. There are wee lassies living in there. Disgusting freak.' He scoffed. 'Funnily enough, he's another one that got off lightly for the sick shit he did.'

'So you can confirm that you not only knew Mr King, but you are also aware of his conviction.' Hazel needed him to say it.

'Yes,' David acknowledged. 'Everybody knew. It was in the papers.'

Hazel watched David's solicitor scribble something down on her pad.

'Can you explain how your prints came to be found at the scene?' Hazel asked and laid a photo in front of him.

David turned away from the scene of horror in the picture, pressing his body as far back into the chair as it could go.

'Jesus!' he exclaimed. 'I didn't do that – if that's what you're about to say. Fucking hell!' he exclaimed as he tried to look again but couldn't.

Hazel tidied the crime scene photos away again into the brown folder. His reaction seemed genuine.

'Why were your prints at the crime scene?' Hazel pressed him.

'All right, we hassled him a bit, might have roughed him up a couple of times but…' He turned his face away then pointed at her folder. 'We never did that!'

'Who's we?'

'Me and Sean.'

'Do you mean Sean Jacobs?' Hazel asked.

'Aye, that's right.'

'When did you and Sean last "rough him up", as you put it?'

David slumped forward. 'I cannae believe you're asking me this!'

'When, David?' Hazel urged.

'About a week ago.'

'What happened?'

David sighed. 'Me and Sean were coming out of the chippy, and we seen him going into the close, so we followed him. We'd hud a couple of cans,' he shrugged. 'He was acting like butter wouldnae melt. Sick bastard.' He stopped for a second, took a brief glance at his solicitor then faced Hazel. 'He touched his ain niece, did she tell you that? His brother gien him a right good kicking fur it. Didnae stop the freak though, did it?'

David's contempt for the man was crystal clear from the tone and venom in his voice.

'What did you and Sean do then?'

'You should ask Rona,' David announced. 'She filmed us when she turned up. Told us to go or she'd call the police.'

'Do you have anything other than my client's prints in a property he admits he's been to on a number of occasions?' David's solicitor finally spoke. 'Do you have eyewitnesses putting him at the scene at the time of the murder, or better still, CCTV?'

David sat quietly while she continued. 'Do you have blood or DNA from anyone other than your victim that matches my client and you said his fingerprints were in crime scenes, plural. Would you care to expand on that?'

Hazel looked at David. 'You broke into the Ramsays' home didn't you.'

David's solicitor looked at him. 'You don't have to answer that.'

Ignoring her, David replied. 'So what?'

'If that's all you have then I suggest that my client be allowed to leave.'

Hazel had to admit that the answer was yes. The prints were all she had. This case was going round in circles and a real break seemed just out of reach. She knew it was there, tantalisingly close, but she couldn't get hold of it. Did Samuel Ramsay want Maggie dead? But what did that have to do with Peter King? It didn't help that Daly had marched in and confiscated King's laptop. What the hell did he want with it? David Wilson was her strongest suspect but still, she was missing something. Hopefully, Samuel Ramsay could help fill in some of the blanks.

Chapter Thirty-Four

Before the next team briefing, Hazel tried Daly's phone again but, like the last time, he didn't answer. Something was going on and she didn't like being kept in the dark. She'd go to his office once she'd spoken to the rest of the team.

'Gerry,' Hazel said, surprised to see Gerry Smith walk towards her.

'Hey, just wondered how you were getting on with your case?' he said.

'Och, you know, slowly, what about you?'

'All right, as it happens; a member of the public has handed us some dashcam footage which is very interesting indeed.'

'Oh yes?' Hazel was genuinely intrigued. 'Come through,' she said and showed Gerry into her office.

'So you're a DCI now, huh?' Gerry smiled. 'Good for you.'

'Aye, it's not bad, I suppose,' she replied, not in the mood for Gerry's small talk. She prompted him to focus. 'The dashcam footage?'

'What? Yes,' he continued and pulled his phone out. He scrolled through a roll of photos and Hazel wondered whether it was deliberate that she was 'accidentally' shown a topless Gerry's surprisingly muscular but pale chest on the beach with the word Barbados on it. 'Sorry, ignore that... ah, here, what do you make of this, then?'

'Is that who I think it is?' Hazel was gobsmacked on seeing the figure she recognised on the screen.

Gerry beamed. 'Yep, Lara Vermeer walking away from the warehouse with a petrol can in her hand.'

Not only that. She had a baseball cap on.

'Wow, that's blatant. Don't you think?'

'Aye, I'm heading up there now to talk to her,' Gerry explained. 'Sorry to spoil any theories you had about the fire being connected to your vic.'

'It's fine.' Hazel smiled but didn't mention their suspect had been wearing a cap like Lara had on in the footage. 'I'm glad you got your man. Or woman, in this case,' Hazel corrected herself. 'I hope she wraps your case up quickly for you.' What she didn't add was that she might also have a word with Lara at some point. But not until David Wilson could be definitively ruled out.

His expression became serious for a second and Hazel was concerned something was wrong.

'Listen there's a band on the night at the Twa Tams that I think you'll like,' Gerry began. 'It's my nephew's band, actually, God are we that old already?' he rambled then blushed. 'Not that I'm trying to say you look old… are old, I mean.' He was tongue-tied like a teenager and Hazel felt awkward. It reminded her of the first time he'd asked her out on a date thirty years ago. 'What I'm trying to say, in my ham-fisted way, is do you fancy coming along? Just as friends… unless…' He coughed and scratched at his beard. A nervous tic. 'I think you'd like them.'

Hazel didn't know what to say. It had been years since a man actually asked her out on a date. A real date. Was it a date? The kind that makes you want to dress up, look your best and impress the other person. Could she really be bothered? Really? His face, though… He was a sweet guy, and it might be fun. She heard the incident room door opening and a burst of voices echo along the corridor. Tom and Andrea would be sitting waiting for her to update them any second.

'Sure, why not? I'd love to.'

'Brilliant.' Gerry's face lit up. 'I'll text you.'

'OK, I'll look forward to it,' Hazel smiled and watched him leave.

Gerry walked past Tom with a wide beaming smile on his face.

'All right,' Tom greeted him.

'Absolutely,' Gerry replied and began to whistle as he walked through the door.

Tom stared at Andrea who was staring right back at him. They both turned to look at Hazel whose face was almost as red as Andrea's hair.

'What?' Hazel asked.

'You tell me,' Tom replied then looked at Billy who had been sitting not far from Hazel's office door the whole time.

'Don't look at me.' Billy held his hands up. 'I know nothing.'

Hazel quickly realised Billy had probably heard everything. She caught him staring at her with a wide grin growing on his face.

'Billy, CCTV from near King's address. Any updates?' She bluffed her way out of the awkward situation hoping nobody would mention Gerry's visit.

'Nothing new, boss, I'm waiting on a couple of businesses getting back to me.'

'OK, Wilson suggested that King's niece had recorded an encounter that he and Sean Jacobs had with her uncle,' Hazel said. 'Tom, could you talk to her. Ask her if we can have that footage and ask her why she didn't mention this before, will you?'

'Sure, no problem, it will be interesting to see if the footage matches where his prints were found in the property. It will help corroborate his version of events at the very least.' He wrote a couple of lines in his notebook.

'Exactly. Not that it rules him right out, but…' She sighed. 'I don't know about this lad. What's everyone else's thoughts?'

'He's volatile enough,' Tom suggested.

'Andrea, what do you think?' Hazel asked.

'My gut says, if they were isolated incidents, then yes, David might be good for it, but I think it's more organised than that. Look at the break-in at the judge's place.'

'What about the firm that's helping the Wilsons with their civil case, are they connected to Peter King?' Tom added.

'On it,' Billy chirped again and hit the keys on his laptop.

'Andrea, can I get you to chase up anything Billy finds?'

'Of course.' Seeing Billy looking at her, that daft smile on his face, Andrea returned his grin.

'Where are we on Samuel Ramsay and the boyfriend, what's his name, Vermeer?' Tom asked.

'I'm going to go back there in a bit, to see what he can tell me,' Hazel told him. 'Once I've spoken to Daly, that is. Did you know he was planning to take the laptops, Tom?'

'What? No! Why would he do that?' Tom asked.

'That's exactly what I want to know.'

'Not only that, why did he not tell you in advance?' Tom added.

'I'll let you know once I track him down,' Hazel told him. 'Right, report back first thing or before. My phone will be on.'

She was about to grab her bag and head to Daly's office when he appeared in the doorway of her own.

'Sir, I was just about to come and talk to you, actually.' Hazel stood up from her chair. 'You've just saved me the trip.'

Daly closed the door after himself and took a seat opposite, a sombre look on his face.

'I'm sorry it's taken me so long to get back to you,' he said.

'What's going on with—'

Daly raised a hand to prevent her saying anything further. 'I'll have to stop you right there, I'm afraid.'

Hazel frowned. 'What do you mean?'

Daly sat back in the chair. 'I need you to stop worrying about what's on Peter King's laptop.'

'I don't understand,' Hazel said plainly. 'How can I possibly do that? There might be something on there that could identify his killer, sir.'

'A very sensitive investigation could be put in jeopardy if you root around any deeper in this but...' He pointed a finger up to stop her interrupting. 'I do have some information that I can share with you.'

'OK.'

'Peter King was in conversation, messages, you know the kind of thing I mean.'

'Yep,' Hazel answered drily, not liking where this was heading.

'He was expecting to meet a young girl that night. A young girl he'd been communicating with. He was pretending to be a boy her age. Now, we don't know if she ever got there that night so...'

'So... what...'

'Let me finish,' he told her and handed her a printout of a conversation. 'This is the last transcript that was found.'

'Diva2008, who's that?'

'We don't know yet,' Daly answered.

'We?'

'Don't ask me any more than that, Hazel.' Daly moved to stand up again. 'That's all I can give you.'

'So...' She didn't quite know what else to say apart from the obvious. 'Are you ordering me to drop this?'

'Yes, Hazel, that's exactly what I'm doing,' Daly confirmed and was gone before Hazel could respond.

She looked out at Billy working at his laptop, hoping he could find out who this Diva2008 was. If not, he'd know someone who could. On top of that, he had friends in the force who had the experience to perhaps also uncover the operation Daly had mentioned.

'Billy, could you come here a minute?' she called out.

'What's up? What did Daly want?' Billy asked.

'I was wondering if you could identify someone for me.'

'Sure, if I can.'

Billy took the transcript that Hazel held out to him.

'Can you track this person for me. Daly is sure it's just a teenager, but can you check? He thinks that King was posing as a teenage boy to lure her.'

'I'll certainly try but there's not much here to go on.' He skimmed through the pages. 'There's no IP address.'

'Thanks, I'd really appreciate it,' she replied, seemingly ignoring his negativity. 'Listen I wondered as well, do you still have connections? You know, the kind that can find out stuff that we're not supposed to know. Covert operations, that kind of thing?'

'Aye, I've got one or two, why?'

'Good, I've got something I need you to find out about. Discreetly, of course.'

'Of course.'

Chapter Thirty-Five

The door squeaked open to reveal a tired-looking Rona King. She yawned then covered her mouth as Tom held up his ID. Tom had to stifle a yawn too. It had been a hell of a long day. John often complained about the long hours Tom did and now that it was gone 7pm he knew John would have a go. Again.

'I'm sorry, hello, Detective.'

'Hello, Rona, could you spare me five minutes? I've got some more questions I'd like to ask you. I know you've already spoken to my colleague, but I'd really appreciate a few moments of your time.'

'Yes, sure.' Rona held the door wide open and pointed towards a door to the right. 'Please go through.'

'Thanks.' He could smell a fruity aroma as he moved deeper into the hall then realised the smell was coming from an orange candle burning on the hall table. That was the fragrance. Oranges.

'Have a seat.' She grabbed a pile of washing from one of the mismatched armchairs. 'Excuse the mess, I'm on a string of night shifts and my body clock is all over the place. The flat has kinda taken a back seat.'

'It's fine,' Tom assured her. 'Where is it you work?'

'I'm a care assistant in a nursing home so...' She yawned again. 'I'm sorry. There's stuff I wanted to ask you, actually. When will I be able to arrange Uncle Peter's funeral? He's not got anybody else that can do it. It's just that I'm supposed to be going on holiday next week and—'

'Not for a while yet,' Tom interrupted her. 'We'll be keeping hold of Peter's body for a bit longer. A post-mortem hasn't been carried out yet.'

'Of course, yes,' she replied. 'I don't know what I was thinking.' Her eyes filled up. 'Ignore me.' She held up a hand and took a deep breath to compose herself.

'It's OK, it's a hard time for you, I understand.'

'Don't get me wrong, I'm not crying for him,' she scoffed quietly. 'I just keep seeing his body. The mess, the blood.' She shivered. 'I never want to see anything like that ever again.' She looked away, her eyes tight shut as she shook her head.

'That must have been pretty awful for you. I'm sorry you had to see that.'

'You can say that again.' She fiddled with the leather bracelet she was wearing. 'What is it you wanted to ask me, then?'

Tom pulled his notebook out of his jacket pocket just as a small dog appeared from behind the kitchen door.

'Is that a French bulldog you've got?' Tom asked.

As Rona turned the little grey dog's tail started to wag furiously and he panted and gambled towards them.

'Yes.' She snatched him up into her arms. 'This is Reg. I did have his brother, Ronnie, too until recently. My next door neighbour comes in to let him out and feed him when I'm working.'

'He's very handsome.' Tom smiled and reached forward to scratch behind Reg's ear. 'Erm, yes, so…' He scanned his notebook. 'A witness has told us that you filmed an altercation between your uncle and a couple of young lads.'

'Do you mean David and Sean?' Rona asked.

'That's right, yes. I was wondering if I could have a look at that footage, perhaps you could even send it to me.'

Rona sighed and handed the dog unexpectedly to him before she walked away. 'Hang on, my phone is charging in my bedroom. I'll not be a sec.'

'Oh, OK,' Tom said and stared into the big brown eyes that were gazing up at him, the dog's tongue lolling as he panted, the stench of dog breath wafting uninvited into Tom's face.

'Here you go.' Rona handed her iPhone over when she returned and lifted the dog back into her arms.

'Thanks.' Tom wiped the collection of small grey hairs from his black trousers and pressed play.

It was haunting to see a living, breathing image of Peter King. Minus the slashes and stabs and mutilations his body had sustained. David Wilson's face was filled with disgust, and it was clear both lads were drunk. How he'd managed to leave his prints in the property was obvious on seeing him grabbing hold of the doorframe and the wall inside the front door to steady himself when he swayed drunkenly. The reason for the huge dent in the door was revealed also when Sean Jacobs landed a heavy blow on it with his boot. Rona's voice could be heard threatening to call the police and Peter telling her not to. Rona had strong words with the two teenagers as they laughed, with expletives aplenty being fired in Peter's direction. Before leaving, David Wilson spat on Peter King's shoes. Tom noted that they should be tested for DNA.

'Do you think either of those two idiots could do that to him?' Rona asked, lowering herself slowly down onto the arm of the other gaudy, plum-coloured armchair.

'Everything is a possibility until we can prove it's not.' He handed the phone back. 'Send that to me, will you?'

'Sure,' she replied and laid the dog down on the cushions. 'Will you let me know as soon as I can sort everything out?'

Tom nodded. 'Of course, but listen, there's something else I want to ask you.'

Rona frowned at him. 'Yes?'

'Why didn't you tell us about that footage before? Surely you must have thought it could be significant.' Tom pressed her for an explanation.

Rona sighed, avoiding his eyes. 'I just forgot. I'm sorry.'

If that was her explanation, it would have to suffice, for now.

'I'm not arranging anything fancy, you understand,' Rona said, seemingly keen to change the subject. 'It will just be a basic cremation. I doubt there will be a big turnout. It will probably just be me, to be honest.'

Tom thought she looked genuinely saddened by that.

'I understand and I promise I'll be in touch as soon as I know anything. If you think of anything else too, please get in touch.'

'I will.' Rona stood and followed Tom back to the door, Reg the bulldog at their heels.

As soon as the front door was opened, Reg started to snarl and growl at a pale, thin woman in a baseball cap who had been about to knock.

'Reg!' Rona snatched him back into her arms. 'I'm sorry, Suzanne, go through.'

Tom smiled politely at the face he recognised as she nodded to him. Once the woman was out of earshot he asked Rona how she knew David Wilson's girlfriend, Suzanne Gerrard. He hadn't expected to hear what she said next: Suzanne was her cousin.

Chapter Thirty-Six

Andrea readied her ID to show Samuel Ramsay as she walked into his hospital room. She noticed that the ward had filled with the evening visitors.

'Hello, Mr Ramsay. My name is DC Andrea Graham. DCI Todd has asked me to come and ask you a few more questions, if that's all right.'

Andrea closed the door after herself and turned to the sight of his frowning expression staring back at her.

'I've told the police everything I can remember already,' he told her plainly and reached for the cup of water on the table.

Andrea noticed right away that his eyes had flicked sideways, and his hands trembled. Was that significant, she wondered.

'You failed to mention that you knew Casper Vermeer,' Andrea said simply as she took a seat next to his bed. His face blushed at her statement, and he looked out of the window at the shower of snow that had people scurrying for cover.

'What about him?' He finally said without facing her.

'How do you know Vermeer?'

'He's doing a restoration job for me.' Still Samuel refused to face her.

'Is that all?' She watched him lick his lips before he took a large gulp from the cup again.

'Yes,' he answered bluntly.

Hazel had given Andrea permission to push him, a little, but to bear in mind he was in hospital because of his weak heart. Just as she opened her mouth to ask again, he beat her to it.

'I knew they were having an affair, if that's what you're wondering.' He sighed and finally looked at Andrea. 'She told me last week.' He sighed again and fell slowly back into the pillows. 'I found Vermeer's card in her bag, and I stupidly thought she was considering having him re-cover that blasted chair that has been taking up space in our garage for the past two years.'

'That must have been quite a shock – upsetting for you to learn that your wife was being unfaithful to you.'

'I was absolutely devastated,' he said, his words filled with emotion. He rubbed his finger underneath his eye. 'It's the last thing I could imagine her doing. We've been through so much together recently. Well, you already know that, don't you?'

A text landed before she could respond. It was from Tom.

> Ask Ramsay if he knows Suzanne Gerrard.
> David Wilson's girlfriend.

Andrea stuffed her phone into her pocket.

'Mr Ramsay, does the name Suzanne Gerrard mean anything to you?'

The blank expression he was giving her was disappointing.

'The name doesn't ring any bells, no. Do you think she could be involved in my wife's death? Who is she?'

'She's nobody important,' Andrea replied and nibbled on her lip, trying to reorganise her thoughts. She'd leave that for now, grateful that he seemed to accept her answer. 'What about Peter King?'

'Listen, I'm sorry I have no idea who these people are.' Ramsay's mood was growing brittle.

The knock on the door briefly disturbed her train of thought.

'I'm sorry, I can come back if you're busy. I didn't realise you had a visitor.'

Andrea looked round to see a plump, greying woman standing in the doorway.

'Hello Sandra,' Samuel smiled at her. 'Detective, this is Maggie's friend.'

'Nice to meet you.' Andrea acknowledged the woman who bustled in with a carrier bag draped over her wrist.

'I've brought you some clean pyjamas,' Sandra began. 'I've done my best to give the place a tidy up for you after what happened. The police said I could after they'd finished taking fingerprints.' She looked at Andrea. 'What a terrible shock I got when I walked in and there he was!' She clutched a hand to her chest. 'Would you like me to call the insurance people for you?'

'I can imagine,' Andrea agreed. Being faced with David like that must have been scary.

Sandra then turned to face Samuel. 'There's some snacks and some bottles of cold water, as well. I know you're not that keen on the water they bring you here.'

'You're a life-saver,' Samuel beamed. 'Thank you and no I'll sort out the insurance when I get home.' Then he focussed his attention completely on Andrea. 'Have you arrested him yet?'

She knew exactly who he meant. David Wilson. 'He's been helping us with our inquiries.'

'What about what he did to our house?'

'That investigation is also ongoing, Mr Ramsay.'

Andrea was relieved when Sandra spoke.

'Oh, there were a couple of letters on the doormat. I brought them, as well. I didn't know how important they might be.'

Distracted, Samuel lifted the envelopes out. 'Sandra has been good to me since...' He stuttered and choked back tears before ripping open the top one. 'Since, everything.'

'You're lucky to have such a good friend.' Andrea smiled at Sandra who was fussing around the locker then turned to Samuel, to see the colour drain from his face. He was reading the typed letter, unable to speak.

'Samuel?' Sandra murmured, watching him grab his chest and struggle for breath. 'Nurse!' she yelled as she thrust open the door and ran into the corridor.

Andrea looked on in horror as Samuel Ramsay's body grew limp and flopped back onto his pillow before becoming still. She grabbed a pair of gloves from her pocket and snatched the letter from amongst the chaos of bodies that were now surrounding the bed where Samuel had just suffered a cardiac arrest.

> *Dear Samuel,*
> *Your wife didn't deserve to live. You're a clever man. Your PhDs in both English Literature and History are evidence of that. You must have known that the scales of justice would have to be balanced. It wasn't personal. I need you to understand that much. I also know you loved her and that you are grieving. Your pain gives me no pleasure. But what it does do is give you a glimpse into the agony she caused.*

Andrea dropped the letter into a clear evidence bag just as the doctor pronounced Samuel Ramsay dead.

–

'OK, thanks for letting me know,' Hazel said then sighed when Andrea called her. 'Get the letter over to forensics, will you, and then get off home. We'll pick everything up in the morning.'

Hazel feared the headache that had started half an hour ago as a dull throb might be turning into a full-on migraine so swallowed down two paracetamol and decided to pop outside for some fresh air. The doctor had told her that because they'd still not found the right dose for her thyroid meds, she'd still get the headaches from time to time. Was she sleeping? Was she eating properly? The headaches she could handle. The patronizing questions from a lad who looked about twelve, she could not.

Tom's text about Suzanne Gerrard had intrigued her. A woman who was connected to both of the victims. As well as David Wilson, of course. Then she'd told Tom to get off home to John.

Hazel sipped from the bottle of chilled water as she looked out onto the traffic on the Dunkeld road, busy in both directions, despite the weather conditions. The new road layout made the traffic move more smoothly even if the roadworks had been a nuisance.

She held the cool bottle against her temple to soothe the ache. She took a few deep breaths and blew them out slowly, hoping that would help shift the worst of the headache too.

—

The man standing round the side entrance to the primary school on the other side of the road watched Hazel rub the bottle across her brow. He wasn't surprised to see she had a headache. She'd been through so much. He'd seen the lights come on in her flat at all hours of the day and night. It wasn't a surprise she didn't sleep much either, given the stress she'd been under. If she would give him a chance to help her, she wouldn't regret it.

He snapped a final shot on his phone just as Hazel walked back towards the station entrance.

Chapter Thirty-Seven

Hazel filled a cup of cool water for herself. She rubbed her fingers across her brow as if that was a magic cure for her headache. An early night had to be on the cards tonight but she knew that wasn't likely. Hazel found it hard to switch off when she had a huge case like this one. A double murder within days of each other. Two people, seemingly so unconnected in life, brutally murdered. Apart from of course the fact they'd gotten off very lightly for awful crimes. Crimes involving children. She was relieved that Lady Campbell was safely hidden given that she was the person who had handed those sentences down. She may be the next intended target. Hazel's head swam with so many thoughts until a text chirped. She grabbed her phone from her pocket.

> I'll meet you outside the Twa Tams at 8.00. We can have a drink before the band comes on at 8.30.

Hazel had completely forgotten she'd said she'd meet Gerry tonight. 'Shit,' she murmured.

> I'm going to have to cancel I'm afraid. Sorry. Something has come up. Another time maybe.

It wasn't a lie. So why did it sound so lame? Hazel was exhausted and the headache was tightening its grip on her skull with a vengeance. She tidied her desk and switched off the lights then checked her phone to ensure Gerry had got the message. She was confused to see he'd read it but hadn't replied. She'd expected to read *No worries* or *Let me know when you're free*.

But there was nothing. Her headache meant she didn't have the time or energy to care about his wounded pride.

The man who had been watching, waiting for her to leave the station, darted in front of a taxi in his haste to intercept Hazel. He waved his hand in apology at the honking of the horn.

'DCI Todd,' he called out a little breathlessly.

Hazel turned to see, in the streetlamps that lit up the busy Dunkeld road, a tall, thin man with long, thick, blond hair tied back in a ponytail, scurrying towards her. He was moving quickly through the emerging daffodil flowerbed, not yet in bloom, almost tripping over in his haste.

'Can I help you?' she said as she unlocked her car, looking the man over carefully. The black rucksack that he had slung over his shoulder looked heavy and his trainers looked worn and dirty.

He pulled a card out of one of the pockets on his khaki combats and held it out to her.

'My name is Grant Erickson. You don't know me but...'

Hazel glanced down at his card before thrusting it straight back into his chest, the force making him take a step back.

'Go away, Mr Erickson. I've told your lot before, I have nothing to say.'

Hazel's headache had intensified as she walked away before she said something she would regret. Something that he would use as a quote against her. It took every ounce of her self-control to get into her car without biting back at him.

'Please, DCI Todd, I just want to talk,' he called out as she closed her car door. He leaned down to knock on the driver's door window. 'Just five minutes.'

Hazel put her car into first gear without engaging him in any more conversation. He was the fourth journalist to try and get her story and she was sure he wouldn't be the last. She would text Rachel Fox when she got home and ask if Erickson had contacted her too.

Chapter Thirty-Eight

That felt better. The headache had finally started to subside on the short drive home. Hazel refilled her glass and gulped another large swig, grateful that the garage across the road had stocked her favourite chardonnay amongst the small selection of whites in the chiller cabinet when she'd stopped in for a frozen pizza to heat up for dinner. She had been positive there were still some garlic bread slices left in the freezer, but she was to be disappointed. Chicago Town bacon and mushroom for one. That would have to do. The headache had almost completely gone after that first glass. Hazel didn't care what had made it go away. She was just grateful it had.

The orange flashing light on her answering machine blinked to attract her attention. Before she could get to it, a text from Daly caught her attention. It wasn't like him to text her. She opened his message, and her heart sank when she read it.

> Sorry to bother you at home but I've been contacted by some mainstream newspapers who want me to confirm what they've been told in connection with our two victims. Come to my office first thing. 8am sharp so we can discuss the matter.

Hazel closed her eyes and sighed deeply. That was all she needed. She tossed her phone onto the worktop and hit the answering machine play button.

You have three messages. Message one.

Hi Hazel, it's Sheila at the home, just wanted to let you know that your dad has a bit of a tummy bug so let us know if you're planning to visit, will you? There's a couple of residents all gone down with the same thing so we're isolating them as a precaution. Don't worry, though. He's still smiling. Ok then, bye.

Hazel grimaced and shook her head as she sipped from her glass. That was the second time since the start of this year the home had got some kind of bug running through it. 'Winter vomiting', they called it. It was almost April. Although when she thought about it further, the weather recently had been more like January than March. She'd wait until morning to give them a ring. The girls had enough on their plate on the late shift. She pressed the button to open the second message.

Message two.

Just me. I hope you've not forgotten that musical is next Saturday at the concert hall. Mind, we got tickets months ago. Well, I just wanted to make sure you got the afternoon off for it. I thought we could go out to tea after it, as well. My treat. Ok then, bye. Oh and, er, I know you're busy with work and that but call me when you get a chance.

Hazel had completely forgotten about *Menopause* – the musical. Cara had bought them tickets ages ago, claiming it would be fun. She'd said the reviews were amazing and they really must see it. Hazel vaguely remembered disagreeing, but the purchase was made regardless. She grimaced as she hit the button again.

Message deleted. Message three.

Hello... you're not in... erm... OK... well my name is Grant Erickson, and my number is...

Message deleted.

How had that weasel journalist got hold of Hazel's home number? She dialled 1471 and jotted down the mobile number, hoping Erickson was the last person who'd called her number. She was about to call it back when the security buzzer blasted, making her jump.

'Fuck!' she exclaimed and clutched a handful of her shirt in her fist, almost dropping her phone in the process. 'Shit.' She exhaled roughly. 'Hello,' she said into the door security phone but was unable to hear what her visitor said because her smoke alarm started to scream as a result of the 'overcooked' pizza in the oven. 'Argh, shit, sorry, hang on...'

With the charred remnants of her dinner lying on the counter, Hazel returned to see if her visitor was still waiting.

'Hello,' she said again.

'Erm, hello Hazel, I hope you don't mind me dropping by, but I was passing on my way home so...'

'Gerry, is that you?' Hazel asked, her eyes wide in surprise.

'Erm, yes, yes, it's Gerry.'

'OK.' she pressed the security button to release the lock. 'Just push the door and come up.'

The sight of the huge pizza box in Gerry's hand was wonderful.

'Looks like I arrived in the nick of time,' Gerry smiled and nodded at the burnt offering on the counter.

Hazel grinned and gulped from her glass before refilling it. She offered the bottle to him. 'Would you like one?' she asked and opened the kitchen window to let some of the choking, burnt smell out.

'Yes please. That would be nice. Thank you.'

Hazel handed him a glass then invited him to sit. 'Thanks for this,' she said and took a huge bite from a slice of pizza. Just a cheese and tomato but that didn't matter. She was famished.

'No problem.' Gerry sipped from his glass, looking at Hazel the whole time over the rim. 'Thanks for this.' He pointed to the wine.

A silence fell gently over the two detectives until Hazel felt she had to apologise for crying off their date. Was it even a date?

'Look I'm sorry for—'

'No need to apologise. It's me that should be sorry. I should have known it was too soon for you.'

Hazel frowned, briefly unsure exactly what he was getting at. Then she clicked.

'Rick and I were divorced so I'm not technically his widow,' she explained. 'You did know that, didn't you?'

The look on his face said that he did not. 'Oh… erm… no, I didn't.'

'Rick left me a year or so before he died,' she began to tell him simply. 'He met someone else, and we got a divorce. So that was that. So like I said I'm not actually his widow.' She ripped off another large slice of pizza before devouring half of it in one bite.

'I didn't know that,' Gerry admitted. 'I'm sorry. That must have been hard for you.'

Hazel shrugged. 'The fact it was my best friend he shacked up with didn't help.'

Gerry's eyes widened. 'Oh.' He gulped his wine and refilled his glass. 'Shit, ouch.'

Talking to him was easy. Perhaps too easy. 'Yes, Cara—'

'It was Cara!' Gerry exclaimed. 'Shit! I remember her from when we were at Tulliallan. She used to come down and see you at weekends, didn't she?'

Hazel smiled. 'I'm surprised you remember that.'

Gerry shrugged. 'Some things just stick, I suppose.'

Hazel's mobile chirped.

Just checking in. The offer of coffee is still there

xx

That made Hazel smile, but she couldn't understand why.

'Good news?'

'What? Erm... no, well, I suppose so,' she stuttered and leaned back to lay her phone on the counter behind her. 'It was Rachel Fox.' Why the hell did she just say that? The wine couldn't be talking already, could it? Hazel didn't talk about Rachel to anybody.

'What? Did you just say Rachel Fox?' Gerry looked shocked. 'Why does she have your number?' Then he held up both his hands. 'I'm sorry, that was out of order. It's none of my business.' He exhaled loudly then sipped from his glass. 'It was just a wee shock, that's all.'

'I know. I suppose our relationship is quite...' She paused to find the correct word, but Gerry beat her to it.

'Unorthodox.'

'That's it.' Hazel pointed a finger towards him. 'Unorthodox,' she repeated.

'So are you two friends now or...' he continued. 'What is she like? I mean, actually like?'

His curiosity didn't surprise her. It made her smile. 'Rachel is just like any of us,' she shrugged. But that wasn't strictly true. 'She's doing her best to be a good person and make a fresh start after all those years behind bars. She volunteers for a charity that helps the homeless.'

'Oh,' Gerry commented. 'That's erm, that's...'

'I know what you're trying to say.'

'I'm sorry,' he shrugged. 'It's just I can't see you and her... You and a serial killer being...' He stopped.

'Being what? Friends?' Hazel said. 'I know how strange it must look to other people, but I suppose we are friends. Kind of.'

'But it was her that…' He hesitated and gulped from his glass. 'You know…'

'Maybe that's what connects us, Gerry.'

Hazel was glad he didn't say it. Hearing the words was still difficult. She supposed her relationship with Rachel was strange after what had happened to Rick.

'I know,' she replied quietly and lifted the wine bottle, offering it to him.

'Yes please.' Gerry held out his glass. 'So you and Rachel, do you meet up for coffee or…'

Hazel laughed and shook her head. 'Not exactly.'

'I'm sorry, I don't mean to pry, it's just…'

'I don't judge your fascination. You're not the only one who finds it interesting. I've had a journalist after my story as well. More than one, actually.'

'Shit, I'm sorry.'

Hazel shrugged. 'It's not your fault. How's your arson investigation going?' She tried to steer the conversation in another direction.

'I'm afraid I don't talk about the job when I'm not on the clock,' he grinned.

'Fair enough,' Hazel replied and wished she could switch off like that.

She was becoming uncomfortable with the way he was looking at her. She recognised that look from thirty years ago. He clearly still liked her. She avoided his eyes and grabbed another large slice of pizza.

'What about you?' she said through a mouthful of food. 'What's happening in the world of Gerry Smith these days?' she asked and flopped back in the dining chair, the effects of the wine sending a warm glow through her body. Her head felt lighter than it had all day. More relaxed.

'My life is boring as hell,' he exclaimed.

'Not a lot has changed then,' Hazel chuckled.

'Oi, cheeky,' Gerry grinned. 'I know I was always just the ginger geeky one.'

'You said it, not me.' Hazel laughed and sank the dregs of her glass, disappointed to see they'd finished the bottle.

'Should I pop out and get us another?' Gerry suggested, staring intensely into her eyes.

Hazel screwed up her nose. 'I have to be up early tomorrow,' she said. 'I've been summoned into Daly's office first thing, and I've got murderers to catch.'

Gerry grinned. 'Aye, no rest for the wicked eh,' he teased and stood up from the table. He pointed to the pizza box. 'I'll leave you that last slice.'

'Thanks,' Hazel gave him a thumbs-up without getting up.

'So, I'll see you soon,' Gerry said and pushed his chair slowly under the table.

Hazel smiled. 'Not if I see you first,' she teased.

There was a brief moment when she thought he was going to kiss her, before it passed as quickly as it had appeared.

'Goodnight, Hazel.'

'Aye, goodnight, Gerry and...' she lifted the final slice out the box. 'Thanks for this.'

'You're welcome,' he winked. 'I'll see myself out.'

Hazel smiled and watched him leave her kitchen. She heard her door close and his footsteps echo down the stairs of her apartment block. The temptation to look out of the window was too much and she couldn't decide if she was disappointed not to see him glance up at her window as he walked back towards Perth city centre.

—

Grant Erickson snapped a couple of shots of the man who'd just left her block. It wasn't a face he recognised. He looked up from behind the parked van where he'd been crouching and saw that she was watching the stranger before letting the curtain fall back down. He scrolled through his contacts and pressed call as he stood up straight, stretching his long legs to encourage the circulation back into them.

'Aye, it's me. No joy yet but I'll try again tomorrow. Call me when you get this message.'

He stuffed his phone into the front pocket of his rucksack and got into his Land Rover. As he reached down to start the engine a loud knock hit the passenger window. He turned to see a familiar face staring at him. Erickson rolled down the passenger window.

'I think you and I need to have a little talk, don't you?'

Chapter Thirty-Nine

Tuesday

Hazel woke suddenly and it took her a moment to focus, to realise she was slumped face down on the pillow and not on the dance floor of a nightclub she and Rick had once gone to in Majorca. The dream she'd just woken from had been so real, and Rick had been so alive. So very alive that she could smell him, touch him. He'd smiled at her in a way he'd done when they first met. Those eyes had looked at her as if she were the only person in the room. They'd danced. They'd kissed. Then Hazel had woken up with a start, reality hammering back into her.

She reached for the glass of water and gulped what was left in it. Her mouth was dry and tasted like shit. A sour thick taste she thought might line a sewer wall. Her breath wasn't much better. The headache hadn't arrived yet, which was nice. A pee was pressing on her bladder, alerting her that she really should make a decision about getting up soon or one would be made for her. The offer that the journalist had made her was a fair one, she had to admit. But it wasn't about the money. Hazel was fine, financially. His face had been a picture when she'd hammered on his car window. It was probably the wine talking, but she'd taken his card and told him she'd be in touch. A loose promise she hoped wouldn't come back and bite her on the arse.

She checked the time on the clock on the bedside table which read quarter past seven.

'Ah hell,' she exclaimed and threw back the duvet. It would have to be a very quick shower, but she had time, just.

An early morning meeting with Daly was the last thing she wanted. As she rinsed the shampoo from her hair, Hazel reflected on the time she'd spent with Gerry last night. He was sweet and really seemed to want to listen to her, which she'd enjoyed. She found herself hoping he'd text her or call and ask her if she'd like to go out for a bite to eat. Hazel could call him. It was the twenty-first century, after all, but there was something nice about wondering when he might call her. Maybe she was being old-fashioned, a sign of her age, but Hazel didn't care.

—

'Have a seat, DCI Todd.' Daly pointed, sombre-faced, at the chair opposite his.

Hazel wished he'd call her by her first name and she did not like the look on his face.

'Sir.' She sat down slowly and waited. Small talk seemed unwelcome in this atmosphere.

'I'll get straight to the point,' Daly began. 'I think it's in both our interests if I do that.'

Hazel swallowed hard. That didn't sound good. 'OK,' she said quietly, the word almost getting stuck inside her throat.

'Like I said, I've had newspaper journalists asking questions. I've managed to put them off until I've spoken to you, but their patience won't last long. You and I both know that.' He raised his eyebrows at her, seemingly to emphasise his point.

This didn't sound as though it was just the local rags that had been pestering him. Hazel dreaded to think which papers they were. She did not enjoy the idea of having her face in them. They would bring up what happened. She was in no doubt about that. Rachel, too – her name would surely be brought up in connection with Hazel's, the two women forever linked by the tragedy that they both wanted to forget.

'I see,' Hazel replied, unsure what else to say.

'Are you any closer to closing this case? And what about Lady Campbell, is she in danger?'

'Erm…' Hazel stopped to take a breath. 'Erm…' She knew she was stuttering.

She had to pull herself together, but it was the shock, the fear of being splashed on the pages of a newspaper. Having everything brought up again and so publicly. It had unnerved her. On top of that, she felt a damn hot flush starting.

'DCI Todd?' Daly frowned at her.

'What? Erm, yes.' She found her focus and looked him dead in the eye. 'Lady Campbell's home has a team in place. If anyone else turns up, they'll be seen. She's perfectly safe. Lady Campbell has gone to stay with a friend.' She coughed to clear her throat. 'We've found the car that hit Maggie Ramsay. It's been burnt badly but…'

Daly sighed loudly and slumped back in his chair. It was then that Hazel noticed the heavy jowls he'd developed. The result of a more sedentary life that went with his status, she supposed. There was a growing paunch around his belly too. What hair he had seemed to be greyer than she'd noticed before. She tried not to look at them. Maybe she should feel sorry for the man.

'That's all we need.'

'Forensics are going over what's left of it,' Hazel said.

'What else have you got, DCI Todd?'

When he said her name like that, it made Hazel shudder. It spilt off his tongue like an accusation. Was he accusing her of not doing her job properly? She thought about David Wilson. His alibi. His grief. His anger. The person who'd run away from Lady Campbell's was a woman. She was sure of it. Someone small, she'd said. Suzanne Gerrard was out of the question. The woman could barely walk, let alone run. But the shock of the situation had made Lady Campbell's mind go blank when asked for a more detailed prescription. The text alert on her phone made Hazel jump.

'I'm sorry, can I get this? It might be important.'

'Yes, yes, go ahead.' He waved a hand towards her.

'Thanks,' she murmured and pulled her phone from her pocket. The text from Billy was like divine intervention. She smiled and heaved a huge sigh of relief.

'They've managed to retrieve a partial print from the inside handle of the car door.'

'That's something, at least,' Daly said with the tiniest hint of approval in his voice. 'Anything else?'

'Nothing conclusive at the moment, sir.' Hazel shook her head.

'What do you suggest I tell the papers?'

For a moment she wondered if he was reaching out and genuinely asking for her help. Did he feel out of his depth? Was his snippy attitude simply a way of dealing with his anxiety?

'You could tell them we are following several lines of inquiry, sir.' She stopped to allow him to mull her suggestion over. 'Which isn't strictly a lie, is it?'

The two veteran officers stared at each other. Two people with almost sixty years' experience between them. Hazel spotted that his expression had softened.

'OK, thank you. That'll be all for now, DCI Todd.' Daly's smile came and went in a blur.

'Sir.' Hazel stood and hoped her rush to get out of there wasn't too obvious.

As she made her way back to her office, she bumped into a flush-faced Andrea in the corridor. Something was wrong.

'Andrea, what is it?' Hazel urged.

'God, there's been a fire up at Lady Campbell's place! One of the surveillance officers is missing.'

Chapter Forty

Hazel was so focussed on the job she didn't notice DI Gerry Smith walking towards her as she pulled on a pair of latex gloves.

'Hello, you,' he said, startling her a little.

'What are you doing here?' Hazel asked and reached into the car boot for a pair of overshoes.

'It's good to see you too,' Gerry grinned. 'You'll not need them, by the way.' He nodded to her feet. 'Fire team are not letting anyone inside yet.'

Hazel looked at what was left of Lady Campbell's beautiful cottage. Even the lavender bed in front of the living room window had been scorched, almost beyond recognition. The stench of smoke lingered in the air. A stunning piece of history was gone in a matter of minutes.

'What a mess,' Hazel tutted.

'Aye, it's a bloody waste. That property dates back to the sixteen hundreds. Did you know that?'

'Aye, I did. Billy told me it was gorgeous inside.'

'She'd put a lot into the house, I gather. Trying to keep it as authentic as was safely possible.' Gerry didn't take his eyes off Hazel as he spoke. 'It must have cost a pretty penny, too. Renovations like that aren't cheap. I should know.' He rolled his eyes.

'Should you?'

'Aye. Me and my ex, we took on an old place,' he scoffed. 'It nearly bankrupted me in the process.'

'I bet it was lovely when it was finished though, wasn't it?' Hazel suggested.

'I'm sure she likes it,' he shrugged. 'She's the one getting to enjoy it and I've got to make do with...' He lifted a hand. 'I'm sorry, I don't know where that came from.'

'It's fine, don't worry.' Hazel pointed to the burnt-out shell of Lady Campbell's house, hoping that would help move the conversation back to the reason they were there. 'Do they know what happened in there yet?'

'Fire started in one of the bedrooms. They've found a device set to go off on a timer.'

Hazel's relief that he'd dropped his bitter words about his ex-wife was tempered by her shock at the news. There was no doubt in her mind that this was a deliberate act.

'Oh Jesus, what about the surveillance officer? Is he...' Hazel wasn't sure if she wanted to hear the answer to that question.

'He's fine.'

'Oh thank God.' Hazel's hand had landed on Gerry's arm before she even knew it had moved. 'I'm sorry,' she corrected herself. 'But,' she exhaled loudly, 'that could have been so much worse.'

'It's fine.' Gerry smiled then looked up at the charred remains of the sixteenth-century cottage.

'He was knocked off his feet and is a bit bruised and bashed but he's all right. Paramedic suggested he might be concussed.'

'Do you think he'll be fit enough to talk to me?' she asked. The concussion didn't sound promising, but she had to ask.

'He's already been taken to PRI by ambulance. Maybe later,' Gerry informed her.

'Of course, yes, of course he has.'

'Do you want me to tell Lady Campbell?' Gerry offered.

'Would you?' The relief on Hazel's face must have been obvious.

'Of course,' Gerry smiled. 'You've got enough on your plate.'

'That's the understatement of the year,' Hazel said and leaned back against her Fiesta. She shook her head. 'I've got Daly on my back about the newspapers wanting the story.'

Gerry leaned in next to her. 'Ouch,' he acknowledged. 'What did you tell him?'

'That we're following several lines of inquiry.'

Hazel frowned when Gerry let out a chuckle. 'That old chestnut, huh?'

'What?' Hazel found herself smiling back at him.

'Journalists know what that means, these days.'

'And what does it mean then, smart-arse?' Hazel teased.

'The square route of fuck all,' Gerry said.

It shouldn't be something to laugh about but Gerry had that effect on her. He was the breath of fresh air her life needed. A cliché but also the truth. Before their conversation could go any further, Hazel spotted a fire investigator walking towards them.

'What have you found?' Hazel asked, moving away from where she'd been relaxing, perhaps a bit too much, next to Gerry.

'Some good news for you, I hope.'

Hazel found herself taking a quick glance at Gerry then back at the officer. 'That sounds promising.'

'There's an area in the location of the device that has a powder residue which we'll be testing but it looks like there's a good chance you'll get fingerprints.'

'That's fantastic,' Hazel beamed.

'We've also managed to recover a small fraction of what we think is the actual device, which can be tested. Fingers crossed, you'll find your man.' The fire officer smiled and looked between the two detectives. 'Which one of you do I send my report to?'

Hazel stared at Gerry but neither spoke.

'I'll email you both a copy,' he said and offered a playful salute as he turned to walk away. Before he'd got far, he turned back to them. 'You can go in now. It's been deemed safe but just go easy.'

'Thanks,' Hazel called after him and reached for the over-shoes again.

'Here, you'll need this as well.' Gerry handed her a face mask. 'The stench of the smouldering bits catches your throat.'

Hazel took the mask from him. 'Listen, just out of interest,' she asked, although she knew the answer already, 'you'll have Lara Vermeer's prints on file now, won't you?'

'Aye and I've got a DNA sample.'

'Good,' Hazel said. 'That's good to know. Given her history with fires.' Because everyone was still a suspect. Until it could be proved otherwise.

'We're looking at an insurance job,' Gerry said. 'A closer look at Vermeer's furniture business has shown up that it's been haemorrhaging money for the past six months. Lara Vermeer was questioned then bailed while we carry out further investigations.'

'Mm,' Hazel replied with a frown.

'Mm,' Gerry repeated and mirrored her narrowed eyes. 'You don't think Lara has done that to Lady Campbell's place do you?' His face betrayed how shocked he was.

Hazel wasn't sure exactly what she thought right then so chose not to respond to his question and the two detectives walked quietly towards the charred property.

Chapter Forty-One

Hazel pressed her hand over the mask and tightened it against her nose and mouth. Gerry wasn't kidding about the lingering stench of smoke choking your throat. She coughed.

'God, I don't know how you cope with this every day,' she suggested.

'Thankfully it's not every day but strangely, I enjoy working the arson cases.' Gerry stepped carefully over the remains of what was once an oak coffee table in the centre of the living room. 'It's more interesting than the work up north unless you find nicking low-level drug dealers interesting.'

'I had heard Highland were struggling a bit with a drug problem. Heroin, isn't it?'

Despite wearing a mask, she could see Gerry was screwing up his face. 'It's not as bad as the media makes out. Glasgow is where the problem is, closely followed by Dundee. Perth is quickly catching up, though.'

Hazel instantly recalled the girls caught up in prostitution to fund their addictions that she had worked with in the past. 'Aye, I think you're right there,' she agreed.

'Aye, the kind of folk that start the fires interest me,' Gerry admitted.

That surprised Hazel. 'Oh yes. How come?'

'Well, arson is a gateway crime, isn't it?' Gerry said as his eyes scanned the burnt-out room. 'It's often a sign that something's no right in the arsonist's mind. I mean, it's no normal, is it? Starting fires? Some then go on to commit truly horrific crimes if they're not stopped.'

Hazel knew he was right but before she could tell him she agreed, he strode away from her, his eyes narrowed.

'What have you found?' Hazel asked, following behind him.

'I'm not sure.' Gerry bent down and picked up what looked to Hazel like a piece of singed fabric. He held it up in his gloved hand. 'Does Lady Campbell wear scrunchies in her hair, do you think?'

'How on earth did you see that in all this mess?' Hazel asked and pulled an evidence bag from her jacket pocket. She took what was left of the white and black, polka dot scrunchie and placed it into the bag. 'No, I can't imagine Lady Campbell would wear something like that. Thanks, Gerry. Well spotted.'

'No problem. Hopefully, there will be some DNA on the few hairs on it. They're a bit burnt but you never know.'

Hazel held the bag up and stared inside at the contents. She spotted a single hair and hoped Gerry was right. *Now who do you belong to, I wonder*, she thought.

Chapter Forty-Two

Hazel hung up her phone from the forensic officer after asking for the fingerprints and DNA evidence to be given high priority which they'd agreed to without complaint. She hadn't had time to eat before getting to the station and then her haste to get up to Lady Campbell's meant she'd been starving. A ten-minute stop at the roadside burger van on the outskirts of Pitlochry had been Gerry's idea. He'd told her he'd stopped there a couple of times and that they did the best cheeseburger in the Northern hemisphere. His eyes had twinkled when he'd said it. His treat, he'd said, and Hazel had promised the burgers were on her next time. The two veteran detectives chatted easily, both needing light relief after their walk around the charred remains of that beautiful house which was unlikely to ever be restored to such a high standard without significant investment in both time and money. Forensics had taken everything they needed and Hazel was keen to get back to the station.

Hazel expected Daly to be waiting for her in her office because she knew he'd be keen to find out how the investigation was going and how Lady Campbell was. She was surprised not to see him.

'Right, let's get started shall we?' Hazel said to the rest of her team who were busy chatting amongst themselves as she joined them but before she could make a start, a uniformed officer knocked on the office door and Hazel waved him in.

'There's a woman downstairs asking for DI Newton. She says it's about her uncle's murder,' the balding officer said as he glanced across at Tom.

Hazel looked at Tom and pointed towards the door. 'Go and see what she has to say, will you?'

'Sure.' Tom dropped his pen onto his desk and headed off after the uniformed officer.

'Thanks, Tom,' Hazel called after him.

'How bad was it?' Andrea asked, referring to Lady Campbell's home. 'Has there been a lot of damage and what about the officer that got hurt. Have you heard how they are?'

Hazel raised her eyes to the ceiling. 'It was horrible.' She shook her head. 'What a mess. I can't see how she'll ever be able to fix it. What's left will have to be demolished. Our surveillance officer is OK as far as I know. They were taken to PRI.'

'Thank God she wasn't in it.' Andrea looked at Billy.

'Aye, thanks to Billy,' Hazel said. 'Well done, DS Flynn. You've probably saved her life.'

Hazel was sure she saw Billy blush. She watched him shrug.

'I was just doing my job. Has anyone been to see her yet?'

'Aye, that's being taken care of,' Hazel replied. 'We do have some good news from the scene.' She tapped her pen on the desk. 'We have fingerprints and possible DNA which I have fast-tracked as well as some hair found on one of those hair scrunchies.'

'That's great. That scrunchie has to be from our girl. I can't see Lady Campbell wearing one of them.' Instinctively Andrea reached for the green one she wore in her own hair.

'My thoughts exactly. If she's got a record, she'll be on the database, so we'll find her.'

Hazel turned her attention towards Billy.

'Billy, that little thing I asked you to do for me...?' she asked.

Before she could continue, Billy nodded. 'I'm waiting on a call back, boss.'

Hazel caught the way Andrea was staring at her and felt guilty but didn't want to explain, not yet. Not until Billy's contact had discovered why King's laptop had been furtively removed from her investigation.

'Good, let me know as soon as you hear anything.'

'I will,' Billy said.

'In the meantime, are we any further on DNA results, from either crime scene or the letter sent to Samuel Ramsay?'

'Nothing yet, I'm sorry.'

'Or the letter Jack gave me from Maggie's pocket?' Hazel pushed him, disappointed to see him shake his head. Why did everything move so damn slowly?

Hazel stared up at the faces of her two victims on the evidence board. Was this really just about simple revenge?

'OK, well, could you chase them up, Billy?' Hazel said. 'You can tell them it's in connection with the Campbell fire. Make sure they realise they're connected, will you?'

'Sure thing,' he replied and made a note in his book. 'Are we doing a full forensic search on the Ramsay place now that the break-in has been cleared up. I gather he made a hell of a mess.'

'Yes, Andrea,' Hazel turned to face her DC. 'How do you feel about leading that?'

'Absolutely.' Andrea jumped at the chance. 'Are we looking for anything specific?'

Hazel allowed her eyes to drift down to her desk, coming to a halt on the gruesome photos from both murder scenes, then she looked directly at Andrea.

'Everything,' Hazel said. 'We're looking for everything. I'll check in with you when I get back from Dundee. It's Carol Wilson's PM this morning and I want to check in with Jack.'

That was the truth. They were looking for everything. Anything and everything that held the clue to who had committed these brutal murders. The email that arrived from forensics entitled '*Fingerprints – Campbell crime scene*' came in faster than Hazel had anticipated but the contents made her heart sink.

No match on the database.

'You told my colleague this letter arrived this morning?' Tom asked Rona as he began to read the letter she'd brought.

'Yes, it was lying there when I got up. God, it was hand-delivered!' She covered her mouth with her hand. 'Whoever this is, they know me and know where I live. What if they come after me?' She twirled the tips of her hair nervously in her fingers and nibbled on her lip.

Tom finished reading the note which said similar things to the one sent to Samuel Ramsay shortly before he died. Its tone read in the same arrogant manner. The last few lines suggested that Rona had herself been one of King's victims.

> *You should be pleased. Now that he's gone you can put the past behind you and move on.*

Her fear for her own life seemed at odds with the suspected motivation for this murderer. Rona didn't have secrets, did she?

'And you have no idea who sent this?' Tom asked.

'No,' Rona said, wiping a tear from the corner of her eye. 'I know Peter was no angel, but he didn't deserve that.' She nodded to the piece of paper in Tom's gloved hand.

'Have you shown this to anyone else?' he asked, then clarified: 'What I mean is, has anyone else touched it apart from you?'

'Erm, just Suzanne. She was at my place early this morning and I showed it to her. She said I should bring it straight here.'

'OK well, listen, Rona, I'm going to have to ask you if you'd consent to giving us a sample of your fingerprints in order to eliminate them from the forensic examination of the letter. Would that be all right?'

It seemed to take her a minute to answer. 'I suppose so… if you think I should.'

'I would really appreciate it.' Tom bagged the letter and escorted Rona to where a uniformed officer took her finger-prints.

Rona looked genuinely scared, Tom thought, as she pressed her fingers onto the fingerprint machine. He offered her a smile of support.

'You did the right thing,' he told her. 'Bringing this letter to me.'

'I know,' she murmured.

'Right, that's you all done,' the officer said.

'Thanks.' Tom nodded as the officer walked away.

'What will happen now?' Rona asked.

Tom opened the door towards the station foyer and held out a hand to let her go through first, allowing the door to close securely behind them.

'A forensic examination will take place to see if the author of the letter left any fingerprints or DNA behind.'

'DNA?' Rona blurted.

Tom frowned. 'Yes, when we sweat we leave behind traces of our DNA.'

'Oh, OK, so if the person who wrote it sweated, then their DNA will be on it. I get it,' Rona said and started to walk towards the station exit.

'Do you need someone to give you a lift?' Tom asked when he spotted the heavy snow shower through the window.

Rona shook her head. 'No, I need some air.' She shrugged gently. 'My head hurts.'

Tom walked her to the door and watched her head back in the direction of the town centre as a blast of freezing cold air smashed right into him. He was about to close the door when a petite middle-aged woman walked up the two steps, so he held it open a moment longer for her to come through. She seemed anxious as she walked past him.

'Thanks,' she said, her mind obviously elsewhere.

'No problem,' Tom replied and headed back through the security door.

'Can I help you?' the desk sergeant greeted the woman, noting her expression was one of serious concern.

'Erm yes, it's my mum.' She coughed to clear the tightness stalking her throat. 'She's missing.'

Chapter Forty-Three

The phone call from the front desk had sent alarm bells ringing through Hazel and she'd asked Andrea to take a statement from the daughter of an elderly woman who had been reported missing. She had to prioritise the welfare of a vulnerable elderly woman. Visions of her own father had swum in her head as soon as the report came in. He had dementia, just like the missing woman. Hazel had called Jack and asked him to send the PM reports on Carol Wilson and King to her by email, apologising that she wouldn't be able to see him. Instead, now that she had redirected Andrea, she was currently standing outside the Ramsay house preparing herself to begin the new search. She tugged on a pair of latex gloves and slipped the blue overshoes on top of her own before joining Tom inside. Before she could get in the door, a text landed on her phone.

> CCTV has just been sent from the shopping
> arcade close to Peter King's block.

Billy's text sparked a glimmer of hope that whoever had done those gruesome things to him might be captured on film. Someone, something, anything would be good right now.

> Thanks. Let me know what you find.

'Who was that?' Tom asked.

'Billy,' Hazel confirmed. 'He's got CCTV from the shops beside King's flat.'

'That's good news.'

'God, I hope so. Come on, let's tear this house apart, Tom.'

'Where do you want to start?' Tom asked.

Hazel stood looking at the 1980s bungalow and hoped the recent break-in hadn't destroyed vital evidence.

'I'll take the second bedroom which I believe they used as an office,' Hazel decided. 'You take the couple's bedroom then can we meet in the kitchen?'

'Sure, sounds like a good plan,' Tom nodded, tightening his gloves as he walked away.

Hazel's phone buzzed just as she was reaching for the spare bedroom door handle.

'What now?' she mumbled under her breath and tugged the phone restlessly out of her pocket then frowned when she saw it was a text from her dad's care home.

> I realise you're busy with work, but could you
> give us a call when you're free.

An unexplained chill ran right through her, starting in her hair, vibrating her scalp, and ending in her feet that began to feel cold. She'd call them back as soon as she was done searching the Ramsays' bungalow.

When Hazel entered the small, immaculately kept room she was hit with a beautiful smell. A fresh scent that filled the entire space. Scanning the room carefully before moving forward, as she liked to do, she spotted an air freshener plugged in under the large mahogany desk which had been placed directly under the window. The upper pane of the window was smaller than the bottom and not large enough for a person to fit through. Hazel noticed that it had been left ajar, just a touch, but wide enough to allow the cold air to drift in, helping to circulate the gorgeous smell. Freesia, if she wasn't mistaken.

Hazel opened the top drawer of the desk, surprised that David Wilson hadn't tossed the contents around. She pulled out the pile of envelopes and quickly noticed that every one of them was addressed to Samuel. Utility bills, phone bills, bank statements, all solely in his name. Thinking of her own marriage, she knew Rick had preferred everything was in their joint names. It was always these odd little moments that made the grief swirl around her again. Hazel had to push the feeling right down and focus on the job.

She laid the envelopes in a pile on top of the desk and lifted out a large folder labelled simply 'Insurance'.

Inside, she found two neatly organised life insurance policies, one in each of their names. Inside the document in Maggie Ramsay's name there was a piece of A4 lined notepaper with a phone number and reference number alongside a date from the previous month. Hazel wondered what that meant until she read further. Maggie's life insurance policy had been increased on that date and Hazel couldn't stop the involuntary sharp intake of breath on seeing the details of the change.

'Hazel,' Tom's voice rang out through the bungalow. 'Could you come here a minute? I think you should see this.'

Hazel kept the life insurance policy document in her hand as she joined him in the couple's bedroom.

'What is that?' she asked on seeing him holding a photo in his hand.

Tom handed her the photo of a much younger-looking Maggie Ramsay, possibly only in her late teens, holding a tiny baby in her arms.

'Why do you think this is significant?' Hazel asked.

Tom pointed to the open drawer in the bedside cabinet. 'Because it was Sellotaped to the underside of that drawer.'

Hazel's eyes stretched wide on hearing that. 'Really?'

Tom nodded. 'Yes. When I opened the drawer, it came right out and I almost dropped it on the floor, but it came out at an angle, revealing that photo stuck to the underside.'

'Interesting,' Hazel said, staring down at the face looking back at her.

It wasn't that of a beaming new mum. The eyes of the girl holding the infant were haunted and sad. There was a hand on her shoulder, but the rest of the person had been cut off – deliberately, perhaps. Hazel turned the photo over and read the name written on the back: *My darling Michelle*.

'Who is Michelle I wonder?' Hazel looked at Tom.

'Do we know if they lost a child? Because from the details we've got, that's not their daughter's name,' Tom reminded her.

'Mm, let's take this and do a little digging, shall we?' Hazel dropped the photo inside an evidence bag.

'What have you got there?' Tom nodded at the folder clutched under Hazel's arm.

'Something else very interesting.' She handed the folder to him. 'It seems Maggie's life insurance was increased *significantly* in the weeks before her death.'

'Oh, is that right?' Tom flicked through pages of the policy, finding the sheet of loose notepaper with the handwritten notes on it. 'Do we know whose handwriting this is?'

'Not yet,' Hazel admitted. 'But this has to be significant, don't you think?'

'Definitely,' Tom agreed.

Raised voices outside drew the detectives' attention.

'What's going on out there?' Hazel commented and walked over to the bedroom window to see Maggie's friend Sandra trying to cajole a much younger woman away. 'I'll go, you keep looking.' She ripped off her gloves and walked towards the front door.

Hazel nodded to the harassed-looking uniformed PC who had tried to stop the emotional younger woman from going inside the bungalow.

'Hello, I'm DCI Hazel Todd, I don't think we've been introduced.' She held out her hand to shake the hand of the girl she now recognised from the collection of photos displayed in the

Ramsays' home. Daly had assured Hazel that he would keep trying to contact the Ramsays' daughter himself. Poor girl must have jumped on the next available flight.

'What's going on?' the young woman snapped without acknowledging Hazel's outstretched hand.

'Detective, this is Louise,' Sandra intervened. 'Maggie and Samuel's daughter,' she added.

Curious onlookers were becoming interested in the raised voices, so Hazel knew she had to divert the conversation away.

'Louise, if you'd like to follow me, I'll try and explain what's happening.' Hazel directed her towards the back of the property.

'Why are we going out the back?' Louise asked angrily. 'I need to get some things from Mum and Dad's. There are so many things I need to organise. I only landed early this morning. I'll be staying with Sandra and...' She was obviously flustered, with tears close to escaping from her eyes.

'I'm sorry, I know this is a hard time for you but if you could just bear with me for a few more minutes.'

Louise looked towards the front door of the bungalow, her eyes glistening, before she walked silently to the back garden.

'I'm sorry,' Sandra whispered. 'I couldn't stop her.'

'It's fine,' Hazel said. 'She's upset. I can understand that.'

'Poor girl,' Sandra continued. 'In less than a week her whole life has been turned upside down. It must have been awful to get that call. To lose one parent, and under such awful circumstances, but to lose them both...' Her words sank away until she composed herself. 'She has had to leave her baby at home with her husband in Canada to rush over here.' Her voice shook, and she grabbed a tissue from her sleeve to wipe her nose. 'I'm sorry, it just sneaks up on me sometimes. I'm still struggling to process this.'

'Don't worry.' Hazel rested her hand on Sandra's arm and squeezed gently. 'I understand.'

'I'll leave you two to it,' Sandra said. 'Tell Louise I'll wait in the car for her.'

Hazel nodded and turned to walk towards the garden gate. She frowned when she was unable to see Louise, then spotted that the shed door was slightly ajar at the far end of the immaculately kept garden. Despite the snow, each of the neatly arranged borders were obvious, with clear lines separating them. A tree at the far end of the long rectangular plot looked like a fruit tree of some kind, its growth delayed by the lateness of this year's spring weather.

Hazel found Louise sitting in a deckchair in the middle of the well organised ten-by-eight shed. Every shelf was tidy and a variety of garden tools – some that Hazel didn't recognise – hung on strategically placed hooks. It smelled freshly painted too. A winter job that Hazel imagined Samuel stuck to like clockwork every year. Just like her own dad. The smell of creosote was a legacy of Hazel's childhood. That and the council grass cutter speeding between the lawns of the scheme, leaving heaps of usually wet grass on the pavements for Hazel to tread into the carpet, much to her dad's dismay.

'Dad loved this garden,' Louise said without looking at her.

Hazel lifted down a much smaller folding chair and opened it out next to Louise. Realising it was possibly meant for children, she quickly regretted sitting on it.

'I'm sorry for your loss,' she said quietly.

'I'm so glad I came back for Christmas,' Louise said plainly then took a breath. 'Their last Christmas.'

Hazel opened her mouth to ask her a question, but her lips had barely moved when Louise filled the silence between them.

'Do you know who did that to Mum? Because they may as well have run down Dad, too.'

'Not yet,' Hazel replied honestly. 'But I'm doing everything I possibly can to find them.'

'I'm sure you are.'

'Do you have any idea who would want to kill your mum?' Hazel asked directly.

'Apart from the Wilsons, you mean?'

'What do you know about them?'

'Only that David threatened Mum.' Louise spoke simply and honestly. 'There were a couple of letters I think, and he came to the house a few times, too. Dad told me. He said I shouldn't worry about it. He was just trying to make me feel better, wasn't he?' She broke down. 'God, I should have done something! Called the police, at least.'

Hazel didn't want to get involved in that.

'Louise, does the name Peter King mean anything to you?' she asked, on a hunch.

The colour seemed to drain from Louise's face on hearing that name.

'What… what did you just say?'

Hazel frowned. 'Do you know Peter King?'

Tears poured from Louise's eyes and she dropped her gaze to the shed floor then nodded.

'Can you tell me how you know him?' Hazel asked gently, seeing her increasing distress. She didn't want to cause the young woman any more pain but this reaction was the biggest lead they'd had so far. She hadn't expected to find this connection.

Louise sniffed back the tears and wiped her wet cheeks. 'I'm sorry.'

'It's fine but I can see that hearing his name was a shock. Why was that?'

Louise took a long, careful breath then blew it out slowly, the slight smell of peppermint drifting towards Hazel's nostrils.

'He raped me when I was a teenager.'

'Oh.' Hazel's mind spun with the revelation. 'I'm so sorry that happened to you.' All kinds of scenarios played inside her head. 'I didn't know that.'

'Yes,' Louise shrugged. 'I had put the whole thing behind me but…' She took another short breath. 'At least, I thought I had but hearing that name… it was just a shock, that's all. Did he have something to do with this?'

'Possibly.' That wasn't a lie. Just not in the way it sounded.

'Please, no…' Louise gasped. 'He couldn't…'

'Was Peter King ever charged with what he did to you?'

Louise shook her head. 'No, there wasn't enough evidence, they said. My word against his because I didn't go to the police straight away. I didn't tell anyone. I couldn't even bring myself to tell Mum for a week.'

Hazel frowned. She'd heard that too many times before.

'I had a Saturday job in the shop that Peter worked in. He seemed really nice, you know.' She shrugged and flicked her eyes sideways. 'I was a rebellious teenager, and he was showing me attention. Mum and Dad hated him. Mum, especially. She was so angry when she found out I'd been on a date with him.' Louise turned her face back to focus on Hazel, her eyes holding her gaze. 'I'd never seen her get so angry before and never again since. It's strange because she never told me why she'd got so angry and believe me, I've asked her many times over the years.' She sighed. 'Mum always told me to drop it and changed the subject. I'll never know why now though, will I?'

Hazel chose not to acknowledge her remark.

'Peter King is dead,' she said instead.

'Oh my God!' Louise exclaimed. 'Do you think it's the same person who killed Mum?'

'We're trying to establish that.'

The two murder victims were so interwoven but the motives for their deaths were confusing in the light of this new information. Was this about Louise? *But why kill Maggie?* Remembering the notes attached to the insurance policy, Hazel lifted a finger briefly in the air.

'Can you hang on just a sec? I'd like you to look at something for me.'

'Sure,' Louise nodded.

Hazel walked back into the couple's office, where Tom was going through the contents of a mahogany chest.

'Tom, have you got that insurance document there?'

'Aye, there you go.' He handed the whole folder to her.

Hazel removed the handwritten note from it and returned to the shed where Louise was now going through a box of assorted broken pencils, bottle tops and pieces of string of various lengths.

'Dad didn't like to throw anything out,' she smiled. '"It might come in handy one day," he always said.'

Hazel smiled back and sat down beside her. Their fathers were alike, it seemed. She handed the sheet of paper to her.

'Can you tell me whose handwriting this is?'

'Erm...' Louise examined the paper closely. 'This is Mum's writing.'

Maggie Ramsay increasing her own life insurance policy wasn't what Hazel had expected to hear. This was just another piece of the puzzle that didn't seem to fit.

'Louise, did your mum have a will?'

Louise nodded. 'Yes, she keeps it...' She stopped to correct herself. '*Kept* it at the solicitor's.'

'Which solicitor was that?'

'Kippen and Dean.'

'I'm sorry could you excuse me just a wee tick again, will you?' Hazel asked and left Louise sitting staring at a collection of rubber bands that her dad had kept in an old jar on the shelf.

Hazel scrolled for Billy's number. 'Come on, come on, Billy boy,' she muttered under her breath while she waited for him to answer. 'Billy, hi. Listen, which solicitor does Suzanne Gerrard work for?'

Hazel could have danced for joy on hearing his answer.

Chapter Forty-Four

'Hello Mrs Latimer, come through,' Andrea greeted the greying woman who looked like she'd seen a ghost. She was dressed smartly as if she'd just come from an office, with neat black trousers and a crisp white blouse.

Andrea led her through the security door and unlocked one of the smaller interview rooms. She switched on the light, momentarily startling the woman, who was clearly nervous.

'Please take a seat.'

'Erm, thanks,' Rita Latimer replied and sat down on the chair opposite Andrea, dropping her bag onto the floor at her feet. Her body looked tight, and her hands trembled.

'The desk sergeant tells me you're concerned about your mum. Is that right?' Andrea laid her notebook on the table in front of her and clicked her pen. 'Tell me what's happened.'

'Well, I generally call Mum three or four times a week,' Rita Latimer began, and Andrea noticed the whites of the woman's eyes were speckled red like she'd been crying.

'It's OK, take your time,' she said. 'Can I get you a glass of water or a cup of tea or coffee?'

'No thank you.' Rita shook her head and clasped her hands together, as if noticing the shaking for the first time. She swallowed hard, then licked her lips. 'I'm fine.'

'OK then, tell me what's happened.'

'Mum, she's not well, you see.' Rita stopped, lifted her bag back up onto her knees and rummaged inside before producing a photo. She slid the picture across the table.

Andrea glanced down at the smiling face of the elderly, silver-haired woman looking up at her.

'What's your mum's name?'

'Sheila,' Rita coughed. 'Sheila Marshall.'

Andrea jotted down the name. 'And how old is your mum?'

'She's eighty-six.' Rita's voice gave into the emotions she was feeling. 'Mum's got dementia – early stages but she gets confused and lost sometimes. Not always but it's been happening more, recently.'

'OK,' Andrea said. 'So when did you last see her?'

Rita sighed. 'I live in Kirkcaldy, and I come through at weekends to do her shopping and take her out for lunch but last weekend I couldn't manage it because my son was ill so...' Her words disappeared into a foam of soggy tears. Andrea genuinely felt sorry for her. She must be worried sick.

'So it was the weekend before last, then?' Andrea suggested.

'Erm, yes, that's right but I did talk to her on Friday night.'

'How did she seem when you spoke to her?'

A thin smile faded quickly. 'She was fine – her usual cheerful self, to be honest. I tried to call her on Sunday, but I couldn't get any answer. My son had been rushed to hospital very early on Saturday morning, so I admit I was a little distracted and didn't think much of it when Mum didn't answer my call. I thought she'd maybe gone to bed with a headache. She gets them sometimes.'

'Right, and you've not been able to talk to her since?'

Rita shook her head. 'I went over to the house this morning and...' Her voice shook. 'There were dishes in the sink and a half drunk mug of tea on the bunker. The dog had made such a mess in the house.'

'Would you say that was unusual?'

'Yes!' Rita exclaimed. 'Very unusual. My mum is...' She had to stop to compose herself. 'She's very particular. To a fault, to be honest. Something that stayed with her from her working life, I suppose.'

'What did your mum do as a job?'

'She was a midwife for nearly fifty years.'

Andrea's eyes widened. 'Wow, that's a long time.'

Rita nodded. 'I know. Mum loved her job. In fact she only retired because she had to. She would have kept going if they'd let her.' She sighed. 'The dementia diagnosis was a blow. I can't describe how devastated Mum was and now she's... She's probably lost out there. Cold and afraid.'

'Listen, I promise you we will do everything we can to find her.' But her words didn't seem to help. She held out her hand and rested it briefly on Rita's arm, squeezing gently before pulling back. 'So you last spoke to your mum on Friday night,' Andrea clarified. 'And she seemed fine. Was there anything else in the house that struck you as out of the ordinary?'

'Yes, the Sunday newspaper was still on the doormat. She gets the *Times* every Sunday.' The same small smile came and went quickly. 'She says the crossword is good for her brain.'

Andrea wrote that down. That was significant. The vulnerable old woman hadn't been there to pick up her Sunday paper. Rita last spoke to her on Friday night.

'What time on Friday did you talk to your mum?' Andrea asked.

'It was eight thirty. I remember because she told me off for calling when *Midsomer Murders* was on.'

'And have you got any idea what time her newspaper is usually delivered?' Andrea asked, hoping she could pinpoint the missing hours from that.

'Yes, actually I do know that,' Rita said. 'Whenever I've stayed with Mum at the weekend the paper lad comes at seven.'

Andrea made a note of everything Rita had said and lifted Sheila's photo. The window between eight thirty on Friday night and seven on Sunday morning. That was a good start.

'What will happen now?' Rita asked.

'A missing person's file will be opened for your mum and a team will go out and search for her very soon. As she's so vulnerable, I'll organise a press briefing and social media push to get Sheila's face out as far and wide as I can. Now, are there any places your mum enjoyed going, or that have sentimental significance to her?'

Rita frowned. 'Only our old house and I've checked there. The new owners said they'll keep an eye out for her.'

Andrea was pleased that Rita had done that already. 'OK and have you contacted other family members and your mum's friends?'

Rita nodded. 'I'm an only child but I've called my cousin and everyone from church that I had a number for. I got them from Mum's diary.'

'Was your mum's handbag in the house?'

Rita nodded sombrely. 'Her big winter coat and her raincoat were still hanging in the hall, too. She'll be freezing out there without either of them, but the weird thing is, her hat and scarf were gone.'

Andrea wrote that down. It might be nothing but worth noting.

'Did you find her house keys?'

Rita nodded. 'Yes.' Then she lifted her finger in the air. 'Something I do remember her saying on Friday though, was that she'd met someone in town that she'd helped deliver as a baby which in itself isn't unusual, but this time she said she had coffee with her.'

'Did she tell you the name of this woman?'

Rita's shaking head was disappointing. 'No, but Mum was pleased to see her, I think. She certainly sounded happy to have seen her.' She rubbed her brow anxiously. 'I don't know, now. My mind is so stressed with the worry.'

Andrea considered whether this was purely coincidence but made a note. She wished she could say something to put Rita's mind at ease. The weather conditions over the past few days had seen a blast of Arctic air sweep down from the north, spreading across the whole of Scotland, causing night-time temperatures to drop to minus ten in some places and covering the country with a freezing dome that the much-needed early spring mild air couldn't penetrate. Neither of them said what they were really thinking. Sheila Marshall was a missing person. For now. Andrea dearly hoped the search wouldn't end in heartbreak.

Chapter Forty-Five

Sean Jacobs knew the Wilsons used to keep a spare key under a flowerpot by the back door. He winced from the pain in his shoulders from trying to fend off David's attack. Knowing how much time David spent with his girlfriend Suzanne and now that Mrs Wilson was gone, he supposed the place would be empty. There would never be a more perfect time to rob the place because he knew that there were at least two laptops and a couple of old phones in there. They might not be top of the range, but he could get a few quid for them. At least enough to get him through the next twenty-four hours. It might even get him something to eat as well. Carol's purse was probably still in there. Maybe he should feel guilty. After all, she'd been good to him over the years, but she didn't need that money now and he did. God, he did. Sean's stomach was churning with the withdrawal and his head was bursting like his brain was banging inside his skull, hammering to be let out.

Yes, there it was. The key. He took a quick glance behind him to make sure the old bag next door hadn't clocked him then let himself in the back door. Just as he'd thought, Carol Wilson's handbag was still hanging over the back of the chair she always sat at when she was eating at the kitchen table. He grabbed the strap from the corner of the seat and dropped it onto the table before flipping through the contents until he found her tatty black leather purse. He snatched it out and unzipped it, wincing from the pain in his hands because even his fingers throbbed then stuffed the wad of notes into his pocket. He hadn't anticipated there being as much as that. Forty quid –

nice result. He stuffed the cash and the debit card into his jeans pocket then flipped through the rest until he found a credit card. He didn't have the pin numbers but with everything being contactless these days, he could use them to get some cider from the offy on the corner.

While he was there, Sean opened all the drawers to see if there was anything else worth nicking. He pocketed the pile of loose change in the drawer next to the kettle – just a few twenty and ten pence pieces but they all added up – then he opened the cupboards above it. A mug filled with pens also had a ten pound note folded up in it. This house was proving to be very lucrative.

He knew that David kept a large sports bag in the wardrobe in his bedroom and decided he'd take whatever he could and carry it away in that. Any more than that would attract unwanted attention. He unplugged the laptop from the charger cable and stuffed it into the bag. An old iPod lying on the chest of drawers under the bedroom window was tossed in. It might be an earlier model but it still had value, to the right people. As did the Samsung tablet that he didn't know David had. He rummaged in the bedside cabinet and found twenty quid in pound coins so pocketed them before moving into Carol's bedroom.

The first thing that hit him was the smell. It reeked in there like old sweat and piss. A fly buzzed round a plate of mouldy chips on the bedside table and a half drunk mug of tea had mould growing across the top. He struggled to stop himself throwing up at the stench. An old laptop lay on the floor and although it was probably more than five years old he'd get a few bob for it. The TV was too big but the DVD player fitted easily inside the bag. He opened the wardrobe door and found a shoebox on the floor. He knew right away what this was.

Sean emptied the contents onto the unmade bed. There it was. The iPhone that had been bought for Liam's Christmas present. All still packed in its box with a brand new pair of

Beats headphones. Liam wasn't going to be able to use this, was he, Sean tried to rationalise with himself. He stuffed them into the sports bag just as a voice came out of the silence.

'Tut, tut,' the accusatory voice said. 'Now that really is bang out of order.'

'What are you doing here?' Sean asked, surprised to see them standing there.

'It's just as well I am here.' They nodded towards the bag that was stuffed so full the zip couldn't close.

'I'm no' hurting anybody,' Sean protested.

'Do you really believe that?'

'Aye I do, as it happens,' Sean said.

'He's supposed to be your best pal.'

Sean clawed the itch on his arm and sniffed. 'Aye, well, Dave will understand...'

'I'll take this.' They snatched the bag and rummaged inside.

'Give that back!' Sean shouted.

'Trust me, you don't want to push me on this.'

'Give it here,' Sean snapped. 'I need that more than you.' He lunged forward but they were too quick for him, shoving him unceremoniously into the open wardrobe.

'Look at the state of you.' Their words exited with every ounce of venom they felt inside. 'What a waste of oxygen. You really are, aren't you?' They tossed the bag back onto the bed and sneered.

Those were the last words Sean heard as the wardrobe closed and a chair was slid in front of it. Trapping him inside. From the darkness inside he heard only cackling laughter and foot-steps leaving, heading down the stairs and out the front door. Banging and then locking it after them.

Chapter Forty-Six

Arriving back at the station armed with the new information she'd gained from their search of the Ramsays' bungalow, Hazel was keen to move things on quickly but made a note on her pad to phone the home because she didn't have time right now. As much as she hated herself for it, her dad could wait a little longer. Given the revelation that Louise not only knew Peter King, but had also allegedly been abused by him as a teenager, Samuel Ramsay's flat refusal of any knowledge of the convicted sex offender was bizarre. The two victims were connected. Hazel hoped the CCTV Billy had now would help the case.

'Hi Andrea, how did it go with the missing woman's daughter?' Hazel asked as she slung her cardigan across the back of her chair.

'The poor woman is going out of her mind,' Andrea confirmed. 'I've already uploaded her mother's details and the recent photo she gave me onto the Police Scotland social media and I'm waiting for a call back from the press team who are arranging a briefing for us.'

'Good girl.' Hazel was impressed with her DC's initiative because that was one less thing she would have to sort out.

'What did you find at the Ramsay house?' Andrea asked.

Hazel laid the insurance document and the photo of the young Maggie Ramsay in front of her.

'Is that Maggie?' Andrea asked and lifted the picture up to look at it more closely. She turned it over. 'Who is Michelle?'

'*Where* is Michelle too?' Tom interjected. 'And why hide the photo like that, taped on the underside of the drawer?'

'Really?' Andrea said. 'Do you think Samuel knew about this child then, or was she a secret from him too?'

'I wish I knew the answer to that one,' Hazel admitted.

'Do we know whether the Ramsays lost a child?' Andrea added, turning to look at Billy, sitting in front of his laptop.

'Not from the research I've done,' Billy Flynn responded. 'Records only show one registered child for the couple.'

'So who is this then, I wonder?' Hazel pointed to the photo in Andrea's hand. 'And where is she? If she's still alive, that is.'

Andrea laid the photo back down and picked up the insurance document. She flicked through the pages and her eyes widened.

'Wow, that's a huge increase in the value of the policy,' she said.

'Isn't it just?' Hazel replied.

'Did the daughter confirm it was Samuel's writing?'

'No, that's the interesting thing,' Hazel explained. 'It was Maggie herself.'

'Why such a big increase? Do we know if she was ill?' Andrea said. 'Didn't the PM suggest she was healthy despite the alcohol abuse?'

Hazel turned to Billy. 'Billy, could you get onto Maggie's GP? I'm sure they'll make a fuss, but I think it's worth having a look – and get in touch with the solicitors. See if they'll show us the will. They might know the reason behind the significant hike in cover.'

'No problem,' Billy replied, starting to tap his keyboard.

'Actually, dig a bit deeper, will you? Check maternity records as well.'

Billy gave her a thumbs-up. 'I'll make us a brew as well, shall I?' he asked and stood up, stretching his arms before stifling a yawn.

'I'd love one, thanks.' Hazel beamed at him. 'You're a good un' you are.'

'So I've been told.' Billy grinned as he headed for the kitchen just as his phone buzzed on his desk.

Hazel picked up Billy's phone and read the caller ID. It was from someone called Jimbo.

'Billy,' she called out. 'There's someone called Jimbo calling you.'

Her words sent Billy jogging quickly back to his desk. He grabbed his phone but was disappointed to answer just as the call ended.

'Shit, hang on,' he said. 'I'll call him right back. He might have news about you-know-what.'

It took Hazel a moment to realise what he meant. 'Oh, of course, yes.'

Jimbo must be Billy's connection to all things secret.

'Great, thanks mate, yes, I'll tell her. Yes and you, bye... Aye, you too, mate, bye,' Billy said and hung up. He turned to face Hazel.

'Well?' she asked.

'It seems Peter King was being watched as part of something called Operation Autumn.'

Hazel frowned. 'What's that when it's at home?'

'It's a covert operation looking at the dark web and the interactions between paedophiles on there. They're looking at a site that's for sharing images. Sick bastards.'

'Do you think Lady Campbell was told about Operation Autumn?' Hazel suggested. 'Is that why she kept him out of prison? So he could be watched?'

'Who knows?' Billy shrugged.

'I think we need to ask her.'

Hazel thought about what the Ramsays' daughter had told her. His conviction for indecent images too. A sickening thought struck her. The fact that when asked about King, Samuel Ramsay denied he'd even heard of him. That was strange in light of this new information She doubted that it was something a father could forget in a hurry. Had Maggie and Louise kept it from her father?

'Is that all your friend said about it?' Hazel asked as she looked at Peter King's photo on the evidence board then allowed her eyes to drift across to Maggie Ramsay's. A missing elderly, vulnerable woman on top of this.

'Yes but he says he'll dig a bit deeper if you need him to,' Billy told her.

'Mm,' Hazel mumbled without looking back at him. 'That's fine for now but text him and tell him we'll give him a shout if we need any more. What about the CCTV you got?'

'Yes the CCTV,' Billy answered. 'Fortunately, this is nice and clear.'

'Some good news at last,' Hazel remarked.

Billy turned his laptop screen round so everyone could see. 'Who is this?' he asked.

Tom's eyes widened. 'That's Rona King. What does the time stamp say?' His eyes scanned the top corner of the screen. 'That's around the same time Jack Blair gave as a time of death.' He turned to Hazel. 'Isn't it?'

'Yes it is,' she replied. 'As close as he could give.'

'Shit,' Tom exclaimed, screwing up his eyes to look more closely. 'Do you think she could have killed her uncle? But she doesn't look like she's going in.' He stared at the figure on the screen, wearing a baseball cap on her head as she hurried away from Peter King's block of flats. 'She seems so...' He paused to think of the right word because 'upset' wasn't exactly true. 'Och I don't know,' he said when the right word didn't spring to mind.

'Well Tom, whatever she is, it's not looking good for her right now. Whether she was going in or not. She was there,' Hazel admitted. 'Go back and talk to her, will you? Get her to explain why she was there and why she chose not to mention it. Bring her in if you think she needs to be formally interviewed.'

'Aye, nae bother. Billy, send that clip to my phone, will you?' Tom asked.

'Right,' Hazel continued. 'Andrea, could you get over to the missing woman's home? Have a look around. It sounds like the daughter has a key. If there's even a hint of foul play, call in forensics. Tell them I gave the order.' Then she added, 'Are you sure you're still OK taking the lead on this?'

Andrea's emphatic nod was good to see.

Hazel was grateful to have such a competent DC. She was sure it wouldn't be long before she was a DS although losing a good DC wouldn't be great. Andrea was ambitious. Maybe one day she'd be doing Hazel's job. Surprised to see Gerry walking towards her, Hazel smiled.

'Hello again,' she said and noticed that he had a sheet of paper in his hand. 'What's that?'

'The identity of Lady Campbell's intruder.' Gerry held the paper up. 'I wondered if the name meant anything to your investigation. They were on file but not yet on the database. They must have been taken recently.'

'Who is it?' she asked.

Every member of Hazel's team stared at Gerry. The CCTV. The fingerprints. It was looking a lot like Rona had questions to answer.

Chapter Forty-Seven

It was horrible to see Suzanne looking so frail as she lay back on the bed in Accident and Emergency. She had insisted she was OK after her fall, but David knew it was more the embarrassment of wetting herself that bothered her. She'd tripped on her front doorstep, at least, and not somewhere more public. Her illness was moving faster than either of them had anticipated. Another flare up so quickly after the last was stealing what little energy she had.

'Hey, you,' he said gently when she opened her eyes.

'I'm sorry, did I fall asleep? I didn't mean to.' Suzanne tried to pull herself into a more comfortable position. 'I'm so tired,' she yawned.

David moved forward and lifted her further up so she could lean on the pillows. He hated seeing her like this.

'There you go. Is that more comfortable?'

Suzanne nodded. 'Yes, much, thanks.' She made the effort to smile for his sake.

'Would you like something to drink? I'll go and get us something from the vending machine in the waiting area, will I?'

'That would be nice,' Suzanne answered realising her mouth was feeling dry. She ran her tongue over her cracked lips. 'See if you can get me a Coke, will you? I'd love something cold and sweet and fizzy.'

David smiled. 'Of course, I'll be back soon,' he told her as the doctor arrived to talk to Suzanne.

David wished he could do something to make her life better. Her multiple sclerosis diagnosis had hit her like a train, she'd told him. Until a year ago Suzanne had been hillwalking and running marathons, she'd said. It was happening so fast. Meeting that day in the solicitor's office had been a wonderful moment for both of them. During the lowest moments in both their lives. The age difference didn't matter to David. Suzanne saw his pain and wanted to make it better. Perhaps she took the place of his Mum, like Sean ribbed him because he'd effectively lost Carol the same day Liam died.

That detective was sure he had killed Maggie Ramsay. Of course he wanted her dead – and Peter King; that sick bastard deserved to die too.

David's phone vibrated in his jeans pocket. He pulled it out after putting his coins into the vending machine and pressed the keys for a bottle of Pepsi, hoping Suzanne would be OK with that instead of Coke. Sean's number came up on the caller ID and David rolled his eyes and tutted. What the hell did he want, he thought, before declining the call. Seconds later, Sean called again. This time David switched his phone off. He didn't have time for Sean's bullshit.

Sean Jacobs started to feel dizzy. His body was moving quickly between sweating and shivering from a cruel combination of claustrophobia and withdrawal. Why had they locked him in there? It was no use, he couldn't hold it in any longer and he vomited into the small space next to him, the smell of his own sick making him retch more. He gripped his stomach against the agonising cramps that were tightening and squeezing his guts and spinning what little content was left inside. Sean started to feel weak. His whole body was trembling as he lifted a hand to bang on the wardrobe door.

'Hello, is there anybody out there?' He tried to shout but his throat burned from vomiting.

He coughed and spat vomit-streaked saliva onto the floor. 'Hey!' He hammered the door with his fist, the sharp sting when his skin made contact with the wooden surface making him yank his hand back. His hands were so cold they ached. 'Please!' he cried out as his body slid to the floor. He kicked out at the door from where he'd collapsed, tugging at the collar of his T-shirt that he now felt was choking him. 'Let me out please, I'm going to die in here.'

Sean started to sob and tried David's number again but all he got was his friend's voicemail. None of this made any sense. He'd kept up his end of the bargain.

'David, mate, please call me back. I'm trapped and...' Sean's words faded as the phone fell from his grasp. His head felt fuzzy, and he was too weak to keep hold of it. His eyes slowly closed.

Chapter Forty-Eight

Andrea thanked Sheila Marshall's next-door neighbour for the key. A lovely old man who had seen her knocking and come out to see if he could help. He'd told her he had a key and was happy to give it to her once he'd examined her ID. He was also worried about Sheila who was a lovely neighbour to have by all accounts. Andrea was grateful that he had spoken to her because it saved her a trip to talk to him. Sadly he couldn't help in her investigation. He'd not seen anything because he'd been staying at his daughter's flat for the weekend. Andrea let herself into the small bungalow which was obviously a retirement home for a single person. That nice old-person smell hit her as she closed the front door behind her, but she wasn't exactly sure what it was. A wonderfully evocative flowery fragrance that reminded her of her own grandmother, Granny Dublin. Her Irish granny that Andrea used to see twice a year when they had a summer and October holiday break in County Kerry.

Andrea pulled on a pair of latex gloves and picked up the post. Charity begging letters, mainly, and a gas bill. She laid the pile of envelopes on the hall table. Dried flowers in an ornate glass bowl seemed to be the source of the wonderful smell. The rest of the table had another bowl for keys and several houseplants, a spider plant being the only one that Andrea recognised. Any other available space was filled with framed photographs of Sheila with a black-haired boy at various ages and school photographs of the same lad, right up to a university graduation picture with a beaming Sheila standing next to him.

The hairstyles in the pictures looked too recent to be a son. A grandson, perhaps.

She stepped deeper inside the bungalow and was saddened to see the dying daffodils in the crystal vase on the fireplace, supposing that would not have been allowed to happen if Sheila Marshall had been there, given what she had learned about how particular she was. The photos on the mantel were a collection of Sheila with different children, mostly babies and toddlers, but not the boy from the pictures on the hall table. More grandchildren, she wondered.

Andrea picked up and read a card that sat next to the vase of dying flowers.

With love always, S x

Who was S, she wondered and why hadn't Rita mentioned them? Andrea bagged the card. She pulled open a drawer in the huge oak cabinet that filled the whole back wall of the living room with barely a few centimetres gap on either end. She lifted out a passport and driving licence. Sheila's face looked stern in both of them. But everyone looked like that in those types of pictures didn't they. She laid them both back in and rummaged through a selection of envelopes that she quickly realised were correspondence from Ninewells hospital. Mostly from the Oncology and Renal departments. So Sheila Marshall had cancer, perhaps. Why hadn't her daughter mentioned that? She'd shared Sheila's dementia diagnosis freely. Perhaps she wasn't aware, but Andrea doubted that. She put the letters back in the drawer and closed it after flicking through several old copies of *The People's Friend* and *My Weekly*.

She opened the drawer next to it and found a green glasses case which had what she assumed to be a pair of reading glasses in it. When she opened it, she found a pair of large framed black glasses and wondered if Sheila was missing them. Next to it was a large spiral-backed notebook with a black biro pen fixed to the spine. She lifted it out and began reading. The first page had a series of dates and initials marked in the margins. What did the initials mean? Was that how Sheila remembered things after her dementia diagnosis?

Andrea pulled out the hospital letters again and realised that the dates matched with some of the appointments. More appointments were jotted down on the next few pages. Chiropodist. Optician. Hairdresser. She flicked to the next page which had a list of names and phone numbers on it. Andrea's eye was drawn to the corner of a telephone book with a smooth black cover, the word 'Telephone' printed in gold lettering, which was also in the drawer. She took it out and, as she suspected, some of the entries in the notebook matched the telephone book. Each entry had a name and two numbers. One landline and a mobile. Except one, which was simply entered as 'S' with only a mobile number. The S from the card? Andrea wondered. That was more than a coincidence. Who the hell was S?

The sound of the front door opening and closing made Andrea jump.

'Oh, Detective!' Rita Latimer clutched her chest. 'You startled me.'

'I'm sorry.'

Rita frowned on seeing the young detective going through her mother's things.

'What are you doing?' she asked.

'My DCI has asked me to come and take a closer look at your mum's home to see if I can see any reason for her disappearance. Your mum's neighbour gave me a key.' She nodded in the direction of the house next door. 'A fresh pair of eyes is always useful. One that can maybe see something that you might have overlooked. It's standard procedure.'

'Other than the fact that she's confused and lost because of her dementia, you mean.'

Andrea gave her a gentle nod. 'That's right.'

Rita sighed. 'Well, at least you're taking her disappearance seriously.'

'Of course. Your mum is a frail, elderly woman.'

A thin smile appeared on Rita's lips. 'She's not as frail as you think.'

Andrea frowned at her remark. 'What do you mean?'

'My mum is a feisty old girl, always has been.'

'Is that right? I'm glad to hear it.' Andrea smiled back.

'What's that you've got?' Rita nodded to the notebook in Andrea's hand.

'It's a book of appointments and phone numbers.'

'Can I see it?'

Andrea handed the notebook over. 'Sure. You might be able to answer something for me.' She was about to open her mouth to ask who S was until Rita beat her to it.

'Who is S?' Rita asked and looked right at her.

'I was hoping you'd be able to tell me that.'

Rita shook her head and frowned. 'I have no idea. The letter S means nothing to me.' She frowned. 'I can't even think of any of her church friends' names beginning with S. I mean, my mum's name does, but why would she...' She stopped when she spotted the card in Andrea's hand.

Andrea handed Rita the card. 'Your mum also received a card from someone who signed it as S. Do you recognise the writing?'

Rita narrowed her eyes at the card. 'No, I don't. God, do you think this S knows where Mum is?'

'There is a phone number here.' Andrea pointed to the entry in the notebook.

Rita snatched the book from her hand, almost ripping the paper in her haste. She grabbed her phone from her handbag and quickly dialled the number before Andrea could stop her. She watched her listen for an answer.

'Well?' Andrea asked as Rita hung up.

'The call just went straight to one of those mechanical voice-mails.' Her mood darkened, and the fearful expression on her face increased. 'Can you lot trace the number?'

'Don't worry, we'll do our very best to find out whose number this is,' Andrea assured her. 'We have a detective on our team who is really good at this kind of thing. The best I've ever worked with.'

'Good, good, and they can trace this S, can they?' She squeezed the book tightly in her hand and held it up in front of her. 'But I'm going to keep trying. Maybe this S is a friend of Mum's that I've not met. Maybe it's a new member of the congregation.'

'I'm sorry but I'm going to need to take that,' Andrea said.

'What, erm, of course yes.' Rita was flustered and grabbed an envelope from her bag and scribbled the number on it before handing the original back to Andrea.

'Thanks,' Andrea said.

Rita closed her eyes then wiped a small tear away. 'God what if my mum's hurt.'

Andrea reached out and ran her hand gently over Rita's arm.

'Don't worry. Billy will do his utmost to find out the identity of S, OK,' Andrea said. 'I'm giving a press briefing shortly. I'll include this.' She raised the card slightly into the air.

Rita opened her mouth to speak as her phone rang.

'It's the number,' she exclaimed before pressing the 'answer call' button. 'Hello, who is this?' she said urgently.

'You called my phone a minute ago.' The caller spoke in barely a whisper, making it difficult to tell if it was a man or a woman. 'Who is this?'

'My name is Rita Latimer and I... hello, are you still there?'

Rita turned to face Andrea, her eyes wide in fear. 'They hung up.'

Chapter Forty-Nine

Hazel ran from the busy hospital car park and raced into the Care of the Elderly ward, relieved that her dad had been admitted straight there and hadn't had to go through Accident and Emergency. God she wished she'd taken the time to call the home. Hazel felt sick that she'd left it. The phone call from the care home manager had come hot on the heels of Gerry revealing that the fingerprints found at the Campbell crime scene were Rona's and Hazel's mind was in turmoil. She felt sick with worry about her dad.

'Hello, my dad has just been admitted and…' Hazel blurted out, sweat pouring from her brow and neck.

'Come with me and I'll take you to your dad's room,' the sympathetic-looking nurse told her.

'What's happened?' Hazel asked anxiously. 'The girl on the phone didn't say very much. Just that he's been admitted.'

The nurse stopped outside a side room.

'Your dad and some of the other residents have recently had a stomach bug.'

'That's right,' Hazel agreed. 'Has he got worse?'

'Not exactly. He's become dehydrated and has developed a chest infection as a result which unfortunately has resulted in pneumonia. We're giving your dad intravenous antibiotics and fluids for now.' She ran her hand gently up and down Hazel's back. A touch that was intended to convey empathy, Hazel assumed. 'If you could sanitise your hands and put this apron and gloves on before you go in.'

Hazel took the protective items from her and held her hands under the sanitiser pump.

'Erm, yes, OK.'

'I'll come back in a bit,' the nurse said before leaving Hazel standing alone outside the room.

Hazel reached for the door handle with trepidation. Her dad had fought back from a bout of pneumonia once before but that was five years ago when he was younger and had carried more weight than the frail man he was now. Her heart rate began to speed up and she had a bizarre urge to call Rick which she couldn't explain. Having his arms round her right then sounded wonderful but that was never going to happen again.

A dull band of pain crossed her brow as she pressed the handle down. Hazel took a breath and allowed the door to swing slowly open.

The sight of the small, thin man lying on the bed in the middle of the room made her whimper. She thought she was prepared but it was such a shock. His face was almost completely covered by an oxygen mask. An IV drip was in each arm. A cold breeze blew in the open window, shifting the blue blind gently. An attempt to get his temperature down she supposed.

'Dad,' Hazel murmured and sat on the black plastic chair next to his bed.

Her dad didn't acknowledge her presence as she took his bony hand in hers.

'Dad,' she repeated and wiped a line of tears that were pouring down her cheeks, the latex of the gloves sticking to her skin. She blew out a trembling breath to control the swell of emotion that she feared might overwhelm her. Hazel felt guilty for not realising how bad his stomach bug had become. She should have phoned earlier. She shouldn't have left him alone when he'd clearly been suffering, but she wouldn't leave him alone now.

The door opened and a young doctor stood in the doorway. 'Hello, I'm Benjamin Delpierro, I'm looking after your father.'

'Thank you,' Hazel mumbled.

'You're welcome.' The pale young man smiled gently. 'We've started your father on a course of quite strong IV antibiotics for the infection which is making him very drowsy. His temperature is proving tricky to bring down. We're also pushing lots of fluids to try and flush the infection out of his system, but given his age and already frail condition, I need you to appreciate that...'

Hazel lifted a hand to intercept what he was about to say. She didn't have to hear the words to know the truth.

'I know,' she whispered. 'I know.'

'Please stay as long as you want to,' he added.

'Thank you,' Hazel replied and as the doctor closed the door behind him, she began to sob, allowing soaking wet tears to pour down her already tear-streaked face.

Chapter Fifty

Tom read the text Hazel had just sent and wished he could give her a huge hug to let her know he was there for her. Her father's condition didn't sound good at all, but he had to keep on top of the case in her absence. He'd been stunned to learn that the fingerprints in the cottage belonged to Rona King, and he began to think the teenager wasn't in as he stood with his finger pressed hard on the doorbell. The sound of barking came from inside. Tom leaned down and opened the letterbox.

'Rona, it's DI Newton. Could you answer the door, please?' He peered along the hall but the only activity inside was the dog jumping frantically to catch his attention.

Tom found Rona's number in his notebook and called her mobile but hung up when it went to voicemail. He sighed and crouched down to peer in again.

'Rona, I think you should open the door. We know what you've done so you might as well let me in. Let's not make things any worse for yourself.'

Tom stood back up and dialled Billy's number.

'Hi, listen, where does Rona King work? I don't seem to have the address.' He scribbled the address into his notebook. 'Cheers, mate.'

Tom turned to leave the block, almost banging into Rona's neighbour, who tutted at him.

'Careful, lad,' the old man said, a heavy-looking carrier bag in each hand.

'I'm sorry,' Tom replied, fearing he'd almost bowled him over.

'Did you tell her to shut that damn dog up?'

'I'm sorry, what?'

'Aye, he's been yapping away all night.' The old man tutted again.

'Has he?'

'Aye, she must be on a night shift again.'

As Tom walked back to his car he considered what he'd been told. Rona hadn't been home all night and hadn't made an arrangement for her dog. She must have realised they would have matched her prints with those found at the Campbell cottage and been too scared to go back to the flat. He didn't think she'd take the chance of going into work either, given the fact that they had her employment details too, but he would try there anyway. As he got closer to his car, the little dog's face came back into his mind. Tom didn't feel right about leaving the wee animal alone any longer, so he returned to ask Rona's neighbour to help.

Tom held his ID up for the nurse in charge of the shift in the care home to examine. Looking around the room, he wondered if Hazel's dad's home was like this one. He supposed they were all kind of similar. The furniture and décor tried to be homely but had to be practical too. A radio played Scottish country music behind the main desk. There was a smell in the air. He couldn't exactly say what it was, but it wasn't something he'd like to smell every day.

'Excuse me a minute,' the flustered girl who'd greeted him said and rushed to help an elderly woman who appeared to be trying to get out of a chair in the day room to the left of them. Looking more closely at the décor he spotted paintings of countryside scenes on the wall, featuring open green landscapes and hills. A huge clock ticked so loudly he could hear it from where he was waiting for the young nurse to return.

Tom lifted his hand. 'It's fine, don't worry.'

He watched her ease the woman back down and tell her that she'd be back as soon as she could to take her to her room but that she'd need to get her colleague to help.

'I'm sorry about that,' the girl said. 'I've been left in the lurch, I'm afraid. One of my care workers had gone AWOL. Not even a phone call, nothing and I've got another off sick.'

Tom frowned. 'Do you mean Rona King has gone AWOL?'

The girl's eyes widened. 'Yes! How did you know that?'

Tom was disappointed but not at all surprised not to find Rona there. If he were in her position he wouldn't hang around places he was known to frequent either – work and home being the major ones. His search would have to be expanded.

'Does Rona have friends or family that she's spoken to you about?'

'Rona doesn't really talk about her family much. I can't blame her really after… you know.' The girl shrugged.

'I do know, yes,' Tom acknowledged. 'You're talking about her uncle.'

The girl nodded and shuddered. 'He made my skin crawl.'

'Did you ever meet him?'

She shook her head. 'No, thank God, but I knew all about it from the papers.'

'How did Rona take his death? Did she ever talk about it?'

'Not to me but Rona doesn't like to chat much, to be honest. I mean, don't get me wrong, she is a sweet girl but she's quiet, you know.'

Tom nodded. 'I see.'

'Between you and me,' she leaned in closer, 'I wouldn't be surprised if he'd abused Rona as well.'

'Mm, I hope not.'

'She seemed so loyal to him,' the girl added. 'Helping him like she did. It was weird. If it was me…' she whispered then stopped taking it any further just as a buzzer sounded. She looked along the hallway behind then said, 'Listen, I need to get that.'

'Sure, of course, yes.' Tom took his card out of his jacket pocket and laid it on the table beside them. 'Thanks for your time and listen, if you hear from Rona or if she does turn up, could you please call me?'

'Sure, yes,' the girl said and jogged away in the direction of the buzzer.

Tom called the station as he walked towards the care home front door, briefly confused by the key system. Of course it had to be locked.

'Press the big pad then type one-two-three into the keyboard.'

Tom turned to see a bald old man shuffling along the foyer in a pair of green tartan slippers with a newspaper tucked under his arm.

'What? OK thanks.' Tom smiled and followed the instructions.

As he left the home he called the station to ask them to circulate Rona's description, stressing the urgency. It was getting late, but he figured there was no reason to rush home, anyway. John would probably be out, so Tom decided he'd check if Rona was hiding out at Suzanne Gerrard's given that the two women were cousins.

Tom rapped the letterbox and waited, listening for footsteps inside. Knowing she relied on her stick, he knew she would take her time answering. When he got no response after ten minutes he peered in the window. The curtains were wide open, and the house was in darkness. Tom tutted and was irritated to leave empty-handed. Again.

–

Rona pressed the bell and the bus pulled into the stop closest to her destination. Thankfully, nobody would look for her there because nobody knew about it. She'd known as soon as she'd given her fingerprints that they'd be looking for her. Luckily for her, she'd been a step ahead of them.

She thanked the driver and started walking the short distance under the light of the streetlamps, tugging the peak of her baseball cap down as the tall man approached with his dog.

'Hi there,' he said warmly, the way people did in this neighbourhood when you passed.

Rona couldn't risk him recognising her in any future police appeals so she kept her head down and said nothing. Trudging through the snow, she was glad to get to where she was going. Her feet were freezing. She opened the door, surprised to find it unlocked.

'It's just me,' Rona said and shut the door behind her, kicking off her boots in the hallway, instantly enjoying the cosy temperature inside.

Chapter Fifty-One

David had stayed with Suzanne for as long as it took to get her settled in a ward for observation overnight. The doctors thought it was for the best. For one night, at least. It was getting late, and she'd looked exhausted. He promised he'd be back in the morning to see how she was. Her condition had relapsed, but he'd tried his best to let her know he'd be there for her, no matter what. The way she'd supported him in his darkest days. They would always be there for each other. He'd promised her.

It's us against the world.

That had made her laugh, at least.

As he got closer to the house he could see through the living room window – because the blinds were still open – that things had been disturbed and a couple of drawers in the dresser had been left wide open.

'What the hell?' he gasped as he went inside. First he'd lost his mum. Now this.

David moved into the kitchen and found the same state of disruption. He couldn't believe they'd been burgled. It couldn't have happened at a worse time.

'Fuck!' he shouted and slammed one of the drawers shut.

Then he remembered the box with Liam's phone in it. The one that had been bought but never given to him.

David ran upstairs, taking them two at a time. He surged into the bedroom, confused by the chair pushed against the wardrobe door. He pulled it away and ripped open the door, stunned to see Sean Jacobs slumped in a heap on the floor.

'Sean, what the fuck?' he exclaimed and grabbed hold of Sean's shirt to drag him out. He dropped him on the floor at his feet. 'What the hell are you doing here?' David looked around at the mess. 'Did you do this, you little shit?' he snarled then frowned when he realised Sean wasn't moving.

David crouched down and grabbed Sean's face between his fingers, slapping his cheek to rouse him from what he assumed to be a drug-fuelled haze. How the chair got wedged against the wardrobe door was a mystery. Sean's eyes slowly started to peel open.

'David,' he mumbled, staring up at his old friend. 'David, thank fuck, man.' His words grew louder but more slurred with each breath. 'I couldn't breathe in there. I thought I was going to die.'

David dropped Sean from his grasp, allowing him to fall onto his back in a heap.

'Shit, argh!' Sean exclaimed then scrambled into a sitting position.

David paced back and forth, the anger burning inside him. He scowled at Sean.

'You did this, didn't you, you piece of shit!' He surged closer and grabbed Sean by the collar of his T-shirt, lifting him up before dropping him back down.

'Argh,' Sean cried out as he bumped back down, banging his head on the wardrobe door.

David snatched the stuffed sports bag from the bed and tipped out the contents. His heart was pounding with rage. Laptops, iPads, watches, cash and two old phones. He was already seething with hate for the lad who was supposed to be his best friend, had been since school, until he saw the phone, still in its box. The one that Liam was meant to get. He picked it up and held it close to his chest. A wave of grief swept through him, and it all came flooding back. That awful day. The police officer's face. The noise his mum made when they told her about Liam. That her beautiful boy had been killed.

'I'm sorry man, I just...' Sean whimpered as he scrambled to his knees. 'I, I...'

That was it. That was the thing that tipped David over the edge. He'd lost Liam. He'd lost his mum. From inside the thick cloud of absolute rage that consumed him he heard the box with the phone in it hit the bed and bounce onto the carpet. David's whole body was filled with such hate for the pathetic creature now sat on his knees begging for forgiveness.

'I'm sorry, man, please...'

That first punch did nothing to quell the tide of anger. Or the second or the third or the fourth or the fifth. Slamming his foot into Sean's ribs, again and again and again didn't stop the pain. He hammered his face until his knuckles throbbed. Until Sean stopped crying for help.

David panted to catch his breath. Sweat poured from his brow, from his neck. He licked the salty taste from his lips, the sound of his hammering heartbeat swimming in his ears.

Blood poured from the cuts on Sean's face, streams of crimson flowing to join each other until they dripped from his chin and onto the floor, staining the beige carpet with a puddle of ruby liquid.

David pulled his arm back and slammed his fist into Sean's face yet again. And again. Until his muscles ached. He dropped Sean's motionless body to the carpet and fell back onto the bed, panting to catch his breath.

'Argh,' he raged and tried to open and close his fist. His hand throbbed and he feared he'd broken it. 'Fucking hell, argh.'

He looked down at Sean. His chest was moving up and down. He was still alive, just. Pity, David thought as he rushed from the room.

Standing in the silence of the kitchen with a bag of frozen peas on his hand, he had time to think as he stared out onto the snow-covered back garden, remembering times that he and Liam had built snowmen out there. Ridiculously big snowmen with eyes and noses and wide smiles. A single tear trickled from

269

his eye and David let it dribble down his cheek until it fell from his face. He sniffed and rubbed his eyes with the hand that wasn't bruised. His breathing had returned to normal. Maybe he shouldn't have done that. He guzzled down the glass of water he'd poured himself, drips falling from the side of his mouth and landing on his sweat-soaked shirt that had spatters of Sean's blood on it.

His head felt like it was going to explode. There wasn't room inside it for everything that had happened. Maggie Ramsay and that sick pervert King had deserved to die. Even that DCI woman must see that.

A text buzzed on his phone, snapping him back to the present, startling him a little. Without thinking, he tried to use his injured hand to retrieve the phone from his jeans pocket.

'Fucking hell, argh,' he cried out and had to give up and use the other hand.

The words on the screen brought more tears to his eyes. This time for a good reason. It was from Suzanne.

Thanks for taking care of me today. I love you x

David tried to dry his face with a damp tea towel he found in a heap on the worktop. He loved this woman so much. He would do anything for her.

Movement from upstairs suggested that Sean had started to recover from his beating. Probably just as well; the last thing Suzanne needed was for David to be jailed for murder. Tempted as he was to kill Sean, it wasn't worth that. The loud knock on the door made David jump. If he ignored it, they'd surely go away. He was disappointed to find that wasn't the case when the doorbell buzzed loudly.

'What?' he snapped after opening the door to the stunned face of their next-door neighbour.

'I was... erm...' The horrified expression on her face on seeing his hand made David move it behind his back, out of sight. 'I heard a lot of banging and shouting, and I was worried—'

'Mind yer ain fuckin' business you interfering auld cow!' David shouted at her and slammed the door in her face.

He stood for several minutes without moving away from the door, watching the irritating old busybody scuttle back next door. But she'd heard the fight and seen his hand. No doubt she'd be calling the police soon. That was all he needed. He'd have to do something about Sean, and quick.

Chapter Fifty-Two

'Tom, come on up.' Hazel answered the security buzzer and pressed the button to let him in through the outside door. She unlocked her front door so he could let himself in.

'Seems the little madam was always a step ahead of us,' Tom said as he closed the door behind himself.

'Come on through. Her work couldn't shed any light on where she might be?'

Tom shook his head. 'Nah. I tried Suzanne's place, but it was in darkness as well.'

'Was it?'

'Aye, do you think they're together?' Tom suggested.

'Suzanne is pretty frail. I can't see her being out and about at this time.' Hazel checked the time on the clock above her kitchen sink. It read ten thirty. She picked up the wine bottle. 'Wine?'

'God, yes please,' he replied and tossed his jacket across one of Hazel's kitchen chairs before sitting on another. He laid his elbows on the table and dropped his head into his hands. 'Shit, shit, shit,' he exclaimed.

Hazel laid a glass in front of him.

'Drink your wine.' She took a swig from her own glass. 'We'll worry about this in the morning.'

Tom frowned. 'How's your dad?' he asked.

Hazel was about to answer when her security buzzer rang out again.

'Excuse me a minute,' she said and walked away.

As Tom waited for Hazel to return he noticed the amount of empty wine bottles in the recycling box. He knew she'd been drinking more since Rick was murdered last year but seeing the evidence literally mounted up was stark. Tom took a sip from his glass as Hazel returned.

'Is everything OK?' he asked.

'Erm, yes, a friend of mine has just turned up and he's brought me a chippy.'

'Ah, OK.' He grabbed his jacket and took a last sip from his glass. He gave a playful, teasing salute which made Hazel smile. 'I'll see you in the morning, boss.'

Tom nodded to Gerry Smith as the two men passed in Hazel's hallway.

'Hello Tom,' Gerry greeted him.

'Enjoy the rest of your evening,' Tom called back to Hazel and closed the door behind him.

—

'I wasn't interrupting anything was I?' Gerry suggested.

'No, no.' Hazel smiled at him and held up the wine bottle. 'Do you fancy a glass?'

Gerry laid the carrier bag with the two fish suppers on the kitchen table. 'Sure, that would be great, thanks. Can I do anything?'

'No, you sit, I really appreciate you coming like this,' Hazel said. 'God, that smells good.' She sniffed the air above the table, savouring that chippy smell. Salt and vinegar and grease. Delicious.

In a moment of weakness she'd texted Gerry to tell him about her dad. Gerry had been lovely enough to call her straight back and Hazel broke down, telling him how scared and worried she was about losing her dad. He had said he'd be over as soon as he could, and he'd bring food. Now that he was sitting in her kitchen she felt weird about it. Unsure what to say to him.

'It's no trouble,' Gerry assured her, his gentle smile causing her cheeks to flare when he looked at her. 'I wasn't up to much tonight anyway. You've saved me from a night of Netflix for one, actually,' he chuckled as he took the glass of wine from her hand. Their fingers brushed together slightly, and Hazel pulled back, scratching her neck awkwardly.

She coughed to cover her discomfort and sat opposite him. Gerry tore open one of the fish suppers and smiled at her.

'Are we having plates or are we savages?' he teased.

Gerry hadn't changed at all in the past thirty years. He was a lovely guy, if a little bit nerdy. Hazel grabbed a couple of forks from the drawer and dropped them onto the table. She opened the fridge.

'I've already got tomato ketchup on yours.' Gerry grinned. 'I remembered.'

Hazel was taken aback by that, and her surprise didn't go unnoticed.

'You seem shocked,' Gerry pointed out.

'I am a bit,' she confessed. 'I haven't seen you for a long time. How can you possibly remember something like that?'

Gerry shrugged. 'I don't know. I just do sometimes.'

Hazel felt a little guilty when he started to seem uncomfortable with what he'd said.

'This was really nice of you,' she said and flopped down on a chair opposite him at the table. She ripped the paper off of her meal and inhaled again. That smell. It was unmistakable and wonderful. Seeing the ketchup made her smile.

Gerry reached behind him and tore off several sheets of kitchen roll. He handed one to her.

'Here you go.' He grinned. 'It's a bit greasy.'

'The greasier the better,' she said through a mouthful of food.

'You haven't changed,' Gerry said and sipped from his glass, keeping his gaze focussed on Hazel the whole time. 'You're still as crazy as I remember you.'

In that moment Hazel realised something. She was actually enjoying herself in Gerry's company. He was a lovely distraction from work and from her dad. Sure, he was more of a bearded Ron Weasley than Jason Momoa, but he actually made her smile. She wondered what had happened between him and his wife and the two glasses of wine must have been the reason she came out and asked him directly.

'How come you're divorced and back in Perth, then?'

Gerry laughed. 'You don't hold back, do you?' he teased.

Hazel shrugged and took a long swig from her glass. 'I realised long ago that life's too short to beat around the bush.'

'Do you really want all the boring details?'

Hazel nodded. 'Absolutely.'

Gerry sank the contents of his glass and refilled it. 'I wasn't enough for her,' he said simply.

Hazel lifted her glass up. 'Snap, I know how that goes. I wasn't enough for Rick, either.'

'He was a daft prick to let you go,' Gerry suggested, the tone of his voice shifting, growing deeper in tune with the mood in the room.

For the first time in as long as she could remember, sexual tension pulsated between Hazel and a man. She hoped she wouldn't regret it in the morning.

Chapter Fifty-Three

Wednesday

It was so early that the sun wasn't yet up as Andrea parked her car in the closest space she could find to the door. The quicker she could get inside the cosy warm station, the better. The weather presenter had said that the cold snap was finally going to come to an end next week. Thank God. Her flat was freezing first thing in the morning. As she made her way inside, she spotted an injured man staggering towards the front door of the station. It horrified her to see that he wasn't even wearing a jumper, let alone a winter coat, given the further snowfall and drop in temperature last night.

'Bloody hell is that…' she mumbled under her breath and quickly ran to where Sean Jacobs was slowly approaching the door.

'Sean, wait a minute,' she called after him and was shocked to see the state of him as he turned to face her. 'Here, let me help you.' She took his arm, momentarily shocked by his freezing skin so close to her face. Even his breath was cold against her cheek. 'Come on, lean on me, it's OK.'

It was a struggle to understand what he was saying with his face so swollen.

'I need some help here,' Andrea shouted as she struggled to help Sean onto a chair.

Once she had managed to get him to sit, she crouched down next to where he slumped. 'Sean, what's happened? Who did this to you?'

Sean Jacobs tried to open his eyes to look at her, but they'd been beaten until they had swollen shut.

'Someone call an ambulance,' Andrea turned and called out.

'No, no,' Sean stammered and lifted a hand before dropping it quickly. 'No.' He gasped for breath. 'Please, wait. I don't want...'

'Sean, I really must insist that...'

'I said no.' Sean raised his voice as much as he could manage. 'I just want to, argh...' He winced and held his ribs. 'I need to tell you something.'

'Whatever it is can wait until you've been examined by a doctor,' Andrea insisted as the door opened again. It was Tom who rushed forward on seeing the state of Sean.

'Jesus, have you called an ambulance?' he urged.

'I don't want a fucking ambulance,' Sean tried to push him away. 'I want to tell you lot something.'

Andrea stared anxiously at Tom, grateful that he'd arrived and hoping he'd take control of the situation. Tom took a breath and ran his fingers across his freshly shaven chin. He chewed on his lip briefly and started to help Sean up, shocked by how light the teenager was.

'We'll take him into the soft interview suite for now,' Tom told Andrea. 'Let him rest on the sofa in there. You call the police doc, will you?'

'But Tom—' Andrea tried to insist. 'Surely it's an amb...'

'Andrea, just do it,' Tom replied firmly.

Tom was relieved to see her walk away with her phone held to her ear. He hated talking to her like that and he imagined she was shocked at his tone, but he was left with no choice. It was a struggle, but he managed to unlock the soft suite door and hold Sean up until he was able to let him fall gently onto the cushioned sofa.

'Argh,' Sean cried out, sucking air in through his teeth as he hugged his ribs tightly in his hands.

'Sean, I'm really not comfortable that you're refusing an ambulance,' Tom told him.

'I don't deserve one,' Sean sobbed, wincing in pain every time he moved.

'Come on Sean, stop feeling sorry for yourself, mate.' Tom perched himself on the edge of the coffee table close to Sean. 'Let us help you.'

'It's too late for that,' Sean mumbled as his breathing became more laboured. It seemed to become harder to take a breath.

When he coughed, the guttural wet sound set Tom's teeth on edge.

'That's it, I'm calling an ambulance.' Tom snatched his phone from his pocket.

'Wait,' Sean gasped and tried to lift a hand to stop him.

Tom stared down at him as he tried to say something. 'Yes, ambulance, please,' he said to the operator, ignoring Sean's attempts at resistance. 'Police station, Barrack Street – it's urgent.'

Tom was growing more and more concerned. Sean's face turned paler. 'It's OK, hang in there, help's coming.' He was angry with himself for not insisting earlier that an ambulance should be called.

'I need to tell you something,' Sean panted slowly, his breathing now even more laboured.

Tom dropped to his knees as a panicked Andrea returned.

'The doctor is on her way,' she said from the doorway.

'Sean, can you hear me?' Tom asked anxiously.

'It was me,' Sean murmured.

'What was you, Sean?' Tom pressed him as the lad's eyes slowly closed. He gently patted his face. 'Sean, listen to me, help's coming. Wake up, come on.'

'What was you, Sean?' Andrea shouted over the top of Tom's head.

'It was me,' Sean repeated, more quietly this time. 'I killed…' Then his words faded away as he sank into unconsciousness.

Chapter Fifty-Four

'Are you two all right?' Hazel was concerned by the pale colour on Andrea's cheeks.

She got to the station just as the paramedics arrived to help Sean Jacobs. Tom quickly filled her in, and she assumed Sean's confession was related to Maggie Ramsay or Peter King. Or both. All memory of last night was swept out of her head completely in the chaos. Probably a good thing. She had been relieved to get a call to say her dad's night had been settled and that he'd managed to eat a little porridge this morning. It wasn't much but it meant the antibiotics must be working.

'Yes, I'm OK,' Andrea replied. 'Just a bit shocked, I suppose.'

'Good, then go and wash your face in the bathroom,' Hazel told her. 'I want you to go to the hospital with Sean.'

'Oh, yes, of course.' Andrea turned and immediately headed in the direction of the bathroom.

'Come on, I'll make you a strong cup of tea.' Hazel gently patted Tom's arm and headed to her office. 'Did you give Sean's phone to Billy?'

'Yes,' Tom replied. 'I did.'

As the pair arrived at the office, Superintendent Daly was waiting for Hazel.

'I'll make the tea,' Tom whispered and left her to talk to Daly.

Hazel slung her cardigan over the back of her chair.

'Good morning, sir,' she said.

'How's the lad?' Daly asked.

'He's stable for now,' Hazel informed him. 'Thankfully.'

'Good, good, I'm glad to hear it. Do we have any idea what he meant when he said he'd killed someone?'

'Not yet,' Hazel replied. 'But I've sent Andrea, I mean DC Graham, in the ambulance with him. I've also given his phone to DS Flynn so he can examine it.'

'Do we have any idea who beat the crap out of him yet?' Daly asked and flopped down in one of the other chairs.

Hazel was shocked to hear the man swear. It must be a sign of the stress he's feeling.

'Not yet but I have an inkling.'

'Yes? Who?' Daly pressed her.

'David Wilson is pretty handy with his fists,' Hazel reminded him. 'It wouldn't be the first time he's kicked the shit out of Sean Jacobs.'

Tom knocked on Hazel's door and she waved him in.

'Here you go,' Tom laid a mug of tea on her desk. 'Can I get you a cup, sir?'

'No thank you, DI Newton, I'm just leaving.' Daly stood up. 'Keep me up to speed, will you?'

'Of course,' Hazel promised him.

Hazel watched the back of Daly disappear then curled her hands into fists before gently hitting her head.

'Argh,' she moaned. 'What the hell is going on with this case?' She snapped her head up. 'I'm sorry, thanks for this.' She lifted her mug and sipped. 'That's lovely.'

'You're welcome,' Tom smiled. 'How's your dad doing this morning?'

'He's better, thanks for asking.' Hazel took another gulp of the hot tea to quench her thirst. She was angry with herself that she'd drunk too much again last night. 'Oh and listen, about last night,' she began. 'About Gerry—'

'It's none of my business,' Tom said. 'If you're happy, then I'm happy.' He gave her one of his wide beaming smiles. The kind that filled his whole face and made his big brown eyes light up like he was telling a naughty joke.

'Thanks, Tom.' She took a breath before returning her focus to work. 'What's happening with the missing elderly woman? I meant to ask Andrea before she left?'

'I'm not sure.'

'It's OK, I'll ask Billy to chase that up,' she said. 'Who do you think gave Sean Jacobs that pasting?'

'Honestly?' Tom replied. 'Sean Jacobs moves in some really sketchy circles. It could have been anyone.'

'Yes but didn't the state of him suggest it was personal to you?' she suggested. 'I mean, his attacker may even have left him for dead.'

'So do you think it was attempted murder?' Tom asked. 'Not merely an assault.'

'Do you know what, Tom? I do think that,' Hazel confirmed. 'I think we need to pick up David Wilson and ask him about it.'

The phone rang on Hazel's desk. 'Hello, DCI Todd,' she said confidently. Tom watched her frown. 'OK, tell him I'll be right down.'

'What's up?' Tom asked.

'That was the front desk.' Hazel downed the last of her cup of tea. 'They said there's a witness who wants to talk to me about Peter King's murder.'

'That's great news. Did they say who it was?'

'No they didn't.'

'Somebody is better than nobody,' Tom suggested.

'Aye you're not wrong. Tom, you go and pick up David Wilson. Ask him if he knows where Rona is will you. I'll see what this witness has to say. I'll get uniform to try Rona's flat and work again. It's a long shot but we have to try. I'll ask them to go back to Suzanne's place as well.'

'Sure,' Tom started to head out of the office as Hazel stopped at Billy's desk.

'All right, boss?' Billy greeted her.

'Aye, I'm all right. Billy, could you chase up Andrea's missing woman case for me? I've sent Andrea to the hospital with Sean Jacobs. The old woman has been missing for too long now. She's a frail, vulnerable person.'

'Aye, sure,' Billy replied.

'Thanks Billy, I'll not be long,' Hazel said and made her way downstairs.

The front desk hadn't given her the name of this witness but the man sitting on one of the black plastic chairs in the reception area was not who she was expecting to see at all.

Chapter Fifty-Five

Billy had texted Andrea to ask her to get him up to speed on the Sheila Marshall missing persons case. She felt guilty that the old woman had almost slipped her mind in the chaos of Sean's sudden arrival, although not completely. She messaged him everything she had and sent a file for him to look at. The look on her daughter's face when they'd last spoken was awful. The poor woman was going out of her mind trying to figure out where her mum could be and what this mysterious S might have to do with her disappearance, if anything.

'He's awake but he's pretty groggy from the painkillers – not as much as some others might be, given his drug addiction issues, though. I assume he has a high tolerance for the opioids,' the doctor told Andrea as she waited outside the cubicle in Accident and Emergency. 'Don't be too long.'

Andrea didn't get the chance to tell him that his patient had confessed to murder because the tall, thin man had walked away. She pulled back the curtain and although Sean still looked horrendously bruised and beaten, he was sitting up in the bed. Andrea closed the curtain behind her and took a seat next to him.

'I know why you're here,' Sean said drily.

'Do you remember what you told my colleague?'

Sean nodded without saying anything. Then he sighed and said, 'Are you here to arrest me, then?'

Andrea eyed him thoughtfully. She took her notebook out of her duffle coat and readied her pen.

'What did you mean when you said you'd killed?'

'What the hell do you think that means?'

'I need you to tell me.'

Sean screwed up his face and lifted his hand to his head. 'God, my head hurts like a bitch.'

'Come on, Sean, don't mess me about,' Andrea said firmly. 'What did you mean?'

'Awright, awright, there's no need to shout,' Sean insisted, squeezing his eyes tight shut. 'This thing goes deeper than any of you know.'

'Oh yes,' Andrea replied. 'What does that mean?'

'The Ramsay woman and King. It's not what you lot think. Not by a long shot.'

'Then tell me about it, Sean. Explain it to me.'

'Argh, my head's pounding, man.' Sean held his fingers tightly against his temples. 'And can you tell them to turn the lights down? My eyes feel like they're burning.'

'Sean, come on,' Andrea pushed him. 'Just tell me.'

Sean whimpered and gripped the side of the bed. 'Argh...'

'Sean, please,' Andrea said gently.

Sean took a long deep breath against the increasing pain crushing his skull. 'Ask Suzanne,' he managed to mumble.

Andrea looked on in horror as Sean's body became rigid before convulsing violently, his head hammering against the pillow with force, white froth foaming from his lips. She tore back the cubicle curtain in a panic.

'Nurse, I need some help in here! He's fitting,' she shouted over the noise of the busy Accident and Emergency department.

A clamour of bodies swept Andrea aside until she was standing outside the curtain. Was this her fault? Had she pushed him too hard?

'Out of the way,' the doctor she'd spoken to not long ago shouted at her. Andrea stepped back as the bed was pushed past at speed. Another voice came from behind her.

'Sean is going to have an emergency CT scan and most likely after that he'll be rushed straight into theatre to drain a bleed on his brain so you might as well go, Detective.' Andrea looked at the nurse who was talking to her now.

'I really think it's best if you go now,' repeated the middle-aged nurse with a shock of grey curls. 'Sean won't be able to talk to anyone for a long time yet.'

'Erm, OK, thank you,' Andrea replied, frozen to the spot. 'I'll try later then.'

The nurse smiled at her before following the sound of a man's voice, shouting for help. Andrea gathered herself together and started to head out of the Accident and Emergency department. DCI Todd was not going to like this. She dialled Hazel's number and waited, a dark, sick feeling in the pit of her stomach.

—

Billy Flynn was glad to be out in the fresh air despite the bitterly cold temperature. He zipped up his jacket as he made his way to his Astra. He was admiring the tenacity of the daffs that were fiercely forcing their foliage through the white carpet, their emerald green shoots a wonderful contrast, when footsteps crunching in the fresh layer of snow behind him made him turn round.

'DS Flynn,' a man's voice called out.

'Who wants to know?' Billy answered the tall, wiry man's request.

The man pulled a card from the inside pocket of his coat, a tatty notebook too, with a page full of writing on it. He held the card out for Billy to take.

'Grant Erickson,' Billy read out loud. 'I know you. You've written some great pieces for the *Scotsman*, haven't you?'

'Aye, I'm not sure about them being great exactly but I have done some work for them, yes.'

Billy handed him back the card. 'What can I do for you, Mr Erickson?'

'I don't know if DCI Todd has mentioned me but—'

'What?' Billy interrupted him and, sensing where this conversation was heading, he turned to walk away. 'I'm in a bit of a hurry, I'm sorry.' As he was turning away, Billy was shocked when he spotted a name he recognised in the man's notebook.

'Wait, please.' Grant Erickson jogged after him. 'I'm writing a book and...'

Billy stopped. 'You're wasting your time. I'm not prepared to talk to you about Hazel or what happened last year, you got that? And as for your book, I think it's sick to profit from tragedy like that.' He walked away, leaving Erickson standing lonely in the snow. He wondered whether he should tell Hazel about the name he'd seen in the notebook. Had they spoken to Erickson already?

The bare-faced cheek of that journalist was still whirling round Billy's mind as he approached the theatre café. He smiled at the small boy who was sitting on a bench playing with a couple of dinosaurs, waiting for his mum to finish buying tickets from the box office. He walked over to the bar area and held his ID up for the pretty, young blonde girl to see.

'Hello there,' Billy began. 'I'm DS Billy Flynn, I was wondering if I could have a few minutes to ask you a couple of questions.'

Sheila's daughter had told Andrea about the café. It was where the church ladies went after the service on Sundays.

'Aye, sure,' the girl replied. 'Just hang on a minute.' She poked her head into the kitchen, but Billy couldn't make out what she was saying. 'Sorry about that,' she added on her return. 'Come on through, we can talk in the back.'

Billy followed her and sat down in the chair that was offered to him. He held up a photo of Sheila Marshall.

'Did this woman come in over the weekend at all, or at the end of last week?'

'I recognise her. That's Sheila, isn't it?'

The girl's answer was exactly the progress Billy wanted to hear.

'That's right. Do you know her?'

'Yes, she comes in here every week with her church pals. It's handy for the North church crowd.'

Billy had to agree. 'Aye, it's barely five minutes away for them.'

'Shame too, about Sheila's dementia, isn't it?'

'So you do know her quite well, then?'

'Aye, she was a bit confused a couple of weeks ago and I had to call her daughter.' This girl was proving very helpful. 'She explained the situation and I said I'd keep an eye out for her.'

'That's very kind of you,' Billy smiled.

The girl shrugged. 'She's a lovely old woman.' Then she frowned. 'What's happened? Why are you asking about Sheila?'

A woman's voice echoed towards them, and the girl sighed before standing up.

'I'm sorry, can you give me a minute?'

'No problem,' Billy replied.

'I'll just be two ticks. We're a bit short-staffed just now.'

Billy smiled and watched her leave the small staff room. He glanced around the room and his eyes came to rest on a pile of flyers on the table. They were marketing material for a play that was coming to the theatre soon. Billy folded one up and slipped it into his pocket. Maybe he'd ask Natasha if she'd like to go. She liked that kind of thing. It had someone he knew she liked in it, too. Someone from *Holby City* or *Casualty*. He couldn't remember which.

'I'm sorry about that.' The girl returned, looking flustered.

'Is everything all right?'

'Och, yes and no,' she sighed. 'The bakers have sent us the wrong order, that's all. What did you want to ask me about Sheila? Is she all right? Well, obviously she's not if you're here, silly question really.'

'Sheila is missing and I'm trying to retrace her last known movements. So did you say she was here at the weekend?'

The girl shook her head. 'No, it would have been Friday. I know that because I've been on all weekend. She usually comes in on a Sunday afternoon for a coffee with the church ladies too – well, not every week but mostly.'

'Was it the church group she was here with on Friday?'

'No, it was a woman I didn't recognise, actually.'

Billy's interest was piqued. Could it have been the mysterious S? 'What did she look like?'

'Mm probably early to mid-thirties, blonde, kind of frail-looking. Really thin, I mean.'

This description sounded a lot like Suzanne Gerrard. 'Did you happen to hear a name?'

The girl shook her head. 'No, but Sheila certainly seemed pleased to see her because they hugged like old friends before they parted ways.'

'Do you remember how long they were here?'

'Yes I do because it was at least two hours.'

'That's a lot of coffee and cake,' Billy commented.

'It was two pots of tea and scones, actually.'

'And you're absolutely sure Sheila looked happy to be in this woman's company?' Billy pressed her. 'She didn't look uncomfortable at all?'

'She looked very happy, actually. It was lovely to see her like that.'

The information was whizzing around inside Billy's head. 'Can you think of anything else about this woman? Did she have any distinguishing features? Tattoos or piercings perhaps?'

'Yes, kind of, she walked with a stick.'

'She did, did she?' Billy's eyes widened and he jotted that detail down in his notebook.

'Yes, I remember now because I thought how frail she looked for someone so young.'

'Thanks for this,' Billy told her as he made to stand up. 'I really appreciate your help.' He pulled one of his cards from his jacket pocket and handed it to her. 'If this woman comes in again or if you see Sheila – with or without her – please call me or the station immediately.'

'Of course, yes.'

Billy headed back to his car, wondering what Suzanne was doing with Sheila Marshall and whether her disappearance had anything to do with the murders of Maggie Ramsay and Peter King. Or was he just putting two and two together to make five? He hit Hazel's name on his phone contact list to ask her what she wanted him to do with this information.

Chapter Fifty-Six

Hazel was stunned to see Casper Vermeer standing in the reception area waiting to speak to her about the murder of Peter King. She'd have understood if he said he'd remembered something else about Maggie Ramsay's murder because of their affair but it seemed this was more evidence that the two victims were connected. The call from Andrea about Sean Jacobs' current condition wasn't what she wanted to hear. She hoped he would improve soon so they could question him further about what he meant. *I killed*. What exactly had he confessed to? Did he kill both victims? Or one. She suggested Andrea come back to the station for now. She could talk to David Wilson with Tom once he'd been brought in for questioning.

Sending Billy to talk to Sheila Marshall's daughter about her mother meeting with Suzanne Gerrard was the obvious thing to do and he was more than happy to oblige. Getting that lead was another piece of the puzzle being slowly put in its rightful place.

'Mr Vermeer, please have a seat.' Hazel ushered him into one of the small interview rooms and took her seat opposite him, grateful that the heating wasn't on full blast like it sometimes was at this time of year. A hot flush in a room with a radiator on full wasn't pleasant.

'Thank you for seeing me, DCI Todd,' Casper said quietly.

Hazel thought he looked tired. She hadn't asked Gerry about how the arson case was going last night. The subject just hadn't come up. Even if it had, she didn't think he'd say. What was it he'd told her? He didn't talk about work when he was off the clock. Hazel was curious to know, although it was looking more like an insurance job rather than anything to do with the piece of furniture Samuel Ramsay had given Vermeer to restore. Perhaps coincidences did happen.

'You told the officer that you have information about the murder of Peter King.'

Casper nodded. 'I read about his murder online last night and I thought you should know something about him and Maggie.'

Hazel turned over to a new page in her notebook. 'What about them?'

'Peter King raped Maggie when she was young and as a result she had a child that was put up for adoption.'

Hazel's mind spun. Why hadn't Samuel Ramsay told them that? Had Maggie kept that from him? The baby in the photo. Michelle.

'Did Maggie tell you this?'

Casper nodded. 'Yes she did. A while back.'

'OK, so, did she happen to tell you what she called the baby?'

'Yes. Michelle.'

The pieces really were starting to fall into place. Hazel remembered the look on Maggie's face in the picture. 'Michelle' scribbled on the back.

'Did Samuel know about the child?'

'I don't think so. Maggie didn't say. It happened about a year before they met at university.'

Hazel had so many questions burning on her tongue. She had to prioritise them.

'So do you know if Maggie had seen the child after the adoption?' she asked as she tapped her pen on the paper. 'As an adult, perhaps? How old would Michelle be now?'

'I don't know. She'd be in her thirties, I suppose. The only reason I know is because she said she saw King not that long ago in town.'

'Did she talk to him?'

Casper shook his head. 'No, but it wasn't just Maggie he attacked either.'

'I know,' Hazel confirmed. 'Louise told me what happened to her.'

'Maggie felt so guilty about what happened to Louise. She said it was one of the reasons she drank so heavily. She feared that he'd hurt Louise to get to her.'

'That must have been very difficult for her,' Hazel acknowledged. Although she didn't have kids of her own, she could imagine the guilt.

'She said it felt like the guilt was killing her – no; *suffocating* her, that's what she called it,' Casper explained. 'Alcohol was the only thing that blotted it out.'

'Did King know about the child?'

'Yes he did. He was a nasty piece of work and, I for one, am not sad that he's dead.'

Hazel knew that seemed to be the majority opinion about Peter King's murder. She had to remain professional. King's death was being treated just like anyone else's. It wasn't up to his killer to carry out the justice his victims deserved and certainly not in the brutal fashion it had been done. If Sean Jacobs had killed them, then why and how did he know what King had done to Maggie. Why kill Maggie at all? If indeed that was what he'd said before being rushed to hospital. They urgently needed to talk to him again. So many thoughts were spinning through her mind that a niggling pain was growing in her temples. Again.

Chapter Fifty-Seven

'He's not in.'

Tom turned to see David Wilson's next-door neighbour locking her front door. She tugged her hood closer to her cheeks against the biting wind.

'I haven't heard him coming or going since yesterday,' she added.

'Thank you,' Tom replied but knocked on the door anyway and waited. 'I'll just check for myself while I'm here.'

'Are you here about the commotion yesterday, then?'

Tom turned to face her. 'What commotion was that?' he asked.

'Oh, what a noise! I thought my walls were going to fall down.' The old woman tutted loudly.

'Excuse me a minute.' Tom lifted a finger as he walked away to answer his ringing phone. It was Hazel calling to fill him in on what Casper Vermeer had just told her. A revelation, to say the least. 'I'm sorry about that,' he said as he hung up. 'What were you saying about a commotion?'

'It sounded like a bomb was going off next door with all the thumping and banging, then David stormed out with a face like thunder. I did go next door to see if he was alright, what with all the racket, but he just slammed the door in my face. Said some words I don't wish to repeat, too.'

'I see,' Tom replied.

'His hand was all bruised and cut as well.'

'Did you happen to see anyone else at the property?' Tom asked, noting that last comment with interest.

The old woman pursed her lips. 'I'm not one for judging people but...' She tutted. 'Some of the people David hangs around with are, well, they're...' She stopped. 'You know what I'm trying to say, don't you?'

'No actually,' Tom shook his head. 'I don't know what you mean.'

'Addicts,' she exclaimed. 'Junkies, whatever you want to call them. One especially. A lad he went to school with I think but he doesn't look anything like he used to.'

Tom took out his phone and scrolled through his photos until he found one of Sean Jacobs. He held it up close to her face.

'Did you see him here yesterday?'

'Yes, that's him.' She pointed at the screen. 'What a state he was in when he staggered out.'

'You saw him leave this address? Are you sure?'

'Yes I'm sure,' she replied and glanced at her watch. 'I'm really sorry but my bus is due in a few minutes.'

Tom had what he needed. 'Of course and thank you, you've been really helpful.'

He watched the back of the old woman until she turned round again.

'I just remembered,' she shouted back. 'That girlfriend of his was kept in hospital last night. You might find David there,' she said and turned to walk away again.

Tom wondered how she could know that but figured she was the type of neighbour who knew everyone's business. Also, the type who enjoyed sharing people's business with others. He hit Hazel's number immediately. That explained why Suzanne's house was in darkness last night.

'Hey, boss, David wasn't here but his neighbour has suggested that he might be at the hospital with his girlfriend, Suzanne. She's confirmed that Sean staggered out of David's place all beaten and bruised. Do you want me to go over there?'

'Could you? That would be great, Tom. It's all starting to look clearer now, isn't it? If he's there, bring him in. That boy knows more than he's been letting on. I can feel it.'

'Will do,' Tom replied.

'Billy is talking to Sheila Marshall's daughter too,' Hazel added. 'To see what she knows about Suzanne Gerrard, if anything.'

Hazel wasn't lying when she said she could feel it. Things really were coming together but she decided to take an hour to visit her dad which meant she could also check up on Sean Jacobs' condition too. She would leave David Wilson to Tom. Tom was a good bit bigger than him. She'd leave Tom and Andrea to talk to him. Sean Jacobs' condition was evidence of what the teenager was capable of.

Chapter Fifty-Eight

Billy quickly read Hazel's text while he waited for Rita Latimer to open the door. She updated him, telling him what Vermeer had told her. Ramsay and King were connected. They'd had a baby. Billy hadn't seen that coming. He slid his phone into his pocket when he heard footsteps coming towards the door.

'Mrs Latimer, my name is DS Flynn, could you spare me a few minutes?' Billy held his ID up for her to examine, which she did, thoroughly.

'Of course, come on in. Have you found her? Have you found Mum?' Rita urged and held the door wide open to usher him inside. 'My boss has given me a few days off. He says I've not to worry about anything and if I need anything...' She stopped. 'I'm sorry I'm rambling.'

'It's OK, it's understandable.' He wiped his snow covered boots and followed her inside.

'So has there been any news?' she asked urgently. 'I'm going out of my mind.'

'Not yet,' Billy told her. 'But I would like to ask you a couple of questions about some new information that has come to light since you spoke to my colleague.'

'Oh yes, of course,' Rita answered and pointed towards a door to Billy's right. 'Please go straight through and excuse the mess, I've been poring through some old photos.'

Billy looked at the various photo albums, loose pictures and newspaper clippings that were scattered over the matching green armchairs and the low pine coffee table in the middle of the room. A grey cat lay curled up amongst one of the piles, startling Billy when it moved.

'Please have a seat,' Rita invited. 'I'll just move these for you.' She lifted a large photo album from the arm of one of the armchairs for him then perched herself on the little bit of space left on the matching sofa.

'Thanks. Mrs Latimer, does the name Suzanne Gerrard mean anything to you?'

Billy was disappointed to see that Rita shook her head. 'No, I've never heard that name before. Is Mum with her?' Her question was urgent, and Billy could see redness in her eyes as if she'd been crying.

'We don't know where your mum is yet, but my enquiries have uncovered that your mum may have met with Suzanne last Friday.'

'Did she?'

'You said to my colleague that your mum told you on the phone that she'd met a lovely girl, is that right?'

Rita's eyes revealed the memory was coming back to her. 'Yes she did, that's right. Was it this Suzanne, do you think?' Then she gasped. 'S! The signature on the card! S, it has to be Suzanne.'

Billy recalled mention of a card that had been sent for forensic examination.

'My colleague mentioned a phone call.'

'Yes, yes.' Rita snatched up her phone and pressed the number she'd been trying since yesterday. 'Every time I call it just rings out and...' Her eyes widened when the call was answered. 'Hello...' she stuttered. 'Suzanne, is my mum with you?' Then the line went dead.

'What did she say?' Billy urged, growing concerned by the fear etched on Rita's face. 'Show me the number.' He held out his hand and took the phone from her.

Billy grabbed his own phone out of his blazer pocket and logged in as fast as he could to trace the location of the number, but he was too late. Whoever had answered the call must have switched it off immediately. 'Shit,' he mumbled under his breath.

'Do you think my mum is with this Suzanne?' Rita urged. 'Who is she?'

A thought occurred to Billy. Maggie and Peter's baby.

'Your mum was a midwife for many years, wasn't she?'

Rita nodded. 'Yes, why is that important?'

'Did she ever talk about babies she'd delivered who went on to become adopted?' he asked on a hunch.

A thin smile crossed Rita's lips but quickly disappeared. 'Yes. All the time. Mum used to work for the adoption agency too. She said she wanted to make sure the babies went to good, loving homes because she didn't want their bad start in life to affect the rest of it.'

'Does the name Maggie Ramsay mean anything to you?' he asked.

'No it doesn't. Do you think she has something to do with my mum's disappearance?'

Billy left that question hanging for now. 'What about Peter King?'

'I know that name, all right,' Rita insisted. 'That's the man who was murdered. I read about that in the paper.'

'That's right. Is that the only time you've heard that name?' Billy asked.

'Yes, why?'

'That doesn't matter,' Billy replied. 'Did your mum ever talk about a baby called Michelle?'

'Detective, my mum talked about hundreds of babies,' Rita told him plainly.

'OK, listen to me,' Billy started to explain. 'I'd like to place a listening device on your phone,' he told her without knowing whether Hazel would approve it yet. 'I'll come back later with it. Is that OK with you?'

Rita looked worried. 'Is that so you can trace where S is? Do you think she is Suzanne? Where Mum might be?'

Billy nodded. 'Yes but if she calls again try not to panic but listen very carefully to what she says and try and write everything down. Listen for environmental sounds. Trains, dogs barking, anything, to see if you can identify where she's calling from.'

'Erm yes, yes, OK, I will.'

'I'll be back as soon as I possibly can.'

Billy raced from Rita's door, scrolling through his contacts, hoping that Hazel would be OK with his plan.

Chapter Fifty-Nine

'Dad,' Hazel said gently and closed the side room door behind her. 'You look much better today.'

His dementia meant that communication was difficult these days, but her dad's smile was a sign that he was feeling better. The colour had returned to his cheeks, too.

'You had us all worried there.' She smiled back at him until a text hit her phone.

> I need a tap for Rita Latimer's phone. Is that OK with you?

Billy knew what he was doing. Hazel trusted him.

> Absolutely. I'll handle Daly if there's a problem.

His reply made her smile.

> Excellent!

One of the nurses walked in to check on her dad as she was putting her phone back in her pocket.

'Is this a bad time?' Hazel asked. 'I realise you guys have a lot to do.'

'Not at all, you stay as long as you like. The doctor will be doing his round soon. Maybe your dad will be able to get back to the home today.'

'Already?' Hazel asked.

'He'll be better off back where he's more comfortable,' the nurse pointed out, but Hazel feared it was pressure on beds rather than a purely clinical decision that his discharge was based on.

She watched the nurse bustle round him, talking to him the whole time, explaining everything she was doing despite the fact he couldn't communicate properly with her. That was a skill Hazel admired immensely.

'I'll leave you to it,' the nurse smiled. 'If you need anything, just shout.'

Hazel stared out of the window at the winter postcard scene outside. It seemed surreal to think it was early spring and not early January as the heavy snow suggested. The gritters had been hard at work keeping the roads around the hospital clear and she watched as the pavements were being cleared and sprayed with salt. A man in a thick brown duffle coat held tightly to the hand of a small boy, probably no more than five or six, dressed in wellies and a thick anorak as they headed towards the maternity unit. Going off to meet a new baby brother or sister, she mused. She watched the pair tread tentatively along the recently cleared pathway, the little boy a step or two behind his dad and trying to keep up, with his arm stretched up to reach the hand that was guiding him. To the next chapter in his young life, Hazel thought.

A jumble of sounds came from behind her.

'It's OK, Dad, I'll get it.' Hazel gently squeezed his hand then poured him a cup of water from the jug he'd been trying to reach. She pointed the straw towards his lips and helped him take a drink.

The frail old man mumbled something which Hazel assumed was thank you, unsure whether he even realised it was his own daughter that had helped him. Perhaps she was just another strange face to him now. She wished she had more time to spend with him, but this case needed her attention too. Hazel looked at her dad lying there. He looked peaceful and wasn't struggling for every breath like the last time she'd seen him. That had to be good news. Hazel kissed his forehead.

'I have to go now, Dad. I'll be back soon to see you, I promise.'

The old man in the bed gave her a smile and a wave as Hazel headed for the door. She wiped a tear from her cheek and closed the door behind her.

If Hazel thought this case was close to being solved, she was to be disappointed. She held up her ID so that the nurse in the ICU could read it.

'I'm here to see Sean Jacobs,' Hazel explained.

The young woman in front of her frowned, her face turning sombre. 'I'm sorry, has nobody told you?'

A sick feeling thudded into the pit of Hazel's stomach. She did not like the look on her face at all. 'Told me what?' she asked tentatively, unsure whether she really did want to hear the answer.

'Mr Jacobs passed away a short time ago.'

Hazel squeezed her eyes tight shut and sighed. At least the lad's drug-ravaged body was at peace, but it was not David's place to give him that peace. He was now going to be arrested for murder.

Hazel didn't have time to dwell. Her phone echoed through the small Intensive Care department, causing looks of disdain to come at her from all directions.

'I'm sorry, excuse me,' she apologised and quickly headed for the exit. 'Tom, what's happening?' she asked, allowing the doors to the ICU to swing closed behind her. What he told her made a bad day worse.

He'd arrived at Suzanne's bedside to find that David wasn't there, and neither was Suzanne. It seemed she'd had enough and discharged herself not more than an hour before.

Chapter Sixty

Hazel hung up the call and headed straight for her car, hoping that the conditions wouldn't make the journey too treacherous. The last thing she needed was to be trapped in the snow on her way to Suzanne's house.

'Come on, come on,' she shouted at the driver of an old blue Citroen who was crawling along the partially cleared Feus road. If they weren't careful she might be tempted to get Traffic to take a look at them. She had asked Tom to meet her there but not to go in until she arrived. 'Thank you!' she yelled as the slow-moving vehicle indicated left and moved out of her way.

Minutes later, she was parking her Fiesta behind Tom's car a little way from Suzanne's bungalow. She locked up and headed to where Tom was waiting for her, almost slipping on her arse as she did. She let Tom have his smirk because she probably did look funny, waddling towards him through the snow.

'Did you realise the place was so close?' Tom asked and pointed to a block of flats just yards from the row of bungalows.

'Mm, Peter King's block. How convenient.'

'That's what I thought,' Tom agreed.

'Are they both in there?'

'I can't make out who is in there, but I've only seen one outline behind the curtains.'

The low winter sun pointed directly into the window of Suzanne's bungalow and Tom was right; Hazel could only see a single figure moving slowly inside.

'What are we doing, then?' Tom asked. 'Are we taking them both in?'

'Sean Jacobs is dead,' Hazel said bluntly, to Tom's astonishment.

'Shit! David's going down for murder. Jesus. The old woman next to his place can vouch for the state of Sean when he left David's and how bruised David's hand was.'

Hazel nodded. 'We'll just take David for now. We need proof to link Suzanne to any of this and let's not forget there's still a vulnerable old woman out there, missing and afraid.'

'OK, let's do this.'

Hazel hammered on the front door and listened for movement inside but there was nothing. She pressed her finger on the doorbell and held it there, knowing that there was no way they could ignore that noise.

'What's going on?' A well dressed, middle-aged woman with short spiky black hair and a cigarette between her lips holding a little brown terrier in her hand poked her head out of the neighbouring bungalow.

Hazel held up her ID without talking which made the nosy neighbour retreat quickly back inside her home.

'Suzanne, it's the police. Open the door please,' Tom called through the letterbox. He spotted a pair of man's legs dressed in jeans rush from one room to another. Tom stood back up. 'It's David, he's definitely in there.'

'David, come and open this door!' Hazel yelled. She tried the handle, but the door was locked. She hammered her fist on the door. 'Tom, go round the back.'

Tom ran to the back gate, glad to find it was unlocked. He rushed through to see David running towards him with a large rucksack in his hand.

'Stop right there.' Tom stood firm, blocking David's only exit. 'I think you and I need to talk, don't you?'

David opened and closed his hand slowly, the pain so intense it was making him feel sick.

'Drop the bag and put your hands on your head!' Hazel shouted from behind them. 'Cuff him, Tom.'

'Argh,' David squealed as the cuffs were placed over his wrists. 'I need help,' he cried out. 'I think my knuckles are broken.'

'I'm not surprised,' Hazel blasted. 'Given the beating you gave Sean Jacobs.'

'David Wilson, I'm arresting you for the murder of Sean Jacobs,' Tom began.

'Wait! What?' David gasped. 'What do you mean? Wait, wait,' he begged. 'What do you mean, murder?'

'Sean died a short time ago, David,' Hazel informed him.

'But I didn't mean to…' David stuttered. 'That's not what I… He was touching Liam's stuff and…'

'Take him to your car, Tom. I'll get a patrol car to come and get him.'

Tom grabbed David's arm tightly and started to walk him back to the roadside.

'She's not in there!' David shouted back. 'Suzanne's gone.'

'Hang on a minute, Tom.' Hazel stood close to David's face. 'What do you mean, she's gone?'

David stood silently staring at Hazel, tears building that he had to sniff back. 'She's gone, I said.'

'Gone where?' Hazel asked anxiously.

David shrugged and looked away. 'How should I know?'

'David!' Hazel snapped. 'Where has she gone?'

'I said I don't know,' David yelled right into Hazel's face, causing her to take a step back. 'She's taken some of her clothes, her phone charger and her iPad.' He took a breath to calm down. 'She's fucking gone, all right?' Emotion began to interrupt his words. 'She's gone.'

'Take him away, Tom. I'll call this in.'

Hazel called for a uniform patrol car to come for David, then walked round to the back door that had been left hanging wide open. She pulled on a pair of latex gloves and stepped inside, directly into the kitchen. Her eyes scanned the room. The scent of lemon filled the air and it was clean, but couldn't be described as tidy. The faint whiff of cannabis wafted into her nostrils. Perhaps Suzanne used that to ease her symptoms.

A pile of plates had been left on the worktop next to a couple of mugs, each with a teaspoon in them. There was a mug tree next to a specially adapted kettle, the kind that was held in place by a contraption to stop the user from dropping it. A walking stick was propped up against the wall next to a tall fridge freezer that had a fruit bowl, heavy with bananas and apples, and a roll of kitchen paper on it.

A photo of Sheila Marshall sitting next to a smiling Suzanne Gerrard was held in place on the fridge by a novelty magnet featuring the Blackpool tower. A loud squawk made Hazel jump and she slid open a hatch that opened up to the living room to see a huge cage with the biggest blue and red parrot she'd ever seen staring back at her inside.

'Bloody hell, don't tell me I've got to call the SSPCA as well now,' she muttered. Sighing, she closed the hatch again.

'What was that?' Tom asked when he returned.

'Don't ask,' Hazel shook her head. 'That was quick.'

'Aye, there was a car nearby, so they've taken him. I've asked the doc to look at his hands as well, but I think he's going to need an x-ray on them. One of his fingers has swollen badly.'

'You saw the state of Sean. I'm not surprised David injured himself doing that.' Hazel took the photo off the fridge and held it up. 'What do you make of this?'

Tom took the picture out of her hand. 'Well, I think we can definitively say the two are connected now, can't we?'

'But what does Suzanne want with Sheila Marshall?' Hazel asked, pointing to the photo in Tom's hand. 'And what does that have to do with the murders of King and Maggie Ramsay?'

'I wish I knew,' Tom said.

'I don't think this was ever about their criminal convictions.' Hazel took the photo back from Tom and stared down at Suzanne's smiling face. 'It was about something much more complicated, wasn't it?'

Chapter Sixty-One

'Hey Billy, how's it going?' Andrea asked on hearing the door open.

'Not bad, not bad, do you fancy a brew?' Billy smiled. 'I am gasping.'

'Nah, I've just had one.' Andrea held up her almost empty mug then sighed.

'Are you sure? I might even throw in a Hobnob.'

That made Andrea smile. 'No thanks.'

'What are you doing?'

'I'm trying to do something useful,' Andrea said drily.

'Are those adoption records?' Billy asked. 'I've been waiting for a call back about them.'

'Aye well looks like I beat you to it, and guess what I've found?' she replied. 'Hopefully, DCI Todd will be pleased with me.'

'I'm sure she will, what have you got?' Billy pulled out a chair and sat next to her.

'Well, this is a record of the adoption of a baby born to a Margaret Williams.' Andrea pointed at the screen. 'Now I then did a record search for a marriage in the name of Margaret Williams, and I found...' She typed the keys on her laptop. 'This.'

Billy narrowed his eyes to read the entry. 'Margaret Williams married Samuel Ramsay. That's our Maggie, then.'

Andrea opened the tab on the screen that had the adoption document on it. 'Do you see this?' She pointed to a name. 'Baby Williams adopted by John and Patricia Gerrard.'

'That created one Suzanne Gerrard.' Billy scrolled to the next document. He frowned, then looked at Andrea. 'Contact was attempted,' he said. 'Suzanne looked for Maggie.'

'Does it say if or when they met?'

'No, it only says contact was made.'

'Do you think Maggie told her about the way she was conceived? About Peter King?' Billy clicked back to the previous entry. 'She was adopted at two weeks and two days old,' he tutted. 'So Maggie had her for sixteen days before giving her up. Wait a minute, the will! Was she changing her life insurance for Suzanne? Have we got the will from the solicitor yet?' He looked at Andrea.

'I don't think so,' Andrea said. 'It's possible, isn't it?'

'Hang on, I'll go and call the solicitor.' He rummaged on his desk for the details. He typed the number into his phone and was disappointed to hear the call go to answering machine.

'But doesn't Suzanne work for them?' Andrea suggested.

Billy hung up. 'Damn answering machine. I'll try again in a bit. What? Yes, I think she works as a paralegal for the firm.'

'What other option did Maggie have than giving her baby up? Suzanne would have been a reminder of what happened to her every day of her life,' Andrea pointed out to him. 'Mind you, I don't expect you to understand, not properly.'

'Why, because I'm a man?' Billy couldn't help sounding hurt.

Before their conversation could escalate into an argument, Hazel and Tom walked in.

'How did it go?' Billy asked.

'Have we got a trace on Rita Latimer's phone?' Hazel asked without acknowledging his question.

'Aye,' Billy replied. 'All done. The tech boys and girls are just waiting for S to call. What did you find out?'

'I need a cup of hot tea,' Hazel said. 'You tell them, Tom.' she added as she walked away.

Hazel switched on the kettle and retrieved her mug from the draining board. She knew Suzanne Gerrard was disabled and couldn't get far but she was still missing and had managed to slip through their hands easily. It looked like Rona King was with Suzanne. She had to be. Sheila Marshall had been gone for days. She must be wondering what was going on. Her dementia already made her confused, now this.

Sheila has to be with Suzanne, Hazel thought, but where the hell are they?

'Boss, you have to see this.' Tom's voice burst into the small kitchen, making her jump.

'Jesus,' she exclaimed and followed the sound of his voice. 'What is it?'

'This... look.' Andrea turned her laptop to face Hazel.

'What am I looking at?'

'I found out the address Margaret Williams gave on the adoption document and—'

'Who is Margaret Williams when she's at home?' Hazel asked.

'She became Maggie Ramsay,' Billy interjected.

'Ah, keep talking.' Hazel's interest was piqued.

'So I checked the electoral register and guess who that address now belongs to?' Andrea asked.

Hazel couldn't believe what she was seeing. 'Wait a minute. Wait a minute...' She stared at her team. 'How does she afford this on her salary and what about the bungalow?'

She stared at the name and address on the screen in black and white. Bingo. Now she knew where to find them all.

–

Suzanne paid the taxi driver and thanked him for helping her carry the shopping to the front door. The numbness in her right leg was the worst part of her illness. Some days it felt like she was carrying round a dead weight. She had to get out of that hospital. For lots of reasons. The doctor hadn't been keen to let her go but she'd promised she'd finish the course of steroid tablets and assured him she was used to this damn illness now.

He said he'd refer her for physio and Suzanne had nodded like a good girl and said she'd go.

'Hello, it's just me,' she called out and closed the front door after her. 'I am so sorry I've been away so long.' She locked the door behind her and lifted one of the bags.

'Let me get them. You go and sit down.' Rona King took a couple of carrier bags in each hand and carried them along the hallway and into the kitchen. 'Do you want a drink?' she shouted out to where Suzanne was standing in the large conservatory, looking out onto the winter wonderland scene in her sprawling two-acre back garden – which was certainly better than that tiny square slab of concrete that the council had given her.

Perhaps she should have felt guilty for taking the tenancy when she had such a luxurious home already, but she deserved it, didn't she? Ever since her diagnosis, Suzanne had re-evaluated lots of aspects of her life. Besides the poky little council bungalow had proved great cover hadn't it. Even if she had lied on the application form to get it. A small price to pay.

'No thanks,' Suzanne called back. 'I'm fine.' She opened the French doors and allowed a blast of cold air to blow in. Thinking about David made her sad. She was genuinely going to miss his sweet face and he'd been so kind, taking her to hospital like that. Maybe she'd catch up with him again some time.

The door to the conservatory opened behind her and the old woman standing in the doorway was holding a cup of tea and smiling at her. Suzanne smiled back.

'Hello, Sheila. I'm sorry I was away for so long but I'm back now. Back to stay.'

Chapter Sixty-Two

Hazel had almost laughed in Daly's face when he'd suggested they should wait for armed back-up but managed not to. Suzanne Gerrard had MS and walked with a stick; she didn't think she posed a huge threat to them. David Wilson was in custody so he wouldn't be a problem and poor Sean wouldn't be able to trouble them. She had considered the possibility of Sheila Marshall's safety but thought if she was still alive then it was because Suzanne wanted her to be. She must have some kind of weird connection to the woman who had helped bring her into the world. Hazel did have an ambulance standing by to examine the old woman, just in case. It was only Rona, whom she was certain was also at the address, that was the unknown entity, but Hazel had Tom with her. His imposing stature would surely be a deterrent.

The view across Perth from the Corsiehill property was stunning and worth every penny of the half a million pound price tag. On a clear day, if you looked in the other direction, she supposed you could see almost all the way to Dundee, across the acres of soft fruit tunnels and the field of rescue horses now working as therapy animals. The low, wispy clouds made that harder today.

On digging deep into Suzanne Gerrard's financial records they discovered that her adopted parents, the Gerrards, had each left her considerable sums of money after they died – more than enough to buy this house. The home she seemed to have discovered was once the family home of her birth mother. It must have felt like divine intervention to her.

'Right, Tom, you and I will go to the door. Keep things softly, softly until we know Sheila Marshall is safe.'

'Yes, sure.' He read the text that buzzed on his phone. 'The ambulance is waiting at the other end of the road out of sight.'

'Excellent. Right, let's do this,' Hazel chirped.

It didn't take long before the two detectives were standing face to face with Suzanne Gerrard when she opened the front door to them after only one knock.

'Hello Detectives. Can I help you?' Suzanne smiled.

'Do you mind if we come in for a few minutes?' Hazel asked calmly despite her racing heart rate. 'I'd like to ask you few questions, if that's OK.'

Rona King appeared behind Suzanne briefly before moving upstairs without saying a word. Of course, Hazel thought, where else would Rona be?

'Absolutely, come on in.' Suzanne beamed a wide grin at Tom, watching him the whole time as she held the door wide for them. 'Go right through.'

'Thank you,' Tom replied and followed Hazel into a huge, immaculately styled kitchen, peering in the living room door as he passed. It was in total contrast to the small, poky one in the bungalow on the grim housing estate Suzanne had passed off as her home.

'Can I get either of you a cup of tea or coffee?' Suzanne leaned heavily on her stick as she joined them.

'Is it just the two of you here?' Hazel asked, feeling the whole scene to be surreal. The contrast between the two houses was indescribable.

'That's correct. Just me and Rona.'

'Is that right?' Hazel asked, glancing around her at the expensive-looking furniture. 'Nice place you've got,' she suggested.

'Thanks,' Suzanne replied.

'Where is Sheila Marshall?' Tom asked.

'Who?' Suzanne replied, directing the word straight at him without blinking.

Hazel was losing patience with this performance. 'Cut the crap, Suzanne. You know why we're here.'

Suzanne frowned. 'Enlighten me,' she said sarcastically and took three mugs from the cupboard. 'Would you prefer tea or coffee?' She looked straight at Tom.

'Tom, search the house,' Hazel instructed, and it was then that Suzanne's mask slipped.

'Stop! You can't do that without a warrant!' She started to follow him, leaning heavily on her stick.

'Hang on a minute, Tom,' Hazel called after him. She caught up with Suzanne. 'Are you going to start telling me the truth then or do I have to get my colleague to strip this house apart?'

'You'll have to get a warrant first,' Suzanne repeated.

'That can easily be arranged.'

Suzanne stared at Hazel momentarily then turned to face Tom. 'Go ahead. I've got nothing to hide,' she shrugged.

Tom glanced back at Hazel who nodded towards the stairs. 'Check upstairs. Cuff Rona when you're up there. We don't want her slipping away again.'

'Do you mind if I sit down at least? My legs aren't very good today.' Suzanne limped slowly into the living room and sat down on one of the cream leather sofas that had been placed under the huge bay window. She fiddled with her silver locket, spinning it slowly through her fingers before allowing it to fall down onto her collar bone.

'The SSPCA came for your bird by the way,' Hazel told her.

Her comment was met with silence. Suzanne stared out at the view without talking. The sun's reflection on the water shimmered, casting a glassy appearance on it as it swept rapidly towards Dundee and the chilly, wild North Sea beyond. Footsteps coming down the stairs made both women turn to see Tom join them, with Rona.

'Nothing.' He shook his head, gripping Rona's arm tightly; her face was sombre.

Suzanne grinned then looked back at the stunning view. 'I told you.'

Hazel followed Suzanne's line of sight to the two wooden buildings at the bottom of the garden. Then it clicked. She took out her phone and texted her instruction to Tom.

Search those sheds

Tom grabbed hold of his phone from his trouser pocket and read her instruction. He nodded gently then flashed Suzanne a smile before walking away, leaving Rona looking at Suzanne seemingly wondering what to do.

'What's he looking so pleased with himself about?' Suzanne asked until Tom came into view walking down to the bottom of her garden.

Before he could get there, the sound of the front door opening and banging shut slammed through the house. Hazel looked in horror. She hadn't noticed Rona King charge out of the room and was disturbed to see she was now hurtling behind Tom at speed. It was then that she spotted that he'd not put her in cuffs. She'd slipped out of the room while Hazel's attention was focussed on Suzanne. Tom heard her in time and turned to stop her attacking him.

'Is there something in there that you don't want us to see, Suzanne?' Hazel nodded to the sight of Tom wrestling Rona to the ground and handcuffing her.

Suzanne didn't say a word.

'Don't move,' Hazel growled and walked outside to join Tom. She stared at a defeated Rona King who was sobbing on the ground. Hazel looked back up at Suzanne glaring at her from the window. 'Open the door.'

Tom lifted the handle of the wooden outbuilding and shook the padlock. 'It's locked, hang on.' He grabbed a large boulder from the rockery garden nearby and smashed it against the padlock which gave way instantly.

Hazel yanked open the door to find a frightened old woman huddled at the back of the shed. Tom helped Sheila Marshall to her feet and gently guided her outside.

'I'll call the paramedics to come up.' Hazel turned to look up to the house, horrified to see that Suzanne Gerrard was no longer sitting at the window. She finished her call as she headed rapidly back inside.

Hazel ripped open every door and searched every inch of every room. She opened cupboards and drawers. Searched under beds and inside wardrobes. Even the chest freezer lid was opened. But Suzanne Gerrard was gone.

Chapter Sixty-Three

After calling Rita Latimer to say her mum had been found safe and well, if a little shell-shocked by the experience, Hazel was now staring at Rona King's sullen face as she sat slumped on the sofa in Suzanne's living room.

'Where did Suzanne go?' Hazel asked firmly.

'I'm not talking to you lot,' Rona answered defiantly and fidgeted with the handcuffs.

'Why, Rona? Mmn? Why were they killed? And why blow up Lady Campbell's place? It's obvious now that this had nothing to do with her.'

Rona's sullen expression was accompanied by silent scorn in Hazel's direction.

'Was it to send us down the wrong track? Make us think it was about that?'

'Hazel, I think you need to see this.' Tom's voice drifted from the upstairs bedroom.

'Keep an eye on her,' Hazel instructed one of the uniformed officers who had arrived to search for Suzanne Gerrard and headed up to find Tom waiting for her with a piece of paper in his hand.

'What's this?'

'Read it for yourself.' Tom handed the paper to her.

Hazel was immediately alarmed by the content of what appeared to be a suicide note.

'Shit,' Hazel exclaimed, realising exactly where Suzanne had gone. The location of the house meant there was only one way she could have headed. A suicide note and their proximity to a notorious local suicide spot. 'She's at the top of the hill. Come on, Tom.'

—

Hazel struggled to catch her breath as the climb grew steeper up the hill path, lit up by the torchlight of Hazel and Tom's phones. 'Can you just hang on a minute?' She took a long breath and exhaled quickly as her heart pounded. 'I've got bloody palpitations.' Her legs stung with the effort, what with the speed they needed to get there and the steep incline.

'Do you want me to go up alone?'

'No, no, absolutely not.' She took another breath and started walking up the hill again. 'I can't see how she's managed this hike, though. Not in her frail condition.'

'You'd be surprised what desperate people are capable of.'

As soon as the two detectives reached the top of Kinnoull Hill they found Suzanne leaning heavily on her stick, close to the edge that led to a sheer drop into the blackness below. Her haunted thin figure lit by moonlight would have been quite beautiful under better circumstances. Hazel ordered Tom to stay back and began to move closer. Careful not to startle her, Hazel spoke quietly as she approached.

'Suzanne, it's DCI Todd,' she paused. 'Hazel.'

Suzanne spun slowly round, the fingers of one hand holding tight to her locket.

'Why don't you come closer, Hazel,' she invited, her hair whipping round her face in the strong breeze, without looking at her.

The gusts blew close to Suzanne, causing her to sway unsteadily on her feet.

'Come back from the edge,' Hazel insisted, fearing the troubled woman would lose her footing any minute and fall into the pitch black. 'Let's talk about this, shall we?'

Hazel feared for Suzanne's mental health and was desperate to talk her down from this. She didn't think her heart could beat any faster.

Another freezing icy blast cut through them both, chilling Hazel to the bone. She was so cold her fingers felt numb. A hot flush would be perfect about now. How Suzanne could bear it she had no idea, because she was standing out there in the full force of the elements with just a thin blouse and trousers on. A buzzard circled overhead, screeching against the sound of the wind. A light flurry of snow began to fall and if it wasn't for the darkness of the situation it might too have been quite beautiful under the moonlight.

'I've got nothing to say to you.'

'That's not true, is it?'

She watched Suzanne frown back at her. 'What's that supposed to mean? What on earth could I possibly have to say to you?' she sneered.

'I know about your illness,' Hazel called back. 'That it makes your mind…' She reached for the right word. 'It makes it cloudy and confused. You're not thinking straight. Please come back down.'

Hazel watched Suzanne close her eyes and shake her head then take a long, slow deep breath before stepping forward.

'No, please,' Hazel called out. 'Don't do this, Suzanne! It doesn't have to be like this.' *Shit! Come on Hazel, think!*

'I know about your mum.' Hazel hesitated. 'Your real mum.'

Hazel was grateful to see Suzanne open her eyes and turn to look at her. She looked haunted.

'I've done what I came here to do.' Suzanne spoke softly, seemingly ignoring Hazel's remark, all the arrogance gone. 'It has to end like this.'

'No it doesn't,' Hazel heard herself begging. 'Please Suzanne, come back from the edge.'

'Why?'

Hazel was alarmed to find she couldn't think of a single reason to give her. 'Just… please… come away so we can talk.'

Suzanne inhaled another huge breath just as another blast of raw wind hit her. She closed her eyes and edged forward again.

'Wait! At least tell me why!' Hazel shouted into the strong wind. 'You can do that at least, can't you?'

Suzanne turned to face her again. 'You mean you haven't figured it out yet?' Her thin smile became engulfed by the tears running down her face. 'I had you down as a smart woman, DCI Todd.'

'I... erm, I know she rejected you,' Hazel stuttered, 'but—'

'You think this was about rejection!' Suzanne blurted angrily.

Hazel remembered the letter in Maggie Ramsay's pocket. 'You asked her to meet you. Is that it? She didn't turn up, did she?'

Suzanne stared right at Hazel without talking. Instead, she squeezed the locket tighter in her hand.

'If it wasn't about that then tell me, please, why.'

'I suppose it makes no difference anymore,' Suzanne began. 'If it makes you feel better, let me spell it out simply for you.'

Hazel waited, saying nothing, fearing that if she spoke, Suzanne would clam up.

'She did reject me. That part is true. But that's not what upset me. What broke my heart into tiny, shattered pieces...' Another gust of wind, stronger this time, almost pushed Suzanne over the edge, catching her breath, stealing the words from her mouth.

Hazel's stomach lurched and she thought she was going to be sick. 'Jesus,' she muttered under her breath.

Suzanne wiped her wet face and sniffed back the tears.

'The thing is, Hazel, I had a great life with Mum – the woman who adopted me, loved me, cared for me, gave me everything I could ever have needed or wanted. I mean, you've seen the house. That wasn't cheap.'

Hazel was confused but didn't have to wait long for an explanation. Suzanne tapped her leg and then pointed to where her trousers were now damp with urine.

'But this,' she shouted. 'This I can't forgive!'

'I don't understand.'

'She gave me this disease. The illness that's going to rob me of my dignity. My life.'

Hazel realised that this was about more than revenge. Suzanne was hurting and her pain was what had driven her to it.

'I inherited this horrible disease from her, and she discarded me like a piece of rubbish.' Suzanne sobbed. 'Mum and Dad are dead. I don't have any brothers and sisters. Who is going to take care of me when I can't do things for myself anymore? David?' She said his name as if it was a question. 'How is that fair? Hasn't he suffered enough?'

Hazel's mind raced. What she knew about MS was limited but she did know that it wasn't directly inherited, although it was more likely to appear if someone else in the family had it. Did Maggie have it? Why hadn't they got her medical records yet? It didn't matter now but Hazel knew that MS could cause depression. Was that what had happened to Suzanne? Was she so seriously ill that she became capable of murder? Hazel had so many questions, but she couldn't deal with them now.

'Did you know who he was when you met him?'

'You mean, did I know Maggie had killed his brother?'

'Yes.'

'No I didn't but it was fate that we met that day. Do you believe in fate, Hazel?'

Hazel had no idea how to answer that.

'Never mind,' Suzanne continued. 'It doesn't really matter, does it?'

The snow grew heavier, and Hazel thought a fresh layer would lie on the roads tonight, for sure. That strange mild air that comes with heavy snowfall hit her face. A small relief, at least.

'Let's go and talk some more,' Hazel said. 'Somewhere warm and dry.'

'Why, what else is there to say? I tried to talk to her that day, but she just left me standing there. She got on the bus and didn't even look back, tried to pretend I didn't exist.'

'I'm sorry that happened to you,' Hazel said. 'I really am.'

'Are you?'

'Yes,' Hazel said quietly. 'I really am, Suzanne.'

Suzanne looked at her and beamed a huge wide smile. Hazel held out her hand.

'In the daytime it really is a most spectacular view from up here,' Suzanne said softly and stepped to the outer edge of the hilltop, the breeze blowing through her hair. 'But this moonlight is perfect. I couldn't have planned it better.'

'Please... no...' Hazel whispered, desperately searching for the words that would persuade Suzanne to step back. 'What about Sheila?' she stuttered.

That seemed to make Suzanne stop and think. She faced Hazel with a soft smile.

'I would never have hurt her.'

'Then why did you take her?'

'I didn't take her,' Suzanne insisted. 'I found her.'

Hazel was confused. 'What do you mean, you found her?'

'I went to her house,' she stopped to take a breath. 'I often did. She was the midwife that delivered me.'

'I know.'

'I went to her house last week and she was in her garden, lost and confused. So I took her with me.'

'You must have known her daughter would worry.'

'She took care of me,' Suzanne said, seemingly ignoring Hazel's suggestion. 'She helped me find the home, the people who loved me. The Gerrards gave me everything.'

'Did you give her a card signed S?' Hazel asked.

Suzanne smiled. 'You already know the answer to that question.'

A silence fell over the two women and Hazel couldn't figure out what else to say. She wished she could just grab Suzanne

322

and drag her back from the edge. But that wasn't possible. If she did, she risked falling into the abyss too.

'Suzanne,' Hazel eventually whispered. 'Please...'

'Thank you for caring.' Suzanne removed her locket and threw it to Hazel. 'Give that to David and tell him I'm sorry. I really did love him,' she murmured. Then she leaned her body back into blackness where it fell slowly, spinning to the rough, cold ground below.

'No!' Hazel screamed and surged forward until Tom pulled her back.

'Be careful,' he insisted.

'Tom, what have I done?' Hazel pleaded, picking up the locket from the snow and squeezing it tightly in her fingers.

Tom pulled her close and hugged her. 'There's nothing you could have done. Nothing anybody could have done.' He kissed the top of her head softly. 'I think this was her plan from the beginning.'

Hazel pulled away and took a long, sharp breath. She opened the locket to see the now familiar photo of Maggie holding baby Michelle. Why had nobody helped Suzanne?

'I get why but *how* did she do it, Tom? How the hell did she kill them? You've seen the state of her. There's no way she was able to do that to them.'

'I think Rona King can probably help us with that.'

Chapter Sixty-Four

Superintendent Daly was waiting for Hazel when she returned to her office.

'Sir,' she said.

'Hazel,' he coughed. 'How are you doing after...' His words seemed to evaporate as if she was supposed to fill in the blanks for herself.

'I'm fine. I'm going to have this lovely cup of tea.' She pointed to where Billy was walking towards them with a mug of hot tea in his hand. 'Thanks, Billy,' she smiled.

'No problem.'

'You and Andrea get off home for the night.'

'Thank you, I'll see you in the morning then.' Billy nodded towards Superintendent Daly. 'Goodnight, sir.'

'Yes, goodnight, DS Flynn.'

Hazel took a long sip from her mug. 'Lovely,' she whispered. 'Once I've had this I'm going to interview Rona King.'

'You do know that going in there without back-up was foolish,' Daly told her, his expression serious.

'I had Tom,' she replied between sips.

'That's as may be but—'

'Sir, please,' she interrupted him. 'I'm sorry but my head is pounding, and I really would like to finish this cup of tea.' Then she thought about the cloak and dagger with King's laptop, and about what Billy's friend had dug up on Operation Autumn. 'If you don't mind, sir, I have a couple of questions for you before you go.'

'Yes?'

'Operation Autumn.'

Hazel watched his eyes stretch wide open on hearing those two words.

'What did you say?'

'You heard what I said,' she replied bravely. 'Why didn't you just tell me that King was on a watchlist?'

'DCI Todd, you have to understand how intricate these operations are,' he told her. 'How delicate, the fewer people who know about them, the easier it is.'

'Even when one of the people we're watching is murdered?' Hazel knew she was pushing her luck. He was still her superior, after all.

Daly didn't respond. Instead, he said goodnight and suggested Hazel take a few days off. She was not to worry; he'd find cover for her without much trouble. She didn't like the implication that she could be so easily replaced.

Hazel yawned as Tom arrived in her office. Maybe she would take a few days off.

'Are you up to this?' he asked.

'Come on, let's get this done so we can get home. There's a tall glass of white with my name on it,' Hazel smiled.

The look of defeat on Rona's face was obvious as soon as they joined her in the interview room.

'My client would like to make a statement,' her solicitor explained before Hazel and Tom had even sat down.

Hazel looked at Tom then at Rona with interest.

'Go on then, we're listening.' It was clear that her solicitor had advised her to cooperate and Hazel appreciated that.

Rona cleared her throat and sipped from the paper cup of water she'd been given.

'I didn't know that Suzanne planned to kill them. I only found out when I overheard her talking to Sean about Maggie's death. About how he was scared he was going to get caught,'

Rona began nervously. She lifted the cup into her trembling hands to take another sip. 'I should have contacted the police. I found out that she was going to kill Peter and…' She swallowed hard. 'I was glad,' she murmured.

'Are you telling me that Sean Jacobs murdered them both?' Rona nodded.

'For the tape, if you could, Rona,' Hazel pressed her.

Rona coughed again.

'Erm, yes, it was Sean that killed them. He stole a car and hit Maggie Ramsay and then he attacked Peter. I was there – well, not there, but I waited outside for him. He took ages and then ran out the back door. It took me ages to find him. He'd pretended to be a girl online and had arranged to meet him that night.' She was becoming flustered, and her cheeks flushed pink. 'Suzanne offered him ten thousand pounds.' Rona's head dropped into her hands. 'But I don't think she gave him it.' She shrugged. 'I don't know.' She looked at Hazel. 'I'm sorry I lied.'

'What about Lady Campbell's home?' Hazel asked. 'What did that have to do with any of this?'

Rona shook her head. 'Nothing,' she whispered.

'Speak up, Rona,' Hazel insisted.

Rona took a short, sharp breath and wiped her wet face. She sniffed. 'It was to make you think it was all about their convictions.'

'Very clever,' Hazel scoffed and watched Rona's eyes fill with tears again. 'But did you really want to go to prison?'

The plan had almost worked too. When they were chasing round trying to pin it on David Wilson, they'd been wasting time. The truth was far different than any of them could have imagined. Hazel wondered if Suzanne felt guilty about using David like that. It didn't matter now. David was probably about to spend the next twenty or more years behind bars for the murder of Sean Jacobs, his oldest friend. Sean's death meant he could never be convicted of killing Maggie and Peter. Hazel supposed he'd paid the ultimate price. She watched Rona break down into floods of tears and reached for the tape.

'Interview terminated…'

This case had taken so much more out of Hazel than in previous years. Her dad becoming so frail had given her more worry than even the divorce from Rick. She headed into the ladies' bathroom and splashed cold water on her face. As she patted it dry with paper towels, Hazel stared at the woman in the mirror. She looked old. Older than her fifty-three years. Her hair sat thin and lank on her head. Her eyes looked tired with dark circles round them. Hazel resolved to take better care of herself. Promised the woman in the mirror she would eat better, take more exercise. Drink less wine. That climb to find Suzanne had taken it out of her.

On her way back to her office, she saw Billy waiting for her. The look on his face said he had something serious he wanted to say to her.

'Billy, is everything all right? I thought you'd left ages ago.'

'Can we talk, boss?' he asked. 'In private.'

'Of course, come on in. By the way, did you get everything sorted out the other day?'

Billy followed Hazel into her office and closed the door after them.

'What? Oh, yes I did, actually. You'll probably find out soon enough and we didn't really want to tell people this soon, but Natasha is pregnant. She didn't feel well. That's why I needed to leave early.'

'Oh Billy, that's wonderful news.' Hazel reached out and hugged him.

'Keep it to yourself for now though, will you?'

'Of course, of course.' She slipped a finger over her lips, but Hazel didn't like the look on his face. It didn't seem to match the good news he'd just shared with her.

'Listen I know this isn't really my business but…' he began. 'A journalist approached me.'

'Was his name Grant Erickson, by any chance?' She wasn't surprised to see him nod. 'What did he ask you?'

'Nothing,' Billy answered firmly. 'I didn't give him the chance.'

'Thanks, I appreciate that.'

'It's not that he approached me,' Billy said plainly. 'I can handle that, it's…' He hesitated.

'What is it, Billy?' Hazel stared at him, her heart rate increasing.

'I saw a name written in his notebook and…' He chewed on his thumbnail nervously. 'It had a tick against it.' Then he shrugged. 'Obviously, that tick could mean anything.'

A sick feeling smashed into the pit of Hazel's stomach. 'What was the name?' she asked quietly.

Billy took a breath. 'It was Cara.'

Hazel's legs weakened beneath her. It made sense. Cara must have given Erickson her address and phone number. Hadn't Cara betrayed Hazel once before? Betrayal seemed to come naturally to her.

'Thanks, Billy, I appreciate you telling me that.' Hazel smiled despite the pain she was feeling. 'You get off home, mate.'

'Are you going to be OK?' he asked.

'Yes, yes, I'll be fine.' She tried to reassure him, unsure whether she believed it herself as the thick knot tightened inside her stomach.

'OK, I'll see you tomorrow, then.'

'Aye,' Hazel sighed. 'I'll see you tomorrow.'

Once Billy was safely out of sight Hazel fell onto her seat and let out a gasp. She picked up her phone. That was it. Her mind was made up.

–

Hazel knocked and waited outside Daly's office to be invited in.

'Come in,' his voice called from inside.

328

Hazel opened the door. 'Thanks for seeing me, sir,' she said and closed the door after herself.

'Please take a seat.' Daly pointed to the chair opposite him. 'What can I do for you? You sounded serious on the phone.'

Hazel stared at him in silence for a moment and nodded. 'Aye, it is serious, and I really hope you're going to be able to help me.'

Between her dad's failing health and the bombshell of yet more betrayal at the hands of someone she had once called her best friend, this was something Hazel needed to do.

'Go ahead,' Daly smiled. 'I'll certainly do my best to help you.'

'Thank you, sir.'

Epilogue

Superintendent Daly had looked pleased that Hazel had taken his advice when she'd asked for some time off. If this case had taught her anything, it was the importance of family. She knew she was leaving the team in capable hands. Andrea had managed to locate Maggie Ramsay's will and discovered that the increase was to ensure Suzanne was given a share. It seemed that she had clearly cared about the baby she had given up. A lot more than Suzanne realised. Hazel was sad that she hadn't known. Then all of the heartache could have been prevented.

'So what do you think of that then, Dad?' Hazel folded the tartan blanket onto the bottom of his bed then sat down in the small blue armchair under the window of his room in his new care home. 'Six weeks of looking at my ugly mug.' She smiled as she stared out at the view from his window.

The weeks of heavy snow finally felt like they were receding, and the daytime temperatures were starting to rise at last. That might even be glimpses of grass she could see out there under the melting snow. Although they didn't want it melting too fast. Flooding had become a regular occurrence in Perth in recent years as a result of rapid thaws. The drifts of daffodils were finally on show. The flowering cherry trees looked like they were also ready to face the spring.

Hazel had managed to get an appointment with her GP to address the medical issues she'd been putting off. HRT was something she'd be discussing with her. Waving goodbye to those hot flushes sounded good. Perhaps it would help with the insomnia, too, although Hazel knew that some of that was still the impact of the trauma caused by Rick's sudden and brutal death. The drinking had to stop too. While she was still able to control it herself. The thought of losing that control and spiralling into alcoholism made her shudder. Maybe she would ask about counselling too, just in case.

Her friendship with Cara was another thing she planned to say goodbye to. Talking to Grant Erickson about Hazel was the straw that broke the camel's back – which might strike people as strange, given that Cara had already stolen Hazel's husband. Shouldn't that have been the thing to end their friendship completely? Like a fool, she'd given her oldest friend the benefit of the doubt after Rick's death. But not anymore. She would attend the solicitor's appointment to discuss the inheritance then that would be the end of it. Perhaps she'd give a chunk of it to charity.

Hazel enjoyed Gerry's company and had decided to allow things to take their course naturally. He was a good guy. The fact that he made her laugh was wonderful. Hazel hadn't laughed much recently.

The early morning sun shone in, casting swathes of natural light into what was quite a small room. The sound of the birds singing came through the open window and Hazel had to admit it was lovely. It was nice to think that her dad woke up to this every day. Being able to look out at the birds coming down to feed on the many feeding stations that the home had put out was lovely. The breeze drifting in on her face was perfect.

Her dad smiled and tried to say something to her. While she couldn't make out the words, the meaning was clear. She took his hand in hers and kissed it gently.

'Do you think you'll cope with that?' she laughed. 'Having me checking up on you every day, making sure you're not up to no good?'

He rambled something incoherent, but he said it with such a wicked grin on his face, it made Hazel laugh.

'Aye, cheeky,' she said just as her phone buzzed. It was a text from Tom.

> This will be the last message, I promise. Give
> your dad a hug from me and promise me you'll
> forget about this place for six weeks. I'm just
> keeping your seat warm for you until you get
> back xx

Hazel smiled and looked at her dad, sitting up in his bed, looking back at her. His eyes were bright, and he seemed happier than she'd seen him for a long time. She typed a quick reply.

> I will xx

Then she switched her phone off.

A letter from Kerry

Hello

To those of you meeting Hazel and her team for the first time – welcome and thank you for choosing this book. To those of you who have returned to find out what she's been up to – welcome back! It's lovely to see you again.

Reviews are a great way to share your thoughts on books you've read so if you have enjoyed reading *Death Sentence* could I ask you to pop a review on Amazon and Goodreads for me so others can give it a try. Tell your friends, colleagues, the window cleaner, the pizza delivery driver, and anyone who will listen. Your support means the world to me.

I can be found on Twitter where I always love to connect with readers. I'm easy to find. Follow me on @kezzawatts-books.

With love and best wishes

Kerry x

Acknowledgments

Where do I begin? The book you hold in your hand was produced by more than me – the simple writer who had the idea.

Firstly, thank you to my family who, without their help, I couldn't have done any of this.

Mark – for your patience in the face of all of my wobbles during my many crises of confidence.

To my children – Hannah and Flynn – who give me joy every day and support me unconditionally.

Dad and Denise – as always, your support is a gift.

I'd like to give a wee shout out to my dad's friend who always buys a book. Cheers Davie!

Thank you to my agent Kate who put my mind at ease during an unexpected situation last year. Thanks. It meant a lot. More than you know.

Thank you to Keshini, Dan and everyone at Hera and Canelo for taking this book from an idea inside my head to the beautiful creation it is today, with the aid of your amazing team of editors and hawk-eyed proofreaders as well as your fantastic cover designers. From the bottom of my heart – Thank you.

To the enthusiastic crime fiction readers of Facebook, Twitter, Goodreads and beyond – Thank you so much for your continued support. To those of you who always recommend my books to people who are looking for a good read – thank you. You know who you are. You are all amazing.

To First Folio who made my dreams come true at York Racecourse in June.

For Theresa, Donna, Livia, Emmy, Billy (and Ted), and Kerry F – your Facebook laughs keep me sane. Also Messrs Tetley and Kipling.

I'd like to also give a mention to a lovely lady the world sadly lost last year. Norma Ormond was a great champion of my books and I always looked forward to hearing what Norma thought of my latest work. She will be missed x